ON THE JERICHO ROAD

Other Books by K.L. Morgan

Chronicles of Fiarah Series:
Castledance
Judges of Light
Lodestar
In Search of Dragons
Guardians of Peace
Beyond the Portals of Time

Briony Series:
Briony Plenipotentiary Princess
Briony Quintessential Queen *

Holiday Series:
A Christmas Angel With Golden Spangles
Love Isn't Love Until . . .
Pioneer Ghost
July's Valentine

Kingdoms of Everley Series
Princess Ilissa's Idea
Princess Mila
Hidden Hobbidew

* Coming Soon

ON THE JERICHO ROAD

BY
K. L. MORGAN

ON THE JERICHO ROAD copyright 2009 by K. L. Morgan
Special edition of "On the Jericho Road" by K.L. Morgan

All rights reserved
No part of this book may be reproduced in any form whatsoever, whether by graphic, visual, electronic, filming, microfilming, tape recording, or any other means, without the prior written permission of the author, except in the case of brief passages embodied in critical review and articles where the author, title and ISBN are mentioned.

Stone Haven Publishing
1579 Monroe Drive, Suite F
Atlanta, GA 30324
800-827-0089

* This special edition distribution license grants Stone Haven Publishing a one-time distribution license to own and distribute this single print-run of the book titled "On the Jericho Road" by K.L. Morgan".

The terms and limitations of this licensing agreement are contained in the written contractual agreement dated July 16, 2010 between the author, owner and publisher of this original work and Stone Haven Publishing.

This special edition printed August 2010

ISBN: 978-1-59936-067-6
ISBN: 978-1-58308-134-1
Library of Congress Control Number: 2008911175
Printed in the United States of America

To my wonderful grandchildren
I adore you all

Mallory Kate
Alyssa Morgan
Kassidy Krystyna
Jake Ryan
Megan Marie
Karly Krystal
Keira Kay
David James
Aubriel Page
Jaden Allen
Sydnie Ann
Linsey Lora

and any more to come,
this is my testimony to you, Jesus lives.

TABLE OF CONTENTS

ROOM AT THE INN 1

A TRULY RIGHTEOUS WOMAN 11

IF ONLY 17

YOU SHOULD KNOW 23

A GOOD MASTER 31

NUANCES OF THE LAW 37

LIVING WATER 41

FREE FROM SIN 49

FIRST LAY YOUR GIFT 55

FOLLOW ME 63

A MUSTARD SEED 71

HE THAT HAS AN EAR 79

THE MIRACLES 91

JETHEN DECIDES 101

SHEEP GATE 107

ASK ME NOT	111
THE KINGDOM	119
BREAD OF LIFE	127
RESTLESS	133
GENTLE HEART	141
JERICHO ROAD	149
A THANKLESS ERRAND	157
FINDING JESUS	163
LEARNING THE WORD	173
SEEK AND YOU SHALL FIND	183
JERUSALEM	193
SACRIFICE AND OBEDIENCE	207
MATCHMAKER	217
THE FRUIT OF THE VINE	227
KIDDUSHIN	235
PROPHECY	245
TEACHING IN THE TEMPLE	255

SPITEFUL MEN	267
GETHSEMANE	271
PREPARATION	277
SHEEP AND GOATS	283
PASSOVER	289
BITTER CUP	293
CROWN OF THORNS	305
KINGDOM OF SORROW	317
JOY IN THE MORNING	329
THE EMPTY TOMB	335
BELIEVE	339
GALILEE	347
WAIT ON THE LORD	359
TONGUES OF FIRE	369
GLOSSARY	377

1

ROOM AT THE INN

Jethen stroked the camel, and leaned into her side murmuring in his deep voice words of velvety comfort. "Let's see it, Sheba," he almost whispered. He didn't want his servants to hear him calling the camel by name.

It all went back to the time his father, Amos, found him weeping over a lamb who had died. "Why are you crying, Jethen?" his father asked the small boy.

"I found Frisk over in the thicket, dead." The little boy sobbed even louder. Giving words to his grief made him realize his favorite lamb would leap over the hills no more.

"Did you take care to dispose of him properly?" At the boy's nod his father then asked, "And did you enter his loss in the records as I taught you?" When his son nodded the second time, Amos lightly touched his son's head. "The animals are our means, son, not our friends. I told you before I do not hold with you naming all the animals. They are your charges, and you must treat them well so they will serve you, but do not make them more than they are. God gave us animals to feed, clothe, and carry us. That is their purpose."

That was why the grown man still whispered the names of his animals when others were about, so no one could hear him. "Let's have the hoof, now there's a good girl, Sheba." Obediently the camel lifted her hoof and he saw a rock had wedged its way in, and cut the flesh around it. "There'll be no more walking for you today, girl," he promised. "I'll fetch my tools, and have that out in no time." Before he left the camel, he called to his overseer.

"Mishob, unload this camel, she's gone lame. I'm going to get my tools and remove the rock, but I want her burden distributed among the other camels. You set up camp here with the others. I'm going on into Magadan, that is where I intended us to stay the night, but this girl can't make it that far. I'll get the food and water for the other camels."

"Yes, Master, will you be asking after your cousin?" Sherai was actually a very distant cousin. It was more a courtesy title from when their fathers had been partners, but they had become friends as children playing together..

Jethen slapped his hand at his side, and curled his fist around the material of his robe. His grey eyes flashed his frustration. "I suppose I will ask after her, Mishob. After all these months, it is unlikely I will find a trace of her here, so far from Sychar. Samaritans aren't too well thought of here in Galilee."

"I didn't know we were well thought of anywhere outside of Samaria, Master." The older servant chuckled, then sobered. "It would be even worse for a woman. We've looked all over Samaria, and Jerusalem, from Jericho to Joppa, and have heard nothing of her."

"I won't give up searching, and neither should you Mishob. Ask everyone you meet." Neither of them ever spoke the thought that she might be forced into some harem, or other undesirable place. In Jethen's heart he knew that Sherai might be a servant, but never a wanton.

"That I will, Master. The poor woman was mistreated, no doubt of that. You'll find her and make it right. I know you will." Mishob then began unloading the camel without further words. Well he knew his master would not wish to speak more, not when there was a chance of the other servants overhearing.

On the road into Magadan on the Sea of Galilee, Jethen did not spend time worrying whether or not his orders were being carried out. He knew that Mishob would handle the animals, and the other servants, with great care. Jethen held few secrets from Mishob because the man helped his father raise and train him to care for their vast holdings. Mishob was more like a friend than a servant. He was also distantly related to him, on his mother's side, and his family always took care of their own. His father pounded that into his head often enough. That was partially why he was so concerned over Sherai.

'Curses on Omini for allowing her to get away from him like that,' he thought for about the thousandth time. He could see Sherai clearly in his mind's eye. Who would have thought that the gangly girl would have grown into the stunning woman she was? He could see her long dark hair, parted in the center to frame her heart shaped face. Her dark eyes were fringed by thick, long lashes, and her skin was the same perfection as a young child's.

The last time he saw her, she was still wed to Maachi. A lack of luster in her eyes, and the way she visited with him only in the garden, and not inside the house told him that she was hiding something amiss from him. One thing for certain, Maachi would never have put her aside for no just cause if his father, Amos, or her own father Ashaah were still living in Sychar.

As children, she and Jethen ran the hills together among the large flocks owned jointly by her father and his. In those days, Amos and Ashaah were partners. When Amos began to sell for the two families, he introduced fine linens to their market. He sold their wool and cloths along the routes from Sychar to Jericho, and Jerusalem and along the coast from Lydda to Jaffa, Appolonia, Ptolemais, and north to Tyre and Sidon.

Amos moved his family to Jericho in order to live nearer the routes between Jerusalem, and Joppa, and the two partners expanded their territory that way. The young people saw one another less frequently after that. When Jethen reached the age of manhood, he accompanied his father on his trips, and yearly they came to Sychar on their route north into Galilee, and beyond to Damascus. It was then that he and Sherai had resumed their friendship. It was as though they had never been apart.

She was past the age of many women to marry when Ashaah gave Sherai to Reuel in marriage. Jethen came seldom to her home after that, for he sensed that Reuel was jealous of him. Then Reuel died. Jethen sighed. The memories were not happy ones. There had been so much death, so much suffering for such a young woman. All that would change, he was now of an age to care for her himself. He moved his business back to Sychar a year past. Some of his servants were now overseeing the building of a rather large house outside the city. As he hefted the bag of feed from the back of a mule, he sighed again. He should have left Mishob there to oversee the building instead of Ziriz, but Mishob was the only one in his confidence. He would need Mishob to take Sherai back to Sychar . . . if he ever found her.

He arrived at the inn long after the evening meal. He was fairly certain there would be a room for him. He stayed there every time he came through Magadan because he liked Mattheu, the owner. But his wife, Mary, was another matter. She bossed her servants and poor Mattheu about like they were chattel. If he were Mattheu, she would have long ago been set aside, even if she did cook like Caesar's finest chef. Even as he thought it, Jethen was certain that Mattheu would never do such a thing.

He suspected that Mattheu asked for Mary because she was the best cook in Magadan. Mattheu's family owned the inn for generations, and one way to keep good custom was to feed the people well. Jethen wondered if Mattheu ever regretted his choice. He never said so to Jethen. Mattheu was a quiet, gentle man who most often sat in his garden and dreamed over scrolls of scripture. Mary would find and scold him, and he would do some chore, and then go back to his meditation.

Jethen knocked at the outer gate, but there was no answer. He hadn't really expected anyone to be awake at this hour. He opened the gate and entered the courtyard. There were no hens to flee his coming, they'd gone to roost.

As he expected, the latch was free, and he opened the door to the inn and stepped inside. A serving woman was slapping her oil cloth to the table and rubbing with all her might. The inn boasted six such long tables. It was obviously her job, before retiring, to oil them after a vigorous last scrubbing of the day. Her back was to him, and so intent was she in her task, Jethen doubted she heard him. A stray wisp of her black hair escaped its binding and hung down, hiding her face. With a weary hand she pushed it back behind her ear and again rubbed the old table with both hands. He heard her sigh. No doubt with Mary as her task master she would have to also scrub the floors before she could retire.

"Is there room at the inn, maiden?"

Jethen saw the woman at the table freeze in place at the sound of his voice. She hung her head low, and in the dimness of the room he could not make out her features. He supposed she was shy, and wary of men appearing from nowhere in the night. "I am sorry for the lateness of the hour," Jethen continued, "One of my camels went lame some miles back, and we were forced to stop and relieve her of her burdens. I will only require a room, and some feed for my animals."

"What is the matter, churl, are you struck dumb?" Mary's shrill voice preceded her into the room, and diverted the attention of the man to herself. "Pardon my servant, Master. We certainly have a room for our most frequent patron." Mary's voice sounded almost fawning. "Jethen, son of Amos, will always have a room in this inn. To the woman at the tables she ordered, "Go at once and prepare a bed."

Seeming grateful to escape, Jethen saw the woman run to do her bidding. Within her hearing Mary's voice continued in diatribe, against her, "Servants are so difficult these days. This one complains of a simple task like oiling the tables. Look at her shoddy work, they'll have to be done again."

Jethen did look. It was a lie. The tables were old, and scarred. Mary was too tight-fisted to put out money for new tables, or pay the local carpenter for planing. He said nothing, but allowed her voice to continue unabated. According to her the serving woman did nothing but complain.

Jethen imagined that any serving woman of Mary's would have no time to complain. When he stopped here in times past, the little serving maid was too tired to even speak. The poor thing worked until she dropped, night after night, into her narrow bed off the kitchen. At cock's crow she was up and stirring the carefully banked coals into a soft blaze with a handful of fuel.

Smoothing the linens over the bed, Sherai regretted whatever fate led her to the very inn her cousin frequented on his many journeys. Tired as she was, her fingers flew as she readied the room for occupancy. With trembling fingers, she lit the oil lamps that cast a friendly glow, and raised eerie shadows on the walls. If the Lord God was kind, she would be finished with her preparations, and out before Mary escorted Jethen to his room.

It was not to be, she was warming the bed with heated bricks when she heard Mary's voice still strident and complaining. "I hope she has remembered to warm the bed. I have such difficulty with servants. They seem not to understand the simplest of directives. Ah, here we are. You are still here, Sherai? What can have taken you so long?"

Sherai could have told her that this room had needed a thorough sweeping and airing, as it lay neglected several days since there was no custom. She held her tongue because she always did, but she heard Jethen draw in a breath at the mention of her name. Though she kept her back to him, he asked as though he could not believe it, "Sherai? Sherai, daughter of Ashaah, is it you?"

"Answer him, woman. Has your tongue deserted you?" Mary could no more resist giving orders than the sun could resist rising.

Reluctantly Sherai turned around, but she drew herself up and stood proudly, and defiantly before him. "It is I, Jethen. I work here for Mary and Mattheu." At his look of angry incredulity, a note of pride slipped into her voice, "It is honest work, and I needed it." What she did not mention was the weary weeks she wandered from village to village looking for work before Mattheu took her in.

She knew she was lucky to have the job. There was very little work for a relatively young woman to do. She received less than kind offers from other establishments. It appeared there was no work for attractive women. They inevitably dissolved into being kept by the wealthier men in the town.

The innkeeper's wife scathingly told her as much when she appealed to them for work. "I need a serving maid and assistant. You would do better with your face and figure as a kept woman. I will have no such woman about enticing our custom." Sherai paled at the woman's coarse cruel tongue, and her heart quailed at the sight of her discontented face. She knew working for Mary would not be easy, and was almost glad the woman did not want her.

Unexpectedly, that day the mild mannered innkeeper reproved his wife. "Do not speak so, Mary. Surely you can see that she is a pious woman of a good family? We could use a hard worker," he told her kindly. "I fear the hours will be long, and we cannot afford much, but shelter and food you shall have." Sherai gratefully accepted, and his wife, muttering under her breath all the while, set her to hauling water before she washed the dust of travel from her feet.

The innkeeper hired her that day, but it was Mary who saw to it that she earned every farthing. As for the innkeeper, he sank back into apathy and did not seem to notice that his wife treated her as less than a servant. Sherai believed he disappeared into his own world to keep from hearing his name screamed at him by his shrewish wife. What ill wind brought Jethen to her hiding place?

Jethen's voice penetrated her memories. "There was no need for you to leave your home, and hire yourself out like this. Omini is worried nigh to death over you. I have searched for you these many months."

"I am sorry to be the cause of any sorrow to Omini, but I could not stay after Maachi . . . Surely, you can see that." It was then that Jethen became aware that the woman, Mary, was listening avidly to their exchange. Deciding to ignore the woman, he took Sherai's hand in his and felt the roughness hard labor impressed upon it. "Go finish your work," he told her gently, "we will talk further in the morning. Do not think to run away in the night. I will follow you until I find you again," he warned. He leaned against the door. At last he found her, here in Magadan of all places. She was living as a drudge, his beautiful Sherai. Anger welled in him. He was glad Maachi wasn't standing there in front of him. He wouldn't be accountable for what he might do.

"I won't run." Sherai was simply too tired. "I'll get back to the tables, mistress," she told Mary.

"Yes, and see that you don't forget the floors. Bank that fire; we'll need plenty of hot water in the morning." Her voice fairly crackled with curiosity, but she was still issuing orders when Jethen closed the door behind her.

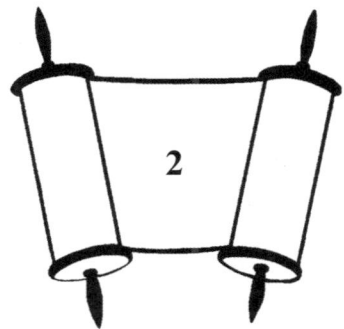

A TRULY RIGHTEOUS WOMAN

Jethen lay propped up in his bed with his arms behind his head. All night he'd wrestled with the problem of how to convince Sherai to do what he felt in his heart she really wanted to do–go home. Conscious of her presence in that tiny room off the kitchen, he'd restrained himself all night from going down there and having it out with her there and then.

It was nearly dawn. The light was breaking over the distant mountains to the east and would rise to sparkle on the waters of Genesseret lapping against the shore eastward of his window.

Protectiveness and something akin to anger washed over him as he thought of his lifelong friend hiring herself out as a drudge. The wish dearest to his heart he did not allow himself to dwell upon, for it conjured longings he couldn't allow in his dealings with her. Sherai needed to be convinced to leave here with him and return to Sychar in a way that would appeal to her.

It was obvious, to him at least, that Sherai was breaking her heart for the only home she knew. Whether or not he could entreat her to return to the city of her humiliation was another matter entirely. It should never have been.

He thought back to the day he discovered her flight. Making his way to Maachi's house, where he supposed her living, he discovered her disgrace from the lips of a triumphant Bethba, who had ousted her rival with no more qualm than eradicating a troublesome fly.

He burned once again with the wrath he experienced when he immediately sought out Omini, her father-in-law, where she should have taken refuge. There he only found more to raise his ire. She fled Maachi's house for a destination unknown. No one in Sychar knew where she had gone, not even her closest friends.

The old man told Jethen of her flight after Maachi set her aside. After all, Maachi was his only remaining son and heir who, with so little concern for her sensibilities, publically gave her a bill of divorcement. While it was true that Omini, shaken by Jethen's anger, implored him to keep his eye out for her on his many travels, there would be no true place in Omini's home for her.

Jethen felt little sympathy for the old man who claimed to be a father to her. "Find her, Jethen," he pleaded. "Tell her I am willing to establish her in a small business in whatever village she chooses." The implication was that her choice would preferably be a place far from Sychar.

"She might prefer to live away," Jethen acceded with barely suppressed scorn.

The old man's voice rose, no doubt stung by Jethen's tone. "I don't understand why she left. I offered her a place in my own house."

Jethen would have liked to shout at the old hypocrite, "What did you think she would do when she was publically humiliated by your goat of a son? Why would she remain in a place where she could daily feel guilt that she remained alive after the death of your sons?"

Instead he listened as Omini admitted, "Maachi is young, and his deep love for Bethba led him to this impulsive act." It was as near to an apology as Omini could give. Then he added, "I love Sherai as my daughter, even so, I cannot deny that she is the focus of many sad memories." Was there a tiny implication in his voice that Sherai might be to blame for all that sadness?

Jethen recalled saying softly, "Knowing Sherai as I do, I wouldn't expect her to remain with you when she was a constant reminder to you of your shared losses." Jethen vowed then to look for Sherai in his own right. He decided he would never tell her of Omini's offer; it would only add to her pain.

It was shame that prevented Omini from admitting that Maachi put her aside without asking his father's advice, Bethba gave away that much, Jethen thought as he stared out the window into the dark night. When he questioned some of Sherai's friends in the city, they were of the opinion that such a son and heir would have been a shame to any father.

His decision to take her into his own home was brought about by one of her friends, Rima, telling him that Omini's new young wife was house proud. Sherai was smart enough to know she would cause friction in such an establishment. There would have been little welcome from his wife, even if Omini did take her in.

Jethen's soul rebelled at returning Sherai to Omini. That sort of charity wasn't good enough for her. She'd done no wrong. He thought of Maachi, the youngest of Omini's five sons, who was now, after the deaths of his brothers, the old man's only remaining heir from his first wife. No matter how Omini personally felt about Maachi's actions, Omini would do nothing to jeopardize his future posterity. Thus far, Maachi's wife, Bethba, was barren, but quite young yet and there was always hope.

Sherai gave Omini one grandchild, but tragically, that small delight, named Talitha, lived only three years. She was the living image of Sherai, his young playmate. Her position would be more secure if Talitha lived.

So far, Omini's new wife produced only daughters. She may in time conceive a son, but until then, Maachi was his only heir, and he was the eldest–it was doubtful younger sons would take the inheritance.

Omini should never have demanded his spoiled youngest son take Sherai to wife. Maachi did so, obediently, reluctantly, but he had no love for Sherai. *'Love,'* Jethen sighed, *'what a pale word to describe such a tempestuous emotion.'*

Jethen's heart caught at the memory of Sherai's eyes beseeching him not to reveal her status to the innkeeper's wife. He couldn't remember a time when he'd not loved her, first as playmate, then as sister, then as his whole world. Even after her father gave her in marriage to that cold Reuel, Omini's eldest son, he kept his thin thread of kinship with her, wanting to keep her a part of his life any way he could. Jethen did not, even now, like to recall his pain. At that time he was in no position to ask for her himself when she was widowed.

'I should have asked for her after Tobiah,' he thought. The truth was, her obvious love for Tobiah ate at his jealousy. *'I wanted more than her gratitude, and like a fool, I waited too long.'* That he was but one year her senior, and too young, and in no position to marry, didn't lessen his frustration when he witnessed Omini foisting her on son after son.

Like a dutiful daughter, Sherai acquiesced. Look where that got her! Divorced! Set aside like an old broom that would only serve in the stables.

'At least Maachi gave me the opportunity to step in and care for her,' he exulted, and vowed at the same time. *'There is no one to stand between us now.'* Jethen shook his head no at the thought. *'She won't agree to wed me knowing that I never wed, and that she is a divorced woman. Pah. Such things don't matter to me.*

'I shall convince her of that. I know she loves me as her kin, and her friend of childhood. It will be up to me to change her friendship to love. It won't be a simple matter; I know I will have her gratitude, the death of love, to set aside first. My care of her will have to convince her of my devotion.'

Thus musing, Jethen spent the early morning devising ways to convince Sherai to return to Sychar. He wanted to offer her something she couldn't refuse. A way out for her, filled with respect for her abilities that would give her every advantage within his power. That was his desire. The cock crowed with the dawn ere he came up with the only scheme he could concoct. Sherai, in spite of her bill of divorcement, was a truly righteous woman. It was something that he doubted a respectable woman would want to do, but it was his only option.

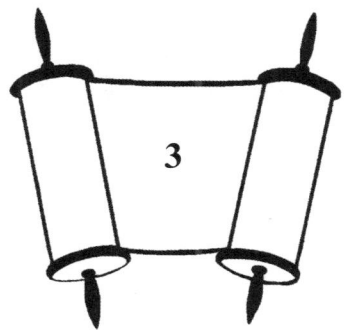

IF ONLY

Sherai woke with the cock's crow at dawn. The light didn't reach her small cubicle, but the hens clucked outside her window, hunting for their feed. She yawned, and stretched, then suddenly remembered. Jethen would demand to speak with her. Evidently he discovered her departure from Sychar and searched for her for months.

It was her place to stir the fires to life before the guests awoke demanding their morning meal. She'd long since gotten used to the drudgery of her work, and her muscles didn't even protest as she swung her legs out of the light cover and stood up. Quickly she dressed, and went to the fireplace where most of the cooking was done. Carefully she laid the kindling so that they caught slowly from the banked embers of the night before. It would not do to fill the inn with smoke.

Her next task was to fill the large urns from the town well. If she hurried, she could make several trips to fill the water urns before the guests awoke. Though Mary bid her fill them at night, it was too difficult to lug the heavy pitchers from the well after a day's work. Sherai preferred to waken early and make the trips when she felt more fresh, after a night's rest.

First, she dipped the last of the water from yesterday into the large pot that hung over the fire. She meant to do that last night, as the last thing, for Mary liked hot water in the morning. She bit her lip. She would rate a scolding for forgetting that.

'If only Jethen hadn't found me,' she thought over and over again as she walked to and from the well carrying the water to the inn. Even with her mind protesting, an elemental part of her was glad that she was to be freed from her self-imposed drudgery. What awaited her back in Sychar was a matter she refused to consider.

Last of all, she filled the large basins where she washed the linens before hanging them over the rocks and bushes to dry. After the washing was done, she would return to the kitchens to prepare the vegetables for Mary's expert hand at changing them to edible dishes. Only then she would be able to sit down and eat her own meager meal. It was something to look forward to each morning.

'Mary is an excellent cook, I'll give her that,' she thought. *'I am a passable cook myself. All young Hebrew girls are taught to cook. Mary's ability,'* she admitted to herself, *'exceeds my own.'* Stretching her back, and rolling her head from side to side, she marched once again to the well with only her thoughts for company. There was one last trip to make.

On her return from her last trip to the well, carrying two large pitchers on either shoulder, she heard Mary stirring in the kitchen. Sherai ran over her tasks in her mind, she didn't want to face an irate Mary, then Jethen. Other than the hot water, she'd done everything. Hurriedly, she filled the last basin, and began scrubbing the linens.

Sherai liked washing clothes, she usually hummed the songs she and Tobiah had sung together during their all too brief marriage. Though the work at the inn was back-breaking, at least it kept her too busy to remember much but the more pleasant parts of her past. This morning, however, the memories she usually kept at bay, came rushing back.

The last time she saw Jethen, he came to visit her in her home with Maachi. He set up his wares in the courtyard, at her insistence, they would show better on the low tables. It gave her a few minutes to visit with him, and ask after his family before Bethba, Maachi's first wife, pounced upon the beautiful scarlet linens, and finely woven bolts of blue, and yellow wool that he produced for her inspection.

It was shortly after that visit, she recalled, that Maachi put her aside, in a bill of divorcement. In pain, anguish, and shame, she left Sychar, and Samaria, and found her way north, far from where anyone would think to look for her, or so she thought. She honestly felt no one *would* look for her.

The end of her flight proved to be here in Magadan on the Sea of Galilee. Here at the inn of Mattheu and Mary, she found a refuge. Now that haven was to be taken from her, for Jethen knew where she was, and Omini, her husband's father, would not allow her to remain a servant in a strange house. It was awful. She would be taken back to Sychar and be forced to endure Bethba's snide comments and sneering glances. Omini would not notice on their visits Bethba coaxing, then preening under Maachi's open fondness. Opar, his wife, would doubtless treat her as a servant. It would be unendurable.

"You have allowed that young fool to reduce you to this?" Jethen demanded at her back as she spread the linens over the rocks. Sherai did not glance at him, but continued to wring out the linens she dipped in the rinse water, and spread them over the rocks and bushes behind the inn.

"I felt it better to be a servant to one of my own choosing, and free, than an unwelcome guest in the home of my husband's father." *'Why can't you understand what that would mean to me, Jethen?'* she asked in her mind what she could not say aloud.

Unexpectedly, Jethen agreed with her. "Yes, I can see what you mean, but Omini is well off enough to establish you in a small home of your own. There was no need to run away in this fashion, and alarm everyone."

"Who is everyone?" Sherai asked bitterly. "There was only Omini to care, and the affront to his dignity was stronger than his true regret. I am much too painful a reminder," she could not bear Omini's pain as well as her own. That was one reason she ran away.

"That is unfair to Omini," Jethen told her bluntly, "and to me, not to mention your other friends in Sychar. I have sought you these many months, at Omini's behest, from Sychar, to Jerusalem and Jericho. I thought you might come to me, my mother would have made you welcome, but there was no sign of you. Instead I find you in this obscure inn in Madagan."

Sherai turned to look up at him then. "I am sorry to have troubled you, Jethen. I meant no ill will to Omini. I didn't think that of your family. I didn't expect you to visit Sychar for a long time. I felt by then I would be forgotten, and everyone relieved I was gone."

"I cannot speak for that pup Maachi, or his simpering wife, but Omini fretted himself nigh to illness. I wouldn't have known about your departure until much later, I admit," Jethen agreed, "but I decided to move back to Sychar now that Amos is gone. I built a house there, and intend to . . .

"Amos has died? Oh, Jethen, I am so sorry." At last Sherai's eyes took in the lines of sorrow, and new maturity on Jethen's face. She reached out a damp hand to him to have it grasped firmly in both of Jethen's own. For a minute they stood silently both thinking of Jethen's father.

Softly, Jethen spoke looking earnestly into Sherai's brown eyes. "Come back with me, Sherai. Not to Omini's house, but to mine. Be my governor, and manage my home for me. I travel so much, I need someone I can trust to look out for the servants and the laborers while I am gone."

"Why not rely upon your mother? She is most capable."

"My mother remains in Jericho, in the house of my father. She says it is time for me to go out on my own. What she means is that it is time for me to find a wife. She will not leave Miriam's children. That is her real reason. You remember Miriam, don't you?" Jethen smiled. "I have no wish to marry, but I do need someone to care for my home. What do you say, Sherai, will you come back to Sychar with me?"

"I should say no, Jethen, in fact I do." Jethen, the fine man, was offering her a home in which she would be welcome, and valued. She looked into his grey eyes, steady and true. No, she could not live with him, even in this most innocent manner. "It *is* time for you to find a wife. Besides, what will the neighbors say if I come into your home that way? The heavens know I've been gossiped about enough, being widowed four times."

"No more than they are saying now, Sherai." Jethen scowled. He hadn't wanted to tell her this. If that's what it took to make her come back, he would.

"What do you mean," she paled, "what are they saying? What could be worse than wondering whether or not I put Reuel out of the way for his coldness? I've endured enough of their evil tongues."

"They say Maachi put you aside because he caught you in adultery, and that is why you ran away."

"That is untrue, why would anyone think that?"

"Perhaps because that fox, Bethba, spread it about to save her own face. I don't know, I only know what I heard when I began questioning them about your disappearance. They felt you ran away because of the shame of it."

"Omini would surely set it right. He knows why I was put aside."

"I doubt they dare say anything around Omini, he would flay them alive for the gossip alone."

She knew this was true. Omini held all his neighbors in high regard, and would listen to nothing that resembled gossip, or backbiting. "I will go back with you," Sherai decided suddenly. "I will establish your house for you, and I will hold my head high. I will go to the well, and wait for Bethba to appear, and stare her down."

"An excellent plan," agreed Jethen, "but I doubt the fair Bethba fetches her own water. Hold your head high regardless, my fine friend, you are more than *her* equal."

4

YOU SHOULD KNOW

"Mistress, a friend named Rima waits upon you. I put her in the receiving room."

"Thank you, Rebbah."

As Sherai hurried to the receiving room she puzzled, *'It is unlike Rima to come to Jethen's home.'* She and Jethen were considered pariahs by most of the city. In the three months she had lived in his house, the friends who crossed their door could be counted on one hand. Sherai wondered what brought Rima. *'I shall have to listen to how much she disapproves of my living with him,'* she reasoned, perhaps Omini sent her. He'd already come himself to endeavor to talk her out of living here. He offered her a generous stipend, but she refused. It smacked too much of charity, and she was proud. *'It is a measure of Rima's friendship for me that she comes at all, I suppose,'* she thought. *'I must find out what she wants.'*

"Rima, when Rebbah told me you were here I couldn't believe it. You are soaked through. Come into the kitchen by the fire. What is so important it brings you over in this downpour?" Sherai took the long blue covering from Rima that absorbed most of the water, and shook it out. "We'll dry this before the fire."

"It wasn't raining this hard when I set out," Rima pouted. "There was something I felt you ought to know. I've debated for some time whether I should tell you."

"Why is it when someone wants to tell you something you ought to know it is always unpleasant?" Sherai asked lightly, and saw Rima bite her lip. "Here, slip off those sandals, and dry your feet," Sherai handed her a dry, soft linen, "then come on into the kitchen, I'll pour you some comfrey tea, that will warm you." Sherai led the way into the cozy kitchen, and lit the fire in the oven set in the wall.

Sherai seated her guest at the table, but she sat on the ledge cut out of the thick wall watching the rain drizzle down on the kitchen garden. At the first sign of a drizzle, she set out the large urns to catch the water from the roof. Outside her window her herbal pots were on the broad shelf doing their best to absorb God's gift. She could hear the water draining down the flat guttering on the roof to the urns. "If this rain continues," she remarked, "I'll not have to walk to the well for days. Why Jethen built his house here in the outskirts of Sychar I will never know. It is at least a mile to the well of Jacob. Ah well, Jethen has offered me this refuge, and I should not complain."

"He also gave you a cart and horse to fetch water," Rima's voice lacked sympathy. "Why are you doing this Sherai?"

"I don't use the horse because I prefer to walk. It keeps me exercised." Sherai told her wickedly. She knew that was not what her friend meant.

"That is not what I meant, and you know it. Why did you come here to Jethen? Everyone is talking about Maachi setting you aside because he caught you... you know, with Jethen."

"Is that what brought you from town? A waggery tongue was speculating on why I was given a bill of divorcement by Maachi?"

"I knew it wasn't true," her friend sighed, "Jethen hasn't been in Sychar for years. Maachi shouldn't have done it Sherai. Your true friends know you did nothing wrong. In fact, I wouldn't blame you if. . ."

Sherai cut her off and sighed, "I don't blame Maachi, not really. He was the youngest son of old Omini and Paaba. After all, I'd already been given in marriage to each of his four elder brothers."

Her friend Rima sighed, "I know, it's such a tragic story. Four husbands dead, and the fifth one puts you aside like an old shoe. You are still so young, Sherai." She sighed profusely then asked, " Is that why you came to Jethen?"

"I think you know me better than to ask that Rima."

"Then why?" wailed her friend. "I am standing by you, but people are asking me things I can't answer. Are you going to marry him?"

"Don't tell them anything, say you don't know. And no, I will not marry a devout man who has never yet married. I am a divorced woman."

"But Sherai, people will think the worst!"

"They already do, Rima," Sherai smiled scornfully, "or you wouldn't be here."

"It was so different when Reuel was alive. You were the most sought after social couple in Sychar."

"Reuel," Sherai sighed his name. "We were wed when my father finally decided he could let me go. He was older than me by almost a score, but he was a just man, like his father. If only he wasn't so cold, so withdrawn." The match was arranged by his father, Omini, and her own father Ashaah when she reached the age of sixteen.

"Who knew that Reuel would die young like his mother? She was only a bit older than him when she sickened and died. When

Reuel died suddenly, Eliphaz took you, at his father's request, to bear up children for his brother. I didn't much care for Eliphaz." Rima was only speaking what Sherai felt, but never said.

Sherai didn't like remembering. "Eliphaz was a hard man. I'd no affection from him or for him. When we . . . when no children came, I was almost glad. When Eliphaz died suddenly just like his brother, I did not grieve. Perhaps God punishes me for my coldness."

"Perhaps you should have shed a few false tears," said Rima sagely. "His other wives were angry with you, and they were cruel. They blamed you for killing him as you killed Reuel."

"Yes, they beat me, and threw me out. I was glad enough to go." She smiled a tender smile. I was so deeply moved when Tobiah asked for me. I always loved his gentle way with children, and animals."

"Tobiah, dear, quiet Tobiah. You were at least nearer in age. We all thought that at last you would live happily together. If only little Talitha lived. She would be of an age with my little Ralla."

"Yes, we were happy." Sherai's eyes became soft brown at the memory. Then tears welled in them. "I have often wondered if after she died, Tobiah died from sorrow. He loved her so." Memories of Tobiah coming across the field from his father's house with their golden haired Talitha on his shoulders brought the same sharp pain she experienced every time she remembered. "It was so sudden, one day she was here laughing and holding out her arms for kisses, the next day she was smitten with a fever, and gone. Tobiah was melancholy for months afterward."

"Do not think of it, Sherai. I didn't mean to bring old sorrows to trouble you."

"If only I could have conceived another child, but I have been barren since. After only a year of mourning, I again mourned Tobiah walking off that cliff."

"You must not say that! It was night, as dark as pitch. He slipped. You saw the slip marks yourself. He would not leave you, he loved you." Rima began to regret her bringing up the subject of all Sherai's past sorrows.

"If only I could be sure he did not blame me. . ." Sherai wept openly.

"I'm certain he didn't blame you." Rima bustled to the window and embraced her friend. *'Think,'* she thought, *'change the subject.'* "How old were you when Tobiah died?"

"I was two and twenty. I mourned him, Rima, how I mourned him. I would have gone gladly to the house of Omini. . ." she trailed off. It was then the women of Sychar had begun whispering that she was cursed.

"But you couldn't. You told me you did not wish to bring death to his house. He'd only recently remarried after a long life alone after Paaba died giving birth to Maachi. Young Opar, Omini's new wife, wouldn't have you, would she? She wanted nothing but to lord it over servants and secure a place for her own children." Rima looked at Sherai shrewdly, "So Omini gave you in marriage to his next son, Nathan. At least he was only a few years older than you."

"I loved Nathan," she said softly, "not like Tobiah, but for his goodness. He was so shy. I think he was a bit afraid of me. We both tried to make it work, and it might have in time if he had not been bitten by that poisonous snake. God cursed me to be a widow," she said with conviction, "even though I do not understand why."

"Not true." Rima spoke without believing it, and Sherai could tell. It didn't matter now. That marriage was over before it barely began.

"Why do you not speak out and blame Maachi for divorcement?" Rima really wanted to know. If only she could silence the gossips with a bit of truth. "I think you were put aside because Bethba lived in mortal fear you would conceive before she could, and give Maachi an heir."

Sherai acted as though she'd not heard her comment. She couldn't bear to admit to Rima that Maachi hadn't come to her even once, not even when Bethba was keeping confinement. "Why would Omini not listen when I begged him? 'Omini,' I said, 'Father to Reuel, Eliphaz, Tobiah, and Nathan, give me not to Maachi. Allow me to live as a servant in your house.'"

"Omini, loves you like a daughter Sherai," defended Rima loyally. "And he still remembers his friendship with Ashaah. I was proud that he gave you to Maachi, at first. You were only five and twenty. For that matter, the same exact age as Maachi. He's always been rather boastful, and sly, but he is so handsome." Rima told nothing but the truth. The youngest of the sons of Omini was handsome like his father. He was so handsome that he was a little spoiled.

"Maachi is of an age with me, but he loved and long courted Bethba, as you well know, Rima. Maachi refused, and rightly so, to make me his first wife. I don't think Bethba ever forgave me for her hastily arranged marriage to Maachi." *'Omini should have known it wouldn't work,'* she thought. *'A younger adored wife, and an older second wife do not abide well with each other.'*

"When Bethba became with child, and lost it, Maachi came to me. I could tell he was upset, but he thrust the paper at me. 'I love you as a sister, Sherai,' he said, 'but my life is devoted to Bethba.'" What Sherai didn't say to her friend was that the shame of it was too much to bear. She'd done nothing to deserve such divorcement, she'd not been allowed to be a true wife. Bethba, if the truth be known, treated her more like a servant in the house, than a sister. Sherai told no one how she suffered at her hands.

As for Omini, he urged her to come into his own house. "No," she declared passionately, "You have a new wife and two small daughters."

"Why did you run away?" Rima persisted, "Omini would have taken you in, I know he would. He felt all the shame of his son's action. You gave him no way to atone for it." Rima could not understand why her friend hadn't turned to her father-in-law.

Sherai decided to be candid with her friend. "This is not to be shared elsewhere, Rima, but the truth is, I couldn't bear to be taken in by Omini. He only asked for me due to his sense of obligation. Think on it, Rima, If Bethba treated me as a servant, what would I be to Opar?" Sherai forced herself to laugh, "I was afraid Omini might have in mind to hold me in waiting until Opar produced a son and he grew to manhood, and offer me to him."

Sherai looked at Rima. Rima studied her, trying to weigh her words. Did she suspect that Maachi never laid with her? No, that would not enter anyone's mind. She doubted her friend understood.

Slowly she said, "I think I was out of my head with grief when I left. I took only a few items of clothing and all my jewelry. I meant to disappear forever, Rima. I was very ill in my mind. It was good that Jethen found me in Magadan acting as a serving maid. He is a distant kin on my father's side. He asked me to come home with him, and care for his concerns. He brought me here and left again on his travels. I've been given time, Rima, time to heal."

"Even if he is your distant kin, Sherai, he is unwed."

"He is a wealthy merchant with a large household. He needs someone to manage it for him. Yes, he is unwed, but he is my distant kin. I am satisfied with the arrangement. Tell them that," she waved her hand to indicate the gossip mongers. Staying with Jethen suited her very well. He honestly told her he wasn't offering her marriage. She wasn't treated as a servant, but was given the privileges of the woman of the house. She kept his home tidy, supervised his servants, and prepared his meals when he was home.

Rima looked at Sherai. Her rich, long, brown hair waved softly from its middle parting, and fell below her waist. Her figure was still trim, and her face, though it reflected the great sorrow she experienced, still glowed with youth, and melancholy beauty. "Has he asked to marry you, and you will not?"

"No, and I don't expect him to," her tone said that the subject was closed. " Jethen is rarely home. That's one reason why he offered me refuge. He told me that the simple pleasure of having someone to return to and talk with after his travels pleases him. We've been friends since we were children, you know that. You played with us yourself."

"I don't think you should stay here, Sherai. You are too vulnerable, and he is just a man. People are talking. Come and stay with me until you can find a place," she invited impulsively.

Sherai smiled at Rima. "No, thank you, Rima. I am happy where I am. If certain gossip mongers in the town whisper that I do more for him than I do, they are welcome to their opinion."

"What will I tell them when they ask me?" she wailed.

"Tell them to beware of bearing false witness. Finish your tea Rima. I made some fresh flat bread this morning, would you like some?"

Rima declined the bread but stayed a while longer to remonstrate with her friend. She couldn't budge her. Rima left some while later after declining both a meal, and the offer to stay until the rain let up. Sherai watched her go. Frustration and irritation outlined her figure as she walked swiftly down the lane. Sherai knew Rima was upset because she'd given her friend no way to fight the fires of gossip.

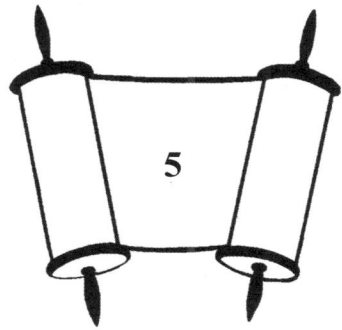

A GOOD MASTER

Sherai seated herself again at the window. She liked sitting where the high rectangular casement provided a frame for the garden. She looked out beyond the garden to the plowed soil beyond. *'This rain will be good for the wheat and alfalfa already greening in the field. God is good to Jethen.'* Her mind wandered to how kind and gentle Jethen was. *'He is too good to me,'* she admitted.

A tiny nudge from her conscience asked her why he was so thoughtful, but she pushed it from her mind and determinedly forced her thoughts to his extensive travels. He told her his trips ranged as far north as Damascus, down to Caesarea Philippi, and the cities round the Sea of Galilee. From thence he traveled to Sepphoris and either over to the sea at Caesarea, or south to Ginae, then home again.

She, who'd never been more than a few miles from Sychar to visit relatives, before running away no further than Galilee, wondered at his familiarity with the wider world. At least once she wanted to travel in his caravan as he made his southern run to Gophna, over to Ephriam, then down to Jerusalem and Bethany. From Jerusalem he went over the mountains to Jericho. She would remain in Jericho, while he traveled back and forth to Jerusalem to trade goods from Jericho, and renew her kinship and acquaintance with his mother and sister.

Since it was spring, and the traders round about had finished their winter quotas, Jethen and his entourage left for Jerusalem and Jericho only yesterday. He left his later planting to his overseer, and the garden to her. Sherai did not expect his return until well into harvest. If the trading was good he could be gone all summer. Meanwhile, she would tend his home, manage his household servants, work in the garden, and make sure there was a harvest to garner.

Sherai ran a hand over the casement along the window. Everything was new. It was built to withstand any weather, a solid construction of highly skilled craftsmen. Jethen wanted only the best for his house, and it was large and comfortable, like this window seat.

Idly she pulled a comb from her basket on the seat and combed out her hair. It became drenched in the initial downpour that morning and again when she had walked Rima partway down the muddy road. Combing out the long tresses soothed her. Her basket of mending sat on the ledge beside her untended.

Her talk with Rima that morning left her limp, and vaguely dissatisfied. Contrary to what she told both Jethen and Rima, she did care what people thought of her, and what they were saying. Running along the back of her mind was the niggling worry that Jethen might be coming to care for her more than he should. If this was so, she would have to leave his house.

In her innermost heart, Sherai admitted she could possibly develop deeper feelings for the man who was her distant kin. Even so, she did not intend to ever admit to that to even herself, aloud. It was time for Jethen to marry, and establish his own house. For that he deserved a young woman, a chaste maiden.

As a widow she perhaps could have bid for Jethen's love, but as a divorced woman . . . After all, she'd entered into marriage with Maachi with her eyes unveiled, as the saying went.

'I should have refused to marry Maachi,' she regretted, not for the first time. *'I was too distraught over Nathan dying so soon after our marriage. I began to believe that I* was *cursed. I didn't resist when Omini said Maachi asked for me. His offer was like proof that at least Maachi did not consider me cursed.*

'I should have confronted Maachi,' she mused, *'and discerned his true feelings before agreeing to the marriage. My acceptance was too hasty. I should have remained free to enter into a covenant with some other man. Perhaps a man like Jethen,'* she thought. It was the simple truth. At the time of Nathan's death, she'd not wanted to be alone to brood over her losses. Four men, and four deaths. It *was* like a curse. *'I doubted any man would ask for me, not with such a curse attending me. That is why I dutifully agreed to Omini's arrangements.'* For an awful few moments Sherai relived the memory of Maachi setting her aside with that humiliating public bill of divorcement, and its attending vicious whispering and gossip. *'He shouldn't have done it,'* was her conclusion. *'The fault rests with him. I have done nothing wrong.'* She pushed thoughts of why Jethen took her into his home from her mind. After all, Jethen was distant kin to her. If he wanted to give her a useful position in his household, she would gratefully accept it. Their arrangement was mutually beneficial. Sherai was not a woman given to long morbid thoughts. Giving herself a shake, she laid aside the comb and pulled the basket of mending to her.

"Mistress! Mistress!" The servant girl Rebbah came running into the room. "The Master is coming up the road. One of the camels is lame, and he's leading it. Two of the servants came with him."

"Call Sachi, Rebbah," Sherai ordered gently, "and run to fetch me linens. You may want to be heating some of this abundant water God has sent us. The Master may wish to wash the mud from his feet. I'll hurry up the preparations for a hot meal." As an afterthought she called, "Tell Sachi to lay a fire in his room." She ran to the kitchen to make sure the fire was stoked up and a pot of water was heating. She deftly began preparation for the little cakes, cooked in mutton grease, he loved eating, to go with the light meal she had planned for herself and the servants.

Jethen entered the house dripping with rain. His long, dark hair separated in rivulets of running water. His trim beard also dripped water. Eyebrows likewise dripped water onto his wide cheeks and starred the eyelashes covering his grey eyes. His travel clothes, over which hung a long cloak, were soaked and clung to him. Sherai handed him linens, and asked, "You returned to settle the lame camel and fetch another? What would you like first: a bath, a fire, or food?"

Jethen stood dripping on the woven rug he had bartered for at the bazaar in Damascus. "I returned," his deep voice rumbled, "because I overheard Ahi bragging to the others that he made Sachi with child. After a sound scolding I returned him here to marry her in haste. I will not have it said that I allow such laxity among my servants. Marriage is a sacred obligation. I brought his brother with me, and only used the camel as an excuse."

"No one said a word to me," Sherai replied with surprise, "and I didn't notice anything out of the way." She felt it a personal affront that she hadn't noticed. Was she so wrapped up in herself that she didn't see what was going on around her? At that moment Sachi entered the room with a flagon of mulled wine. The steam was still gently rising, sending out vapors of rare spice upon the air. Sachi's eyes were red rimmed, and she was trembling. She offered the wine to Jethen and stood before him waiting to be dismissed.

In a voice gentler than one would have deemed possible due to his deep voice, Jethen addressed Sachi. "Is all well with you Sachi?"

At his kindness her reserve melted, and she wept with her face in her hands before him. "I see that all is not well," he said kindly, "but do not weep. I have brought Ahi with me, and there will be a wedding. We shall have a feast worthy of such an event. You must call all your friends and family. Sherai, will you be able to prepare such a festivity within the week?"

Sachi, who was overcome, tried to stammer her thanks but succeeded only in wetting her Master further with her tears.

Drawing the girl within her arms, Sherai gently led her out of the room. "I shall," she replied quietly to Jethen. To the trembling girl she said, "It will be a marriage feast long to be remembered."

Having turned the affair over to Sherai, Jethen strode to his rooms to shed his sodden clothes. *'It was wisdom itself to open my home to Sherai,'* he mused. *'Surely it will not be long ere she recognizes my love for her. Perhaps she has even begun to return it in some measure.'* Jethen felt quite satisfied with himself and life that day. It was a feeling that would not long last.

NUANCES OF THE LAW

Several men walked together on the dusty road leading toward the Samaritan city of Sychar. It was obvious that they traveled far, for their feet were dusty, as was the hem of their robes. The countryside outside of Sychar, yet so near, was dotted with sheep grazing and new lambs frolicking. On the terraced hillsides, vines were flaunting their large green leaves protecting the small racemes of white blossoms that would soon become globules of green growing beneath them.

Rainfall has loosened the earth, but now that it was dry, dust abounded. The travelers, walking from Jerusalem where they attended the Passover worship, seemed equally oblivious to both the cultivated beauty, and the dust. They were deep in discussion with one another.

"But Jesus," argued Jude, his younger brother, "the Law of Moses says "eye for eye, tooth for tooth, hand for hand, foot for foot, burning for burning, wound for wound, stripe for stripe." How can this accord with turning the cheek? Is not God the same yesterday, today, and forever?"

James, who always walked beside his brother to buffer him from the others, inserted, "Can you not see that Jesus is weary of your questions, Jude?"

"Stay James, I will answer him." A gentle yet firm voice *was* tinged with a touch of hoarse weariness. "Jude, have you not asked me this question in other ways? How is it that I must contend with you on this matter? I tell you that our God is a God of love. He gave those weak in the faith such rules to live by that He might have peace among His people. Now that He has sent the Son of Man to redeem his people, the old laws will be replaced. A new commandment is given. From you, Jude, it is required to forgive all men. *'Vengeance is mine,'* said the Lord God. How can this equate to an eye for an eye?"

"It seems that much is expected of His children," Jude answered aloud. "Perhaps more than they can bear," he muttered in an aside to an older man named Philip who accompanied them.

"Where much is given, much *is* expected, Jude," rebuked Jesus softly. "You will come to understand. Let us speak of other things. I am tired and hungry. We have, it appears, reached the city of Sychar. I see a well there ahead. Is there coin in our treasury?"

They were traveling from Judea into Galilee, and walked for some miles without food, water, or rest. Since his ministry was not yet formally begun, most of his disciples lived near his own home in Nazareth, and were anxiously pushing on to their homes where there were comfortable beds, and familiar food. Though they'd been on a pilgrimage to Jerusalem, and the temple there, their minds were sore from grappling with the new doctrines taught by their beloved leader. Yet, their souls were exalted by the holy beauty of his words. When *he* said the words, they sounded so wondrous, simple, and easy; but living them, as he wanted them to do, as he *did*, was another matter.

"Very little coin remains."

"It is sufficient. I will rest here at the well while you and the others enter the city to buy us meat. Refresh yourselves in the city. Speak to those you meet with kindness. There is work to do here."

"Here?" His brother was horrified. "This is a city of Samaria!"

Jesus smiled at Simon. "It is written that He knows the secrets of the heart, Simon. What the Father knows, I know. There is a work here for me to do," he repeated. So saying, he seated himself upon the well, and settled himself, and closed his eyes, as though in prayer. His disciples well knew what that meant. He was in communion with the 'Father'; they must do as he said.

There was no use arguing with him that the Samaritans were not to be associated with, that the Jews would look down upon him with disfavor for this association. It was utterly useless to mention that he, being a Jew, should have nothing to do with them. With the exception of Philip, who followed them from Jerusalem, and Simon who was a Zealot, and Jesus, who did carpentry, they were all poor farmers trying to eke out a living in Nazareth.

Besides, the city beckoned, and they were to refresh themselves. It would give them an opportunity to sit and discuss the teachings of that day without his presence. If the Samaritans wanted to listen to their discussion, they might learn something.

"Let's be going then," James, the next eldest, urged on his friends.

"You don't have to rush me," boasted Philip, slapping his wide girth. "I am near hollow." The dull thud of solid flesh elicited a spontaneous laugh from Jude, and at least a smile from the others.

"Remember, we are messengers on God's errand," reminded Simon. So chaffing one another, and talking, they walked into the city on well-worn paths.

They were not to argue with people, Jesus had been most specific about that, but there might be the chance to practice some of his teachings in their dealings with these people. A good word must be spread, even, it appeared, among the Samaritans.

When all was quiet, Jesus opened his eyes, and looked far to the west. He absently brushed some of the dust from his robe, and ran his fingers through hair tangled by the breeze. Idly he swung his foot, and allowed his mind to be filled with thoughts of the work he was to do. He opened his thoughts to that quiet voice speaking in his mind. His eyes sought out the distant hill.

Nestled against the hill was a house, located outside the city of Sychar, but quite prosperous looking. His eyesight was excellent, and even from this distance he could see the servants bustling about the house and garden. He waited patiently, and watched. At last, one of them detached themselves from the others, and came walking to the well with a pitcher on her shoulder. Jesus' eyes softened. Now was the time.

LIVING WATER

"Rebbah, I'm going to the well to fetch some water." Sherai entered the house and fussed about the pitchers, selecting the tallest.

"Mistress, the barrels are still full!" protested her servant. "I'll run and fetch you some water to drink and enough for the others as well." Sherai, and some of her women servants had been out gathering in the tender leaves of shard, and weeding the garden. They'd been at it for over an hour, and it was time for a break. Rebbah flushed, thinking her mistress rebuked her for forgetting to bring them a drink of water. The rain was plentiful, and the barrels were still nearly full, they could drink their fill.

"I have a taste for water from the well, but do take water to the others," answered Sherai. "I need to stretch my legs, my back aches from working the field, and the walk will do me good."

"Yes, Mistress," Rebbah answered her and shrugged. If her mistress wished to walk all the way to the well after bending for hours over the garden on this hot day, it was nothing to her.

As Sherai walked down the long road to the well, she reflected that life was good. The wedding of Sachi and Ahi was a memorable occasion, and Jethen was pleased. Sachi walked about the house once again with her head high, and a merry smile upon her face.

Immediately after the wedding, Jethen left again with a laden camel, and his servants, but not before he assured Sherai she handled everything to his satisfaction. A small new house was to be built onto the compound to accommodate the newly married couple, and the work was being done. Jethen was a just and good Lord, just like his father.

As she neared the well, Sherai could see that a lone man was seated there. She hadn't expected anyone to visit the well after the abundant rain, except travelers, perhaps. The closer she came, she realized that he was no one she knew, and that he was a Jew. She saw that he looked steadfastly upon her, and she lowered her own eyes. If he'd been of her city or a traveler from her own Samaria, she would have greeted him, and offered to draw him water. This stranger might also be thirsty, but she saw no pitcher.

Why was she always to be confronted by these awkward situations? Her sojourn among the Jews in no way lessened her feelings of antipathy toward them. Still, she felt no ill will. The Jew was still watching her, she could sense it.

She drew nigh the well, and took care to stand on the side opposite the stranger. Keeping her eyes lowered she prepared to draw water from the well.

In a voice stirring and gentle the stranger said, "Give me a drink."

Sherai raised surprised eyes to the man. Most Jews would have jumped from their seat and strode off in the distance when she appeared. The memory of the Jews who passed through the inn demanding her to serve them as though she were a slave rather than a hired servant raced through her mind. None of them spoke as softly as this stranger. She dared to look into his eyes, and saw only kindness reflected there.

"How is it that you, being a Jew, ask me, a woman of Samaria, to give you a drink from the vessel of my house?"

The man answered her, "If you knew the gift of God, and who was saying to you, give me to drink, you would ask me, and I would give you living water."

Within Sherai's heart something leapt. This man spoke as no other she ever heard, with assurance, and authority. A tiny flame kindled within her. Something urged her to know more of this man. Tying off the rope she threw over the metal rod at the top of the well, she attached it to her pitcher to send it down into the depths. She then dared to respond to his words. "Sir," she said, "I see that you have neither a vessel, nor rope to draw from this well, and it is deep. How and from where will you draw this living water?" Sherai dared another look into his eyes. They were steadfast, and she perceived that he was trying to tell her something very important. Somewhere inside her a voice whispered at the edges of her mind that she came to the well this day purposely to hear what he had to say. Without knowing how she knew, she accepted that he was a prophet.

Taking a deep breath she added, "Are you greater than our father Jacob, who gave us the well, and drank thereof himself, and his children, and his cattle?" Most Jews would bristle at her claim this was Jacob's well. She knew that many wells were so claimed.

The man did not answer her directly, but looked down into the well as though he could draw up the water if he would, then raised his eyes again to her and said, "Whoever drinks of this water shall thirst again: but whoever drinks of the water I shall give him shall never thirst." He looked kindly upon her and added, "The water that I shall give him shall be within him like a well of water springing up into everlasting life."

Never to thirst again, cried Sherai's hungry heart. Here was a man of God, and he was offering her more than her mind could comprehend. Still using his own words she spoke again. "Sir," she cried, "Give me this water, that I am never thirsty, nor come again to the well to draw."

The man smiled. He seemed to understand the hunger of her heart. Without words he communicated to her that he spoke of water of the spirit, not water from a well. She knew he was a man of God. How had she dared to ask such a thing, and of a Jew? Once again she lowered her eyes, and drew her water from the well. Taking her full pitcher, she offered it to the man, and he drank freely.

When his thirst was slaked, he returned the pitcher to her. She refilled it, but still did not depart. "You wish to know more of this water I spoke of," he stated. Sherai nodded, but did not look up.

"Go, call your husband, and come back." His voice was calm, but distant.

Sherai realized that the man properly wanted to show her no disrespect. Her heart lifted at his tone of consideration for her feelings. Wanting desperately to hear what he might tell her, she nevertheless admitted, "I have no husband."

"You speak the truth," said the man in a satisfied voice, as though he'd known she would tell him the truth, "for you have no husband. You've had five husbands, but the man you are now with is not your husband. You speak truly." Sherai was overcome. Daring to look once again into his face, she saw sadness for her, and compassion in his eyes.

Sherai began to tremble. He knew! She felt the sting of tears in her eyes and the ache of tears in her throat. The man *was* of God. "Sir, I perceive that you are a prophet." His words stirred within her a desire to deepen her knowledge of God, and to live as God would expect of her. A question sprang to her lips. "Where ought I to worship? Our fathers worshiped in these mountains, yet the Jews say that the place where men ought to worship is in Jerusalem. Should I then move to Jerusalem, Rabbi?"

The master held up his hand to still her speech. "Woman, believe me, the hour is coming when you shall neither worship in this mountain, nor in Jerusalem."

The man was quiet, and gazed out toward her house. "You do not know what you worship, but we know, because salvation is of the Jews."

"I would know. . ." she began.

He stilled her again with his hand, "The time has come for true worshipers to worship the Father in spirit and in truth. For the Father seeks such people to worship him. Those who wish to worship him must worship him in spirit and in truth."

Her heart sang within her. Here before her was succor for her soul's depletion. This man of God could heal her, she knew it. With awe and trembling she said, "I know that the Messiah is to come, which is called Christ:" she looked into his eyes and dared to add, "when he has come, he will tell us all things."

So caught up in their conversation was Sherai that she didn't notice that his disciples, returning from the city, came up behind in time to hear her comment, but Jesus had. Raising his voice slightly so that there could be no doubt, what he said to her he said clearly, "I who am speaking to you am he."

His disciples spoke among themselves.

"He is speaking to that Samaritan woman!"

"Is this not casting his pearls before swine?"

"Why does he tell her these things not fit for her ears?"

"Did you hear what he said?"

Not one of them had the courage to ask him directly why he spoke with her, or why he declared himself the Messiah. Perhaps they feared to hear his answer.

Sherai, however, was past noticing their displeasure. A fire burned inside her, the cleansing fire of truth. Inside her a witness grew that before her sat the very Christ, and he *could* give her this living water. Sherai believed. All thought of harvest, and work was forgotten. She was saying in her heart, *'I must go, I must bring others to hear what this man says. Living water. I will share it. We will all return and hear his words.'* Thinking she said all this aloud to the Messiah, as perhaps she had, she smiled, for the first time.

Sherai turned from him and hurried off to the city, leaving her water behind, to gather her friends. First, she went to the house, and sent her servants far and wide to spread the word. Not content to leave it to her servants, she ran all the way to the city, and on to Omini's house. Once there she told them, "A man has told me all I ever did, he is truly the Messiah. Come to the well! Come hear him."

"What do you mean, daughter? Some sorcerer has come to Sychar?"

"No revered father of my husbands, he is Messiah, the one who is prophesied to come. I have heard his words as I fetched water from the well. Bring your household, and hear his words. He is a man of God. He knew of your sons, and more."

"Why should we heed the words of a wanton woman?" Opar's lips curled, and scorn dripped with her words.

"Silence, Opar!" demanded Omini.

"You know I am no wanton, Opar." Sherai defended herself, then ignored the woman. Once again she appealed to Omini. "This man knows, he knew of all my husbands, and he knew of Jethen. He knew also of my sadness, my longings. I tell you he is a man of God."

Ophar snorted, and Omini reproved her, "Hush wife. I will hear more of this." To Sherai he asked, "This man is a man of Samaria?"

"No," admitted Sherai, "he is a Jew. The prophesies say the Messiah would come of the Jews. Don't they? I know you are a righteous man, Omini. Come and hear this man who knows your sons."

"We will come," declared Omini. "I would have Maachi hear him. Opar, take him word to come to the well. Do not trust to the servants for this. Go yourself." Opar left the room, but not before she had cast angry eyes on Sherai. Her look said as loud as words, "You are not in my house five minutes, and you have Omini treating me as a servant."

Sherai turned her face from her, and concentrated on her former father. "Thank you, father of my husbands. I must go now and tell others, I shall see you at the well."

"I will go and tell a few of the rulers of the synagogue. We will meet you at the well, daughter," replied Omini.

8

FREE FROM SIN

As the Samaritan woman departed, the disciples gathered about the man sitting at the well. "She has left her pitcher. Let us take advantage and drink." The disciples each drank from the well. It had been a long day, and their thirst had not been slaked in the city.

"I have no thirst," said their Master.

"She gave you to drink?" asked the youngest of the disciples.

She did, Jude," the Master answered.

"Then we should be setting out again. We have a long walk before us."

"First Jesus must eat," rebuked Simon. "He's had nothing to eat all this day. Here, Master, we have brought you meat. Take it, and eat."

"We must tarry here awhile, Simon. She will soon be returning with many of her friends. I don't need meat, I have been filled already," Jesus smiled at Simon, then at the perplexity on the face of his disciples. He laughed softly and his voice was filled with quiet happiness. "You don't understand as yet, but you will. I am filled by the Spirit. Pray with me, my friends. Soon there will be a multitude here, and I must speak with them." He then bowed his head and closed his eyes.

He did not speak a single word, but not one of his disciples doubted that he spoke directly to the one he called, "Father."

He taught them a prayer for when they did not know what to pray, and Jude began it, with the others taking up the rhythm of the beautiful words. "Our Father, who art in Heaven, revered is your holy name. May your kingdom come, and your will be done on earth, as it is in heaven.

Give us this day our daily bread, and forgive us of our trespasses as we forgive those who trespass against us. Lead us not into temptation, and deliver us from evil, for the kingdom, power and glory are yours. Amen."

Their short prayer concluded, they looked up and saw that their Master slipped from the well, and was walking a little apart from them, away from the city. He often slipped away from them to think on what he wanted to say, or to continue his prayers. They settled about the well. The saying of their simple prayer established a feeling of peace among them, and they remained silent for a time.

"Why," began James, "do we delay here among the Samaritans?" James heard him say only a few days past that the word was to be spread throughout Israel, but no one considered Samaria as an integral part of it.

"I think he means that he has someone here to teach, James," said Philip quietly. He was the least of the disciples, he felt, in their eyes. He was a follower of John the Baptizer when Jesus found him listening to his words at the temple. The man felt his heart swell within him. Gladly he left his home to follow this man.

Bartholomew wiped his brow with a sleeve, "I would rather he taught in the shade, this sun is hot." Nathaniel, or

Bartholomew as he was known among the Romans, was introduced to Jesus by Philip. He was an older man, and not used to much exertion. In fact, he was resting beneath a tree when Philip found him and brought him to Jesus.

"There is plenty of water to quench our thirst," Simon, the Zealot dropped the vessel into the well once again. "I think I'll pour some of it over my head as well. Shall I share with you, Nathaniel?"

At the older man's nod, he began pulling up the filled pitcher.

Jude frowned on general principle. The man, Simon was always doing something that seemed to Jude to be irreverent, or uncouth. Truth to tell, everything was irritating him today.

They planned to return to Nazareth to begin their speaking tour. They'd been away since early spring in Judea awaiting the Passover. Jude sighed.

Simon, also, wanted to reach Nazareth. He wanted to confer with his old associates, the Zealots who shaped his youthful philosophy. Here they were wiling away precious hours in Samaria.

Andrew must have felt his discontent for he came up and said quietly, "I imagine you are most anxious to go on, Simon. I know that James is."

"I am," the burly disciple admitted. "How is it you are so patient? You and James never complain, how can you be content?"

"His words, his message, do you not feel the depth and breadth of them? I can't speak for James, but for me his words fill my heart and mind when he speaks, and sustain me when he is silent. I ponder each one," Andrew scratched his head. "You know I've never been able to convey my deepest feelings."

"You do well enough, Andrew. I'll admit that when you came from that wild man, John the Baptist, I labeled you a dreamer..."

"Not for the first time," Andrew interrupted and grinned. "I heard Jesus say that he intends to return to the Jordon to hear John, and be baptized of him.

Simon sobered at once. "This is news, indeed."

"Philip, Nathaniel, and I are traveling on to Capernaum. We will then go to John. It is likely we will see you there, if you attend him."

"I will attend him. You are right about his words they are what pulled me to him. Have there ever been such words, such a message? I don't understand half of what he says. Take his being filled with food by the Spirit for an instance, but some of his sayings are so simple. I never thought of religion as simple, did you?"

Andrew shook his head, but his eyes were on the small crowd of people moving out from the city. "Here come the people the Master predicted would come. I believe I recognize some of the people we spoke to, Simon. Perhaps we are doing better at spreading the message the Master has taught us. Let's go out to meet them."

Simon looked up and saw Jesus returning, as though he knew the people were nearly there. His heart gave that strange tug it always did when his Master seemed to know what was going to happen before it took place.

The Master looked out over the crowd. He noted the one man he wanted to meet. Jesus' kindly eyes stared steadily into his, and he nodded to him. The elderly man met his eyes, and then bowed his head as if ashamed. His young wife beside him jangled with bracelets and adornments hanging from her ears, and hair, and about her neck. Her restless movement stilled only when she looked at the woman he met at the well. Then her concentrated look of enmity was very apparent.

Jesus looked over the crowd. Most of them seated themselves on rugs or on the ground. "You have come," he began, "expecting a prophet, or at the very least, a diviner, one who can tell you your future. You think that perhaps I may give you this water I spoke of so that you will never again thirst. You err in thinking I speak of a drink, I speak to you of eternal joy welling up in your soul. First, you must be born again of the water and the spirit that you may gain eternal life."

Andrew heard these words before, and still they thrilled him as they had when he had first heard them. He'd been baptized by John in the River Jordan, and was John's ardent disciple when the man introduced him to Jesus. He invited Jesus to his home, and heard him speak, and had joined with him for a while to hear more. His ruminations ceased when he realized that Jesus paused for a moment as if waiting for a question, but the crowd was silent.

"Many of you look for a messiah to come and deliver you, but it is you who must free yourselves from the bonds of sin. If you are free from sin, you are free indeed.

"You have heard the law. I bring you fulfillment of the law. If you would be free, follow each commandment with a new determination. If a man asks alms of you, give to him abundantly; if a man asks for your cloak, clothe him completely. If a friend asks you to walk a mile, walk with him to journey's end. Give freely of yourself, and all that you possess. Treat others as you would desire to be treated.

"What if you have been grievously wronged?" Omini asked, looking sideways at Sherai. "It is not so easy to treat that person as you would want him to treat you."

"Hold no grievance to your bosom. If you would make an offering to your God, first offer forgiveness to those who have given offense. Then bring your gift."

Jesus ceased speaking for a moment, but the crowd still willed him to continue. He smiled at them. "If you would have others love you," he looked at Omini's young wife, "you must first love them. When you are the master, you are more truly the servant of all. Those who serve you are your stewardship and your treasure here on earth. Longsuffering, patience and kindness beget longsuffering, patience and acceptance. If your yoke is easy, the burden is light.

"I do not come to deliver you from vile oppressors, but from sin. I have come to bring the message of good tidings. The message I bring is of love. The Father loves you, and wants you to return to his presence. I am the way you may return; I bring truth and light to mark your path. No man may come to the Father but through me. Come, take my yoke upon you, and learn of me; for my yoke is easy, and my burden is light."

"How can we take this yoke, Rabbi?" The old man rose to his feet with tears flowing down his face. "What is the first step we must make?"

"Do you not recall I said that you must be born of the water? Your first step is to repent of your old ways, and be cleansed from your sins. Take upon you a covenant of baptism for the remission of your sins."

"Then I must find sufficient water to cover me." The old man hesitated, not certain of the reception his next words would be given. "Will you come and abide with me and teach me . . ." he paused and looked about at all the people sitting around him, "teach us more of these good tidings?"

Jesus looked over the people once again. A look of compassion suffused his face. "We will come," he replied softly.

9

FIRST LAY YOUR GIFT

Omini was sitting in the only room in his house where he could find peace from his active small daughters, and out of the way of his busy wife. There was one window in the north wall that allowed light and air. He was looking out that window now, over his olive garden. Within the room were tables and scrolls, and all those things which a man of means needs to run his household, his weights, his ledgers, and his pillows. Along one wall ran a couch for reclining, covered with a bright blue cloth that had the stamp of Amos' wife's making. He thought often of his old friend, and was glad Opar had purchased the cloth from Jethen.

Thoughts of Jethen always led him back to thoughts of Sherai. If he had done his duty, Sherai would not be in such a position. When Jethen had first brought Sherai back to Sychar, he was privately relieved that he'd not been asked to take her in. Sherai insisted she would work for Jethen. It solved his own wife's worry, and gave him peace. At this moment, however, he felt no peace. Although the waters of baptism cleansed him, he still had one more spot to scrub free–Sherai. He felt an uneasy suspicion that Jethen would not thank him for this day's work.

Omini shifted uncomfortably, and the scroll on his lap rolled to the floor. Retrieving it he smoothed it reverently, and began rolling it back up. These past several days were among the most memorable of his life.

His heart swelled within him to recall the words of the young rabbi who spent two days with him talking to him of the holy writings, and explaining their meaning. Omini's hands cradled the scroll that represented not the law of Moses, and the prophets, but his own family's line from Adam.

In a nearby room he heard Opar's voice raise in berating tones, then lower and continue more softly. He smiled, and his heart softened toward his young wife. She was trying very hard to live Jesus' words. The Master not only changed his life. It was because of Opar that he had sent a servant to fetch his former daughter, Sherai. It was Opar who told him of all Bethba had said and done, and then shamefacedly admitted her own part in making Sherai feel unwelcome. "You must send for her, Omini, and offer her a rightful place among us."

At that moment in his musings, sounds came of the jangling of Opar's bracelets. The curtain over the door was drawn back, and Sherai came through the door followed closely by Opar. "Seat yourself, Sherai," Opar offered her the plumpest pillow and set another at her back. "Could I bring either of you refreshment? I made some little cakes for the children." At their negative response she continued, "Nevertheless, I will send a servant with goblets, talking is thirsty work. Here is a linen for your face, Sherai. You can use this fan, I know it must be hot walking from Jeth . . . I mean I know that walking must have tired you."

Sherai, in not a little surprise, took both the damp linen and the offered fan and stammered her thanks to her hostess. She was still reeling from Opar greeting her at the door rather than being met by a servant, and the woman ushering her into this room with so much ceremony. Sherai looked wonderingly at her, and saw her blush at her surprise. Opar had changed!

Since the coming of the Messiah to the well, a large portion of Sychar changed. "I will leave you for a nice talk, I must check on the children. If there is anything you need, Omini, you have but to ring this." She walked to a table and took a small bell from it and placed in near to hand. She then hastened to leave them as if she'd said too much.

Recalling her own training Sherai remembered just in time to call after her, "Thank you, Opar, for your care and thoughtfulness. I feel most welcome in your house."

"My home is yours," called Opar from the hall.

Sherai looked at Omini as if to call for an accounting of Opar's demeanor.

"Welcome indeed, Sherai, most dear of daughters. I have called you here today to make what amends I am able for the mistakes of the past. I have treated you unfairly, my daughter. I allowed my only remaining son to put you aside, publicly."

"I attach no blame to you, Omini, for your son's action."

"But you did not choose to live in my home. I am not so unaware as you think. My young wife has not made you feel a part of our family. Perhaps it was not in her nature to do so, but you must know that you are here today, in part, because she felt you must be." The old man stared at the door through which his wife departed as though he could still see her there.

He rubbed his eyes, and then opened them to gauge Sherai's reaction to his words. "I have called you here to make reparation to you, if you will accept it. Maachi's inheritance will be great when I depart from this life, in spite of any new little sons I might have also gaining an inheritance. I intend to see that you receive a goodly amount of what would have been Reuel's portion. It is your just due, Sherai.

"Though Tobiah's loss still haunts me, I know that he would not have me leave you penniless, so also a portion of his inheritance that would have come to Talitha will also come to you. Since I have no immediate plans to leave this earthly toil any time soon," he added wryly, "I wish to settle Tobias' share upon you now."

"But Father Omini . . ."

The elderly man raised his hand against her protests. "I will hear no arguments, my daughter. I must right this wrong that my son has done you as far as is possible."

Neither of them heard any outside noise so intent were they on talking, so when Maachi broke into their conversation, they both started.

A handsome young man, a little taller than Sherai, stood before them. His hair was neatly combed, and his beard was trimmed. He wore his robe with a belt woven of fine linen tied at the waist. "No, Father, it is my place to make reparation to my sister. Forgive me for intruding in your private conversation, but I came to see you, Father, about this very thing. When I told Opar, she told me where you were. I wanted to ask your advice about what I should do. I think you answered that question most adequately, but there is something yet I must say. If you will allow me, Father, I would like to speak to Sherai."

"It is up to Sherai, Maachi. It is she you have wronged."

Sherai blushed crimson, and tears sprang to her eyes. Omini was admitting his son's wrongdoing in front of her. She turned her back on them both and walked to the silk hanging over the door. Never in her life had she felt so much pain mingled with joy. This was her first time in Maachi's presence since he had so publically denounced her, except for listening to the Master's sermon at the well. Suddenly the memory of the man at the well and his teachings came to her and she came back to Maachi, but she could not bring herself to meet his eyes. "What is it you wish to say to me?"

"Father, I wish you to stay." Omini had risen as though to leave the room. "You must hear what I have to say to Sherai, for I also brought disgrace to *your* house with my actions."

"The Master said it best, didn't he Sherai?" Maachi continued. "He said we must deal with others as we would wish to be dealt. When he said that, it was as though a sword pierced my heart. It came to me like a lightning flash in darkness what I did to you. For the first time I felt deep shame for my actions.

"This is no excuse, but I allowed my love for Bethba to blind me to honor. It is also no excuse for me that I was uncomfortable taking one to wife whom I regarded as a sister. I allowed my father to overrule my deepest feelings, but it was because I would not articulate them. Please understand me, Sherai, I could not be a husband to you."

"Did you fear you would be cursed by me as it seemed your brothers were?" she blurted. Then she was mortified that she shared her secret shame with him.

A look of profound pain crossed his face, and deepened the color in his eyes. "I do *not* think you cursed them, Sherai," he told her earnestly. "I was too young to notice other than how kind you were when you were married to Reuel. I did know you gave Tobias and Nathan more happiness than they ever knew. For that alone I loved you," his voice faltered, and he breathed deeply to control his emotion.

Sherai suddenly realized she was not the only one to suffer loss, Maachi also lost his beloved brothers, one after the other, and he was the only one left of a once large family. "I loved you Sherai, as a brother," he repeated. "I should have told my father of my feelings rather than give in to his demands."

Maachi turned to his father, and held out his hands in entreaty. "I should have told you, Father, that I could never be a husband to Sherai. Instead, I gave in to your importuning when I should have been strong. There are so many things I should have done and said differently. There is no way I can undo the past, and the pain I caused, but this I can do." He reached out to his father who met his gesture by taking his son in his arms. "Forgive me, Father, for failing you and bringing disgrace to our family."

"No, it is I who should ask your forgiveness. I knew you didn't love Sherai as Tobias and Nathan did. Forgive me, my son," said Omini.

Sherai's heart was full. She watched as father and son wept together. It was as though a breath of fresh air was sweeping through the room and cleansing them all of pain and bitterness. Sherai once again lowered her eyes to the floor when Maachi brought his hands up to his father's shoulders and stepped back from him. She saw that he once more returned to her, for his feet were almost toe-to-toe to her own.

Maachi took Sherai's hand and waited until she looked into his face. Her own eyes were washed in tears. He then said softly, "I will have it read in the synagogue that you did me no wrong, and that I put you aside for my own selfish reasons. If you so wish, I will declare that I was never a husband to you."

"You would admit this before all of Sychar?"

"If you wish it, I will declare our marriage void because of it."

"It would be all my heart could desire, but the embarrassment, the disgrace. Bethba . . ."

"Do not worry yourself about that. Bethba will be required to apologize to you for her ill treatment during our marriage."

"No, Maachi, Bethba is very proud, I would rather not . . ."

Maachi drew a breath of relief. He'd not wanted to force his young wife to a public apology, but his sense of justice felt it was due to Sherai. Now that Sherai relieved him of that burden, he acknowledged, "Then I will allow Bethba to make her own reparations as she sees fit. Nevertheless, I will do all I see fit to do. I intend with this letter," he withdrew a packet from his robes and held it out to her, "to settle upon you that portion which came to me from Tobias and Nathan." He pressed it into her hands.

When she opened her mouth to protest he hurriedly added, "It is the least I can do to make amends. This parchment also settles upon you a portion of my own holdings that I will settle with you annually at each year's end. Here is payment for the past two years." He placed a coin bag in her hand that was full. The sack was heavy. He must have sold some of his sheep to accumulate this much so quickly.

Maachi said to his father, "I will not have you paying for my wrongdoing."

Omini looked proudly at his youngest and only remaining son. Then he smiled upon Sherai.

Maachi, with none of his former arrogance and pride petitioned humbly, "Will you forgive me, my sister, for the wrong I have done you?"

Sherai felt free, just as the Master said she would. "I will forgive you only your part, Maachi. I allowed Omini to give me to you with very little protest, and I knew that you did not desire me for a wife. You are more than generous, but I will accept your kind offers. My heart is at peace with you, my brother, and with Bethba. Tell her that I bear her no malice, and that I wish her a long life with many fine sons to fill her days with joy."

Sherai, smiling the first smile he'd seen since Nathan's death, said, "I came to tell you, Omini, that I intend to follow the Master to Galilee. It was his words that first healed my heart. Now that you have so generously dealt with me, I can hire a servant to attend me, and take such provision as I can provide for myself. I will find a dwelling in Galilee, perhaps in Capernaum, for I want to hear more of this Messiah's words. I can sew well enough to earn my way, and now that I need not . . . now that I am able to provide somewhat for myself, it should sustain me."

"What of your . . . what of Jethen? I thought you covenanted to him to oversee his properties?"

"I have sent word to Jethen, and I will wait until he sends Mishob to take my place. Meanwhile, I can prepare for my journey. Omini, will you care for my portion, and administer it for me until such time as I have need of it?"

"Gladly with all my heart," Omini answered her.

"There are some articles that you left with me . . ." began Maachi uncomfortably.

"I would have you send them to Jethen's home if you would," Sherai immediately said.

"Then so shall it be," Omini broke in, "Maachi had them all sent to me." What he did not say was that Bethba piled them all in a cart and instructed her servant to dump them at his door. His own wife took what she liked from the pile, and would have given away or sold the rest, but he firmly restored all she took and put the items in a closet against her return.

Sherai smiled upon them both. "I thank you for your goodness to me. I know you will be happy." To Maachi alone she said, "I do love you as a brother, and I understand." At last she did understand. She could not refuse to acknowledge his sincere feelings. Maachi watched her happiness with Tobias and with Nathan, and rejoiced to see it. His own heart was bestowed elsewhere, and she prayed in her heart that Bethba might come to be worthy of him.

FOLLOW ME

Jethen stomped about the room. His emotions rode a fulcrum between exasperation and anguish. He had been seething since Levi reached his caravan two weeks past with the news of Sherai's intended departure. Instead of returning Mishob to Sychar, as Sherai expected, he left his caravan in Mishob's care and returned to Sychar with Ziriz, Mishob's hand picked successor. Ziriz was his overseer in Sychar since the beginning and only traveled with him since Sherai came. Mishob, in his old age, preferred to travel with his master.

On the journey back to Sychar, Levi was full of the words the rabbi spoke in Sychar. The man admitted that he, along with many others were baptized by the disciples of this Jesus of Nazareth. From what he heard, Jethen feared trouble might be brewing over this itinerant rabbi. The fat, self-satisfied High Priests in Jerusalem would not revere him, and the Romans might consider him a threat to their supremacy–if the crowds following him got big enough.

Close questioning of Levi, the servant who told him the news of Sherai's defection, brought out all the details of the visit of the man at the well. Jethen thought Omini to be too canny to be taken in by a charlatan, but the old man, according to Levi, invited both Jesus and his followers into his home. Omini was the first to step into the waters of baptism. From all he could gather, they remained several days preaching and baptizing many of the inhabitants of Sychar, including Sherai, and most of his own household servants. How could this be?

Jethen wouldn't admit to himself that even second-hand, some of the man's words stirred him. Do unto others as you would have them do to you . . . bah, no one did that.

According to Levi, he taught the people to be peacemakers, meek, humble, poor in spirit, and to seek after goodness. His words didn't sound seditious, but coupled with the power to heal the blind, halt and lame, they were a powerful draw. Others besides Sherai were leaving Sychar to follow him.

Yesterday, Sherai seemed unconcerned about his return yet again so soon after the wedding. Had it only been two months? She assumed that he came to make sure the transfer of duties to Ziriz went smoothly. If she was surprised Mishob wasn't chosen for the task, she hadn't said. What she did after his arrival was quietly gather her belongings, and leave. Jethen didn't want Sherai in Galilee. For that matter, he didn't want her out of his house, or his life, but she was gone.

Outside the sun shed a soft yellow haze over the saplings he planted around his house. They seemed to stretch and preen in its warmth. The garden was wafting verdant fragrance through the window, and out in the vineyard, the leaves protected the fruit beneath. Busy bees were humming around the small red flowers that dotted the land in spring.

The lure of all he built did not appeal to Jethen as he paced the floor. Early this morning he sent for Sherai, and was waiting for her to appear to his summons. Could he say anything to Sherai that would change her mind? What he wanted to say went something like, *'You can't leave me like this! You and I have a covenant. How will you care for yourself? Why do you feel you must follow this rabbi? Do you love him?'*

None of those accusations or questions would convince Sherai to remain, and he knew it. Jethen clenched his fists and hit the wall. The motion set his shelves to jangling, and caused a cloth tacked to the wall to fall. Rescuing the fine cloth from the floor, he smoothed it through his fingers as he imagined what he would say to her. In his heart he knew there was nothing he could say to keep her, not even that which he most wished to say, that he loved her, and wanted to marry her. Some instinct told him she would not listen. He wadded the cloth and threw it in a corner somewhat relieving his feelings.

Now that Omini and Maachi both provided for her, she did not need his charity. Sherai no longer carried the stigma of shame. The city was abuzz with the news that Maachi withdrew his bill of divorcement, and that their marriage had been dissolved. *'Do unto others was a difficult command, nearly undoable, but Maachi and Omini did it.'* A voice in his mind reminded him. Jethen hardened his heart. This Jesus robbed him of the one thing on this earth he treasured–Sherai.

After some investigation by Ziriz, the man told him that she was staying with Rima until she could purchase a mule. The rumor was that she was leaving Sychar for good. She acquired a young maid, Mazar, from among her family, and planned to travel to Galilee with all her worldly goods, and that young woman for company. At least he would have his way about that! He would travel with her bringing a small band of his servants. They would see her safely settled in Galilee.

So deep was he in contemplation he missed hearing Sherai step into the room until she spoke. "Jethen, I have come. What was so urgent? Ziriz said you wanted to speak with me. Have I forgotten some vital account?"

While his back was still turned, he heard her drawn in a deep breath. "Before you tell me whatever it is, I must say something to you. I know there are no words with which to thank you for all that you have done for me since you found me in Magadan. Yet I must try to tell you how much your kindness has meant to me." Sherai faltered and came to a stop at the sight of his face when he whirled from the wall against which he had been leaning. Jethen knew it was a thundercloud, but there was no hiding that he was not pleased with her decision to leave Sychar. The words he was not saying hung in the air like slivers of ice on a frosty morn.

When he at last gave words to his feelings, she was stunned to hear, "Why Sherai?" he almost pleaded. "Why are you rejecting my kindness? Have you been unhappy, has someone dared to make you feel unhappy in my house?"

"No!" she protested, but her smile faltered. "I was most happy here." Just as she did when still a child, she took a piece of her sash and twisted it between her hands, showing she was agitated. Jethen listened to her with tight lips, and scowling features.

"Your offer came at a time when I was in despair. It was well meant, but my living here with you is wrong. The rabbi made me see it clearly. I was living with a man who is not my husband. It wasn't right, Jethen, I knew it, but I closed my eyes to the impropriety of it. Now that my marriage to M-M-Maachi has been dissolved," she stammered, "it is even more inappropriate. Now that he and Omini have settled with me, and provided a modest living, I am free.

"I know you took me in to care for me. It offended your sense of fairness to see me working in that inn. You did it to give me a place, and a sense of worth, but you did not really need me here. Ziriz admitted to me that he has been Mishob's assistant for years." She caught a fleeting look of chagrin cross Jethen's face. Softly she said, "My only regret in leaving Sychar is to be found in losing your friendship."

"You haven't lost my friendship," he told her gruffly, then softened his voice. "What is it about this rabbi that entices you to leave your life here in Sychar, your home, your religion? He is a Jew, and you are a Samaritan. How could you allow him to affect your life so? Who is he to you, and the others," Jethen waved his arm to include all who had fallen under the spell of this traveling rabbi.

Sherai softened her voice to almost a plea as she answered him, "If you would only listen to Jesus, you would know that he is the Messiah. Look at Maachi, he listened to his words, and set me free . . ." Sherai faltered, what could she say to convince him? Realizing that he might never understand her following a Jew after all she had been taught as a Samaritan, she whispered, "I know you are disappointed with my decision." She studied his face as she spoke.

Jethen tried to mask his pain. *'Disappointed? Merciful God help me!'* Jethen wanted to stalk over to her and administer a sound shaking. He wanted to take her in his arms and rain kisses upon her beautiful face. He did neither of those things, but stood before her. Finding his tongue he said, "I cannot find it within me to be convinced by Maachi. The man must have said sufficient to stir his conscience regarding you. For that, at least, I thank him. Maachi treated you abominably." Finally he wrung words from his innermost self and admitted, "My reasons for taking you in, Sherai, were partly selfish."

Sherai shook her head, she didn't understand his meaning. "There is no selfishness in you, Jethen. You must admit that our arrangement was the scandal of the city. I was not thinking at all clearly or I would have realized I was damaging your good name, but I was the selfish one, I was too hurt and angry with Maachi to care about what my coming would mean for you. Rima came and told me, and still I stayed until the Master came." If it were possible, her face became even more beautiful as she spoke of him. Jethen felt a stab of the pain of jealousy.

Sherai looked up into his eyes. Her own were shining with deep happiness, "As kind and well-meant as your offer was, it was wrong of me to accept it. In your heart you know that is true, Jethen.

I must follow this rabbi, and learn all that I can. He told us he is going to teach in Galilee. If I move there, I will be near him. I will be able to hear him preach and teach. His words fill my heart, and his actions are those of a holy man. I wish . . ." She broke off whatever she was going to say and substituted, "You will visit me when next you are in Galilee, won't you? I'm going to set up a small shop near the market. I'll sell my needlework."

"There are many towns and villages in Galilee, which one have you chosen?"

Sherai blushed and answered him readily, "I have chosen Capernaum."

There was no doubt in Jethen's mind that this rabbi also lived in Capernaum. "I'm going to see you safely settled in Galilee, Sherai. There are no markets in Capernaum, only a strip along the shore of the lake where people set up stalls on market day by laying their goods on cloths along the shore. The spacious rooms in Sychar will not be found in your small town," he said firmly.

"It doesn't matter," she said. "I can be happy in a small house near the sea of Galilee. It is so beautiful there."

His tone said there would be no argument. "I'm going to see you to Capernaum. After I've seen you to your new home, I'll go on down to Jericho. It has been some time since I visited my mother. I shall add more camels to my caravan before I rejoin Mishob in Damascus. I'll stop and see if you are settled well on my return." Perhaps she would be lonely, or tired of living among the self-righteous Judeans. *'Perhaps she will be married,'* a nagging voice said in his head.

"But that is out of your way," Sherai protested. "You will see me to Capernaum, go back to Jericho, then return? I will be safe enough traveling with your servants. You must not put yourself out for me."

She did not need him. Perhaps she did not even want his company on the journey. Jethen stiffened, and assured her gruffly,

"I have business to see to in Hippos. It will be no hardship for me to see you there. The camels can carry your goods to Capernaum, or wherever you settle. Why not in Tiberias? It is a beautiful city. They have a market, and much more custom for your wares."

"Jesus and his disciples are going to live in Capernaum," Sherai admitted. "I heard word of it from one who follows him. Tiberias is a Roman city, built for Romans."

Jethen heard the finality in her voice, and gave in. "I will pack additional camels to carry the goods I'll be adding to my caravan in Hippos. The cloth I trade for in Hippos I will sell in Jerusalem before I travel on to Jericho. It is a part of my regular route as you know."

Sherai looked doubtful, but accepted gratefully. "It will be good to have your company on the journey. I want to tell you more of what Jesus taught. His words remind me of you."

Jethen didn't know whether to be offended, or gratified. "I am nothing like him, but if he causes me to be in your remembrance, I am satisfied. If you are ready, we will leave early on the day following the Sabbath."

"I'll be ready. I planned to leave in the morning. Rima found me a mule, and I purchased a small cart, but it will be better this way, I won't be traveling during the Sabbath. A few more days in Sychar will give me time to visit my friends. I'll go and visit Omini and Opar. They were reluctant to bid me farewell so soon. I will be here early on the first day of the week to help load the camels," she promised. "It will be agreeable to you for me to ride in the cart with Mazar? I really should bring the mule with me."

Jethen saw that she was determined to abide no longer under his roof. Her aloofness both angered and pained him. There was nothing he could do or say to change her mind, so he said gruffly, "Of course you must bring the cart and mule. Levi will see to your goods, there is no need to transport them twice. Where are they? At Omini's?" At her nod, he paused then ended abruptly, "Then I will expect you." She turned to leave the room, and he called after her, "Ziriz tells me that you have managed my concerns as well as he could, and for that I have never thanked you. For a while, Sherai, you made my house feel like a home." He could not keep the longing for such a place from his voice.

Sherai turned back to him and spoke as a sister might, "There is a cure for your empty house, Jethen. Let Mishob sell your wares this season, and find yourself a wife. There are many beautiful young women here in Sychar."

Jethen smiled in spite of the pain her words caused. "Now you sound like my mother." He couldn't resist adding after a slight pause, "If you wish for me to have a wife, Sherai, remain and marry me."

Sherai blushed and yet held his eyes with hers. "Do you seek to save my name when it no longer needs saving? Or is it that you wish to save yourself the pains of looking for someone to fill your life? You know you should have a young wife, and many children. I . . ."

Jethen cut her off quickly, before she could tell him she did not love him. "I will have a wife in my own time, Sherai, one of my choosing. Neither you nor my mother can hasten the day."

A MUSTARD SEED

    The departing sun sparkled over the lake with the shine of light hitting jewels. Fish were snapping at the sparkle. A breeze caused the sails to billow sending the boat sliding through the waves like a plow through moist earth. That same wind also soothed the brows of the men drowsily resting on the deck, or those tending the net they cast. There was no reason to let a good catch go by.
    Once the net was cast, the wind picked up a bit. Peter, once called Simon eyed the clouds the wind was pushing before them. The ship should reach the far shore in good time. It was only about thirteen miles from one end of the Sea of Galilee to the other, and even less from side to side. They were tacking a zig-zag course, but it wouldn't take long if the wind favored the direction they wished to take.
    Their destination was a city, a fortress really, in the land of the Gadarenes on the far eastern shore in the Decapolis area, built by Greeks, comprising, as its name implies, ten cities. There was a city built over tombs on the eastern shore called Hippos. The land about it was mostly desert.

Peter wondered why Jesus chose that desolate spot filled with infidels. He knew the Master became tired of the crowds of people surging against him, and that his body was weary. It was no wonder he requested the sea trip to have a rest. It was typical that many of his followers took to smaller boats and were bobbing along behind them like so many sheep. They were avid to see more healing, or hear more words, or see what Jesus would do next.

In the months since his ministry began, ever larger crowds followed him to listen to his words, and see the miracles he performed. It was no wonder they followed him. He healed a centurion's servant, and in Nain he raised a widow's son from the dead. In their own Capernaum Jesus healed Simon's mother-in-law, and others. Before he even officially began his ministry he accrued followers, Andrew, Simon's brother being among them.

Jesus was already asleep in the stern of the largest boat of the Zebedee and Bar Jonah fleet. They'd walked through the small towns around Capernaum, and he taught large crowds for several days. Jesus performed many miracles. While Simon Peter mulled over the teachings of the Master that day, he forgot the nets, and the wind.

He looked over at the sleeping man in awe. It hadn't been so long since Andrew brought the man to his home. Andrew told him of his words, and his turning water into wine, and healing a nobleman's son. Simon had known no peace since that time. Soon followed that glorious day when Jesus walked past his boats and called to him, "Come, follow me, and I will make you fishers of men." He, Andrew, and the Zebedee boys left right then and there and followed him. *'Look at me,'* he told himself. *'He walks along the shore, calls to us to follow him, and Andrew and I leave our nets and follow him. And we weren't the only ones. Even Levi, the tax collector followed him.'* Simon looked over to where Levi was seated clutching the mast. Simon pondered the change that came over Matthew, as they now called him. His very countenance was changed from the days he walked the shore waiting for their boats to come in with a catch.

Simon wondered if his own countenance differed from the past. He glanced again at the man sleeping in his boat. Jesus' teachings were so simple, his parables so beautiful, and yet so difficult to understand. While he taught the multitudes in parables, he would expound and explain later to his disciples. That didn't always make for understanding, and Jesus would have to expand on his statements.

Darkness covered the lake as Simon ruminated over the parable of that grain of mustard seed. Was Jesus telling them that their faith was too small? He often told the Pharisees that they had little or no faith. What was faith, exactly? Simon hardly knew. Why was faith so important? Once he thought that faith meant what religion you believed in, whether you were a Pharisee, or a Sadducee, but Jesus kept saying it meant so much more than that. "Faith is different from knowing," the Master said to them.

Take, for instance, the sea. Simon knew its many moods. He needed no faith to know it. Jesus said that to understand his teachings, faith was needed. Peter wanted whatever this man said he should have. The truth of Jesus' words chimed in his heart and mind. There was something in his words that stirred the soul, and gave . . . a fat drop of rain hit his face, followed by another. A streak of fingered lightning slashed the sky and outlined the sleeping man in the stern.

These swiftly gathering clouds and the sudden wind accompanying them gave Simon concern. He knew this Genesseret. It was capricious. What could begin as a sailor's delight could end in a sudden squall, and if those clouds displayed by the lightning were anything to go by, that was exactly what they were in for in a matter of minutes.

He called to the men to pull in the nets. He took one more look at his sleeping Master, and got up to give them a hand. The catch was small. There would be enough to feed them, and the other small boats following, if they could get a fire lit in the rain. "Take an oar," he yelled over the rising wind, "and John, grab that tiller. Make for shore. I'm going to get these sails down." While he had ruminated, the sky covered with black clouds filled with rain. As they worked to bring the boat to shore, the wind whipped more clouds across the lake and the only light to see by was the occasional flash of lightning as the clouds clapped together in their rush to meet.

Rough waves began to spill over the boat, and Simon began scooping out the water. The waves tossed higher and higher as they rowed. They were being pushed away from the shore. Simon looked over at his sleeping master during the flashes of light. *'How can he sleep through this,'* he wondered. The man must be exhausted from teaching and healing all day.

They all knew that when he healed the sick it often left him weak as though his own strength went from his body to theirs. Today he healed the many that came to him. They all praised God, but their healing had taken its toll on Jesus.

"Matthew," Simon called over to the former tax collector. The man was nearly useless on a boat. He was hanging onto the mast looking terrified. "Come and bail out this water while I grab an oar," he roared over the noise of the clapping thunder. Obediently Matthew came to take the bucket. Simon lashed him to the boat, and the man began bailing out water.

"Put your back into it," admonished Simon. Dutifully Matthew dipped and poured faster. "We'll make a sailor of you yet," approved the gruff fisherman, clapping him on the shoulder.

"If we live through this," rejoined Matthew.

"You fear this small breeze?" scoffed Simon.

After much rowing and bailing, the water still poured over the boat. Rain lashed Peter's face as he looked up to see whether the clouds were breaking, they were not. The sailors were losing the fight. Higher waves sent more and more water over the sides. The smaller boats that set sail after them would be lost if they hadn't returned to the west shore already. All the disciples not manning oars were pushing the water back into the sea with whatever they could find. The wind was tossing them about like a leaf rather than a sea-worthy boat. Philip, who was never much of a sailor either, was clearly frightened. "Master," he called urgently. Others took up his cry.

Philip called, "Don't you care that we are about to perish?"

Nathaniel, who was nearer Jesus, shook him awake. "How can you sleep through this? Look, your robe is wet. If we cannot ride out this storm we will perish. Come, help us steady the boat. James, John and Andrew are rowing, but to no avail."

Jesus came slowly awake, and looked up into the face of his disciple. He looked down at the water lapping against his robes as though wondering that it hadn't wakened him. "The rain lashing against my face should have wakened me, if nothing else. My pillow is sodden." He sat up, pushing the water soaked hair from his face, and looked out over the tempest.

The boat was heaving mightily from the waves, but Jesus stood to his feet as though on dry land. When a wave lashed against him drenching him to the skin he turned to the sea, holding onto the rigging. Over the sound of the howling winds, rebuking the elements he called out, "Cease your blowing, winds of the sea. Peace, be still."

The high winds ceased at that moment. The waves stopped rocking the ship, and the waters calmed. The clouds parted, and the night lights in the sky twinkled overhead once more. The oars once again cleaved the waters and took the ship toward the shore. Every man on the ship stopped what he was doing and stared at the man standing in the hinder part of the ship. The now gentle wind was whipping his hair back from his face, and gently drying it.

"Did you hear what he said?" Simon the Zealot asked no one in particular. "He told the storm to stop, and it did."

"What manner of man is he?" Judas Iscariot whispered to Simon.

"Don't you know?" Simon growled his answer to Judas.

"Even the wind and waves obey him," breathed Andrew.

"We nearly died," Philip loudly stated the obvious. "I thought we would." Fear and awe clearly marked his features.

"Yea." Several of the disciples agreed with him.

The master turned from looking over the waters and asked, "Why did you fear? Did I not teach you this very day about a mustard seed, and how such a small seed could grow to house many? You may recall I spoke of its size compared to faith, and told how as small a measure of faith could move mountains? Is cloud, wind or wave any different? Why should you fear so, have you no faith?"

"Master," said James humbly, "tell us again of this faith."

Jesus seated himself and asked, "Have any of you seen the Father?"

There were several who answered, "No."

"Then how is it that you know He exists?"

"We have been taught in the synagogue," answered Nathaniel.

"We have His word, and the words of His prophets," said James who was not a Zebedee.

"We see His handiwork all around us," John added. "Something in our minds tells us He created it."

"That *something*, John, is the Holy Spirit, witnessing to you of the Father, just as I witness of Him," Jesus began. John seated himself near him.

Simon looked out over the water to see whether all the small boats survived. Quietly he counted them, and noted that some were turning back to Capernaum. Not one appeared to have foundered, perhaps they'd had more faith.

"Faith cannot be seen," Jesus continued. The other disciples leaned against the side of the boat, or hung onto the mast. Due to the shift in weight, the prow lifted out of the water a bit. Simon Peter quietly issued orders to the oarsmen, who shifted their seating. He unfurled a sail on the mizzenmast he furled only minutes before as he listened.

12

HE THAT HAS AN EAR

Jethen sat back with his back to the wall at the small outdoor eatery outside the gates in Hippos. It had been a long day, but his business was concluded successfully. Various buyers visited his stall and bought all the finely crafted pots filled with the medicinal herbs prepared by his mother. Other pots held spices he traded for in Joppa.

Trinius, one of his customers who knew a bargain when he saw one, bought all his dyed cloth from the city of Lydda. It was on his route to Joppa he found the expert dye maker. Due to Jethen's own shrewd trading, he loaded his camels down with pottery and baskets to take to Jerusalem. He also owned a substantial box of coins stowed beneath the goods.

He looked out over Gennesseret, as the Greeks and Romans called it, and Sea of Galilee as the natives termed it. He and his fellow diners were actually sitting on a rooftop beneath swaths of cloth spread to discourage the sun. Hippos was a military compound, and walls surrounded the bustling city hiding the view of the lake. Innkeepers resolved this by serving their visitors on the roof.

The water's tranquil lapping at the shore helped Jethen relax as he sipped his wine, and occasionally dipped bread in the dish of olive oil and herbs. A serving woman brought him baked fish caught fresh that day. A pungent cheese plate to nibble, accompanied by grapes was set before him, and he was replete. Still sipping and nibbling, he unbent enough to look out over the harbor.

His business was done, but there was one personal favor to fulfill. His mother requested a Galilean weave. She gave him a piece to replicate if he could. He took the piece to Caprias who assured him that in a couple of days he could locate or have a bolt made for him. He'd waited for a week, but, he reflected, if he must wait a couple more days, there would be time to visit Capernaum again before traveling on to Jerusalem.

He would leave Mishob here in Hippos with the goods, camels and servants, and travel by boat over to Capernaum to see Sherai one last time. She should be settled in her new home, after two weeks, and perhaps lonely enough to appreciate another visit.

Certainly the small city was not what she expected. The houses were set up along narrow winding alleys with high small windows, and no outward signs of beauty. The flat roofs were a simple timber arrangement topped with reeds, and covered with mud to protect them from the rain.

Jethen could not help but compare it to the home she left in Sychar. His wide rooms, with their Romanesque windows allowing light inside, the balconies, the tiled roof, all spoke–no shouted–of affluence and comfort. How she could leave it for that . . .

He felt grimly satisfied to see her recoil at the waste lining the area ways and the bleating of goats from within. When they looked for a house she drew a veil over her face to minimize the stench. They eventually found a house near the Sea of Galilee. At least the breeze from the sea reduced some of the smells, but there were no windows with vistas of beauty. It's rooms seemed slammed together around a central courtyard. It was a large home for two women, but it was the best to be found. In the courtyard was a pen for her goat, but she and Mazar took it down and made a stable of one of the far rooms for the chickens, goat and mule. His servants quickly unloaded the camels, for there was no room for them in the town.

After unloading and moving her into her new home, he sent Mishob and the others around the lake to Hippos. They were to stop in Bethsaida, and other towns along the eastern shore to look for items to trade in Damascus and Jerusalem. Mishob knew what to look for.

Jethen remained in Capernaum for several days, boarding with Mary and her brother Jacob and his family, who sold the large house to Sherai. He helped her settle into her home. When all was made ready, he returned to Hippos, and business.

The last time he saw Sherai two weeks past, she was standing in her doorway swept as clean as the courtyard beyond. Her home was as cheerful and lovely as she could make it. He admitted that she knew how to make a house a home. A small olive press adorned one corner of the courtyard, and a grinding stone and hearth each graced other corners. Several stone jars of varying heights stood about and held water fetched from a well, while others held oil and grains. Cheery baskets hung from the ceiling, painted with palms and olive leaves, contained what vegetables and fruit that could be purchased.

The rooms were small, but the hard dirt floors were covered by the mats woven of reeds that she brought from local vendors. Some of his cloth, which she would not accept as a gift, she bought from him to cover the doors that opened onto the central courtyard. At least it gave a more cheerful aspect to the place, and afforded a little privacy. He smiled as he pictured her delight when he presented her with more mats found in Hippos. Yes, he would take them to her early tomorrow morning.

He also found a low table in a small carpenter's shop. It would do as a worktable in the courtyard. The well-made table, with her daintily painted pottery on it, would be the finishing touch.

Wiping his hands on a square of linen, he then tossed it onto the table, and sought for further excuses to return to Capernaum. If he called upon the metal workers he might find something . . . no, there were no metal workers in Capernaum, but he might find enough items in that carpenter's shop to give reason for his return so soon after leaving her there. It would be a long time before he saw her again if he waited until after his long journey to Damascus. He must go on to Jericho to visit his mother. In addition, he would return again to Jerusalem before his run to Joppa ere the season ended and he went back to Sychar.

Jethen was musing over the idea that he could return to Hippos to stay the winter instead of Sychar, and be nearby in case she needed him. Loud voices from the table next to him broke his contemplation, and he heard the name, Jesus. All the countryside was agog over Jesus. Jethen couldn't help but notice that the man who mentioned Jesus' name was also staying at the inn. His garb indicated a Jewish man of business, but he wasn't talking business with his associates.

"You know there was a storm last evening, Judas. I tell you, Simeon, I heard it directly from Simon Bar Jonah. I've known the man for years. What reason would he have to lie to me? I am one of his customers. He said that the wind and waves ceased when Jesus told them to. It was a miracle."

Jethen had heard this story both in the market, and from the serving maid, and was about to tune out on the men when one of them said, "I have heard him speak several times. This Jesus speaks with authority, not like the scribes."

"He wears no priestly robes," argued another companion.

"Matthias thinks he is a prophet, robed or not," claimed the man addressed as Judas, "like that one in the desert over by the Jordan." He slapped his goblet down on the table and some of the wine splashed onto the table.

The man seated nearest Jethen shook his head. "I think, Judas, you seek to jest at my admiration of the man. You forget, I was there the day he came to be baptized of John. John told us to behold the Lamb of God. I don't think any of us knew what John meant. He went on to say he would take away the sins of the world."

"I thought your being baptized did that for you, Matthias," laughed another friend.

The man referred to as Matthias did not rise to the baited tone. "I think he meant something more profound than that, Simeon. I have listened to this preacher. His teachings touch on the law, but go deeper, and get to the root of our lives."

"How do you mean?"

Jethen was wondering what the old Jew would say to that, and listened avidly. His grapes, cheese, and wine were forgotten.

"He taught that the commandments forbid us to commit adultery, but this Jesus said a man looking on a woman to lust after her is committing adultery in his heart." Matthias looked pointedly at Judas who was eyeing the comely serving maid each time she passed their table.

"Then that proud beauty would be stoned," Simeon indicated the serving girl.

"You miss the point, Simeon. It is the man lusting after her who has sinned." Matthias spoke gently, but there was no mistaking the sincerity of his tone.

Judas' retort proved that he had been stung by Matthias's criticism. "You'd do better to look to your business, Matthias, and quit following after that rabble rouser. You haven't taken your goods to Jericho yet, have you?"

"No," Matthias sounded abashed. "The Master calls it laying up treasures in this world that can be corrupted, or stolen." Matthias looked around and noticed that Jethen was listening to him. He gave a small tentative smile as though he, a Jew, did not notice that Jethen was a Samaritan. Then he answered Judas' taunt. "I want to hear him speak again while he is in these parts. You should go with me, Judas, and you also, Simeon. Then we can talk again. There is plenty of time to travel to Jerusalem. I'll finish my regular route with what few items I bargained for here, and I'll take them on to Jericho. There is still some time before winter sets in."

Jethen thoughtfully paid for his dinner, and walked down the outside stairs, through the city and out of the gates. On his way out of the gates he heard people talking of a man being healed by Jesus. Making his way along the rocky shore, he thought of what the old man said. Seating himself upon a rock, he looked out over the lake where the supposed miracle took place. It was true that late yesterday there was a sudden squall. Many merchants shut down and just as suddenly reopened when the storm passed.

Matthias truly believed that Jesus of Nazareth was holy, just as Sherai did. She was also righteous, a true Samaritan in the religious sense of the word. That is why it surprised him so when she became a follower of a Judean claiming to be the Messiah. The Samaritan's strict religion did not acknowledge the Jewish place of worship, their interpretations of the Torah, nor their prophets. His own father scrupulously followed the way of the Children of Israel–as the Samaritans referred to themselves.

When Amos died, Jethen and his mother fell from the faith. His mother gave up some of the more strict practices, as he did. They lived much as they always had, without their worship being centered on Mount Gerizim or making a yearly pilgrimage there to offer sacrifices.

Omini, and his household in Sychar was another such family, but his household always adhered strictly to the faith, as did Sherai.

It occurred to Jethen that Sherai might wish for a more righteous companion in her life than he was. Perhaps that is why she accepted Maachi, he at least adhered to his father's faith.

When he and Mishob first brought Sherai to Capernaum she urged him to go listen to this rabbi. He jestingly told her that there was no need to listen to the man; he heard his words wherever he went. This was true. Everywhere he heard about this Jew from Nazareth. Whether he heard good or ill depended upon who was speaking.

Take Matthias, there was no doubting the old man's dedication. There was something about his countenance that spoke of quiet happiness, and peace within. Jethen wished that he felt that peace.

He looked out over the lake, and saw the sinking sun playing with the small waves. Once in a while he saw a fish leap for an insect or other edible he couldn't see. The beauty did not touch him, nor calm him as it usually did. He wanted to see Sherai once more before he continued on his journey.

On an early visit to the caravansary the next morning Jethen saw Matthias set out with his friends. The old man left his small band of two servants, and three mules. Matthias hailed him, and invited him to join them. Simeon and Judas looked as though they would like to bathe from just looking at him.

Jethen just smiled and shook his head. They would likely visit the inn again that night to discuss the teachings of the day. He wouldn't be there to hear them, he thought without a tinge of regret. Jethen wanted an early start, so he headed for the harbor. Eagerly he scanned the skies. There was not a cloud in sight. The squall of two days past was truly over. In a matter of an hour, he would see Sherai. He would tell her about Matthias, and allow her to tell him more of this Jesus.

Rather than brave the streets, Jethen walked along the wide shore toward Sherai's house. It was early morning, but the fishermen were already out on the lake. Their boats dotted the surface like the water birds nearer shore bobbing for food.

Mazar opened the stout, strong wooden door bound with metal strips. A waft of scented oil drifted from within and minimally covered the smells outside. "Will you inform your Mistress I am here?" he asked politely. "I brought more reed mats, and this small table."

Mazar took the mats from him and said, "If you will be seated, sir, I will tell her you are here." The maid showed Jethen to the same seat he occupied on his other visits to them. Depositing the small table near the door, Jethen waited.

Sherai entered the room wiping her hands on a square of linen. "Jethen," she said as she extended her hand in greeting, "this is a pleasant surprise. I thought you to be already in Jerusalem. Thank you for the mats. Where did you find that small table? It will be perfect for the courtyard. You must allow me to pay you for them."

"No pay," Jethen denied, "they are a gift."

Sherai smiled. "I can accept the mats, but I must refuse the table unless . . . how much was the table?"

"If you insist on knowing, it was a trade, and I can only accept some of your work in trade." He picked up a long scarf. "This, and perhaps a few of these," he selected some of the snowy napkins bordered by sheaves of wheat. I am glad to find you at home this morning."

"Do not think to change the subject. You must take this table cover with the napkins, and this shawl for your mother. As for finding me at home, Mazar and I intend to leave Capernaum to travel north this morning to where Jesus is teaching. You would have missed us if you came an hour later."

"Then this Jesus has returned from the Decropolis, I heard that he was to preach there. Do you think Mazar to be sufficient company on the road?" asked Jethen. He did not approve of Sherai following after this man. A tinge of that disapproval shaded his voice.

"Oh, we do not intend to travel alone." Sherai sounded shocked. "I expect we will meet up with Mary and her brother, Jacob, on the road."

"Yes, and about a thousand others," drawled Mazar.

Jethen looked about the room. Sherai chose this house for its proximity to the water, and because right inside the door, where they were sitting, was a large room where she could display her wares. Her stitching lay out in ordered rows, bread covers, table linens, delicate veils, and small pillows, all decorated tastefully with palm trees, flowers, or palm fronds. He doubted she would have much custom for such dainty items in this agrarian and fish town. Perhaps he should set her up with an established trade route.

He said aloud, "I should take some of your stitchery on my trade route. He fingered the delicately edged cloths she thrust upon him, and studied their pattern.

"We've already had some customers. There's to be a wedding." She pointed to the veil, and to a set of table linens. Hesitantly she then asked, "Jethen, would you like to come with us today? I'm sure Mazar and I would be glad of your company."

"I would be happy to remain here, Madam. I know you will tell me all that was said and done when you return. I should tend the garden, and feed the animals."

Jethen looked at Mazar suspiciously, "Where did you find room to grow a garden?"

"We share a plot between the houses in back and to the south side. It saves money to raise our own food." Her cheerful rejoinder convinced him. Her voice held the same glad note as Sherai's voice these days. No doubt Mazar was one of those followers of Jesus, who heard him speak in Sychar. All Jesus' followers seemed to have, if not smiles on their faces, at least the same look of contentment. That old Jew Matthias also had it.

Jethen glanced down the lane through the open door and saw Mary and Jacob carefully choosing their path down the narrow street. He would have liked spending the day with Sherai, but not in the company of others. "I see your friends coming to join you," he gestured with his head down the street. "Thank you for your invitation, Sherai, but I best get back to Hippos," Jethen admitted. "I plan to travel on to Jerusalem, and I may as well start today. I don't mean to keep you, but have you heard the story of the grain of mustard seed and the storm at sea? I've heard then from at least five people at Hippos."

"I have heard Jesus speak of a grain of mustard seed, but a storm at sea, I have not heard that story. Will you share it with us?" Mazar spoke before her mistress could reply.

When he opened his mouth to begin, Sherai said, "Wait until Mary and Jacob get here, they will want to hear it." She went to the door, and called, "Come inside, Mary, Jacob, make haste. Jethen has a tale of Jesus from Hippos." Mary and Jacob hastened their steps, and they all moved to the courtyard where there was more room. Jethen carried the small table to the center of the room, and deposited it on the floor. He sat on a reed mat, and leaned his elbows on the table, and began. "I guess you recall the rain here two nights past?" Sherai's were not the only eyes lit with wonder as Jethen found himself unfolding the story to them.

When he concluded his tale he asked, "Surely none of you believe the storm stilled at his word?"

"I do believe it," Mary answered him. "You have not seen him heal the blind, and the lame, or the palsied as I have."

Jacob added, "I believe Jesus of Nazareth can do anything."

"I don't believe it. You make him sound like a God," Jethen protested.

"He certainly is sent from God," Mazar asserted.

"Did I not tell you that he is the Messiah?" Sherai reminded him.

Jethen recalled that Sherai told him the man said he was the Messiah, and something about living water. The thought that a man would declare himself *the* Messiah was too much to swallow. How he dared such a claim in this day of Roman occupation was beyond him. Telling a good story was one thing, but Messiah?

"You did say he told you that, but I am unconvinced. Storms come up at sea and vanish just as quickly. Who could say what happened out there on the water? Why do you forsake all to follow this man?" he asked them in exasperation.

"His words are the way to eternal life," Jacob said simply.

Jethen growled to cover the fact that the man's simple sincerity touched him, "You must be anxious to depart. I will take my leave. Sherai, I hope I didn't outstay my welcome. I doubt I will be in Capernaum again soon."

Sherai stood up and lightly hugged him, then seemed embarrassed. "We will be happy to see you, whenever you return," she said politely, she paused, "Thank you for coming and sharing that story with us, Jethen. And thank you again for the mats and table."

Jacob stood and thanked him for his story as well, and Mary. Mazar brought him a basket for the goods Sherai pressed upon him. He thanked them and bid a farewell. He hastened toward the harbor. If he hurried he could catch the same boat back to Hippos. The city he would bypass and go directly to the caravansary. Mishob would ready the camels for Jerusalem. Whether or not Caprias had the cloth for his mother, he'd wasted enough time. Sherai was not going to return to share his life in Sychar no matter what he said.

Anger and confusion filled his mind and heart. So much for the words of Jesus, it would take a mountain full of mustard seeds dropped on the small town to move Sherai from Capernaum.

THE MIRACLES

Sherai sat in the small garden atop her roof. She and Mazar hauled up soil, and filled boxes with seeds from last summer's flowers. Already they were pushing through the soil, and seeking the sun. Now that winter was giving way to spring, all her neighbors were busily cultivating the winter wheat, and coaxing their vegetables to grow. Her roof overlooked the plot of land where she and neighboring houses kept a garden. She smiled to see Mazar bending over her plants as if urging them to grow faster. Droning bees flitted around to plunder nectar.

Her needle flew over the small cloth she was embroidering that would sit beneath a menorah. Since the wedding she had sewn linens for, many came to her home to purchase the delicate handwork she displayed. Embracing the Jewish faith brought many to her door that might not otherwise have come.

Mazar preferred working in the garden to produce the vegetables that she and her neighbors shared. Sherai would rather sew and clean than bend over a garden. The two women were able to divide the work between them. In a week they would have early vegetables to take to the improvised market stalls along the shore. Some markets, such as the fishing stalls were already open. She would take her sewing, the more practical items, and show her work.

She was glad her hands were busy, because then her mind could wander over the things she'd seen and heard in the past few months. She thought of nothing these days but the teachings of Jesus, and his power. It seemed to her that anyone listening to the words of Jesus, or witnessing the miracles he performed, could not doubt that he was the one promised by prophesy. She smiled over his promise that those who hungered and thirsted for righteousness would be filled. His words satisfied a hunger within her soul she was unaware of before he came to the well that day. No matter how often she heard him teach, however, she still wanted more.

She, Mazar, Mary and Jacob followed him from town to town, even during the early winter months, absorbing his words, and witnessing the miraculous healing power. It was as though they lived on clouds of glory. Even the rulers of the synagogues and the city would come to listen and argue with him in their jealousy.

Sherai looked around her and breathed in the air laden with moisture from the Sea of Galilee. She wanted to sing, or shout aloud in her joy. It seemed like only yesterday she brought all her worldly goods to this small town, and made it her home. Either it was just yesterday, or she had lived here all her life. Was it truly only months? Her mind lingered over the memory of Jethen escorting them into Galilee.

The talks they shared on the way were a good memory. Eagerly she told him all that Jesus said and did in Sychar, but Jethen remained unmoved. He actually seemed shocked when she told him she was converting to Judaism. He felt that was going too far, and said so. What was Jesus to her, he asked her once.

There was no good answer for that. Jesus was everything, but she was certain if she'd said that, Jethen would have misunderstood. She wasn't a young girl enamored of a man, she was a woman enthralled with righteousness. It was very difficult to explain. It was as though a whole new world opened up within her. There was an urgency she didn't understand to absorb and learn as much as she could. Every word the Master spoke seemed a treasure to lay up in her soul. One thing was certain, she had never been this happy, not even when Tobias and Talitha were a part of her life.

Each day was a new joy to be added to the day before. She would never forget how she felt being part of a crowd following the Master to the home of Jairus. Jairus was a ruler of the synagogue in a nearby city whose daughter was dying. The Master was teaching when the man came to him asking Jesus to come see his daughter. Jesus agreed to go. He got up and departed with his disciples and Jairus. Many of those he taught followed along. There was a great crowd. She, Mazar and Mary were content to follow behind with the other women and children, but Jacob pushed on ahead with the men.

Once they reached the town the streets were so crowded there was barely room to move. It seemed the townspeople added to the throng. While they were pushing past jars, donkeys, and houses, a heavily veiled woman merged into the masses, and began to make her way through the crowd. When she stumbled into Sherai, it was as though the woman was so frail and dizzy she could barely stand. As she steadied her on her feet, Sherai noticed her heavy veiling, and wondered at it on so hot a day. She heard her again in memory as she murmured wildly, "If I can but touch him." It seemed to Sherai that the woman's mind was not on her humble apology. "Forgive me, but I must get to him." Then the woman said to herself, "If I can but touch the hem of his garment, I will be healed." She continued to push her way through the crowd.

One of the women near Sherai said, "Isn't that Anna, the woman with the issue of blood? She shouldn't be here, she is unclean."

Many of the women covered their face to avoid contamination, but Sherai looked ahead in pity to where the woman was shoving and squeezing her way through the crowd. People were pressing about Jesus so closely it was unlikely that the woman would be able to reach him at all.

Sherai saw Jacob, who was closer to Jesus, make room for the woman as with her arm outstretched she pushed her way past him. She watched the bright blue of her veil as she shoved her way closer to where the press of people was densest. Her hand reached out from between several men to touch Jesus. When she stood still and let the men surge around her, Sherai knew Anna either must have touched him or given up in despair. When Sherai reached her, she saw intense emotion radiating from her eyes which was all that could be seen of her face.

Sherai stopped to offer to help the woman reach Jesus, and then noticed that everyone had stopped moving. Sherai heard Jesus speak and ask, "Who touched me?"

Many in the crowd laughed. She heard Simon bar Jonah's deep booming voice ask him how he could ask who touched him when people were all around him. The crowd backed away from him a bit as he turned. He studied each person's face and stopped when he saw the woman, Anna, with tears dripping down her veil.

When Jesus met her eyes, the woman wept aloud, and came toward him, the crowd separating to allow her to fall at his feet.

Sherai's heart felt like it rose to her mouth. What would Jesus say? What would he do? The woman was unclean.

"Forgive me, Master," Anna sobbed. "I have been ill for many years with an issue of blood. I sought healing, but no one was able to help me. For these twelve years I have been shunned and tormented with this plague. When others told me of your great healing power, I knew that I might be healed.

"I was in seclusion when I heard that you were coming to my village. Following behind you, I found the courage to push myself through the crowd so that I might touch you. When I touched you, I felt immediately that I was healed." She stopped speaking, and the tears continued to fall down and soak her veil as she looked up, waiting for whatever Jesus would say.

Jesus said to her, "Daughter, your faith has made you well."

"Thank you, Lord Jesus," she almost shouted in her exuberance.

"Go in peace, and be well." His words echoed and reechoed through the throng, and they parted to allow the woman to return to her home.

Sherai thought she would never forget the woman's face as she undid her veil, and walked with confidence and steadiness down the pathway. Her face glowed with health. Her eyes were clear, and sparkled with unutterable happiness.

'That is what Jesus can do,' Sherai thought. *'His touch, or his words, it doesn't matter, they are the same. He makes you whole.'*

She was so wrapped up in rejoicing over Anna, Sherai didn't even notice that, along with the rest of the crowd, she continued on until they reached Jairus' house.

They were met by mourners beating instruments and wailing. The daughter died. Abruptly the euphoria vanished.

Finally, the servants crying that his daughter was dead came out to meet them. They assured Jairus that he was too late in bringing Jesus, and that they should trouble him no more.

Sherai was close enough to see Jesus look into the grieving father's face and say, "Jairus, believe." He chose three of his disciples, and bid the others wait outside. Those disciples and Jesus went with Jairus into the house.

Jacob, Mary's brother, and a few others slipped into the house behind Jairus' servants. Sherai would not have known what happened if he'd not boldly entered the house. Jacob told them he barely hid behind a pillar when Jairus' wife came out to meet Jesus and tell him in her grief, "You are too late. Our daughter is dead."

The mother went to Jairus and buried her face on his shoulder. Jairus was filled with grief, and his body shook with sobs.

Jesus, filled with compassion for them, said, "There is no need to grieve. She is not dead, only sleeping."

The mourners inside the house stopped their professional wail, and some of them laughed. "We know the difference between sleep and death," one was bold enough to say. Simon gripped the shoulder of Jairus and said, "Come with us into her room, we will wake her."

At this point in the story, Jacob told them that the people inside the house, including himself, crowded outside the door. It was only covered by curtains, and they could clearly hear what transpired. The light from a window casement showed the shadow of Jesus taking the young girl by the hand. Then they heard his voice, "Damsel, I say to you, arise."

Many of the silent watchers leaned into the curtain to see what would happen. Gasps of awe and worship escaped from their lips when the little one sat up. She arose from the bed and went to hug her mother and father. Then she walked out of the room and stared at the people as if wondering what they were all doing in her house. All the people waiting outside the room saw her alive and well. Some of them, including Jacob ran out of the house shouting.

"She is alive!"

"Praise be to God!"

Jacob was still telling us what transpired when we all saw her. She came to the door to bid Jesus farewell. Sherai sank to her knees. Others all around did also. A shout of "Hosanna" filled the air. Sherai was shouting and waving her hands in the air all the while tears were pouring down her cheeks. People all around were shouting and praising God. Had anything so miraculous occurred before in this small town?

Directly afterward they returned to their homes. It was as though nothing more could add to the day. Everyone praised

God and rejoiced on the way. Jacob, who was usually silent on the long walks, could not stop talking about the miracles. "Surely he is sent of God," he kept repeating. "He is the Messiah." Sherai's heart was too full for words.

Tears welled in her eyes just at the memory of that day. She almost wiped them on the linen before she came to herself and realized what it was. Smiling at her absentmindedness, she wiped her eyes on her apron instead. Gathering up her sewing she made her way down into the courtyard. It was getting too warm on the roof.

Seating herself near the small table Jethen brought, she once again became lost in thought. All that mild winter Jesus taught, and performed miracles. As often as she and Mazar could, they went where he was teaching, and witnessed even more miracles. Two blind men received their sight, a dumb man was healed, and lepers were cleansed. The sick that were brought to him were healed. As wondrous as the miracles were, to Sherai it was Jesus words she loved. His words healed her broken heart.

There was so much to ponder, and relive. The memories alone kept her faith strong. For a while there would be no teaching, and no more miracles, at least not in Galilee. Jesus went to Jerusalem for the Passover. Many of his disciples traveled with him, but Sherai did not wish to travel to a busy city during Passover.

Jesus would return to Galilee, and the crowds would follow him again, but meanwhile, she was glad for time to absorb the things he taught. "Don't worry so much over what you will eat, or what you will drink. It is needless to worry over what you should wear. Seek first for the Kingdom of God and His righteousness. All these other things will be of little importance to you, but you will have them."

"The Kingdom of God," Sherai murmured.

"You said something to me, Mistress?" asked Mazar. Sherai was so deep in thought she'd not heard Mazar return. The woman was dusting the room with a damp cloth. It was difficult in the warmer months to keep the dust to a minimum. The rugs needed to be taken out and beaten weekly, and the floor was watered down rather than swept, for the swirl of dust sweeping created made it difficult to breathe.

"What does the kingdom of God mean to you, Mazar? What do you think the Master means when he talks of it so stirringly?"

The servant girl answered promptly. "He is the Messiah. He will drive out the Romans, establish a Kingdom, and be the ruler of it. All the children of Israel will be united once more, and live together in harmony."

"I'm not so sure," Sherai murmured. "I believe that he will rule, in a sense he does hold the hearts of the people. Look at the thousands who follow him. It does not seem to me that he needs to set up His Kingdom by warring with the Romans."

"How could he otherwise become king?" Mazar asked. "Perhaps someone will ask him, and He will explain it. Then we will know for certain."

"I hope that will be so. Often he answers questions with parables, or examples, and it is difficult to get to the meaning of his sayings. Haven't you found that to be true?"

Mazar stopped wiping down the furniture and walls long enough to formulate an answer. Her brow wrinkled with the effort. "I think that the Rabbi's words are easy to understand with our heart. When we try to understand them with our mind that is when we become confused. Oh, I am not saying what I mean well, Mistress, but . . ."

"On the contrary, Mazar, you have put it very well. I was just pondering why he would tell us not to worry about food, or clothing, or a place to sleep. It doesn't seem rational."

"He wears robes, and has a hearty appetite from what I have seen."

"You are right. Some of the Pharisees accuse him of being a wine bibber," Sherai laughed. "He does have a very nice robe."

"Just the same, he observes all the holy days, and the Sabbath."

"You have reminded me that tonight our Sabbath begins. We must prepare. I will put aside this sewing and help you dust." In harmony the two women worked to prepare their dwelling for the Sabbath.

JETHEN DECIDES

Jethen bolted up the stairs to the roof. Frustration lent speed to his long legs. If his mother took ill again . . . he didn't even finish the thought in his mind. How could Miriam allow their mother to walk these steps, and risk the weather when they just pulled her through her last bout of sickness nigh to death?

"You are angry, my son?" queried a soft voice.

Jethen walked rapidly to his mother and placed the back of his hand against her cheek. It was warm, but not feverish as he feared. His mother ignored his anger and taking his hand held it against her face. "Mishob and your sister helped me up here. I'm feeling so much better I insisted on a bit of fresh air. After being indoors all winter, I wanted to be a part of spring and assure my worn-out body that I am going to live. It is a beautiful day."

When Jethen didn't say anything she continued with spirit. "Smooth your frown, Jethen. There is no cause for it. When I woke this morning I was hungry. I ate with enjoyment, and felt strength returning to my body."

He looked over the fields and willed himself to calmness. "You look as though the air is agreeing with you," he finally said.

"I feel well, or at least I am assured that in due time I will be well, thanks to the care you and Miriam have lavished upon me. I believe I feel better than you do at this moment." She looked up into his face in as penetrating a study as he just gave her.

Uncomfortable with her scrutiny Jethen walked to the edge of the eastern roof and looked out over the olive vineyard. He and Mishob supervised the grafting on some of the trees just this morning. His mother called out to his rigid back, "Are you pining for travel again after the long winter? Have you missed your home in Sychar? Or," she added slyly, "are you pining for a certain person?"

"Sychar?" Jethen chose to ignore her last pointed question and answer the second. "I have not given one thought to the house I built." That, at least was true. When Sherai left Sychar, it no longer seemed like a home. He hadn't lived there long enough for it to seem like his.

"Then it is travel you miss, I have kept you at my side when you wished to be elsewhere."

There was too much truth in that statement for Jethen to openly refute it. He chose evasion. "Now that you are feeling so much better, I will be on my travels soon enough. I was concerned that Miriam allowed you out of your sick bed too soon."

"Since you find me well enough to be out, and there is still a wrinkle across your brow, *someone* else must be bringing that look to your face," his mother probed.

Jethen forced his face to relax, took in a deep breath, and took her hand in his. He didn't relinquish it as he sat down beside her on the stones used for grinding wheat and barley. "We have spoken of this before. During those long nights when you couldn't sleep, we talked of my future, and how you wished to see me marry and bring children to you. To make up to you for my frown, I will admit that I have a longing for a family. I built in Sychar for . . . I think you know me enough to guess the woman I have always loved."

"You speak of Sherai," his mother said softly. "You have always loved her, even as a child."

"You also know that although I have her friendship, she has never loved me in return."

His mother softly snorted in denial as if to say she believed him not one whit. "Why did you not ask for her when that whelp of Omini's put her aside?"

"I hoped to persuade her to come here to you in Jericho, and ask for her away from Omini's influence. I built that house in Sychar to take her to if . . . I'm sure Mishob has told you that after Maachi's bill of divorcement was read, she ran away. The humiliation was more than she could bear. I devoted most of that winter to finding her. When I did locate her, she was hired out as a servant in Magdala. I took her home to Sychar. It was almost spring, and I needed to begin my rounds again. At the end of my trip, and harvest, I was intending to bring her here for the winter."

"Then I became ill," his mother regretted, "and you remained in Jericho to care for me."

"No," her son denied. "It was nothing to do with you, her not coming here, I mean. Nor would it have mattered if she agreed to a betrothal. I would have remained with you even if she said yes."

His mother let out a long sigh of her own. "I feared that you might have quarreled over me," she admitted.

Jethen took a deep breath. He didn't like telling his mother this part. "The truth is—I did not ask for her in so many formal words. There is something I haven't told you yet. Sherai is no longer at Sychar. A teacher, a Jew named Jesus of Nazareth, came through Sychar, and preached to the people there. He converted many, including Omini."

"I know, Jethen. Mishob has told me. This Jesus touched Sherai's heart as well. Even some of your household now follows him." The old woman sighed and continued, "I may as well admit I was relieved to hear that Maachi rescinded his divorce, and absolved their marriage. He and Omini settled money on Sherai. Now there is nothing to stand in your way."

Jethen blurted, "She thinks this Jesus is the Taheb who was promised to us, and she left Sychar to follow him." Jethen lifted a stone lid and withdrew some dates offering some to his mother. His mother took a date and nibbled at it. "She is living in Capernaum in Galilee, not at Sychar."

"I won't pretend I did not know this, my son. Nothing much happens that I don't know about," Miriam admitted. "Mishob's son brings me most of my news, but I know about Sherai because Mishob, himself, told me. So, Sherai chose to follow this Jesus. Does she love *him*?"

"It is more devotion than love, I am hoping. She truly believes that he is the Messiah. Has Mishob," he asked drily, "told you of his words, and the miracles?"

"He has," she colored a bit, nodded and bit her lip before adding, "I begged him to tell me until he feared for my health, and told me all to put my mind at rest." She tugged her hand from his and hid her hands in the sleeves of her robe.

His mother looked into his eyes and said softly, "I have heard the words of this Jesus from sources other than Mishob. 'We are the light of the world, a city that sits upon a hill.'" she quoted. "He certainly wasn't speaking of Jericho." She chuckled and coughed reminding Jethen that she was not completely recovered.

"Should I take you inside?" he asked anxiously.

"No, please. I am enjoying the warm weather, and that light breeze from the river. Besides, our conversation is not finished. Don't think you can change the subject. If you love Sherai, you must pursue her. It isn't like you to give her up this easily."

Her son grinned at her like the young boy who never gave up loving his animals. "Now that you are recovered, I'm leaving next week for Hippos. That's why I was so anxious on learning you were outdoors instead of safely tucked in bed. If you became ill again, I could not go."

"If Sherai is in Capernaum, why will you go to Hippos?"

"I find the accommodations there more amenable than those in Capernaum. It's a military fortress turned into a city. It is only across the Sea of Galilee from Capernaum. The distance isn't a problem. What is more likely, she will be off with the crowds following Jesus."

"Then you must follow him too, until she sees you as her husband."

"That I won't do," denied Jethen. "I won't pretend to espouse something just to win her. I will go on up to Damascus, and down to Joppa, Tyre and Sidon, then stop in Sychar, and go on to Jerusalem, my usual routes. I want to marry her, and I may ask for her formally even though I know she doesn't love me. I may ask her to come visit with you and Miriam." He paused, and rubbed his hand over the stubble on his chin. He really must take better care of himself. "I suppose I would marry her knowing that she does not love me in the way I . . . I would like for her to feel the same way I do."

"She may, in time."

"Not as long as Jesus is everywhere teaching and performing so-called miracles."

"Jesus is not in Galilee. I hear that he passed through here on his way to Jerusalem. Some of our workers in the vineyard followed him there. Why not go to Jerusalem first, and see if Sherai is there?"

"She might be there, and I could bring her here to see you." He didn't say that perhaps his mother could persuade her to accept him. "Perhaps I will go to Jerusalem and practice some of that faith Jesus talks about."

"Faith, I like that word. You must have faith in Sherai. Was it you or did Mishob tell me that Jesus said it only takes the amount of a grain of mustard seed to move mountains? Sherai is much smaller than a mountain," his mother teased him gently.

"But only slightly less immovable," Jethen grumbled, but he was smiling.

15

SHEEP GATE

Jerusalem was teeming with pilgrims who came to offer sacrifices, and join together in the Passover. In the caravansary north of the Mount of Olives, within walking distance from the Sheep Gate, Jethen settled all but one of his pack animals, and paid for their lodging. Not liking the looks of a few of the extra men hired for the religious observance, he bade his servants remain with the animals and their goods. "I'll be back later to assume the watch, and you may enter Jerusalem then," he promised.

"Come Nam, we have work to do." Walking beside his donkey out of the enclosure, he met the old man he encountered in Hippos. He was about to pass him with a nod when the man stopped him with a hand on his arm. "We never introduced ourselves. My name is Matthias, son of Thomas. Didn't I see you in Hippos last year? Have you come for the Passover? Is all well with you?"

Jethen was surprised, but pleased that the old man would speak with him. "How is it that you speak with me, a Samaritan?"

"Jesus has taught us that we must consider all men as our brothers."

"Then, brother, my name is Jethen, son of Amos. Yes, all is well. And with your family, also?"

"All is well. I have been here several days. Right now I am on my way to the temple. Would you care to walk with me?"

"Nam and I will pass by the temple. I would be pleased to join you."

"You call the donkey Nam?"

Jethen looked uncomfortable for a moment then admitted, "I call her Nam because when I load her down one gerah more than she wishes to carry, she pretends to be lame, and refuses to walk."

"Ah, a clever one. Nam is a good name for her."

Jethen decided it was time to change the subject. Perhaps Matthias did not believe in naming animals either. "I am not surprised to see you here in Jerusalem at this time. Isn't your Jesus here also?"

Matthias did not seem surprised to be questioned about Jesus, nor to claim him. "Yes, the Master is here. He came to observe the Passover. He created quite a furor by healing a man on the Sabbath yesterday. Would you care to have me relate it to you as we walk to the gate?"

"Tell me, Jesus healed a man on the Sabbath? I don't suppose the High Priests liked that."

Matthias chuckled, "There were quite a few disgruntled, devout men, as you so shrewdly deduced. Are you familiar with the area north of the Sheep Gate? There is a pool there, with a colonnade of five porches around it. In the Hebrew tongue it is called Bethesda."

"Yes, I am familiar with it, it is a beautiful spot."

"There is a tradition that at a certain time the Lord sends an angel to trouble the waters, and the first person into the pool is healed of their infirmity. There is always a large group of halt, lame, blind, and other folk waiting for the moving of the water.

"Jesus came to that pool and saw a man who had been crippled for thirty-eight years. Perhaps he noticed him there before. The man waited patiently though there was little hope of him making it into the water. He was alone, you see.

"Jesus went up to him and said, 'Will you be made whole?' The man looked and told him, 'Sir, I have no one, when the water is troubled, to put me into the pool. While I am trying to reach the pool, another steps down into it before me.'

"Jesus said to him, 'Rise, take up your bed, and walk.' I watched as the man felt the strength returning to his limbs. He seemed filled with ineffable surprise and joy."

"I can well imagine it."

"My friend, he arose from his bed, took it up, and walked. Jesus passed into the crowd with us, but the man made his way through the porches carrying his bed.

"As he walked, several Jews confronted him and told him, "It is unlawful for you to carry your bed on the Sabbath."

"He answered them, "He who made me whole bade me to take up my bed and walk."

"Then they asked him, 'What man said to you, "Take up your bed and walk?"'

"The man did not know who it was who made him whole, and could not tell them. Later that day, Jesus found him in the temple, and told him to sin no more lest a worse thing should come upon him. They talked for a while and the man discovered it was Jesus who healed him. He went and told his accusers who the man was. Today, Jesus is speaking in the temple. It is likely he will be challenged by those same accusers."

Jethen thought to himself that the man, Jesus, was making enemies by flouting Jewish laws and customs. They reached the end of the story, and the gate at the same time. He asked, "What do you think Jesus will say to his accusers?"

Matthias shrugged, and a worried frown appeared on his face. "I believe he will say what he often says to his accusers, "I must do the will of my Father."

"And who is his father? Does he mean . . ."

"Ah, that is the crux of the matter. We, his followers, believe he means the one who is God." Matthias looked anxiously at Jethen as if afraid he went too far in speaking so before a foreigner.

"He equates himself with God openly?" Even Jethen was shocked to hear the man make such a claim. "Your Master is asking to be stoned as a blasphemer."

"He is no blasphemer. His words and works proclaim him. In the name of the Father he does all his healing. Perhaps they will try to stone him, he is not so well known here as in Galilee. He plans to teach about the Father in the temple. I must find Him in the Court of the Gentiles as soon as possible. Do you wish to accompany me?"

"I must take my leave of you," Jethen told the old man politely, but without regret. He'd no wish to become embroiled in trouble. Brawlers and rioters tended to get flogged by the Romans first, and asked questions later. Perversely, he hoped Sherai was not in Jerusalem. "I have business to transact in the market place, and then I must journey on to Galilee." He told the old man.

Matthias nodded as though he heard, but Jethen could see his mind was already with Jesus. The old man took his leave and hurried off through the crowds and on up the stairs to the temple.

Jethen made his way slowly past the temple to the upper city. There he would find Herod's palace. He would soon meet with Gera, chief buyer for the King, and his best customer. Gera would be surprised to see him so early in the year.

After leaving his donkey with Gera he would make his way back to the temple. If Sherai were here she would be wherever Jesus was. He would find her.

16

ASK ME NOT

The one-masted fishing boat pulled into the harbor of Capernaum. Other fishing boats were already bobbing on the waves, from which men were casting their nets. A few older men dotted the shore, sitting on rocks smoothed by water, mending nets in the pale spring sun. The air was filled with the smell of water, and nearer shore, fish.

Nearby, several women were washing their clothes on flat rocks rolled to the shore for that purpose. These same clothes would soon flap in the breeze on rooftops and in courtyards. Mazar hefted her filled basket higher on her hip, and made her way to the shore. That is how she happened to see Jethen when he first stepped from the small boat.

Her heart sank within her, for she knew this meant that she and Sherai would not be free to follow the Master if he came today. It was rumored that Jesus was returning to Galilee after the Passover, and was again going to be teaching in the synagogues, and on the hillsides. She had kept an ear and eye out for his return the last two days.

She shrugged her shoulders and dropped her basket on the rocks. It was none of her concern if the man could not see that Sherai was uninterested in him. He would do better to follow after Jesus than to visit a woman who looked upon him as she might a brother.

Sherai answered the knocking on her door with a preoccupied air. That morning, while Mazar was out with the laundry, she was sweeping her courtyard, and straightening it from the ravages of the winter. She was wearing her oldest robe. It had been washed and mended until the color faded to a pale apricot. A large apron was tied up to her waist to keep it clean, and a square of linen protected her hair from the cobwebs and dust.

"Jethen," she cried, half in glad welcome, and half in vexation. Swiftly she brushed down her apron, and tore the kerchief from her hair. "Come in, and welcome. As you can see, I am doing some much needed household cleaning this morning. What brings you to Capernaum so early in the day?"

"Sherai," he took her hand in his, disregarding the traces of dust, and cobwebs that clung to her. "I was hoping to persuade you to accompany me on a walk. There is a matter I wish to discuss with you. I think it would be better to take you away from the distractions of house and home."

"How like a man not to notice that I am in my oldest clothes, and in no fit manner to go abroad on the streets," she mock scolded him.

"It won't take you long to ready yourself."

Sherai looked at him in exasperation. It wasn't so much that she couldn't get ready, it was that she was prepared to clean. She looked about her entry, and on into the courtyard and sighed. "If you will come in and be seated," she offered, "you can wait while I freshen myself."

"No," Jethen hastily denied, "it wouldn't be seemly to come in while your serving woman is away. I will wait for you outside."

When Sherai raised a questioning brow, he explained, "I saw her with a basket of clothes heading for the shore. She seemed displeased to see me," he blurted.

"Laundry day is Mazar's least favorite. She frowns at everyone on wash day. Wait for me outside then," she agreed. "I'll make haste." Sherai shut the door and mused that his sudden concern for her reputation was more impatience and wanting to pace outside while he was waiting for her than propriety. He knew she would hurry more if he waited outside. Untying the apron from her robes, she scurried to her room. The cleaning would have to wait for another day.

They stood looking out over the city of Capernaum, and the Sea of Galilee. The sun was sparkling over the water. A light breeze was puffing at the sails, and rippling the water. The climb to the nearby hilltop wasn't arduous, but Sherai's cheeks were becomingly flushed from the exercise. She looked at Jethen to share the beauty of the day with him, and found him observing her with a serious look on his face.

"I looked for you in Jerusalem," he said.

"You have come from Jerusalem? You are more courageous than I. I would not brave the Passover crowds. Mazar and I kept the Passover here in Capernaum with Mary and Jacob."

Jethen frowned. "You are keeping Jewish customs now?"

"When I was baptized by Jesus' disciples, I became a part of the tribe of Judah," she told him. "I thought you knew."

"I suppose if I gave it more thought, I would have realized it. I mostly think of you as that young girl running with me among the sheep, or that woman who left me in Sychar."

"Jethen, I . . ."

He interrupted her quickly, "I would have come sooner to visit you, but my mother was ill."

"Is she . . .?"

"She is well. It is really because of her that I sought you out."

"You need me to go and care for her while you travel?" Sherai's heart sank. She wanted to be in Galilee. Jesus would be returning soon from Jerusalem. She squared her shoulders and lifted her chin. If Jethen needed her, she would go. She owed him at least that much.

"No, no. Miriam is there with her. I am only saying that my mother urged me to see you."

Sherai looked as puzzled as she felt. Why would Jethen's mother urge him to see her?

Jethen saw her look and gave an exasperated sigh. "My mother told me to come to you because she knows what you refuse to grasp, how very much you mean to me. How much you have always meant." Jethen reached out and cupped her shoulders with his hand. "She knows that I love you, Sherai. I have loved you since we were children together. She wants me to bring you home as her daughter."

"You . . ."

"I want to marry you, and care for you all the rest of our lives."

Sherai looked up into his eyes. There was no denying what she read there. Jethen did, indeed, love her. She purposely blinded herself, seeing only friendship, when something far deeper motivated her friend. She thought that his desire to help her stemmed from their distant kinship, and their long ago association. Sherai looked away from him, and felt a blush rising in her cheeks. She admitted, now that she was faced with his declaration, that she wondered at his devotion. Her heart slowed its beating. Her cheeks, that blushed so rosily, were now pale with dread.

"Jethen, I scarcely know what to say," she managed to get that much out.

"Say you will marry me and go first to Jericho for my mother's blessing, then home to Sychar."

She said the thing uppermost in her mind. "You have never been married."

"Because I was in no position to ask for you when we were young. We were of an age together, and Omini's son was already well established. Your father would not have considered me. You must not think of my single state in your answer to me, Sherai. There is no other woman I ever intend to marry." He said it with such finality she was forced to believe him.

"But I have been married many times. I am now a Jewess. I must marry a Jew, and you must marry a Samaritan. That is your law, and my law."

"Such things no longer matter to me. You are a Samaritan woman by birth."

She said as gently as she could, "These things do matter to me, Jethen. If I wish to marry again, which at present, I assure you, I have no wish to do, it must be to a member of the tribe of Judah. I am no longer a Samaritan."

"You wish to marry this Jesus?"

"Me? Marry the Taheb?" Sherai actually laughed. Taheb was the Samaritan name for the Messiah. She hoped that by using it she was conveying to Jethen the man's importance in her eyes. "Where did you get that idea? He is my rabbi, my teacher, my king, but that is all."

"Then there is no reason to reject my offer."

"There is every reason, Jethen. I have just told you. Aside from the reasons I cited, I have no wish to be married, and if my heart was inclined to do so . . ."

Jethen dropped his arms. There was no use. He had known it before he journeyed to find her, but his mother had given him hope.

Pulling his breath deep into his lungs as though they no longer wished to draw breath, he asked, "What does your heart tell you?"

"My heart tells me to follow Jesus. I must hear every word that he teaches. I must be his ardent disciple for as long as I can be. He has the words of truth, and eternal life. His teachings absorb my every thought, and fill my heart. I wish..."

"What is it you wish?" Jethen's voice was strained, but his question proved he was trying to understand.

"I wish that you would listen to Jesus, see his miracles, follow his pathways," she said bravely, and looked up into his face.

Now it was Jethen's turn to look elsewhere. He faced eastward to the city, and admitted. "I have heard him speak. It was at the temple in Jerusalem. I went there to look for you, thinking you might be in Jerusalem with him. He was talking about his relationship with the Father. It seemed to me that he was saying that he was a God, Sherai. Do you believe this?"

"Though he said it in my hearing only once, I believe he is the son of God, yes. Who else could do all the miracles he does?"

"There are others I have heard of who go about the country preaching and performing miracles. They do not profess to be a god, only a prophet."

Sherai shook her head, "Not the miracles I've seen. Jesus mostly calls himself the son of man. It doesn't matter. I know within myself that his words are the words of eternal life." Earnestly she entreated him to believe her.

"I can't believe it," he said heavily. "I can't believe that he is the son of God." He looked into her eyes again, this woman he loved with all his heart, and he saw that his words hurt her. He knew what she would say to him before she even spoke.

"With such a fundamental difference between us, Jethen, I cannot marry you. You would come to resent my beliefs, and I would always long for you to embrace my faith."

"You say this, but you would overlook these things if you cared for me. That is what you are truly saying, you do not care for me."

Tears came to Sherai's eyes. She reached out her hand to lightly touch his sleeve. "I'm sorry, Jethen," she whispered, and she ran from him down the hill toward Capernaum. She knew as she ran that she just lost her dearest friend.

Jethen watched her run from him down the hill. His mind and heart were seething from her rejection. She must have known he would convert to Judaism for her sake, he left the Samaritans long ago both philosophically and religiously, so that was not it.

She did not want his love; it was his love she was rejecting. No matter what she said, it was this Jesus she loved. He felt his resentment toward the Galilean grow. His hand went to the pack at his side. Digging deep, he scooped up the grains of mustard seed buried there. He scattered them on the ground. Faith didn't seem to work for him.

He stood looking after her until she disappeared into the outskirts of the town. Feeling as though his heart was beaten raw, Jethen made his own way back to the shore. Pain and anger dogged his footsteps. He'd known heartache before, but never this pain of a heart severed forever from its reason for beating.

17

THE KINGDOM

Mazar came running into the courtyard. "They've returned!" she cried joyously. "They are traveling through Capernaum toward Bethsaida, and there is a multitude following them."

Sherai didn't need to ask who was back, for they long awaited this day. Hastily she wiped her tears. She didn't want Mazar asking her awkward questions, at least, not yet. There was little her servant could not wheedle from her, but her heart was too sore to be questioned. This was what she needed to reaffirm her resolve.

The long winter months of waiting resulted in a few gatherings to hear the Master in Capernaum, but he traveled. A few persistent men who followed him brought back reports of his healing two men of their blindness, and healing a man, unable to speak, who was possessed of a devil. He was vilified by both the Pharisees and Sadducees for eating with sinners. Also Jacob brought word of His parable of the two debtors before he had left for the Passover. Mazar was as hungry to hear more of Jesus' words as she was.

Mazar's glad cry meant his Apostles returned from their journey with Jesus. When the woman came in with her basket of wet linens Sherai told her, "Then we follow along with them."

"What of Jethen?" Mazar looked around the courtyard. "Will he travel with us?"

"No," Sherai told her casually. "He left for Hippos, and then he will travel on to Damascas. There will only be the two of us." Taking a small bag similar to ones used to store grain, Sherai walked to the room they used to store their food. She thrust into the bag a loaf of bread, a round of goat's cheese, and some olives. From a simply carved box she selected a knife, and inserted it in the bag also. Food would be needed if they were to be gone all that day. "You had best take one of the wine skins."

Mazar looked at her piercingly, but Sherai, with a stern frown, made it clear she did not wish to speak further. Her servant shrugged her shoulders as if to say, *'then don't tell me,'* and said aloud as she picked up the woven reed basket she dropped, "I'll have to hang up this wash first. I nearly forgot it in the excitement. I'll hurry as fast as I can," she promised.

"It will go much faster if I help you." Now that she knew she wouldn't have awkward questions to contend with, Sherai was content to hurry Mazar along. Chatting about the crowds, and what they should take, the two women hurried to the roof. Sherai cast an anxious glance at the sky, but there wasn't a cloud in sight. They would chance leaving the clothes on the roof for the day.

Sherai shut and locked her door, and she and Mazar set out to find the crowd. It wasn't difficult to find Jesus because everyone was going in his direction. The streets were crowded with travelers all going toward the road that led to Bethsaida.

As they passed through the small villages and towns in between, the crowd following Jesus increased. Just as they joined the throng, others along the way left their homes to follow. People were shouting out questions to Him, but he seemed oblivious to their entreaties. He was talking quietly with his Apostles. They were all talking at once, but Jesus seemed to hear every word.

When they reached Bethsaida, they journeyed on through the town and out into the desert. There was no room in the town for the large company of thousands that thronged Jesus. They traveled until they came to a hill. It was large enough to accommodate all who followed.

Once there, Jesus climbed to the top, and seated himself on a large rock. He spoke quietly with his disciples around him until all the people arrived and seated themselves on the hill.

Sherai and Mazar seated themselves as near to the man as they could, but many younger and stronger men had pushed their way to the very top, and were seated closer. Sherai saw Mary and Jacob, and waved, but the crowd was too dense for them to make their way to each other. It had been a long walk and most of the people were tired.

"Rabboni," called out someone in the crowd, "What of this kingdom of which you speak. Is it a throne in Heaven, or will some other kingdom come? When will it come?"

Sherai and Mazar caught one another's eyes and smiled. The very question on their own minds was asked.

Jesus motioned for his disciples to be seated around him. He looked out over the large crowd assembled, as though looking for the questioner. It seemed he found him, for his eyes rested on one person as he said, "I will tell you of the kingdom."

His voice reverberated as though he cupped his mouth with his hands and shouted, but though he sat atop the hill and spoke, loudly, it was true, he did not shout. Yet everyone seemed to hear his words as though he spoke to them personally. The crowd quieted, and everyone settled to listen, even the children.

"The kingdom of heaven is like leaven that a woman takes and places in three measures of meal. She leaves it there until it all is leavened. The kingdom is also like a mustard seed, the least of all seeds that a man took and sowed in his field. When it is grown it is the greatest among herbs, and becomes a tree so the birds can lodge in its branches."

"We understand that the kingdom is to grow, and that it will be great, but when will it come? Where will it be established?" These questions were raised by certain Pharisees who followed Jesus, mostly to heckle him.

He looked at them and replied, "You recall that I said to repent for the kingdom of heaven is at hand?"

They nodded their heads, but one of them said, "That does not tell us where this kingdom is to be found."

"The kingdom of God does not come with observation," Jesus answered him. "No one can say, *'Lo it is here,'*" he gestured toward Jerusalem, "*'nor lo it is there!'*" he gestured toward Tiberius. "This none can say, for behold, the kingdom of God is within you."

"Then the kingdom of God has come?" persisted the Pharisees. "How can that be when there is so much wickedness and oppression in the world?"

"The kingdom of heaven is like a man who went and sowed good seed in his field. Then his enemy came in the night while he slept and sowed tares among the good seed and went away. When the blade sprang up and began to grow, the tares appeared also.

"His servants came to the man and said, "Master, did you not sow good seed in your field? Why is it filled with tares also?"

"He said to them, 'An enemy has done this.'

"The servants said, 'Do you want us to go out and gather up the tares?'

"'No!' said he, 'lest while you gather the tares you also root up the wheat with them. Let both grow together until the harvest and in the time of harvest I will tell the reapers to first gather the tares and bind them in bundles to burn them, but gather the wheat into my barn.'" Jesus finished his parable and looked at the Pharisees as if expecting them to question him further.

Sherai looked at the Pharisees, but they did not seem any more satisfied than before. Could they not see that the tares were the wicked? It was as though they heard all his words but did not understand his meaning.

Finally one of the scribes seated near Sherai, who wore the emblem of his trade on his robe, stood and asked, "How can we find this kingdom within us?"

Then he said to them, "Every scribe who is instructed about the kingdom of heaven is like a man who is a householder, who brings out of his treasures things both new and old.

"The kingdom of heaven is like a treasure laid in a field that a man found and hid in a field. For the joy of having such a treasure, he sells all that he has, and buys the field.

"Again, the kingdom of heaven is like a merchant seeking good pearls. When he finds a pearl of great price, he sells all he has, and buys it." Soft talking broke out all over the hill as people tried to wrest the meaning of his words.

Jesus ceased speaking for a time, and some young children who had been waiting for such an opportunity ran to him and began trying to reach him. His disciples gathered round Jesus to prevent them.

Jesus had been speaking quietly to one of his disciples, but when he saw them forbid the children he was displeased and said, "Let the little ones come to me, don't forbid them. Of such is the kingdom of God. He who will not receive the kingdom of God as a little child shall not enter there."

The children gathered round him, and he touched them, and blessed them. One climbed onto his lap, and laid his head on his chest. Another stood with his arm about his neck, several little girls knelt at his feet. He had a smile and a word for them all. Sherai and Mazar took the opportunity to move closer themselves.

Sherai saw Jesus look up and ask his disciples, "Who have I said is the greatest in the kingdom of heaven?"

Simon bar Jonah said, "He who is the servant of all."

One named John answered him, "He who humbles himself as a little child is the greatest."

"Yes, and whoever receives a little child in my name, receives me," Jesus sought the crowd and seemed to single out a swarthy man who had been watching him intently, "but whoever offends one of these little ones, who believe in me, it would be better for him that a millstone were hanged about his neck and that he were drowned in the depth of the sea."

"I understand that," whispered Sherai excitedly to Mazar. "Little children believe with all their hearts. They have no doubts, or fears, they accept what they are taught . . ." she ceased speaking because Jesus was still speaking.

Still looking at the man he continued, "Woe unto the world because of these offences. It must be that offences come, but woe to that man who offends. If your hand offends by striking, or your foot by kicking, cut them off, for it is better to enter into life halt or maimed than having two hands or two feet to be cast into everlasting fire.

Sherai followed Jesus' gaze, and it seemed he was speaking directly to the swarthy man. The man was staring him down, but a deep red had suffused his face and neck.

It is the same for your eye, if it offends, pluck it out and cast it far from you, for it is better to enter into life with one eye than that by having two eyes be cast into hell fire.

"Take heed that you despise not one of these little ones," he held up the child in his arms, "for I say to you that in heaven their angels always intercede for them before the Father."

"Who would want to offend a little child, or hurt them?" asked Mazar.

"I'm sure I do not know," whispered Sherai still looking at the man who now had hung his head as if in shame, "but there must be some here who do or the Master would not speak of it so plainly and with such authority."

Jesus put down the older child with a pat on his head, and leaned over to pick up a toddler tugging at his robe. One of the nearby Pharisees, overhearing that conversation, took that opportunity to ask another question.

"Do you seek to fill the kingdom with children? Is not the kingdom of God for men?"

"The son of man has come to save *all* who are lost."

There was no mistaking, in Sherai's mind that he addressed the man he had been looking at previously. His voice took on a gentle tone, and it was as if he willed the man to look up at him. The man did raise his eyes to Jesus, and they were filled with tears.

Jesus said, "Ponder this, if a man has a hundred sheep, and one of them has gone astray, will he not leave the ninety-nine and go into the mountains to seek the one which has gone astray?

"If it be that he finds that one sheep, does he not rejoice more over that one sheep than of the ninety-nine who are in the fold? In the same way it is not the will of the Father that one of his little ones should perish." Sherai watched the man, with tears running down into his beard. She saw his face change from intense pain to a dawning joy. It was as though she was watching him repent and enter into the joy of the Lord.

It was almost an intrusion when another out of the crowd asked Jesus, "What must we do when our brother has committed a serious offence against us? Will you listen to our grievance?"

Jesus looked at the man as though he were seeing his innermost thoughts, and answered him directly, "If your brother trespasses against you go and tell him his fault between you two alone, if he acknowledges his wrong and asks forgiveness, you will still have a brother. If he will not admit his wrong, or apologize, take one or two witnesses, that by the mouth of these two every word can be verified. If he won't hear them, tell it to the church, but if he won't listen to the church, he will be to you as a heathen, or a publican."

Some lawyers standing nearby did not like this advice. Sherai heard them saying among themselves, "Is he saying that this man should have no recourse to the law?"

Jesus perceived their ire and added, "Whatever you bind on earth shall be bound in heaven likewise that which is loosed on earth shall be loosed in heaven. Again I say, If two of you agree on anything on earth, and ask, it shall be done by my Father in heaven. For where two or three are gathered together in my name, there I am in their midst."

Jesus sent the children back to their parents and answered many more questions. He taught even more parables about the kingdom, and the crowd lingered with Jesus until it was dusk.

BREAD OF LIFE

Sherai, Mazar, and Mary all enjoyed a glorious spring and summer following Jesus as he taught in Galilee. Sherai lost count of the endless healing and miracles performed by him. It seemed to her as though the Messiah brought Heaven down to earth with him. The earth seemed to respond to his presence. The sky was bluer, the grass was greener, and that year the wild flowers were more abundant.

She and Mazar talked often between them about the change in their lives because of Jesus' teaching. It seemed like the Kingdom of God, that Jesus talked more about than any other single thing, really had come.

When Jesus let it be known that he was returning that fall to Nazareth, she and Mazar remained in Capernaum. Sherai was staying at home in case Jethen chose to visit. She couldn't quite work up the courage to confide in Mazar about what happened between them, and her servant did not ask.

They heard that Jesus traveled on teaching in other towns and cities beyond Nazareth. Jacob, who followed him, brought back stories of his trips. Mary came to visit and related all Jacob told her and added, "Jacob said that Jesus did no mighty works in Nazareth as he has done elsewhere, because his own people have no belief in him."

"How can his own people of Nazareth reject him? Of all people, they know him best," protested Mazar.

Sherai disagreed. "I think that those closest to us we understand the least. Our familiarity with them leads us to assume we know all, but we seldom look below the surface."

Mary snorted, "I knew my husband like the back of my hand. I know Jacob, too."

Mazar added, "Often our own families don't seem to appreciate us."

"That is what I think," Sherai agreed with her. "Mary, you know many things about your brother, Jacob, but do you know his deepest thoughts?"

Mary laughed, "I don't think Jacob has many of those."

"Perhaps before Jesus began teaching this was true," Sherai nodded, "but do you think any of us cease to ponder deeply now? There are those we think we know, along with all their thoughts and motives, but inside them, their longings, and desires are seldom revealed to us. Even with long association we barely begin to understand them."

"Surely you don't mean Jesus. He lays bare his thoughts for his followers daily." Mary defended.

Mazar thought she could guess to whom Sherai referred. They had not seen Jethen since that day he had stepped from the boat on the quay. Sherai would often look afar off, and Mazar wondered if it was then she was thinking of him. Jethen did not come to Capernaum.

When Jesus returned to Galilee it was nearly spring. Huge crowds followed him as he taught them. Sherai and Mazar where there the day the disciples of John came to Jesus and told him that Herod feared him because he thought Jesus was John the Baptist raised from the dead. Jesus departed into the desert, but many followed to hear his words.

Sherai and Mazar followed him, whenever they could, since his return. Taking provisions, they followed on foot into the desert region. For many days he taught them. Jesus' popularity had grown since the years he had begun his ministry. Crowds that once had numbered into the hundreds now numbered in the thousands. They followed him everywhere.

Because of his miracles, they brought their sick and afflicted to him, hoping that a miracle would be given them. Often the scribes and the Pharisees would follow him trying to expose him and his works as being of the devil. He was forced by their large number to travel far from the cities and teach in the countryside where the large crowds could spread out.

One such day, shortly before the Passover, Jesus taught them all the day long, but it was getting late. The sun was lowering in the sky, and shade was stealing over the landscape. Soon it would be cold in the night desert. He stood to his feet, and all those on the hillside stood with him. He could sense that they did not intend to leave. "Bring me those in need of healing," he called.

Many surged toward Jesus, and he had compassion on them and healed them all. Sherai whispered to Mazar, "I suspect that many of them are not seriously ill, they just want to be touched by his power."

Mazar's eyes filled with tears. "I can understand that wish. To be touched by a God is no small thing."

Sherai hugged Mazar, "His words seem to me like a touch to my heart. I have never heard anyone speak as Jesus does, not even the rabbi. Are you hungry, Mazar? I'm afraid we long ago ate the meager portion of food we brought with us."

"Oh no, please Mistress, I don't want to go."

"I have no wish to go, either, never fear. Very few of our number have gone away to seek food, or rest. I think it must weary Jesus a great deal to have such huge crowds pressing him about all the time."

"It's because when we are with him, we feel more alive," Mazar sounded sure, "look, the healing is almost finished, His disciples have come and surrounded him."

Sherai, who had pressed closer during the healing, heard one of them say, "People are getting hungry, Master. Send the multitude away so that they can go into the towns and country nearby and get food."

"Give them something to eat." Jesus answered him.

"We have only five loaves and two fishes unless we go and buy more for all these people. There are about five thousand men here, and that doesn't include the women and children. How could we buy for so many?"

"Have them sit down by fifties in a company."

The one called Simon turned to the crowd. "My friends," he shouted, "sit down in companies of fifty. We are about to eat."

There was a great deal of talking and shifting, but the people complied. Sherai and Mazar were in one of the first groups. When everyone was seated again, Jesus took the five loaves and two fishes. He looked up to Heaven, and he blessed them. Then he broke them into bits and gave them to the disciples to pass among the multitude. From somewhere more baskets appeared, Sherai contributed her empty basket, and the disciples filled all of them. Afterward they walked among the multitude distributing the food inside. The baskets never seemed to empty. Food was passed to a company and dispersed among them.

Sherai bit into her bread, and though she knew she ate it, her bread did not seem to diminish. She looked about her and everyone seemed to be holding bread. Likewise, her fish multiplied in her mouth, and each small bite grew to two, or three. There was adequate food in her portion to satisfy her hunger, and yet bread and fish remained. She looked about her company and noted that everyone still held portions of food in their hands, and they were all eating! Still the disciples handed out more.

When everyone was satisfied, they took up the remains, and there were twelve baskets full. It was a miracle!

When all was done, Jesus stood to his feet again. "You must return to your homes," he said. "My work calls me and my disciples north to Tyre and Sidon. I promise to return to Galilee later this spring. Watch and wait for us, and think on all I have said." Jesus then cloaked himself and disappeared down the hill surrounded by his disciples. All walked down the hill marveling at the feast they shared from five loaves and two fishes.

"The bread," Mazar marveled as she told Sherai as they walked, "multiplied right in my hands."

"I know, it was the same for me. Did ever any fish taste so good? Salted fish would have me drinking water to slake my thirst, but I wasn't thirsty beyond the normal. Were you?"

"Only, as you said, for the normal amount of liquid with a meal." Sherai and Mazar hurried back to Capernaum along with others. "I wish we could follow him and see his miracles."

"So do I, Mazar, but my time of confinement is nearly upon me. We will hear word from Jacob, he at least can follow Jesus wherever he goes. At times I envy men their ability to go when and where they will."

19

RESTLESS

Lugging the large basket of laundry, Sherai made her way to the shore. It was usually Mazar's chore, but today she intended to hand wash the linens she so painstakingly stitched, and she did not trust anyone but herself to wash them. She included in her basket most of the cloths that hung over her doors inside the house. It was time to rid her home of dust.

For the first time in a long while, Sherai was feeling frustration. It was nothing dire, just a small longing–for what, she didn't know.

Reaching the shore, she sat her basket down, and shading her hand from the morning glare, looked across the lake. While fishing vessels dotted the surface, there was nothing to be seen heading for Capernaum. Idly she found herself wondering whether Jethen was in Damascus, traveling the shores of the Mediterranean, or perhaps as near as Hippos.

"Even if he is in Hippos, he won't be coming to see you," she reminded herself. Inexplicably, Jethen's grave face, and unusual grey eyes formed in her mind. An unexpected pang of homesickness swamped Sherai for all that was familiar and dear in Sychar. If Jethen was a large part of that homesickness, she wasn't consciously aware of it.

"I'm just restless because usually at this time of year I am following the Master around Galilee," she told herself. Jesus, she knew, had gone to Caesarea Philippi with his disciples. It was summer, and he would soon return to Galilee, then on southward, perhaps. It seemed that his days of limiting his ministry between Galilee, Nazareth and Jerusalem were over.

Stooping to wash her linens, she carefully rubbed the wet cloth with sand, careful to avoid the delicate stitchery so laboriously applied. She'd already lowered the basket filled with cloths into the water allowing the wet cloths to anchor the basket in the shallow water and soak.

"Greetings, Sherai."

Sherai jumped up, startled to be wrested from her thoughts. "Why Mary, I didn't see you. Greetings."

"You were very deep in thought, Sherai. I stopped to tell you Jacob returned home yesterday. He says that Jesus and his disciples are on their way home from Caesarea Philippi. They are planning to travel on through Samaria, Judea and Perea on their way to Jerusalem. Jacob said he was planning to send out the disciples to preach the word. That will be an interesting experience. I would like to be able to go along with each of them to see how they fare, wouldn't you? Fishermen, tax collectors, and zealots," she snorted, "what a group for preachers."

Sherai chuckled at Mary's disdain, but added, "They may do better than you think, Mary. They've been listening to the greatest teacher of them all, remember. Is Jacob going with them?"

"Jacob will go," Mary affirmed. "He never stays home these days. Naomi's about to set his shoes outside the door."

"Naomi will never do that. She loves our Lord as much as Jacob."

"Yes, but she has mouths to feed and backs to clothe."

"And you help her with that, I know, good woman. I imagine you are here to do some shopping at the market, confess it."

Mary colored, and admonished, "You shouldn't be praising me for my duty. Next you'll be taking away my blessing."

"Are you going with Jacob on this trip, Mary? I may go with them as far as Sychar. I have been thinking of my friends there, and wondering about them. Would you like to go with me? I think you would like Samaria," she teased.

"Jacob's going to preach," Mary snorted. "I sure won't be going with him. I wouldn't like going to Samaria either. Why do you want to go there?"

"I want to take Mazar to visit her family, and I have some business that needs attending."

"Well, you know your own business best, but be wary of those Samaritans."

"Mary," Sherai reproached her, "Remember that I am from Samaria myself, I have converted to Judaism, yes, but I am still a Samaritan."

"Yes, but you are one who came to her senses." With that parting rejoinder, Mary turned on her heel and made for the market stalls.

Sherai looked after her and wondered aloud, "Now when did I decide to visit Sychar?"

Carrying the wet basket back to her house proved to be a heavy burden. " "It's too heavy for one person to carry all this wet material. How do women with children do it all? I'm going to help Mazar with the laundry from now on," she decided.

She reached that conclusion and her door at the same time. Opening the door she called out, "Mazar, are you within?"

There was no answer, so she lugged the heavy basket up the stairs to the roof. On such a sunny day as this the clothes would be dried in no time, and she could hang them back up over the doors. Then she'd pull out covers for her furnishings, and prepare them for her long visit in Sychar. She hummed as she hung the laundry even though a stiff breeze slapped some of them in her face, and wrapped them about her legs as she worked.

It would be good to travel with Jesus and hear him speak again. On the road he tended to teach the deeper meaning of his sayings to those who followed him.

It was not to be. Jesus and the twelve were making the journey with only a few of the newly chosen seventies, and they were not traveling near Sychar. Simon Peter, along with James, had come personally to her home. At once Sherai perceived something different about the men. While Simon Peter still looked the same, and dressed in his same homespun robes, his countenance had a gentler aspect, and his air was one of serenity and quiet knowledge. James had always had a gentler mein, but now he seemed to radiate a quiet authority. She greatly wondered what had brought this about.

They proceeded to tell her as gently as they were capable, that it would not be seemly for her to join them on their journey. "In the late fall we are going to return to Capernaum, but will set out again for Jerusalem, this time taking the road to Jericho. You may travel with us then if you wish," James concluded.

Disappointed, Sherai put the best face on it she could. "I thank you, Simon Peter, James, for coming personally to tell me," she always called the older disciple by his two names, one of which had been given him by Jesus. "I will put my restlessness and travel-longing aside, and wait for the fall."

The leader of the disciples smiled at her and approved," You would do well to continue inscribing all the words and events you can remember of the Master. I'd like to tell you what happened in Caesarea Philippi if you have the time."

"Let me get my quill and some parchment." She hurried into another room leaving the two men in her courtyard. She found Mazar and quietly asked her to take some refreshment to them. Beneath the scrolls she had already written, she found some loose parchment, and hurriedly attached it to a wooden scroll. In a nearby box she found quills, and grabbed several. It might be necessary to sharpen them, so she found a small bladed knife she used. Lastly she reached for the ink. It was a blend that she had brought from Sychar, and it was nearly gone.

After the two men left, she studied her notes. It was a wonder she could read them at all. Her hands were still trembling after they had taken their departure. Taken up to speak with Moses, and Elijah–imagine! No wonder they had changed so. What they had only believed in their hearts they now knew for certain. It was all true, and Jesus was indeed the Messiah, the one prophesied for all those years, and truly the Son of God.

He had also spoken of his death, something about a second coming, and what it meant to be a disciple. They had climbed up Mount Hermon, and there they had met with the prophets of old. Then they had returned to Galilee. Jesus had healed a lunatic boy, and taught his disciples more about his death, and tribute money, but mostly he had talked about the principles of humility, service, and forgiveness.

Her favorite part was a parable of the unmerciful servant. It seemed there was a servant who owed his Lord a certain sum of money and when the Lord demanded it, he could not pay. He begged for mercy, and the Lord forgave him his debt.

This same servant then went out and found a man who owed him much less that he had owed. He demanded the money from the man. The man had no money, and begged for mercy, but the servant showed him no mercy. Instead he had him thrown in prison.

The King found out about the man's treatment of his friend, and had him thrown in prison until his debt was paid. Sherai finished reading what she had written and said, "Jesus was the same as telling us that if we expect mercy, we must show mercy. That is very different from the days of Moses I have been studying. Then it was an eye for an eye. I'm going to take my scrolls to Sychar this fall. Omini will be very interested in reading them, and discussing them with me.

"Mazar," she called. Her servant came running into the courtyard. "Mazar, we will be traveling with the Master in the fall. We will most likely stay the winter in Sychar. Will that work well for you?"

"It is well for me, I *have* been homesick for my people, as you must have guessed."

"Mazar, would you be more content to remain in Sychar? I could likely find another young woman, perhaps one of your sisters to accompany me."

Mazar burst into tears, "Oh, no, Sherai, I want to remain with you. I will be content just to see my family again." She picked up her apron to hide her face inside it.

"Then perhaps another of your sisters would come with us when we return. She would be company for you, and I could always use more hands."

Mazar's face came out of the apron. She forgot her tears, and smiles broke out immediately. "Oh, Sherai, that would be of all things most to be desired." She came over and hugged Sherai. "You are the best Mistress in all the world."

"Thank you, Mazar, I will try always to be." Mazar curtsied, and left her. Sherai looked around her home. It was as comfortable and lovely as she could make it. All around her were the things that for her made a home. In spite of all that, for some reason, Sherai still felt discontented, and edgy. She had longed for the trip this summer to run away from this odd feeling. There was a nagging feeling inside her that there was something important she should be doing. There was an edginess to her spirit that she couldn't define.

There in her courtyard she knelt and lifted her face to the heavens. "Dear Father," she pleaded, "What is wrong with me? Why do I have these feelings of being unfulfilled? Why am I unsure of what I want, and long for things I can't have? Surely there is something out there for me to do? Perhaps I can't go out and preach and teach, but isn't there anything I can do for the Kingdom?" Suddenly she was seized with a feeling of envy, even rebellion. Other women had homes, families, and children to care for. Their lives were fulfilled, and happy. Why had God chosen her to be alone? A sense of shame washed over her. She was being ungrateful. Sherai wept. "Father, help me accept this life I have been given. Help me do some good with it."

20

GENTLE HEART

Jethen stood on the rooftop of the house where he rented a room for his stay in Jerusalem. This rooftop offered a view of the temple mount, the temple, and the surrounding valleys of the city. Also, it was cooler up here, and less noisy and crowded than the streets below. That was not to say that other rooftops were unoccupied at this hour of the morning. Women were busy laying out washing to dry, or sweeping up dust, or working at varying tasks.

His business in Jerusalem was done. He had sold nearly all of the items he accrued in Sidon, Tyre, and Joppa. There were a few items bought here in Jerusalem, but most of what he acquired in Hippos was for Jericho. It had been strange to be in Hippos, so near to Sherai, and not see her. He dreaded the questions his mother would ask.

He pummeled the palm of his hand with his fist. 'What more could I have done to persuade her?' he asked himself. Pushing thoughts of her from his mind, he contemplated the remainder of his travels.

After visiting his mother and selling what remained, he would bargain for goods: dates, figs, and the balm for headaches and eyes that was made only in Jericho, with which to begin his long journey to Damascus once more before the harvest. Not, however, before he hired laborers for his mother's vineyard, and fields. He would return to Jericho after harvest and sell her grain. The grapes would be made into wine in Jericho.

This led to thoughts of his own vineyard in Sychar. It was newly planted, and would not make good wine, but the grapes would be harvested and carefully labeled for their juice just the same. Then cutting and grafting would begin to strengthen the vines and blend the best. He trusted no one with that duty but himself. His own fields would be harvested by Ziriz, and the reaping either sold, or poured into the stone storage vaults carved out beneath his own home. This year he sowed barley, and wheat. Lentils were already drying on his rooftops.

Business was good. His immediate future was so well mapped, he could afford a few days here in the most bustling city in Judea. Jethen wanted neither to go on to Jericho, nor to remain here in Jerusalem. Indecisive restlessness bound his skin like new wine in an old bottle. If he could do exactly what he wanted to do . . . That was precisely the problem, he could not do what he most wanted to do.

He was a wealthy man by most standards, but he was not a happy one. His loneliness was even more apparent here in Jerusalem, one of the busiest cities in all the land, and he was virtually alone in it.

Mishob housed the camels outside the city, and remained to care for them, and watch over his goods that remained. His servants, other than those sharing Mishob's duty, were most likely spending their wages at this moment in the market stalls, or other pursuits offered in such a city.

He considered the theater, or strolling along the streets, perhaps visiting the temple, but the thoughts of avoiding the pious Jews on the streets deterred him. What he wanted, he could not have. He wanted companionship. Not just any companion, he wanted Sherai. She would not be with him on his travels, but he could always look forward to returning to her. When she was a part of his household, that is exactly what he had done. He'd looked for reasons to return to her.

Usually he remained away from home until all his travels were concluded, she did not know this, so she wasn't surprised by his frequent returns to Sychar. That was all over. She chose to follow Jesus. Jethen allowed his heart to fill with anger against the man. Just when all his hopes and dreams looked like they would be fulfilled, Jesus went to Sychar.

A gentle somewhat familiar voice broke into his thoughts, "Jethen, son of Amos, Greetings."

Jethen looked up and saw the old man he met outside the Sheep Gate over a year ago. "Matthias," he spoke involuntarily in his surprise.

"You do remember me, my friend. What a pleasure it is seeing you again." The man seated himself near Jethen.

Jethen flushed and inwardly cursing his impulsive tongue said, "I still don't understand how is it that you, a Jew, would speak with me a Samaritan."

"I do not despise any man," replied Matthias. "Once I may have despised anyone who lived in a manner I thought wrong, or evil, but not simply because he was different than myself. I no longer even despise the man who is wrong or evil, only the evil itself do I despise."

"And did Jesus teach you this?"

"You have come to know Jesus of Nazareth?"

"I have no acquaintance with him, but one cannot fail to hear his words everywhere," Jethen replied.

"In a small village outside Jerusalem, not two days past, I was dining, and in the corner farthest removed from my table sat a priest and a rabbi. Judging by the priest's mein, and fine apparel he was merely passing through that place and could hardly bear to sit at table with the local rabbi. I knew he would wither me with a glance if he caught me staring. He was holding forth to the rabbi his opinion of the man called Jesus of Nazareth. If I understood him rightly, he did not approve of him, or his teachings."

"Did you happen to hear his name?" queried Matthias.

"I believe the rabbi called him Annas."

"Ah, yes, he would find Jesus' popularity most difficult to bear. He was appointed to his high position, you see, and Jesus is voluntarily followed by the people."

Jethen chuckled. "I heard him say scathingly of Jesus that he sups with publicans and sinners. He also accused that his teachings were no more than stories to tickle the ears of the credulous."

"That sounds like Annas. He would resent Jesus preaching of a Kingdom of God when he feels that the religious life of our society is his to reign over."

"I saw him arrive with the rabbi to dine. The man had pulled his robes tightly to his body when approached by a beggar, who seeing his fine clothing, had begged for alms. The priest had nodded to the rabbi who shooed the man away with a coin from his own shabby purse.

"I watched the man heap upon the table every delicacy the inn afforded, and could only conclude that the rabbi's humble home did not provide sufficient quality for the priest's palate. It was no surprise to me that the priest was not staying at the inn. Your people rarely stay at inns, Matthias. Why do you?"

"I have traveled much on business, as I'm sure you do, Jethen of Sychar. I find it more convenient to pay for my amenities than to require them from a friend. It also gives me more freedom to make acquaintances such as yourself," the old man bowed by tilting his head toward Jethen. "I am captivated by the teaching of Jesus of Nazareth. He preaches of a society where all is shared, and none are in want. Our just and equitable God requires that no man go hungry, or naked."

"Those are certainly noble thoughts, but I fear many do go hungry."

"That is why I am on my last run. My purse after I sell all should feed the hungry for a while."

"Do you intend to sell all you have?"

"Yes, then I will follow Jesus. He is sending us out to teach and preach his words."

"You cannot mean it."

"Yes, that is what I intend to do. My wife, Lydia, will support me in this. We have no children to leave an inheritance, so it will not matter. Jesus' ministry needs our meager funds. You see," he added with shining eyes, "I believe his words. Outside influences like the Romans, or the Greeks, have nothing to do with our faith, and our true devotion."

Jethen could not doubt the man's sincerity. He really did see it as his responsibility to do something about the poor and indigent. He wondered if he might dare to ask the man about the miracles. "Have you seen his miracles, Matthias? Is that why you wish to follow him? I heard tell of a young girl raised from the dead, and a woman healed by simply touching the hem of his garment."

"His miracles are only a small part of why I follow him. To answer your question, yes, I know Jairus personally. He is a distant relation on my wife's side. The girl was dead, now she lives. To me this is proof that our God does still care for and remember his people." The old man lowered his voice and leaning closer to Jethen almost whispered, "Some of our people lost their faith under the iron fist of our oppressors, but Jesus returns our faith to us by showing that our God is not dead, nor sleeping."

"Does Jesus tell his followers to do as you are doing, to sell all, give to the poor, and follow him?"

"To some of them he does," he answered honestly. "His disciples have forsaken all to follow him. To most, he makes it a matter of choice, but his chosen Apostles, the twelve, he has required it of them."

"Does he require this of women, as well?"

"No, but many women support his ministry. Jesus has many of the rich among his followers. Some of them might surprise you."

"I know one," Jethen admitted gruffly.

At the thinly veiled animosity in his voice, Matthias reared his head back and looked searchingly into the younger man's face. Jethen was unable to sustain his scrutiny eye to eye, and dropped his own. Understanding and compassion shone in Matthias' eyes in that moment. "You would do well to emulate her, my young friend," he said softly. "May I suggest that you take the time to find Jesus for yourself. His is the only way to true happiness in this life, or the life to come."

"I wish I could believe that," Jethen admitted.

"You will come to do so," Matthias assured him, prophetically. They spoke together for a long while. Matthias talked, that is, and Jethen listened as the old man expounded on the teachings of Jesus. He wove a tapestry of words that sank deep into Jethen's heart, and shook him to his foundations. Phrases like, a light unto the world, salt of the earth, give your cloak, and your coat also, care for the widows and the fatherless, love your enemies, do good to them who curse you, do not light your candle and hide it under a bushel basket, all these teachings filled up his heart like hearty broth filled his stomach–rich and satisfying.

Sherai had repeated some of those same words on the way to Capernaum, but his heart had been filled with thoughts of her, and he hadn't listened. The familiarity of them from Matthias' lips seemed to stamp them upon his mind, and seal them in his heart.

He was unaware of time passing as he listened to Matthias, but when the old one drew breath, he looked up at the sun which was lowering from its zenith and toward the west.

"I am glad to have seen you again, and spoken with you, Jethen of Sychar. I suppose I have begun my preaching early. You should not have presented such a listening ear. I must take my leave of you now, for I am beginning my journey home."

"Where is home?" He asked Matthias.

"I live in Jericho."

"I lived in Jericho for many years," said Jethen

"I know, my boy. I knew your father. He was a good man–for a Samaritan." his eyes twinkled showing he bore the Samaritan no ill will. "I hope to see you again, perhaps among the people listening to Jesus."

Jethen stood, and clasped the man's arm to help him rise. He could not explain the bond he felt with this old Jew, other than that he sensed the man truly cared about him, and not just him, but all mankind. Matthias' God was a just, loving God.

Jethen, when he thought about God always saw him as harsh, jealous, and stern. Trying to live up to the exacting standards of his own people had caused him to withdraw from his faith.

Matthias, on the other hand, seemed to find no difficulty in embracing his faith and making it his life, he exuded love for his fellow men.

"I will think on what you have said, Matthias, and perhaps I will someday find this Jesus and listen to his words."

The old man smiled, and bid him farewell, and left the roof as quietly as he came. Jethen seated himself again, and pondered the words of Jesus that he learned that afternoon. He found himself hoping in his heart that this kingdom of God would come. 'I didn't think to ask him if he thought Jesus was a God,' he pondered.

JERICHO ROAD

The morning was bright and clear. The sun shimmered over the white walls of Jerusalem dazzling the eyes of Jethen as he turned in his seat atop his camel for a last look at the city before entering the mountains. He and his men elected to leave before sunrise to drive their caravan over the road northeast of Jerusalem through the pass on the long lonely road. They watched the sunrise over the nearest peaks as they made their way through the mountains before going down to Jericho.

The going to Jericho from Jerusalem was always easier than a return journey. The elevation dropped considerably from the high mountains surrounding Jerusalem toward the Dead Sea. Herod's Jericho was rebuilt about a mile nearer the old Jericho where Joshua, obeying God's command, in the days of old, brought down the walls.

Amos, his father, settled outside the city when he moved his family to be near the famous trees that gave the milky-white sap that became a balm for headaches and bad eyesight. Amos also planted many date palms, and a few fig trees besides the vegetables they grew, and the sheep they grazed. They also planted a large vineyard, but his father always said Sychar produced better fruit of the vine than Jericho.

The road to Jericho was as familiar to Jethen as the well-laid streets of Jericho. Every mile marked a familiar sight. They were nowhere near the rugged terrain where thieves and bandits plied their trade against unwary travelers. He and his men would travel that stretch with swords drawn. Seldom did they attack as large a caravan as his, but it happened a time or two.

The camels were not so heavily laden that they couldn't make good time on the fifteen mile stretch between the two cities. Jethen chose to ride in the early morning on one of his camels, but Mishob was riding one of the donkeys. Later they would walk, and be alert. One of his men, perched atop the lead camel, kept a lookout ahead. It was better to be wary on the road.

Jethen's mind that morning was filled with the words he heard from old Matthias. The stories of Jesus, and his miracles were enough to fill the mind of any traveler. He questioned closely his decision to sell all and follow Jesus. His arguments did not convince Jethen, however one provocative phrase repeated itself over and over in his mind. *'Lay not up for yourselves treasure upon earth, where moth and rust corrupts, and where thieves break through and steal: but lay up for yourselves treasures in heaven, where neither moth nor rust corrupts, and where thieves do not break through nor steal; for where your treasure is, there will your heart be also.'* Imagine having a place to lay up treasure where it could not be corrupted. Jethen doubted that Jesus would consider hoarded gold, silver, or grain a proper treasure. Those he would expect to be shared with the poor. What then would this treasure be? Matthias obviously felt that the only treasure worth seeking was the one you used to serve others. What would his treasure be?

As the sun climbed to its zenith, a trickle of travelers passed them coming from Jericho. It amused Jethen to see a small entourage of the High Priest Annas pass to the other side of the road giving his caravan a wide berth as he hurried back to Jerusalem. Jethen wondered what had taken the fastidious man to Herod's Jericho. He had seen him only a few days past in Jerusalem. If his expression was anything to go by, nothing pleasant drew him there, or perhaps it was something unpleasant he was going toward in Jerusalem.

Dismissing the priest from his mind, he also ignored another traveler on the road hurrying to Jerusalem. He considered again on the phrase that had so captivated his mind. In his heart Jethen knew what his treasure was. It was presently residing in Capernaum, and a bit more of his treasure resided in Jericho. For him, the only treasure worth counting was family, but he had no family other than his mother, and sister. His own family was merely a dream of Sherai. He allowed his mind to drift off in dreams of Sherai, and the beautiful children they could have. He was teaching their young son to sow a proper field when a sharp call broke into his dreaming.

"Master, master, come quickly." Rama sighted something from atop his camel.

Jethen kneed his donkey, and then alighted when he caught sight of where Rama was pointing. A man badly beaten and left for dead was lying at the side of the road. He was robbed of even his clothing. He ran to the man and turned him over. It was Matthias! Bending low over his face he could hear that he still drew breath.

"He lives," he told Mishob who came to stand beside him. "Fetch some water," he demanded of his men. "Find me some ointment, and cloth. Tear it in strips, I need something to bind his wounds." Taking the water skin from Rama, he gently lifted and trickled some water into his mouth. The old man swallowed with difficulty, and moaned.

"The robbers are becoming bold if they will plunder this near Jerusalem," Mishob commented.

"Or desperate. Since the Roman legions have begun patrolling this road, their pickings must be few. I wish I would have asked this man to travel with us."

"You know this Jew?" Mishob was surprised out of his habitual calm. He stooped down so that he could see him.

While Jethen answered him, he was cleaning and binding the man's wounds. "Yes, I met him in Hippos, and again in Jerusalem. He is one of those followers of that man Jesus. He is a kindly man of great faith." He thought to himself, 'That's why that haughty Annas' face could sour milk and he was in such a hurry to reach Jerusalem. He must have passed him by as he lay here because it would take a month of purifying ablutions to cleanse him of a brush with death. I took him for dead myself,' he added honestly.

"Here, help me carry him to a donkey. We'll have to tie him on. We'll stop at that inn outside Jericho, what do the Romans call it?"

"I don't recall the name, Master."

"No matter, I know the innkeeper there, he'll take care of him for me." Loading carefully on the donkey, and binding him, Jethen walked beside him for the remainder of the journey tending to him, and giving him water.

"Lucius, just the man I want to see! What brings you out of doors on a hot day like this?"

"Jethen! Have your camels acquired a thirst, or is it the man who has a thirst for the finest wine my inn serves? I even have a room, if you want one." The man, Lucius, was laughing and jesting, for he knew Jethen's fairly large family home was in Jericho.

"I do have need of a room," he replied. Slowly Mishob came through the gate guiding the donkey on which he rode.

"Oh ha," Lucius stopped laughing. "One of your men? What happened?"

"This man is known to me, but not one of my men. We found him on the side of the road badly beaten and robbed. He did have three camels, and a couple of servants. I am wondering if the servants did not beat him and leave him for dead in order to steal his goods. He was returning to Jericho with quite a load."

"He looks pretty bad. Does he live in Jericho?"

"I believe he does, but I do not know his family name. Tonight I will care for him here at the inn."

"Why do you take so much trouble for a man you know so little?"

"I only met him briefly, but there was something about him. He is a good man, Lucius. I . . . I envy him."

A short burst of laughter erupted from Lucius. "Now I know you jest with me. This man can be the envy of no one." Then he sobered and became the man of business he truly was. "I have a room, and you are welcome to it for the night. Bring him." He then turned and walked up the stairs to one of the open rooms above the stables.

Jethen and Mishob cut the man down from the donkey and carried him carefully between them. They were puffing by the time they reached the room, and both sighed relief when they placed him on the low bed.

"You can settle with me in the morning," the innkeeper looked upon the man with curiosity. Seeing nothing in him to engender so much compassion in Jethen, he shrugged, and commented, "If you have need of anything, send a servant for me."

"I have everything I need to tend him, but some of your best wine would not come amiss. I used most of mine pouring it over his wounds."

"I have some healing oils," offered Lucius.

"That would be most kind. Mishob, go with him, and find us some food. We've gone all day without meat. I want to change his bandages. I have the wrap for them with me."

Lucius shook his head in disbelief, and turned for one last word as he followed Mishob out the door, "I am not being kind, Jethen," the innkeeper warned, "I will expect to be paid. Since the Romans appointed me to this caravansary, I have had more trouble than pay." The burly man departed and pulled the curtain across the opening behind him.

The morning came after a long night. Matthias developed a fever and Jethen was forced to bathe him down with water fetched from the well in the courtyard below. He suspected from his breathing that he had been kicked in the ribs. He bound him tightly, and his breathing did ease some. One thing was certain, he would not be able to travel on to Jericho.

Mishob had elected to remain with the other servants and the animals, and he knew his old servant wanted to move on to Jericho. Lucius wasn't the only one who didn't understand Jethen's compassion for the old man.

When Mishob finally did appear Jethen said, "Remain here with him while I settle up with Lucius. We will travel on to Jericho, so when I return, you must make ready."

"I have made ready, Master. The animals are fed and watered, and the men also. Will this Matthias be accompanying us?"

"No, he is too ill to travel. I hope to come to some arrangement with Lucius about him. See if you can get him to drink some wine."

"Yes, Master." Disapproval was in every line of Mishob's back as he bent over the man.

I would like to leave him here in your care, Lucius, while I try to locate his wife. He is fairly old, as you see, and I think they were alone." Jethen didn't like appealing to the innkeeper. He had spent more minutes than Jethen wanted to spend complaining about his business. Also, he had paid him a large sum for his night's lodging and amenities.

"I can take him in, but it will cost you, Jethen. This is my busy season, and new travelers come here for rooms daily. Not every traveler wants to stay in Jericho these days."

Jethen opened his pouch, and shook out two silver pence. They were older coins from Herod, stamped with a date palm. "Use this to tend him until he is well. Whatever more you spend, I will repay. Meanwhile, I will look for his wife. When I come again, if you have used all, I will make it good, you have my word on it."

"What is this man to you that you would do so much? He's only a jew."

"If this is too much to ask, Lucius, I will leave one of my servants . . ."

Lucius eyed the silver pence, and rubbed his thumb over the stamped palm. It was always good to have a rich man owe you for a favor. He stuck out his big hand and clasped Jethen's arm. "I will have him moved to my own rooms," he promised.

Jethen completed the gesture by gripping Lucius's own arm in salute. "My thanks to you."

22

A THANKLESS ERRAND

The market place in Jericho was crowded with booths. Sellers and buyers haggled over the wares displayed there. Others loudly proclaimed their wares to every passer by. Jethen was hot and tired. It was mid-summer, and the hottest time of day when the sun stood directly overhead and there was little shade to be found.

His entire morning consisted of going from stall to stall looking for someone who might know Matthias and where he might find his wife, Lydia. Most of the vendors denied knowing any such person and pointed out that their own wares were vastly superior, and he should buy from them. Others who admitted they knew of Matthias would not admit they knew where he lived, or even where his stall could be found on market day. It was quite a task wending his way among the stalls manned by Greeks, Romans, and other foreign traders to find those of a Jew.

Jethen was beginning to feel that his idea on how to find the man's wife was not so dazzling after all. He was glad, at least, that he had not sent Mishob. They would have divulged nothing to his old servant. At last, nearer the upper city end of the market, Jethen stood before a stall selling exotic oils and lamps. The owner was a Jew of about Matthias' age, if he was any judge of age.

"How can I help you, young man? I have the finest oils to be found in Jericho. Some I extract myself, and others I trade for as far away as Rome." While he was talking he pulled the stopper from one exquisite bottle, and waved it beneath Jethen's nose.

Answering automatically Jethen challenged, "I have smelled sweeter oils from Persia than this."

"Ah, a discerning customer. For you I have the finest oils from the orient. He dove under a table and pulled a small, ceramic bottle painted and trimmed in gold leaf. He pulled the stopper and a sweet fragrance of rain washed violets, and something Jethen could not define, filled the air.

A woman, her arms filled with bundles stopped. "What is that fragrance, Jakim? You showed me nothing this sweet when I shopped with you earlier this morning."

The man was scornful. "The cost of this small bottle would feed your large family for a year, Deborah." The woman sniffed, and walked away.

Jethen knew the man spoke truly. Such a bottle alone would cost a fortune. "I will have it," he decided, "but I will only pay one half a year's take of the best vintage in my vineyard."

"I have no need for wine, I grow my own fruit. This bottle cost me more than my entire vineyard is worth. I would part with it only for vast quantities of gold, and not Herod's gold."

As the talkative old Jew stoppered the bottle and put it under the counter, Jethen observed, "It is a wonder you are not robbed. I will meet your price, but I really came to ask you about a seller named Matthias. I am looking for . . ."

"I doubt very much you could meet my price, young man. The perfume is not for sale. Of course I know old Matthias. He has operated the stall across from mine for over thirty years.

His nephew is running it now, and into the ground, I might add. He holds on to pence so tight he rubs off the image, as we say. Matthias mostly travels and sells these days."

"You know where he lives? It is rather urgent that I find his wife."

"I can direct you to his home, but I doubt you will find anyone there. He and his wife follow that man Jesus, and he is teaching near Jericho out of the city northward about a half day's journey. The crowds are too big to allow inside the walls."

"Three bags of Roman gold for the vial?" Jethen wheedled.

"Not for five," admitted Jakim. "I bought the oil for my only daughter's dowery. You cannot even marry her to get it," he cackled a wheezy laugh that broke into a cough, "she is promised to another."

Jethen laughed. "It is a princely gift for any man. I concede my defeat. Direct me to Matthias' home, and we will be quit of each other."

The man directed him through the city and to the outer walls. It appeared that Matthias had more land and property than he let on to Jethen. The house was situated in a beautiful garden. A large vineyard, nearly the size of his father's, grew against a small slope. Date palms lined the walk up to his walled house.

Jethen picked up the mallet and flailed it against the large gong residing outside the gates. He rested on a bench looking out over the garden obviously intended for the purpose of waiting for someone to answer the summons. A very young maid answered the door, and Jethen inquired politely for Lydia wife of Matthias.

"She don't live here no more," the girl spoke with difficulty. It appeared that she spoke only Greek, so Jethen switched to that language, and discovered that Lydia had already turned their large estate over to her nephew.

"May I speak to the nephew?" Jethen asked in Greek.

The young girl smiled, and ran to fetch the owner of the property. Jethen had known a little what to expect from Jakim's description of the nephew.

A Jew, younger that he, came to the door. In his hand was an abacus, and he was still pushing the beads as he came. When he caught sight of Jethen, he stiffened. He was one of those Jews who would have nothing to do with Samaritans. Before he could turn on his heel and leave, Jethen spoke, "I am looking for the wife of Matthias with an urgent message. Do you know where I might find her?"

Scorn dripped from the nephew's mouth. "I am not in the habit of requiring an accounting of my aunt as to her whereabouts, and particularly, if I knew, I would not divulge it to strangers, or foreigners," he added with a sneer. Jethen was unable to tell him of Matthias before the door was firmly, and not quietly, shut in his face.

Jethen doubted the man was even interested in the message he carried, or he would have inquired before shutting the door. Shrugging his shoulders, Jethen turned from the door and began the long walk to the other side of Jericho to his own family home.

"Jethen, I thought I'd find you up here. Did you find who you sought?"

At the sound of his mother's voice, he turned to face her. She was looking so much better. His sister Miriam had returned, with her children, to her own home, and only looked in on their mother once or twice a week now. His mother must have heard him return and run up the stairs to the rooftop. She would know he was upset.

"I only met a young man too busy counting his shekels to give me the courtesy of a hint where I might find her." Jethen related all that had transpired that day.

When he had finished, she commented, "Ah well, you have done all you could, I suppose. You surely own this man, Matthias, nothing more."

"Perhaps in courtesy I owe him nothing more. I'm certainly not in the mood to tell that upstart nephew anything, he would probably leave him to rot. In friendship . . . I think I know where I might find her."

"Oh? Where is that?"

The words seemed to drag from Jethen's mouth. "I think she might be following that man Jesus. If I go to him, he might direct me to her."

His mother looked at him in surprise. She knew of his feelings of antagonism against the man, for Sherai's sake. "Yes, he is preaching somewhere outside of Jericho, I hear. Some of the servants have gone to hear him."

Now it was Jethen's turn to be surprised, "You encourage them in this?

His mother answered him evenly, "I think I would have gone with them if I possessed the stamina for a day's journey. I like what he has to say, or what they tell me he says, I should say. I've also heard that he heals all who come to him. That is amazing in itself, aside from his words."

"I find many of his words astonishing. Matthias told me stories of him in Jerusalem, and not a little of his teachings. I think I might have gone to hear him without needing to find his Lydia, if not for . . ."

His mother nodded. Jethen confided in her his failure to win Sherai. Her heart ached with pity for him. There was great humility in Jethen, almost nobility. His father, Amos, had been a good man, and a good provider, but his outlook and compassion did not match his son's. Miriam was almost in awe of Jethen's goodness.

Jethen accepted Sherai's refusal, and was attempting to live his life with her decision. Sherai followed this Jesus, and he would see her again if he went to him. The pain it would cause him seemed so unnecessary, especially for an acquaintance such as Matthias had been.

"I could go for you, or with you, perhaps," she offered.

Jethen grasped his mother's out held hand, accepting her sympathy. "No, you were right to remain home. I hope I am enough of a man to put aside my own feelings, and seek him out. Something about Matthias touched my heart, as well as my mind. He has a simple, deep faith in God that I have lost. I wasn't even aware I missed it until I met him."

Miriam knew by the tone of his voice that he meant what he said. Her heart stirred with a hunger for her own lost faith.

"Then you must go find Jesus. It is possible that you might find more than Matthias' Lydia."

"At least I will finally see for myself," he said grimly.

23

FINDING JESUS

Jethen didn't go alone. In the stables he encountered Mishob, who insisted on accompanying him. "I have long been curious to hear the man speak," he admitted.

"Then come with me and both of us will have our curiosity satisfied. We'll ride the mules. If we walk, we'll miss hearing him speak. I wonder where he chose to stop and preach?"

"I think I know the place. There is a hollowed out hill set back from the road less than a half-day's journey on foot from here. It forms a sort of natural theater that the Roman infidels are so fond of building. With so many following or listening, it would be a natural spot. It should only take an hour to reach it if we push the mules a bit."

"Then we'll saddle light."

"Yes, I'd say take Shy Bit and Nibble, they're our fastest with a light saddle." Jethen looked at Mishob quickly to see if he made a jest at his expense. Mishob caught the look and smiled, "My almost-like-a-son, I have known of your names for the animals since you were old enough to talk. I call them by their names as often as you, I expect. You have a gift for names; they all seem to fit them, especially Nam. The animals respond to names just as humans do. Your father, Amos, was a good man, but he had no imagination."

Jethen chuckled as he took the tack from its accustomed place across the side of the stalls. "Then I am riding Nibble, she's the fastest."

"Only because she knows you'll give her a treat at the end of the ride. It's the proverbial carrot dangled before the donkey."

"We'll have to take more water bags, I only snatched two for myself."

"I'd like to take the bags for the feed, as well. I'll put them on Shy Bit. I'm a bit lighter in the saddle than you."

"Then we'll need water for them also."

"Naturally. I don't think I would undertake such a journey in this heat without water for the animals." Mishob's tone was a light rebuke.

"The filled pannier is at the door. I had no intention of neglecting the beasts, but I am in haste."

"Then less talk and more action is our law."

They rode as quickly as they dared in the heat. The harsh sun was west of the road making some shade where large rocks or shrubs grew. Taking care to travel in the shade, where it was available, made the ride less arduous. They did not meet another soul on their way. Mishob tried a time or two to make conversation. When Jethen answered absently because he was inwardly steeling himself for the encounter ahead, Mishob contented himself with studying the landscape.

They had traveled this road so often neither of them needed to consult the landscape. When the land began its upward slope was soon enough to begin looking for the crowd. Jethen went over in his mind what he would say, but never got further than, 'Your disciple, Matthias, was injured on the Jericho road.' What if Sherai was with him? Would his eyes single her out in such a large gathering? Would instinct draw him to her as he always sensed her presence in the past? Would it distract him from his purpose? Could he endure the pain? He almost groaned aloud.

Most often he felt anger against Sherai for her rejection of all he offered. He used that anger to fortify himself against her. It made losing her so much easier to bear. But when her image came to his mind, his anger at her dissolved, leaving him helpless and suffering. Would it be even worse to see her?

Jethen wished, not for the first time, he had not heeded his mother's advice. Had he never asked for Sherai he could have gone on cherishing the hope that someday she might be his. Hope was dead.

How many times he mulled this over in his mind he couldn't remember. Mishob rode up beside him and said, "They are just ahead."

Jethen looked up, and sure enough, a large crowd decorated the hill. Below the hill, seated on a large rock that seemed to have been rolled there for that purpose, a man sat talking. Because they were behind him, his voice was thrown up the hill, and they heard little of what he said. Alighting from their mules, they led them around the outskirts of the crowd seated in fan shape outward from the speaker.

Settling on a spot not quite half-way up, Jethen watered and fed the mules while casting covert looks at the man who had taken Sherai's heart. As for Jesus, he spoke with ease, and seemed comfortable in his role of rabbi. He was tall, perhaps taller even than Jethen, for his long legs stretched out from the rock. His beard was well trimmed, and his hair, which fell to his shoulders, seemed well kept. Jethen felt there was nothing striking in his appearance that would so easily captivate a woman, unless it was his eyes. They seemed . . . wise.

Jethen was unaware that he had stopped working, until Mishob's mule nudged him. Even that did not budge him, for by then, Jesus had noticed the newcomer and was looking directly into his eyes. Though his voice did not falter, his eyes seemed to be probing Jethen's deepest thoughts. He smiled slightly, and then his eyes seemed to move directly to another in the crowd. Jethen followed his gaze and froze. He had looked directly at Sherai! It was as if Jesus knew.

Then he heard what he was saying, "As I have said before, the son of man is come to save that which was lost. What do you think a man would do if he had an hundred sheep, and one of them went astray? Does he count the sheep he has remaining, and rest contented, or does he secure the ninety and nine, then go and seek the one which is lost?"

Jesus looked again at Jethen, and said, "If it should so be that he find that sheep that was lost, he rejoices more over that one sheep than the ninety and nine safe in the fold."

Jethen looked down at his feet. It was as though Jesus of Nazareth was speaking directly to him. It was as though he was saying, "I know you are lost, but I have come to find you. I rejoice that I have found you." Jethen looked up to meet his gaze, but Jesus had turned away from the crowd and was saying something in a low voice to his disciples who sat directly behind him. Many people in the crowd leaned forward as if they were trying to hear his words. Jethen looked again to where Sherai sat. She was looking directly at him. She moved as if she would rise and come to him, but Jethen gestured for her to remain seated.

A man rose from the crowd. Jethen recognized him. He was a lawyer from Jericho. What was his name? Oh, yes, Isaac.

He seemed to almost taunt Jesus as he asked, "Master, what shall I do to inherit eternal life?" From what Jethen knew of him, he doubted his sincerity. Isaac of Jericho was more interested in adding to his stores than piety.

All eyes turned to Jesus to see what he would say. They didn't have long to wonder, "What does the law say? How does it read?" Jethen wasn't surprised at Jesus knowing the man was learned. Isaac wore his learning and affluence like a cloak.

The man seemed to puff himself up, and in polished tones, as though he were addressing a prelate he answered, "Love the Lord God with all your heart, with all your soul, with all your strength, and all your mind; and love your neighbor as you do yourself."

Jesus answered him again, "You speak the truth. This do and you shall live."

Isaac threw his arms wide and said, "Yes, but who is my neighbor?" He seemed to indicate the large crowd and was asking how much of it should he include in his love.

Jesus looked at Isaac, and turned once again to look at Jethen. Isaac followed his gaze, and his lips curled. He knew that Jethen, who still stood by his mule holding a handful of grain in his hand for the mule to eat, was a Samaritan. Certainly, his gaze said, this man is not my neighbor. Jethen saw his look, but Jesus captured his eyes, and he couldn't look away. Jesus smiled at Jethen, and began speaking.

"There was a certain man traveling down from Jerusalem to Jericho," he spoke in a storytelling tone. Jethen hadn't known what to expect, but he hardly imagined a parable to vanquish the self-satisfied lawyer. He waited to hear how the story would unfold. "And he fell among thieves, and was robbed, wounded, stripped of all he had, and left for dead along the side of the road." Jesus paused and looked again at Jethen.

Jethen felt the hairs on his head rise. His fist closed over the grain in his hand, and his mule protested in huffed breath. His heart gave a painful jerk then continued beating in heavy strokes. In that instant thoughts were colliding in his head like chaff in the wind. What would this man say next? What had Sherai said about her first meeting with him? That he told her all about herself?

Jesus looked away out over the crowd, and spoke directly to Isaac, "And by chance there came down a certain priest that way, and when he saw the wounded man, he passed by on the other side." This time there was no mistake. Jesus looked again directly into Jethen's eyes. Jethen saw again the self important Annas pass him on the other side of the road as he journeyed that morning. The crowd murmured a displeased reaction to the story. Most of them depended on their priests to lift them up, and care for them as a shepherd would care for his flock.

Again Jesus looked away, and Jethen caught the breath he was unaware he had been holding. Unbelieving what he was hearing he looked to Mishob for confirmation. Mishob had been there that day. His old servant was staring at Jesus with tears in his eyes, and did not notice Jethen's glance.

Jethen heard Jesus continue, "Likewise, a Levite, when he came to that place came and looked upon him, and he, too, passed by on the other side."

Jethen felt the blood drain from his face. Well he remembered the other man hurrying along the road after the priest. All at once Jethen felt light-headed and dizzy. It couldn't be possible? Did Jesus really know? He shook Mishob gently, and the man looked at his Master tearfully, and shook his head slightly before returning his gaze to Jesus.

Like a magnet, Jethen's eyes once again met those of Jesus. Not until he was certain he had his gaze did Jesus continue, "But a certain Samaritan, as he journeyed, came to where the wounded man was." Jesus' eyes then sought out Isaac. "When the Samaritan saw him lying there, he had compassion on him." Jesus paused again and looked directly at Jethen. "He went to him, and bound up his wounds pouring in oil and wine." Jethen heard Mishob draw in his breath in a gasp, and felt him grab his arm in a punishing grip.

Jesus looked out over the crowd to tell the rest of the story. "After caring for the man all he could, he put him on his own beast, and brought him to an inn. There the man continued to care for him through the night." Jethen felt tears rising up and choking his chest. It simply wasn't possible, but it was happening. Jesus was relating to this crowd the story he had come to tell him.

It appeared that Jesus was not yet finished with his story. Jethen fought down his emotion to hear what else he might say. "In the morning, when the Samaritan left the inn, he gave two pence to the innkeeper, and said to him, 'Care for this man, and whatever more you spend, when I come again, I will repay you.'" Jesus glanced once more at Jethen, then turned to the lawyer and asked, "Which of these three was neighbor to the man who fell among thieves?

How could this man possibly know what had taken place on the Jericho road? How could he know unless he was the son of God as Sherai claimed? Sherai's words came clearly to his mind concerning her first meeting with Jesus. "He told me all about myself, all that had happened, he knew, and best of all, he did not condemn me."

Jethen barely heard Isaac's reply, "He that showed mercy upon him."

Jesus said, his eyes taking in Isaac, and then the crowd, "Go and do likewise." He paused again, and then said, "My disciples and I will be traveling on. We will take our leave of you. Are there any among you who desire healing?"

A few got up from the crowd and walked toward Jesus, but Jethen paid them no heed. He fell to his knees disregarding the dirt and gravel. His heart and mind were churning with the clarity he experienced. Over and over in his mind he prayed, "Forgive me, God, I didn't know." Every word that he had ever heard that Jesus said played into his mind. Every miracle he had heard about on his travels, he recalled, raising a young child from the dead, healing the blind, calming the sea. He recalled every word taught him by Matthias, but most especially he heard the words of today, "If it should so be that he find that sheep that was lost, he rejoices more over that one sheep than the ninety and nine safe in the fold."

"He has found me,' Jethen thought. The raging hurt, confusion, disappointment and anger were washed from his heart as he contemplated. He experienced a sensation similar to a wave of water washing over his soul, making him clean, and whole.

How long he was lost in such meditation he had no way of knowing. He felt someone kneel next to him, and soft arms encircle him. Opening his eyes he noticed first that Mishob knelt beside him. It was possible that he'd pulled him down when he fell to his knees. On his other side was Sherai, and when he looked up he saw that the tears he had forbidden to fall from his own eyes left dust tracks down her face. No words were necessary between them.

A voice above them said, "I see, my children that you have found one another." Jesus stood before them and at his side was an older woman. The hair at her temples was white. However, her eyes shone with serenity. Her skin had some wrinkles around her eyes and lips, but other than those, her skin was smooth and soft looking. At once Jethen knew who she must be. His own tears then fell, without his permission. "I have brought Lydia, as you see," Jesus said, then called him by name, "Jethen, is there something you wish to tell her? We are traveling on, perhaps you would care to come with us, and tell her on the way. We will stop at the inn."

"I don't know you, do I?" Lydia asked, "Except perhaps that we are sister and brother in the Lord?" Her eyes took in his tears, and compassion settled over her features.

Jethen rose from his knees, and pulled Sherai and Mishob up with him.

He took Lydia's hand and said, "I bring you news of Matthias. You will find him at a caravansary midway between Jerusalem and Jericho. I left him there in the care of the owner, Lucius, a friend of mine. Matthias was robbed, and left for dead on the Jericho road." Jethen blushed a crimson red when he admitted, "I took him there and cared for him. He will live," he hastened to add, "but I fear he will be laid up for some time."

"I was worried for him. I knew something must have detained him," she responded. "He was one of the seventy who went out to preach, but he was to have been here with me today. Thank you for your care of him. You knew this, Master?" she asked Jesus.

"The Father knows when a sparrow falls; what the Father knows, I know." Lydia nodded as though she believed him implicitly.

"I will go with you," Jethen told Lydia. "You can ride my mule, and use him for Matthias to journey on when he is ready." What he didn't say was that he would not be parted with Jesus for a bag of gold. He gave a small start when Sherai spoke, for he had forgotten her for the moment.

"Master," she said, "I would like to present my friend Jethen to you, but it seems you know him already."

Jesus extended his hand in greeting and smiled at Jethen and Sherai, "I think you are more than a friend."

Jethen did not see Sherai blush or he might have wondered at it. Placing his hand on Jesus arm in Roman fashion, he confirmed, "We are distant kin. Our fathers were partners long ago." It was then he noticed that Sherai still held his other arm through hers, and he looked at her.

24

LEARNING THE WORD

"Master," a muscular fellow with a long beard who stood somewhat shorter than Jesus interrupted them. "All the people have gone on. Are we returning to Galilee?" His voice was rough, and it brought to Sherai's mind the folk along the shores of Gennesseret.

"No, Peter, I must travel to Bethany, and beyond. I will remain in the south until the spring."

"I would be honored if you would stop in Jericho at my home for the night before continuing on."

It seemed Jethen didn't want to be parted from Jesus.

"I must travel on to the inn," Jesus reminded him, "with Lydia."

"I should go with you, and settle up with Lucius."

Sherai interrupted before anything else could be said, "I will gladly go on with you to Jericho, Jethen. Mazar and I are traveling on to Sychar. She is going to visit her family there, and I am going to see Omini. I would be happy to renew friendship with Miriam. I have never seen young Miriam's children." Sherai knew she was babbling like a young girl, but she couldn't help it.

She was so happy to see Jethen again. Even more, she was happy to see that a change had been wrought in his life. That much was apparent by the joy in his face. It was an echo of the joy her own heart had experienced at the well. Sherai knew it had something to do with Matthias, Jethen was undoubtably the man in the parable. No wonder he had fallen to his knees.

Sherai wanted to dance there in the dust. She wanted to fall to her knees and dust the gravel and dirt from Jethen's knees. She wanted to shout for joy. What she didn't want was for him to know that before her journey began she had determined to go into Jericho to his family home. At the time she had felt it unlikely that Jethen would be in Jericho at this time of year. He usually traveled the coast up to Maritime Caesarea to meet the ships, then on to Damascus. It was an unexpected joy to see him here with Jesus.

Jethen blurted, "There is need for me to be baptized." He spoke to Jesus, but his words were in answer to Sherai as well. "Rabbi, I would be a disciple, if you would accept one such as I. I would go with you from this moment."

Sherai held her breath. She heard Jesus say many times that he was called to teach repentance to the Jews. True, he stopped in Sychar and taught there, but to her knowledge, he had never returned. Many who had followed him from Sychar had fallen away.

Jesus seemed to study Jethen before his reply. "I sent no disciples, nor will I send seventies into Samaria, Jethen," he paused and looked down at the dust that covered both their feet. Then looking up he grasped Jethen's upper arms in his strong hands. "The day will come when my disciples teach all the world, and you will be among them. Before that day, I desire you to return to your home, study the scriptures, pray earnestly to understand them, and begin teaching my words."

"I don't as yet know your words, Master. I must first learn them," said Jethen. It was a humble supplication to learn those words at the Master's feet. Sherai knew exactly how he felt. Jesus' words were a feast for the soul.

Gently Jesus shook his head, "There is another thing you must do. Matthias taught you many of my words. Your kinswoman also knows my sayings, she will help you. Together you will study the scriptures, search out the prophets for they will teach you more of me. Meanwhile, use your abundance to help others, the poor, and the widow." Jesus smiled at both him and Sherai.

"Go forth now, and serve. Bring him in early spring to Jerusalem for the Passover," he said to Sherai, "You both must be there with the other disciples. John," he called one of his chosen to him. A younger man came through the crowd of disciples waiting to depart. His face was sparsely bearded. His hair was bleached by the sun, his arms were tanned a deep brown. It was his countenance that captured Jethen's attention. His whole face shone with utter love for his Master.

"John, I want you and Jude to accompany our new disciple to Jericho. There you will baptize him, and see that he is instructed in the ways of the Lord. Then come to me in Bethany."

"I will," he said simply. John then addressed Sherai and Jethen, "Will you wait here while I find Jude?" His speech was the speech of Galilee, but softer than the burly man who had spoken earlier. He disappeared into the throng still pressing around Jesus.

Jethen went to where Mishob was preparing the mules. He was going to turn them over to Lydia as he had said.

Meanwhile, Mazar found her way to Sherai, and stood talking quietly with her. "We are stopping in Jericho?"

"Yes, then we will travel on to Sychar, perhaps with Jethen and his servants. Jesus has told Jethen to minister to the people in Sychar, and I am to tell him his words."

"You?"

"Who knows the Master's words better? I'll speak more on this later," she whispered to Mazar because Jethen came back to them announcing that the mules were ready for travel.

"I'm sorry," he addressed Sherai stiffly, "that the Master has involved you in my teaching. I could perhaps speak with him, and request another."

"No, Jethen, I want to do as the Master said. I have written many of his words. I'm thankful to my father every day for teaching me lettering, and reading. It will be my greatest joy to share them with you. Meanwhile, John is one of Jesus' favored disciples. He has a heart much like yours. He will teach you many things before he travels on to Bethany. Jethen, did you truly succor Matthias as Jesus said in his parable?"

"You heard me tell his wife so."

Sherai sighed, "Then you have seen the same miracle I saw at the well. Jesus is the Messiah, and he knows all things. Can you believe now that he is a God?"

"I believe he is the Son of God, just as you said he is."

John had returned just as Jethen answered her. With him was a man slightly older than John who carried himself with the same ease and confidence that Jesus displayed. A closer look convinced Jethen that this Jude was probably related to Jesus. He was relieved to see that they both carried water skins that were nearly full.

He was not ashamed that John overheard his declaration. In fact he was delighted when he said, "You have accepted on faith what it has taken many of our Lord's chosen disciples long to acknowledge, Jethen. It's no longer a wonder to me that he is sending you to Samaria to spread his word."

"I depend on you to teach me during our short time together."

"It will be my pleasure to teach you anything I can. Jude is my travel companion. We went preaching together. He is Jesus' younger brother. You've possibly noticed the family resemblance. Say something, Jude, something profound."

"You could learn of compassion from Jethen, John," Jude responded, but his countenance was unruffled. "You say enough for the both of us. I am pleased to be of service to you, sir," he told Jethen as he clasped his shoulder. "How profound anything I say may be, you will have to be the judge."

Jethen chuckled, "I have heard it said that we are to judge not."

Jude smiled, and his relationship to Jesus was even more pronounced, "I see that you do know some of the Master's sayings. Do you know that he once said, "You are like a city upon a hill, like a burning candle in the darkness, and you are not to hide you light, but to shine forth for all men. It seems that you are to be such a candle, Jethen. I am glad to make your acquaintance. I hope that in some small way I can teach you to shine."

"Tell me more about this candle," begged Jethen.

"Come," said the impatient John, "we can tell him more along the way. The sun is sinking and my stomach tells me it is nigh time for food."

Sherai recalled that John had been one of the men with Jesus on Mount Hermon. She smiled because she realized he still had his feet firmly on practical matters.

The four men, Mishob, Jethen, John and Jude, and two women, Sherai and Mazar made their way to Jericho together. John, now that they were on their way, walked beside Jethen, "Perhaps before you begin to shine," he smiled at Jude to show he meant no offense, "you should first understand why there is a need for you to be baptized." At once his youthful and more playful mein left his face. His voice even took on an expression of spiritual guidance, "To be fit for the Kingdom of God, man must be born of the water and the spirit. The Master calls it being born again. First you repent of all your sins. Then you are presented to be washed clean of your sins, symbolically, in the water. You are then immersed in the water by one having authority from God."

"After that you take upon yourself a new name," Jude contributed.

"I am no longer Jethen son of Amos? Who will give me this new name?" Jethen asked.

"You are Jethen son of Amos, the disciple of Jesus," Jude smiled. "You are not less than you were, you are more–more righteous, more centered on holy things than the treasures of this world. I meant that you will be a disciple of Jesus the Christ."

"You will begin your life of service in righteousness. You have already begun this journey toward righteousness by what you've done on the Jericho road, and in parting with your mules," John added.

"Lydia needed them for Matthias," Jethen was unworried about parting with them. "If I am to be baptized, we must first journey to water." Jethen sounded so eager, so happy.

Sherai traveled along, sometimes listening, but more often thinking her own thoughts. Mostly her heart was full, and she kept remembering Jethen on his knees with his eyes fixed firmly on Jesus, and filled with tears.

She looked again at her distant cousin and saw him in a new light. She saw him for the man he was, the good kindly man who had taken her in, saw that his maid Sachi was married, cared for his mother, cared for her, even after she left him, and succored a near stranger. He was remarkable, and now he was a disciple of Jesus. He would always be like this, caring and giving. She tuned in again to what they were saying.

John, disciple of Jesus of Nazareth, was telling Jethen, "Then he said 'if there is anything you wish for mankind to do for you, do it also for them, for this is the law, and the prophets' way.'"

Jethen repeated, "If I want a person to treat me a certain way, I must also treat them in like manner. For instance, if I want courtesy from a servant, or respect, I must give the same courtesy and respect to them, is that what he meant?"

"That is precisely what he meant," affirmed Jude. "We are not to look for faults in others, but within ourselves, and rid ourselves of that fault before we look at other's faults."

"That ties in with judge not, doesn't it?"

"Yet," Jude broke in, "we are not to blindly accept all things. We study the fruit that a tree bears. A good tree brings forth good fruit, but a corrupt tree brings forth evil fruit. By the fruit that they bear, or their actions, we can separate what is good from what is not."

Sherai was the first to notice that the man, who had inquired of Jesus who was his neighbor, had been following them for some time listening to their words. When she wasn't paying attention, he had worked his way to them, and frankly listened to all that was said.

While Jethen pondered on what Jude imparted, the man took the opportunity to speak, "If we are to know people by the fruit they bear, is that not a form of judgment?"

Jude turned to the man unsurprised. Often on the road he had been approached by people in the crowd who wanted clarification on some point, but dared not approach Jesus. When he noticed that it was the man who seemed to mock Jesus at the gathering, he gave thought before he answered him. "I believe it is more a form of discernment. If a man sees a mold growing on a fig, he does not eat the fig. If he sees a scum on the surface of the water he doesn't suffer his beasts to drink. If he sees a flaw in a garment, he does not buy it." Jude paused for a bare second and continued, "If he sees a sneer, he does not expect humble sincerity."

"We've been taught to avoid evil." The stranger bristled and was quick to defend himself.

"Yes," agreed John, "but first we must know what is evil. Is a race of people evil, or the act that one person of that race may do evil? Should we avoid all men because one might do evil deeds? Jesus says to love, to forgive, to serve others. If a man asks for our coat we should also give him our cloak, if he asks us to walk with him a mile, we should walk with him two. Tell me, what sort of man would ask for a coat?"

"A beggar, one who does not care for himself."

"Or a man who cannot. We do not know for certain, but we are to give whether or not he is worthy."

"We would have no substance remaining for ourselves," the man cried in protest.

"Then we would be equal with him, and understand his plight."

The man turned to Jethen, "Surely you do not accept this philosophy? You are a merchant, a man of vast holdings."

Briefly, Sherai wondered how the man knew Jethen. She avidly listened to what Jethen would say.

"I would impart of my substance to the poor, yes. I would also work to get more substance that I might have more to give."

The man seemed incredulous, "You would stop by the side of a road to succor a man who was beaten and robbed and left for dead?"

"I did stop to succor such a man. I was the Samaritan who stopped to succor the man who fell. Without my telling him, Jesus knew every detail. I intend to listen carefully to such a man so touched by God. Should you not do the same?"

"You were the man in the story? When had you told it to him?"

"I said, I told him not," Jethen repeated, "Still he knew."

The man pondered this before repeating feebly, "He knew you had done this without your telling him? What of another, could they not have told him?"

"No one knew but me. There was no one to tell him. Why do you think I fell to my knees?"

"I supposed it was because you were a Samaritan and he was saying something good about them."

"It was because my eyes were opened, and I saw that he was a man of God, Isaac of Jericho."

There was complete silence for a moment on the road to Jericho. The man, Isaac, visibly softened, "Then he knew that I mocked him, yet he answered me not with sharpness, but with a story a child might understand. He meant for me to see that all men are my neighbors and I must love them?" He said it as a question.

Jude put in softly, "He knew you mocked him that is why he asked you to answer your own question. Jesus loves all mankind. He wants all people to love and care for one another. He wants to banish hatred, envy, strife, and malice. Most importantly of all, he wants all to gain eternal life."

"Though it sounds simple and beautiful, it is a very difficult life to live," Isaac remonstrated.

John agreed, "Straight is the path, and narrow is the way that leads to life eternal, and few people find it. Jesus said that himself."

Unexpectedly Isaac said humbly, "Though I mocked, I do wish for eternal life with God."

"Then the path is laid before you, Isaac," replied John. "Repent of your sins, be washed clean in the waters of baptism, and take upon yourself a new name. Become a follower of our Lord."

"You call him Lord?" Isaac was startled.

Jethen said firmly and with a humble assurance, "He is the Lord."

"Then you follow him?" He asked Jethen.

"From this day henceforth and forever," vowed Jethen.

"I would hear more," said the man, his voice now humble, and entreating.

"Well said–for a lawyer," Jethen told him with a touch of humor, but with brotherly kindness added, "Think of the good you will do among men."

Sherai shook her head in near disbelief. Jesus drew all to him. Physicians, high priests, lawyers, and even the rich came to him. It would have to bring a better world, this Kingdom of God.

Joy welled up in Sherai as she understood that here was the answer to her prayers in Capernaum. It was God's will for her to help Jethen, and assist him in his work. He was going to convert many souls with his simple goodness.

Jesus had as much as told her that her travels with his disciples were over. Instead of feeling affronted, or sad, a sense of responsibility, and deep contentment settled in her heart. Jesus had read her heart, and given her work to do.

Inexplicably, there was also a stirring of excitement within her. It seemed she had come around to close a circle. Almost three years ago she had met Jesus in Sychar, traveled to Capernaum, followed his ministry, and now she was to return to Sychar.

Tears filled her eyes as she listened to John teaching with authority and assurance. She looked at Mazar and Mishob also absorbed in John's words. No one but her seemed to notice as his mules, with Shy Bit carrying Lydia, passed them by to travel on to the inn with the rest of the disciples, and Jesus of Nazareth.

25

SEEK AND YOU SHALL FIND

Sherai had spent a delightful hour in this spacious home of Miriam's. The young wife had tastefully furnished her home with both old and new design. Without overstating the obvious, it was clear that wealth was involved.

Unlike the home of her mother, it was built after the manner of the Greeks and Romans. There was an openness to the house that reminded Sherai of Jethen's home in Sychar. They were outdoors on one of the open loggias overlooking the orchard of olive trees. In the distance against a rise, she could see the fields of grapes, the fruit of the vine, as the Master called it. The long walk that led to the house was lined with date palms.

"Miriam, your baby is enchanting. I could do nothing but hold her all the day long."

Miriam laughed and teased, "If you did, you would become extremely wet before long, and you would have a very cross, hungry baby in your arms. I must admit that you look natural with a babe. Why don't you marry again? Mother told me you were freed from Maachi, there is nothing to keep you from finding a good man to marry."

Miriam's warm frankness colored Sherai's face a deep red. She could feel the heat in her face and neck. She didn't know what to say. Jethen had brought her to Miriam's house to say goodbye before they left for Sychar. He had gone off with Miriam's husband, Tahan, to inspect their sheep pens. Tahan had taken over Miriam's father's sheep folds when he died.

It had been delightful playing with the small children, and holding the baby. "I have no thought to marry," Sherai finally said. "I was content to follow the Master and learn of him, and to ply my small business in Capernaum. Now that I am returning to Sychar, there are few eligible men there . . ." she mumbled, then blushed even more when she recalled that she would be working closely with one very eligible man.

"You could marry my brother. He is of an age to marry, and needs someone to care for him. Mother and I worry that he will never marry."

Sherai looked up at Miriam, and saw that she knew of her brother's feelings for her. She wondered if she also knew that Jethen had asked for her, and was turned down. "He is young yet, and he has never married. Don't you wish for him a bride who is young and unmarried as well?"

Miriam came over to Sherai and took her baby from her. She sat little Miriam down in a basket of reeds that had been prepared with straw and covered with blankets. It was her outdoor bed. The baby fussed a moment for being put down, and Miriam expertly changed her linens. Then the little one settled into the softness and began to coo. Miriam touched her cheek. When she looked up at Sherai she saw such a look of longing on her face, she felt she had intruded on her heart. She walked over and took Sherai's hands in hers. With great deliberation she then said, "I want my brother to be happy. I think that you could make him happy. Perhaps you are the only one who could."

Sherai protested, "Jethen has been very happy since he met Jesus. John and Jude have taught him so much. It has been like a school for me, too. I feel that I have very little more to contribute to his learning on the words of Jesus."

"Yes," Miriam let go of her hands, "I have noticed his joy. He whistles as he did in the old days, and his voice is even gentler with me. I think he would give me all that he has if I needed it, or even if I asked for it. The other day Mother asked for a hand in making the wine, and Jethen, who had just come into the room with Jude and John said, "Both hands are yours, Mother, right John?"

"He has worked day and night to prepare the house for his departure. All that, and Mother is going with him!"

"I didn't know your Mother was going to Sychar. She hasn't been there since he built his house. She will love it. It is so open, and spacious."

"Yes," said Miriam, with a sly glance at Sherai, "she is going with what you said earlier in mind."

"What I said?"

"Truthfully, I don't believe she will return until she has found him a wife. She told me as much while I was helping her pack up for the journey." Miriam turned away with a smile when Sherai involuntarily frowned at the news. What Mother Miriam had told her daughter was, *'They will have need of a chaperone if they study together. I won't mind learning, myself. I have no intention of returning until I have convinced Sherai to take Jethen. I want some grandchildren from him before I die. I won't tell Sherai that, mind, I have another idea.'* Miriam was thinking furiously how she might help in the project. "While she is there she might make a match for you. An older man might be pining for a younger second or third wife."

"I've had enough of being a second wife, thank you." Sherai was adamant about that. She might marry again, but it would be to a man with no wife. In spite of herself, Jethen's serious face that day on the hill came to mind. Yes, she would have a man like him, perhaps a widower.

So Jethen's mother wanted a young wife for him that much was clear. Sherai's mouth drooped a bit. When she saw Miriam's eyes were twinkling wickedly, she said cooly, "Perhaps I can help your mother find a wife for him. I want to see him settled with a family." Sherai tried to imagine a young chaste bride who could bring him a dowry, and lots of healthy babies, but she couldn't think of a single one. Not one of the young girls she knew was good enough for Jethen.

"You do that," Miriam told her.

What Sherai, his sister, nor his mother knew was that Jethen had not yet been baptized. John taught him the Judaic law during their stay in Jericho. He also discussed with him certain principles that Jesus outlined in his ministry. Unknown to Jethen, he was preparing him to become a true disciple of Jesus, just as he had been instructed.

This was the last day of his instruction. Each day John had put him off when he asked about baptism. On the following day he and Jude planned to go on to Bethany. Jethen was certain that on this last day he would speak of his baptism, but John talked most of Jesus' miracles with a smattering of his words. He then told him. "Jethen, do you understand what Jesus meant when he said, 'No man can serve two masters. Either he will love the one and hate the other, or he will hold to the one, and despise the other. You cannot serve both God, and man. Jesus said to lay up treasures in heaven, not build larger barns here on earth. We are to care for the widows and the fatherless."

Jethen knew this law, "That is a part of the Mosaic law that is also recognized by the Samaritans." He interrupted John's teaching to ask a question that had in times past deeply troubled him, "How does Jesus perform the miracles you have told me about? What is it that makes him able to raise a man from the dead like that widow's son, and that little girl? These are the acts of a God, not a son of man as he claims himself to be."

"Or they are the acts of a man sent by God," John told him. He quoted from Isaiah, "'the Lord himself will give you a sign; Behold a virgin shall conceive, and bear a son and shall call his name Immanuel.' His name means God is with us."

Jude said then, "Would you like to hear about the birth of my brother?" He then told Jethen of Jesus birth, and the signs attending that birth. While he was expounding the various points of Jesus birth, something curious happened, Jethen realized that he believed every word.

Jethen found he was hungry to hear more, and asked John, "Were there more prophecies concerning this birth?"

"Many more from Isaiah and other prophets. I would have to have scrolls to read you all the prophecies where a Messiah is mentioned."

"Then I must have these scrolls," Jethen declared. "Jesus told me to study the prophets, he did mean more than Moses, and Joshua, didn't he?"

"Yes, I think he meant for you to study the Torah. These contain the words of our prophets. There have been many since Joshua, my friend. Their words and study of them are available to Jews, as these prophets and judges came to them," John told him then added, "that is why I have told you many of the words of the prophets myself."

Jude inserted, "A few of Jesus' converts who wish to understand more, who are Gentiles–meaning non Jew–convert to Judaism."

"Then I must convert."

John smiled, but Jude, always the more grave of the two, said, "It is a serious step to take, Jethen. You must forsake your old beliefs, and promise to adhere to the Torah. I know that you were once a devout Samaritan, for you have told us. You must forsake Mount Sechem, and acknowledge Jerusalem as the center of your worship. You will be traveling back to Sychar for your study and worship. You will be among your former Samaritan friends and relatives. They will surely berate you for your decision. Can you do this?"

"I can, and I will. How can I deny what I know to be true?"

"If that is so, there are three steps to converting, the first is circumcision, and I believe that you have already complied with that commandment, being a devout Samaritan in your youth."

"Yes, I have complied. What are the second and third requirements?" Jethen asked eagerly.

"The second is that you must be baptized by a priest of the Sanhedrin before two other witnesses, Jews who can vouch for your integrity and intention."

Jethen looked at his new friend, John, then at Jude, and tears came to his eyes. "That is why he sent the two of you to teach me. He knew I would want to convert, and there must be two of you to witness it. Now, tell me the third requirement."

"The third step is that you must make the appropriate sacrifice at the temple."

"Of course. For all these things we must be in Jerusalem. That is why you wanted to go tomorrow."

"That, and the fact that we have taught you all that we can. The rest you will have to study for yourself," agreed Jude. "I thought you would want to convert, but it had to be your decision."

The next morning, just as dawn was peeking over the plains, Jethen roused everyone in the house. He wanted to get an early start. He planned to stop at the inn and inquire after Matthias, and settle with Lucius. Though it was uphill most of the way, he wanted to reach a caravansary outside of Jerusalem by nightfall. That meant that everyone must ride.

He woke Mishob to help him load and saddle the camels and mules he would be taking to Sychar. He told the older man, "Most likely I will sell many of them. I won't be making any more long trips. I'll keep enough to travel between Sychar and Jericho, but my long travels are over. I might sell John and Jude's mounts in Jerusalem. They should fetch a good price there.

"Thank you for remaining here in Jericho to look out for Mother's holdings, Mishob," Jethen was grateful to the older man for staying. The house and concerns here in Jericho were too vast to be left to even Mishob's son to look after alone.

"I'd like to go with you and learn more of Jesus' teachings," Mishob admitted, "but I won't mind staying here with my family. I haven't seen as much of my children as I'd like, and I'm getting too old for travel." Mishob's wife had died many years past, and he'd never remarried. His children lived in Jericho, and most of them worked for Jethen's mother. "Besides, John and Jude have stuffed my head so full of knowledge I was sure I'd drown from being so heavy when I was baptized."

Jethen chuckled in sympathy. "I know what you mean, my head is full of thoughts and ideas and stories. It was a good thing I wasn't baptized before they began teaching me in earnest."

"Everything's ready, we just need the riders."

"We're here, Mishob. The sky is clear. It is going to be a beautiful day." Miriam, knowing Jethen's liking for setting out early was already at the doors of the stable with a few extra items she couldn't do without. She'd brought her own maid, Sarah, with her. "Sherai and Mazar are behind me, and John and Jude are still talking with young Amos."

"Jude will have him converted before he goes," said Mishob. "He's been working on him for two weeks now."

"May all your children come to accept the Messiah," Jethen took Mishob's arm in the usual clasp of farewell. "Wait outside, Mother, I'll bring the animals out to you." All Jethen's servants that went with him on his travels were also traveling with them. Their numbers were so large there would be no fear of bandits along the road. They would stop in Jerusalem to sell their dates, wine from their vineyard, and some of the medicine for the eyes his mother had made.

When they were all assembled, Jude and John came to mount. John was still talking with Amos, and reached down to whisper something to him just before he turned to the others and assumed an air of command, "Is everyone ready?"

Jethen deferred to John as though the former fisherman was the owner of his vast holdings. He stood aside while John helped Sherai to her camel, and saw Miriam safely tucked into a canopied seat atop another. Mazar, he and Jude, then mounted mules, and all were settled.

"Hoah," he yelled, and the camels rose and the mules led the way.

Lucius pulled Jethen aside, and in a hushed voice said, "You did not tell me that Matthias was a person of such importance."

"I did not think it necessary to tell you. How did you come to learn of it?"

Lucius hiked his foot up onto the watering trough where the camels and mules were drinking for their long journey, and folded his arms across his chest. "A large group of people came to get him, that's how. Let me tell you, One day last week, a crowd came walking into my caravansary. There were men and women in the group, and two of the women were riding mules. One of the women turned out to be the man's wife. She had come to bring him a mule to ride onward. He was still not well from his beating and I doubted he could yet be moved. I told her so." He stopped speaking to yell to his servant, "Hey, feed those mules some hay."

As though he had not stopped his story he continued, "Then a man stepped forward out of the crowd. He was a bit taller than most of them, and his face was–well, I can't describe it. He asked me to take him to Matthias. I did so, and when we went into the room he called, "Matthias, rise, and come with us." He stretched forth his hand and touched the man's brow. Immediately the old man arose, and before my eyes his cuts and bruises seemed to vanish. His eyes were bright, and he walked out of the room like he was a young man, bouncing and eager. I've never seen anything like it in my life. I thought for sure he was nearly dead. Then off he goes toward Jerusalem, striding beside his wife on the mule like a young man in his prime."

"Lucius, you have been honored to see one of the miracles of Jesus the Christ."

"The Christ? Isn't he the one whom the Jews have been waiting to come for many centuries? Is he the one? He seems rather ordinary to be . . ."

"The Samaritans have also waited for this Messiah, my friend. Was what he did for Matthias ordinary?"

"No, but. . ."

"That is because he is in no way an ordinary man. Tell me, how much do I owe you for Matthias' care? I have need to settle up and ride onward. I want to reach Jerusalem by nightfall."

"You owe me nothing but to tell me more of this Jesus the Christ."

"Learn of him yourself, Lucius, that is much the better way. I must go on. He will be teaching at Jerusalem, and beyond."

"I can't leave my business, my servants would rob me blind," Lucius said, then trailed off. He recalled that was what had happened to Matthias, and the man had ridden off happy.

Jethen put a hand to the man's shoulder and said, "Consider this, Lucius, to know such a man would be worth all the gold in the world."

Lucius shook his head and pulled two of the camels away from the trough and gave them the command to sit down. The women and others who had gone to refresh themselves inside came out and mounted. Jethen did the same with the other two camels.

John came over to Lucius, "I believe you are the man who cared for our friend. Thank you for all you have done. May God shine upon you." He shook the man by the hand, and then went to draw his ride from the trough and gave him a carrot he had found inside.

Lucius leaned over to Jethen, "He's one of the followers of that Jesus, isn't he?"

"Yes," Jethen answered him joyfully, "and so am I." Mounting his own camel, he clucked to him to rise, and when John said, "Hoah." He turned his back on Lucius and the caravansary and moved on to Jerusalem without a backward look. If he had looked he would have seen Lucius staring after him with his mouth hanging open.

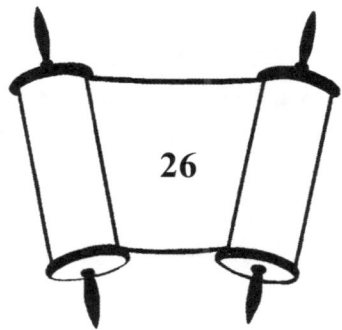

JERUSALEM

Jethen seemed in no hurry to continue on to Sychar. Instead he got his mother, Sherai, and their maids comfortably settled in rooms where he always stayed in Jerusalem, told them to take tours from the temple if they were interested, go to the market with Levi, whom he had left as a servant for them, and attend the theater or the baths if they wished. Then he disappeared with John and Jude.

He had taken a room for himself, John and Jude up near the roof, and was never, according to Levi, to be found in it when his mother inquired for him. Sherai thought he was busy selling some of his goods that had come on the camels with them, and she knew he intended to sell some of the animals.

Jethen was sweating. After two days, they had finally managed to make an appointment to meet with a priest of the Sanhedrin. It would be he who would interview Jethen, and then, if he was found worthy, baptize him. For those three days, Jethen had fasted.

John told him how important it was to repent of his sins before he stepped into the waters of baptism, and he spent much of those days in prayer and preparation. He and John bought the clothing that Jethen would don after his baptism and wear thereafter to signify to the world that he was a Jew. That clothing he reverently kept in a box.

They also sold two of the mules, and two of the four camels. They sold the goods that the camels carried. Jethen gave money to Jude to give to their treasury, and some he spent on scrolls of the prophets–bought through John. A large portion of the money he set aside to put in the temple treasury for the poor.

A scribe came to conduct them to the priest. They were in the temple's south colonnade, and they were escorted to the east apse where the Sanhedrin met. In a room set aside for the scribes, and other offices of the Sanhedrin, they were ushered inside.

In the room was only a table set with a menorah, and a few scattered cushions. A rich thick curtain was tied back to allow air into the room. The priest was seated on the only chair in the room. It was a cushioned seat covered with what appeared to be silk.

The priest was dressed in the white robe of the temple priests. His bearded face was as solemn as the occasion required. "You wish to petition the court to be converted to Judaism?"

"I do," Jethen replied for himself.

"You will remain silent and allow your two adjuncts to speak for you," the priest said.

The priest appeared surprised when John, clearly the younger of the two replied, "We petition that this man be accepted for baptism into the faith. He has studied the halakha (Jewish law) and understands and accepts the duties thereof."

The priest looked Jethen up and down. His face showed his clear distaste for his task. "This man is a Samaritan by birth?"

The priest shifted uncomfortably in his seat as though just saying the name spotted him in some way.

"Yes, he is," replied John.

"You have questioned him and he is prepared to abandon his belief that the true center of worship is on Mount Secham, and is prepared to accept the Torah?"

"I have questioned him, and he is prepared," Jude answered this time.

"You have questioned him and he has been circumcised?" The priest very well knew the answer to this, but it was a ritual question.

"We have questioned him, and Jethen, son of Amos, was circumcised shortly after birth, as declared by the law of the Samaritans."

"Humph, yes, well, then has he duly repented of his sins, and prepared himself to enter the waters of the mikveh[1] for his tevilah[2]?

"He has," replied John. The priest looked at Jude.

"He has," he echoed.

"Then tomorrow before sunrise you will present yourselves at the mikveh in the inner court. Bring robes befitting his status as a Jew in which to clothe him. Is he prepared to offer the proper korban (sacrifice) at that time?"

"He will be prepared."

"Then I will prepare the certificate of conversion, and sign it after these deeds have been done and witnessed."

"We will be at the assigned mikveh before sunrise," John agreed.

The priest stood up, signaling that the meeting was over. The scribe appeared as if by magic, and the men, who had been standing, all followed him out into the court.

Before the scribe left them, he showed them where they were to come the following morning. When the scribe left, Jethen let out a long sigh of relief. "Whew, that was not what I expected."

"What did you think would happen?" asked John.

"I thought it might be more difficult, or he would ask me questions to which I wouldn't know the answer."

"That was what we were for," John smiled at him.

"When will you make the sacrifice for me?" asked Jethen.

John clapped him on the back and said, "Like any good Jewish man, you will present your own sacrifice. I imagine you have made sacrifices on the altar at Mount Secham?" Jethen nodded in the affirmative. "It will be much the same except you will lay your gift on the altar in the temple."

"Then I'd better have one," he said.

They had been in Jerusalem three days when Miriam became exasperated, "You would think that my son would tell me of his plans, or have a meal with us."

Sherai told Miriam, "I imagine that Jethen is at the caravansary outside Jerusalem. He stays with the goods and animals to give his servants a chance to see the city. Why don't we do the same? Let's go get a closer look at the temple."

"But I am not a Jew," Miriam protested. "They won't let me in."

"There are places where anyone can go," Sherai assured her. "Besides, I have converted, and I can't miss this chance to see the temple," she coaxed her.

Miriam was a trifle shaken by this news, "You have converted, Sherai? Jethen didn't tell me this."

"Yes, after I was baptized, I converted. I don't think it was a requirement to follow Jesus, but I wanted to do it. It did make life a

---

[1] (ritual bath
[2] immersion

little easier in Capernaum," she readily admitted. "So, you are consorting with a Jew. Can you bear it?"

Miriam smiled wryly, "I can bear it if Jethen can. I suppose he will be converting next."

"He might," she agreed. "I know that he asked to be a disciple of Jesus."

"He did? And what did Jesus say? I don't suppose he was happy to have a Samaritan ask him that."

"I would have thought Jethen would have told you all about that, Miriam. I know that he confides in you a great deal."

"Humph, he did tell me, and what he is going to do. I imagine Jesus will make him a disciple when he returns to Jerusalem in the spring. In a sense, he is a disciple already," she sighed. Then her eyes narrowed, and she added, "Jethen also told me that he asked for you last spring, and you refused him. Was it because you are now a Jew and he is a Samaritan?"

Sherai quailed inside. She hadn't expected Miriam to bring up the subject, but she should have known that a woman as forthright as Miriam wouldn't let her off so easily. Licking her lips that had gone suddenly dry she said, "Partly, that is, that was one of the reasons I gave him. Another reason was that he made light of my new beliefs, and I . . ."

"Yes," prompted Miriam.

Mazar who had been helping Sarah straighten the room moved a little closer to the two women. She began dusting surfaces that had no dust, and leaned in to hear. Sherai saw her, but answered Miriam steadily enough, "I want Jethen to have a home and family with a woman who is young, strong, and able to give him many children. He deserves no less. I intend to help you find such a chaste young woman while you are in Sychar."

"Excellent," Miriam surprised her by saying. "I was hoping you would. It is the fondest wish of my heart to see him married. Since you do not want him, I want the matter concluded as swiftly as possible. He wants to be married, and that is half the battle."

Miriam patted Sherai's hand. "With both of us working for him, we'll see him happily settled soon. I believe that the Jews expect their men to marry."

Sherai had mixed feelings at best. It appeared that Miriam was intent on finding a bride for Jethen. Miriam thought Sherai had rejected him because she didn't want him. Now it was Sherai's turn to sigh. She wanted to be married, too.

Miriam saw it in Sherai's face, and she got up from her seat so that she couldn't see her satisfied smile. Sherai's resistance was already crumbling. "I believe I would like to see the temple. It looked so beautiful from afar with it's gleaming white. Sarah, fetch me my veils."

Sherai quickly braided her hair and bound it up. It was unseemly for a woman to be seen with her hair unbound. It was unlawful for either a Jew or a Samaritan woman's hair to be seen at all. Both women, suitably veiled, ventured forth on the streets of Jerusalem accompanied by their maids, and Levi.

Jethen, John and Jude walked over to the pens where the animals were kept. Jethen was to select and buy his animal for sacrifice. On this occasion he wanted only the best, and kept John and Jude standing out in the hot sun while he examined each sheep.

When he had decided on a sheep, Jude smiled. "Did you know that when Jesus was baptised, John the Baptist said that he was the Lamb of God?"

"What did he mean?" asked Jethen.

"We aren't sure, but your choice of a sheep reminded me of it. As you mean to become a disciple of Jesus, that is an appropriate choice."

"I chose a sheep because of his story of the lost sheep. In a way, I am offering myself, I am that lost sheep."

At last he found a thick woolen sheep without spot or blemish that had perfect markings. It was this sheep he selected and paid for asking the man to keep the sheep separate for him until the following morning.

"What do I do with the remainder of the sheep here in the temple?" Jethen knew that on the Mount, all those who attended the sacrifice with him ate of the sheep, as did the priest, except for the part that was completely consumed in the flame.

"You may give all but a small portion, which you must eat, to the priests."

"I'm glad you will be here with me for my first time."

"We are happy to be of service to you," said Jude. "Shall we go see if old Abinah will part with the Jeremiah scroll you were interested in yesterday?"

"Yes, as long as we don't have to go past food stalls," groaned John, who was also fasting.

"It will do you good to sacrifice your appetites," rejoined Jude as they made their way out of the Golden Gate and down the long steps.

Levi, who knew the city well, led the women deftly through the narrow streets of the upper regions of the lower city where they were lodged. He brought them past Herod's lavish theater, and the Hasmonean Palace, from there they turned south toward the temple mount. They walked past the Hippodrome, and made their way to the first of the Huldah Gates. The stairs led up into a wide court busy with vendors and white robed members of the Kohanim or Jewish Priests roaming about on errands from the Sanhedrin, or conducting large groups of tourists.

Levi said in his best tour guide voice, "The structure behind you is supported by its pillars."

"How high are they?" asked Mazar. Sherai was glad her friend asked, she'd been bursting to ask about every building they passed. Never in her life had she seen such opulence. Even Herod's Palace in Jericho wasn't as magnificent and ornate as this.

"They are twenty-five cubits," he replied. "They're made of one piece of marble. It's called the Royal Stoa." The women walked over and ran their hands over the smooth marble.

"It's so smooth," Sarah said in awe, "and so high. What a beautiful place to escape from the sun."

The sun was at its height, and many had elected to walk in the shade of the cloisters.

"The Sanhedrin, that's their court of law, meets in the apse at the eastern end. This," he spread his hands wide, "is the Court of the Gentiles. As you can see, over there," he indicated the other end of the court, "a great deal of trading is transacted. It is there we will exchange some of our currency for Jewish money."

He led them over to the tables, and produced a rather bulging coin bag he wore about his neck under his chiton, or tunic, as the Romans called it. The money changer pulled out his weights, and studied the coins Levi dumped into his hand.

After the money was changed he led them to the enclosure for the actual temple. Along the side there were gates through which they could see many men standing in groups.

On the west side there were steps leading up the inner courts. "Only the Jews may enter these gates," he said. They could glimpse through the gate the Women's Court.

"Further inside is the place for the ritual sacrifices."

Levi showed them one of the signs on the wall that threatened death to anyone who entered those gates who wasn't Jewish.

Everywhere they went there were throngs of people. Many were tourists, just like themselves, anxious to see all the sights. Sherai wished with all her heart that she was alone so that she could explore inside the beautiful gate. There was music, dance and song coming from the inner court.

On around the inner wall to the northeast, they could see the towers of the fortress of Antonia. Roman soldiers patrolled the upper walls and towers reminding anyone who noticed them that Palestine was now under Roman occupation.

"It certainly doesn't excite me to religious fervor out here," Miriam remarked.

"No, it's too busy and noisy. I imagine inside in the innermost part of the temple it is much more quiet and reflective."

"Judging from the sounds of music and dancing, I doubt that," drawled Levi.

"That is only in the Women's Court," Sherai told him. "The Priest's Court we glimpsed through the gate on the south side was much more decorous."

"True," acknowledged Miriam. "It almost makes me want to convert myself, just to see it. Sherai, if you would like we will wait out here while you go inside. Then you can tell us what it is like."

"No, I thank you. I brought no papers with me to prove that I am a converted Judahite, and I'd rather not be hauled before the court and have to be tried."

"I see what you mean. Let's go to the market. Levi, you know where that is, don't you?"

"I do, Mistress, I think you would prefer to go to the market in the upper city. It's a long walk," he warned. "It's up near King Herod's Palace."

"I don't care. I want to see something a little more down to earth."

The young girls were excited to go to the market in a large city like this, and Sarah said as much, "Oh, Mistress Miriam, I do hope they have jugglers."

"I hope they have arm bands," put in Mazar. Her own arms were presently was adorned with four each, metal bands of differing design.

It was said that the women of Palestine wore their wealth on their arms and in their ears. Sherai thought she wouldn't mind seeing some arm bands. She'd heard they even had silks from the east.

Jethen parted with his friends who promised to return that night so as to be ready to return with him to the temple early the next morning. John and Jude had acquaintance in the city, and wanted to visit them. Jethen was glad to be alone for a while. He returned to his room, and found that his mother was out with Sherai. In a way he was glad.

He had not stopped for anything but prayer in all the time he had been in Jerusalem. Until late at night he had met with merchants to sell some of his goods. Then there had been shopping for a Torah, and clothing. He smiled to think of John's wide eyes when he had purchased more than three robes. He also bought some thick sandals in which to walk, and more than one drape which had tassels sewn on the four corners. He supposed that John thought he bought too much, but he didn't say so.

He took one of the cloths from its wrapping and smoothed it reverently with his hand. Slipping to his knees beside his bed he prayed for his mind to be clear in the morning, and for his heart to be right before God. As he prayed he felt a sweet peace settle over him. He knew that when he stepped into the waters of baptism he would be a new person. He would be born again, as Jesus said.

He stood up, and put the shawl away, and washed his face preparatory to taking a short nap. It was not to be. One of his servants, Tab, entered the doorway. "Master, one of the camels has gone lame. She is bellowing, and the owner of the caravansary says we must do something."

Jethen sighed. He knew it must be Sheba. She was used to him giving her his personal attention, and he hadn't been to see her for days. Her hoofs were sensitive, and she would only allow him to check them. He would have to go.

He wrapped a turban about his head, and wrote a note in Aramaic for Jude. He didn't know how long it would take him to return to the inn. He had hoped to have dinner with his mother and Sherai, but knew he wouldn't make it. "I'm ready, Tab. Let's go."

The market was overwhelming. None of them, save Levi, had ever seen such a large display of goods, not even Miriam and Sarah who were used to the markets in Jericho. The young girl's eyes glittered at each new sight.

Each stall or shop was ornate and designed to lure the customer to their wares. They rubbed shoulders with the elite of Jerusalem whose chitons and himations were embroidered with fancy designs sewn in gold or silver, and beaded with the finest of beads or jewels. Their veils covering their faces were decorated with beads and jewels as well.

A few of the women had their hair uncovered except for a veil over the back of their hair which was ornately bound with scarves or braided with jewels–obviously Greek, or Roman women. Women of Palestine kept their hair completely covered except in their homes. Most of them, even in their homes, kept their hair tied back with a small scarf that covered their hair and kept it from the dust.

Oh, the sights to behold! There was blown glass from Hebron, vases and bowls in bright colors. There was brass ware, candlesticks, bowls, and goblets, plates and platters. There were wall hangings, rugs, cushions and pillows some plain, but most of them decorated in intricate detail with scenes and stories that Sherai had never before seen. The girls ooh-ed and aah-ed over the beads and medallions that hung from wooden branches, or glistened against black cushions.

There were bangles and bracelets, earrings and necklaces to delight every eye. Mazar found her arm band, and Sherai bought delicate earrings for Bethba, Opar, and Rima. She bought beads to give to Rebbah and Jethen's other servants. She bought silks to work into her own designs for tablecloths.

She and Miriam delighted over the pillows, tablecloths, napkins and linens found in abundance.

Miriam, sure that Jethen had not suitably purchased for his house, bought lavishly.

Sherai became enchanted with a small olive wood box she had to have. But when she saw the camel leather bags and belts, purses and himations, she had to exert great discipline not to fill her arms with the delightful display.

At last they came to the food market. Everywhere delectable smells assailed them. They came to the baker who displayed the small seed cakes, and nut honey confections that filled the air with mouth-watering goodness.

"I didn't bring enough money," mourned Miriam, whose arms and Sarah's were laden with her purchases.

"Nor I," echoed Mazar who had spent every mite.

Sarah just smiled. She hadn't spent anything except for a small bag of exotic spice that she intended to sew into small packets and place in her clothes to scent them.

"Don't worry," Sherai, who had nearly spent all on her silk, consoled her, "I have enough to buy us each one of those cakes, and one of the honey confections."

"I'll buy us all drinks," offered Sarah.

"Sarah, you angel," was all Miriam had time to say before Levi interrupted.

"Master Jethen gave me this purse just to spend on you," he informed them. "I shall buy all the cakes and drink you can hold. I'm feeling rather hungry myself. They all selected several of the delectable treats and took them to a table provided on which to eat them. While they were thus happily engaged Levi told them they were to each select things to take back to the rooms to supplement their dinner.

Miriam did not hesitate, once the food had refreshed her, to fill Levi's arms with dates, nuts, pomegranates, figs, olives, more of the nutty sweets, cheese, and plenty of bread and honey.

"Miriam," Sherai accused, "you have a sweet tooth."

"I do," the woman admitted, "and I'm old enough to indulge it. I'm not buying all this for just me," she assured them. "We'll all enjoy them later when we're hungry again."

With their arms full of purchases, they all made their way back to their rooms. Levi excused himself saying that he would go to the caravansary and return in the morning.

"Not too early, Levi," Miriam instructed him. "I'll need some rest after today. We would like to go and take a closer look at the theater tomorrow, wouldn't we girls?" Levi bowed and left them.

Sherai could see that Miriam was tired, and she excused herself and left with Mazar and all their packages.

Miriam waited until Sherai had gone to her room, and said to Sarah. "Go and see if Jethen is in his room. I want to speak with him."

The young maid ran off and came back in almost an instant. "No one is there, Mistress."

"Humph, he can't avoid me forever. Where has he been? Sarah, go to the cook and get something to eat. After you've eaten, go to his room and sit outside the door until he returns."

"Yes, Mistress." Sarah ran off to do her bidding.

SACRIFICE AND OBEDIENCE

When John and Jude returned to the room, rather late, they found the faithful little Sarah sitting outside the door of the room.
"Sarah," asked John, "what brings you here so late at night?"
"Is someone ill?" probed Jude.
"Is my Mistress' son not with you?" she asked sleepily
"No, we have been to see other friends in the city. Your Master had other chores to do."
"Then you don't know when he'll be back?"
"I am sorry, no," admitted Jude. "Why don't you go to bed? He might not return until quite late."
"No, I am to wait for him," she insisted.
Leaving her at the door, the two men entered the room, and were soon sleeping. Sarah slumped down against the wall, and slid to the floor. Listening to their gentle rhythmic breathing had her yawning, and nodding as she waited.
Jethen returned long after she was soundly asleep, lying on the floor in front of his door on a pillow provided by John.

"This is Mother's doing," he knew as soon as he saw the young girl. "I suppose she wants to talk with me. I doubt she is even awake. I'll just carry this little one to her room, and see."

Jethen scooped up Sarah and carried her to his mother's room.

There was a small lamp burning, and his mother's eyes were closed when he entered the room and laid Sarah on her cot. He covered her with a blanket, and turned to leave the room.

His mother's eyes opened, and she said softly, "Where have you been all these days, my son?"

He leaned over his mother and kissed her cheek. "It is very late," he evaded. If he told her all he would get no sleep. "I must be up before dawn. You will know all on the morrow. Now go to sleep, and do not worry. I am well, and happy."

"Tomorrow I will know all?"

"All," he patted her grey hair, and smoothed it away from her face.

"Then get some sleep, and we will talk tomorrow."

"God be with you, Mother."

"And with you, my son."

Jethen blew out the lamp, and left the room. He hoped she would be happy with his decision, as happy as he was.

It seemed he had just closed his eyes when John shook him awake. Rapidly he pulled the tunic over his head, and attached the himation around him in the desert chill of the morning. It was the last time he would wear these garments that labeled him a Gentile to the Jews.

Reverently he opened the box and removed his recently purchased clothes. The day before, he had tied them in a bundle. He looked about the room. He was leaving it as Jethen son of Amos, the Samaritan, but he would be returning as a disciple of Jesus.

"Are you ready?" asked John.

"I'm ready."

"So are we," Jude told him. "We have a walk, but we should have plenty of time." They should, Jethen thought as he looked out the window, it was completely dark. Only the stars lit the night.

It was ghostly walking in the empty streets. No one was about, not even the persistent beggars who thronged the streets during the day. Jethen stretched his legs. He was in a hurry. It seemed he had waited forever for this moment. He should have listened to Sherai all those months ago. He could have had this joy all the sooner. There was work, good work, for him to do in Sychar. He felt excited about his future for the first time in years. The only way he could be happier was with Sherai. What would she say when she found out about his conversion? Firmly he put all thoughts of Sherai from his mind. It was the God of Israel he should be thinking about at this moment. This was a big commitment, and he was ready for it.

The temple mount rose out of the darkness of the night. A few discretely placed torches eerily lit the exterior so that the men could make their way up the steps and into the courtyard. From there they made their way toward the apse. They were met by the scribe who led them inside through a series of halls, and into an archway that led to stairs downward.

They traveled down into a series of tunnels and took a tunnel due west. They walked under the temple mount until they must have traveled the entire distance of the courtyard of the Gentiles. Jethen knew they must be very near the western wall. They had passed several arches leading to other tunnels, but their course had been straight. Another arch at the extreme end led them to another series of downward steps into a lower tunnel to the south.

Through the arch they entered a room twenty meters high and 10 by 10 meters wide. At the bottom of the room was the mikveh. The walls were well lit by torches placed at intervals. It was here that the priests did a ritual cleansing before entering the temple grounds.

At the foot of the stairs within the room that led to the mikveh was the priest clothed only in his loincloth. Jethen looked at the smooth plastered walls painted in the color of eggshells. There was no decoration save in the floor, covered by Roman mosaic tiles. On the wall above the font was a conduit for fresh water that still dripped a few drops into the still pool below.

The priest spoke. "Disrobe the Gentile, and let him come forth."

Jethen slipped off first the himation, then his short tunic. Last of all he removed his sandals. They were the only item he would be putting back on. John held his clothing, and Jude escorted him to the font. Then Jude took his position at opposite end from John on the side of the pool of water.

The priest watched the timed candle that burned in the sconce on a level with the edge of the pool. John had told him that the ceremony would not begin until just before sunrise, signaling a new day. Jethen had wondered how they would know the time down here. The candle burned to a marker, and sizzled a bit when it reached a thin layer of red ribbon.

Without words, the priest gestured that Jethen should take his place in the water. Jethen stepped down the steps. He forgot he was going to count their number, but he knew it was at least ten. The last step into the pool of water was deep, and it covered his waist as he walked toward the priest already standing nearly chest high in the water.

There was a shimmering air of fervor in the room as the priest raised his hand in the air and spoke. "Blessed are you Lord our God, King of the Heavens and the Earth."

To Jethen he said, "The water will cleanse you from your past. You are to immerse yourself in the water until every part of you shall be covered. The two witnesses will verify this."

It was then that Jethen noticed that the priest's hair was still dripping water. He had already cleansed himself for his day at the temple.

Saying a prayer in his heart that he would always serve God in whatever he was called upon to do, promising to abide by the commandments, and live a worthy life, Jethen sank into the water. He propelled himself downward until he felt the water close over his head. Holding his breath he remained under the water for several seconds until he was certain his hair had also submerged. When he rose from the water he felt lightness permeate his being. It was as though he could have floated on up to the high ceiling. With joy he looked for John to share his joy, and saw John's serious nod toward the priest, then to Jude, following the priest's eyes. Jude also nodded. They signaled they had witnessed his complete immersion.

Jethen had never in his life felt so clean, so new. It was as though the priest read his thoughts. "From this point forward, you are renewed. Rising from this water marks the beginning of your elevated religious state. You are as a babe born of his mother." The priest then placed his hand on Jethen's head and intoned, I declare you are Jethen son of Amos and are now one with the tribe of Judah."

Removing his hand he looked Jethen in the eye and solemnly told him. "You are now a Jew in every respect. Clothe yourself in your new robes, and come with your witnesses to present your sacrifice."

The priest then climbed out of the water, and donned his own robe that had hung from a hook near the steps. He crossed the room and swiftly went up the stairs leaving them alone in the room.

"Is it appropriate to say Hallelujah?" whispered Jethen.

"It is most appropriate," smiled Jude.

"Hallelujah to the Most High God," said Jethen aloud.

"Hallelujah," said John.

"Hallelujah," echoed Jude.

Jethen's exuberance needed an outlet. His overwhelming joy needed words, but he had none that fit the occasion. Then he recalled some words of Matthias. He did not know he was paraphrasing a psalm of King David. "Let all those who put their trust in You rejoice, let them ever shout for joy; for You defend them, let them also who love Your name be joyful in Your service."

"Praise be to God," said Jude quietly.

"All praise, honor and glory be to God," added John, and held out the robe ready to slip over Jethen's head.

When they reached the Gentile's court once again, the sun had gloriously burst forth. The morning was radiant, and the walls of the temple court gleamed white in the dazzle of the sun. Never had the sky seemed so blue, or the air smelled so clean as it did to Jethen that morning. He greeted everyone he passed, and smiled on them all. Those who had come early to the temple to ask for alms each had a pence pressed into their hand.

He, John, and Jude made their way to the animal pens. There the man brought forth the sheep that Jethen had purchased the day before. Jethen hugged the sheep to him before he slipped a lead over its head. "Thank you for being sacrificed for me," he told it softly.

The sheep bleated as though it answered him. Jethen felt moved that an animal would be sacrificed for his sins so that he might live. He had always felt that way, even when his father sacrificed a new lamb during the Passover. Walking over to the steps leading into the inner courts Jethen's heart pounded. Yesterday he could only climb the steps and read the dire warning on the bricks. Today he had a right to enter inside the Gate Beautiful.

Knowing he wished to contribute to the treasury, John told him, "I'll take you to the treasury after the sacrifice."

They walked straight past the Court of the Women, the Court of Israel, and into the Court of the Priests, straight to the altar where a priest stood ready to accept the sacrifice. The High Priest, knowing that Jethen was a convert asked, "Who offers this sheep to the Lord God?"

After John dug an elbow in his ribs Jethen answered, "I, Jethen son of Amos, offer it."

"Do you bring this sheep willingly as a sign that you do take upon yourself the laws of the Torah?"

"I do take upon myself these laws."

"Is this animal without spot or blemish?"

"It is."

"Then bring it forth. This is a sacrifice of Thanksgiving," informed the High Priest, "therefore you will take some of the meat, and consume it today in thanksgiving that you have been received into the tribe of Judah."

Jethen brought the sheep to the altar, and with practiced ease the priest heaved it upon the altar and expertly sacrificed it in one deft stroke, offering up a prayer for it. Then other priests came forward, and the animal was butchered as was the custom. The fat went into the fire, and a portion of the meat was brought to Jethen in a container. At once his thoughts, for the first time that day, went to Sherai. She, too, had gone through this ritual. She had stood at the Women's court, but she was given the meat to consume.

Jethen pushed thoughts of Sherai from his mind, and concentrated on worshiping God. This was the way, the Law of Moses. He would obey this law. In the spring it would be a lamb. Unbidden to his mind came some words of John as they walked to Jericho. He had said that the Baptizer called Jesus the Lamb of God. The Lamb of God. No, surely not! Jethen opened his eyes and looked at John. He saw John looking directly across the court. Following the direction of his eyes, he saw Jesus standing there watching the sacrifice. His eyes met those of Jesus. His own were filled with tears.

Jesus turned and disappeared through the crowd. Jethen made a move as though to follow him, but John caught his arm. The priest who interviewed him the day before had come up to them. He touched his shoulder. He was holding in his hand a parchment. It was his Certificate of Conversion. "Take care not to lose this," he told him. "It will not be easy to get another to take its place. Go with God."

"God's blessings attend you," answered Jethen.

Clutching the certificate in one hand, and the portion of meat in the other, Jethen allowed John to lead him from the temple court to the Treasury.

Jethen was too overwhelmed to speak on their journey back to the inn. All joy he had experienced in that small room had faded. What could it mean, the Lamb of God? Had he known the rest of the quote he would have been weeping. John, however, did not seem in the least upset or unsettled by the sacrifice. Perhaps it was because he had not made it.

They went directly to the kitchen where the cook agreed to prepare the meat for eating. She sprinkled some herbs on it to mitigate the freshness of the kill, and roasted it over the coals already warm from breakfast. Jethen, John and Jude sat in the common room waiting. They had not yet broken their fast, and would partake of some of the meat with Jethen as further witness.

When the meat was set before them, Jethen could only look at his brethren eating their portions with relish. At a sound he looked up, and Jesus came into the room. He took a chair at their table, and reached for a small portion of the meat. "Eat," he said to Jethen, "It is a part of your willingness to take upon you this new life."

Jethen picked up a piece of the meat, and brought it to his lips. He was sure he would choke on the meat, but it was tender and sweet to his taste. It was as though it was dipped in the finest honeycomb. The herbs tingled in his mouth exciting his palate, and before he knew it, the entire portion was gone. Replete and satisfied, Jethen leaned forward to ask Jesus questions.

Jesus forestalled him with a negative shake of his head and raised hand, "I must go and do the will of the Father," he told him. "You have another task set before you. You must study the prophets to learn of me. When you have learned, you must teach others. Remember, come to Jerusalem for the Passover. Come well before to secure a place, I will be teaching in the temple."

"We'll be going as well, Jethen. Our time with you is over," John sounded regretful to be leaving his new convert.

"Only for a short season," Jesus told John, and laid a hand on his shoulder in comfort.

"I will take my leave of you, Jethen, disciple of Jesus," smiled Jude. When he smiled, he looked most like Jesus.

"I thank you for all you have done," began Jethen "I wish . . ."

"Learn of me," said Jesus. "Then I will be with you always."

Tears again came to Jethen's eyes. Jesus knew even the thoughts of his heart. "I will," he promised.

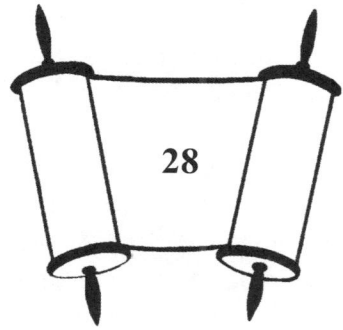

MATCHMAKER

Jethen came in from his fields in time to wash the dust and chaff from his face and arms, and brush his clothing. He had been harvesting in the fields with Ziriz. The harvest had been plentiful this year. There would be enough grains for his household for the winter months, and enough to share with others.

Since his return to Sychar, Jethen had seen to it that there was not one family in that city that suffered from want. Work in his fields had been offered to those able to work. Gleanings from his harvest had accompanied each of his workers home. Those who couldn't work were also given from his stores.

He appointed Levi to find those in need, and tell him. Often together they would go to a poorer home to repair the structure, and bring what was needed to care for them, whether it be food, or other practical items. Levi kept records of people in need so that in the years to come they would all be remembered.

People from the city came to his home with their troubles, knowing that Jethen the Jew, as he was referred to, would see to their needs. Children wore shoes. Cloths from his storehouse went to make them warm clothes for the winter. The sick were sent the finest of Miriam's soups and herbs to see them well again.

That wasn't all, when he realized there was no place for the followers of Jesus to worship, he began building a small synagogue on his land where they could gather. From his window he could see the work in progress. He hoped it would be completed before the rains. He wanted a place to read from the Torah, and discuss what particular passages might mean.

He was so busy with all this, he had to remember to find time to study as Jesus had commanded him. He chose the afternoon, in the heat of the day. Usually, it was then Sherai visited Jethen and together they poured over her notes of Jesus works and words. He never tired of reading the wonders that Jesus performed. His words settled in his heart like live coals warming him. Many of the longer passages he memorized, and he repeated them to himself as he worked alongside his workers in the fields, or orchards, or in his olive press.

Still, at the back of his mind was the echo of John's words, "The Lamb of God." When he and Sherai poured over the scrolls of the prophets and the Torah he looked for references. Between them they agreed to read the entire works from start to finish. They were seeking, in particular, for references to the Messiah, as Jesus had bidden Jethen to do.

When he came from his room clean and brushed, Sherai was already in the large room they used for study, talking to his mother.

Miriam was saying, "Tonight Heber ben Gera and his family will dine with us. We'd like you to come, Sherai. I've already asked Omini and Opar. Heber's young daughter, Hodesh, is a lovely young woman, and just the right age."

"Just the right age for what, Mother? You aren't matchmaking again?" Jethen, since his return, had dined with every family in Sychar with an eligible marriageable daughter, or so he thought.

"Yes, I am. I am determined," she paused and took Sherai's hand, "we are determined to see you married. After all, you do want to follow all God's commandments, don't you? Isn't marriage an important commandment? Multiplying and replenishing and so on . . ."

"Sherai, are you a part of this?" Somehow, that hurt more than annoyed.

"I . . . er . . . Jethen, she is right, you know. You should be married." She took a deep breath, "I'm sure Hodesh is a lovely young woman." Sherai didn't know where to look. Promising Miriam she would help her was one thing, but facing Jethen with it was another.

"I believe that I have already discussed this subject with you both," he gave a stern glance to his mother, and an equally probing look at Sherai. "I should think you would both know that I have much more important work to do right now than worry about a wedding. Sherai, would you care to discuss my future, or study?"

Sherai scooted to the table where the scrolls lay ready, one already open from their reading yesterday.

"Let's study," she decided, and sat down and began pouring over what she had read the day before. "Here in Numbers it says, '*There shall come a star out of Jacob, and a scepter shall rise out of Israel.*'"

"That is one prophecy that the Samaritans also accept. I know we said we'd read all, but it seems like covering old ground to read them."

"We did say we'd write them all down, remember," Sherai dutifully wrote it down on a parchment selected for the task. "This is the last book the Samaritans accept. I know you've been reading ahead, what did you find?"

Jethen seated himself opposite her and opened a scroll that was already easily unwrapped from much reading. At night he poured over the Psalms of David. They seemed to bring happiness and contentment to his sore heart.

"A couple of things. I would study the words of the prophets all the day long, and happily for the rest of my life," sighed Jethen.

"You mean that you would read the Psalms of King David, don't you?" teased Sherai.

"There are words here that may speak of the Messiah," he defended himself. "What do you think this means? *'The assembly of the wicked has enclosed me, they have pierced my hands and my feet. I may tell all my bones they look upon me and stare at me. They part my garments among them and cast lots upon my vesture.'* Who is he talking about?"

"Perhaps he speaks of what his enemies would like to do to him, King David, I mean."

"There is another passage that refers directly to the kingdom. Here is the portion I read last night, *'All the ends of the world shall remember and turn unto the Lord; and all the kindred of the nations shall worship before you. For the kingdom is the Lord's, and he is the governor among the nations.'*"

"That does sound like he is speaking of what Jesus teaches. He talks of the kingdom. Is there any other passage that sounds like he is speaking of the Messiah?"

"Well, I did read another, just let me find it." Jethen rolled, then unrolled the scroll further. He read passages that were already becoming dear and familiar to his heart. "Ah, here it is, listen to this, *'Then said I. Lo, I come; in the volume of the book it is written of me. I delight to do thy will, Oh my God, your law is within my heart. I have preached righteousness in the great congregation, I have not refrained my lips, O Lord, you know this.'*"

"I like that, *'your law is within my heart.'*" that's the way I feel.

"You feel that way, too? About the law, I mean? I have come to feel that way more and more as I talked with John, and have read for myself."

"Jesus said something to me similar to this at the well when he talked about the living water. I think he was talking about his words and his law."

"I wish I could have been there." His voice sounded so wistful Sherai reached across the table and patted his hand in sympathy.

Miriam, who was still sitting across the room saw the pat, and smiled. Things were certainly moving along well. Now if Hodesh reacted to Jethen's wealth as she thought she might, having met the young girl on one of her visits to old friends, Sherai just might be given a jolt. Hodesh had a lithe young body, and beautiful eyes that she knew how to use behind those thin veils her father made her wear. She was also shrewd enough to recognize a wealthy handsome young man when she met one.

What was it Sherai was saying now?

"I read just the other day that to everything under heaven there is a time and purpose. I think that your time is now, Jethen."

"Where is that passage? I'd like to read it for myself."

"I'll find it for you, but first tell me, did you find any more in Psalms that sound like Jesus?"

"Yes, one more so far, let me find it. Ah, here, *'My heart is inditing a good matter: I speak of the things which I have made touching the king: my tongue is the pen of a ready writer. You are fairer than the children of men: grace is poured into your lips: therefore God has blessed you forever.'*"

"That is truly beautiful, and it does sound like Jesus. Now I'll find that passage I spoke about, it was past where I'm reading so I'll have to wind back to the place . . ."

As Sherai wound the scroll, Jethen watched her face. Didn't she understand that she was the only woman in this world for him? If it was true that there was a time for everything, and that now was his time, surely soon she would come to see him as her companion, her mate, her protector.

"Here it is, I've found it. I'll just scoot it over to you, so you can read it. It's quite long." Sherai looked up and saw Jethen studying her with gentle eyes. She felt a blush covering her face, but she couldn't seem to look away. Jethen was such a dear gentle man, he was everything... Tearing her eyes away she tugged to move the heavy scroll to his side of the table.

He said, "Don't bother moving it. I'll bring my chair over and sit beside you. We can read it together." Suiting words to action, Jethen brought his chair and put it close to her's. Head to head they bent over the passage and read the beautiful words together, *'To every thing there is a season and a time to every purpose under heaven. A time to be born and a time to die . . .'*

To honor Jethen, and to hold her own with Miriam's guests, Sherai took special care to put on her best robes and veils for the dinner. Sherai was staying with Omini and Opar, so together they walked the few short miles to Jethen's home. Opar also felt the festivity of the occasion and dressed her best. Every bracelet and necklace she owned adorned her person. She even wore tiny jewels suspended from the veil covering her forehead. Her brown eyes sparkled with excitement.

Sherai's eyes were sparkling, too, at least they were until they arrived, and discovered that the other guests were there before them. Miriam waited at the door to welcome them. "Omini," she greeted them, "Opar, so good of you to come. Enter and be welcome. Sherai, you look lovely this evening. Come in, there is someone I long for you to meet. Perhaps you already know him, Heber, come and meet my lovely guest."

A man nearly as tall as Jethen, and every bit as handsome came striding across the room. He was no longer young, but he still had a trim body and a healthy aspect. He walked uprightly and with ease. "Heber ben Gera, this is Sherai daughter of Ashah.

Sherai, Heber is widowed these three years now, he tells me. Sherai is also widowed, Heber. You have a lot in common."

"I am most pleased to meet you, Sherai. Miriam has told me so much about you." Sherai's eyes flashed suspiciously to Miriam. It appeared she *was* matchmaking, but exactly who was she trying to match?

A nudge from Miriam reminded her of her duty. "I am the one more pleased," said Sherai. "Did you perhaps know my father, Ashah?"

"I knew of him. I moved from Sychar, and have only recently returned. Much has changed in my absence." Ah, that would explain why Sherai had not known him. She thought she was acquainted with everyone in Sychar. "Come, I would like you to meet my son, Aichri, and my daughter, Hodesh."

Sherai heard Jethen laugh, and looked across the room. He was standing at an open fire with a young man with brown curly hair, and a girl wrapped in diaphanous veils who reached only as high as his chest. Her dainty figure could be seen even through the robes she wore with such grace and aplomb. Immediately Sherai felt like a behemoth beside her. The top of her own head came to Jethen's nose. Truth to tell she was an even height with Heber, and perhaps a bit taller.

Hodesh laughed in response to Jethen's laugh, and her laughter tinkled like little silver bells. She looked up at her father and Sherai as they came over. If her eyes were anything to go by, she rather resented their intrusion. Sherai was impressed with her wide eyes that tilted at the corners. They were surrounded by thick lush lashes that owed nothing to artifice.

"Sherai, this is my daughter Hodesh, and my son Aichri."

Aichri smiled and bowed. "There is no need to invoke God's blessings upon you," he flattered, "it is easy to see he has already lavishly supplied them."

Jethen frowned at the silly speech, but Sherai laughed. "I see that we shall become good friends," she teased.

"That will be all from you silver tongue. Soon you will be stealing your father's thunder," Heber rebuked him, but not seriously.

"Jethen tells me you are good friends," Hodesh acknowledged her. Her voice was as smooth as cream. Before Sherai could form some suitable reply, she had already turned away from her father and Sherai, and placed her hand daringly on Jethen's arm. "You said you would show me your scrolls," she invited. Her veil over her eyes, like Opar's, shimmered with bangles that caught the light from the fire. Her beguiling eyes flashed with a shine like the spangles that decorated her headpiece. There might have been no one else in the room.

Jethen slid from beneath her hand and said, "Aichri, you will be interested in seeing my jeweled daggers from Damascus. Come with us."

"I hope to know you better," Aichri said sincerely before he left with them.

"And I you," Sherai called after him. There was no need to say anything to Hodesh, she was talking to Jethen in a low seductive voice he had to bend over to hear her.

Sherai looked up at Heber when he apologized, "I'm afraid that growing up without a mother these past few years has made her a little spoiled."

"Perhaps she feels that any other woman is a threat as she has so recently come to her own womanhood. That will pass as she comes to more confidence."

"I fear she has too much confidence," her father laughed, "but it is kind of you to be so charitable."

Sherai felt she didn't deserve the praise. Inside she was thinking that Hodesh was a slightly younger version of Bethba.

At that moment she heard another laugh from the door, and saw Maachi and Bethba enter to Miriam's greeting. It would be interesting to see how Hodesh and Bethba reacted to one another. Meanwhile, she worried for Opar, who would be swallowed up between the two of them.

"Come with me, Heber," she said. "I want you to meet my delightful host and hostess, or do you know Omini from before?"

"I do know them. They came to make me welcome when first I arrived in Sychar. I would much rather spend the time getting to know you better."

"Now I know from whence Aichri gets his silver tongue."

Sherai was certain that during the course of the evening, Hodesh had appraised every item in Jethen's home. She had commented on every treasure on display. Jethen, as proud as a boy over his decor preened under her flattery, and eagerly explained each piece. Hodesh laughed, cooed, and flirted with every male in the room, and left the women strictly alone. Most of her attention, however, was focused on Jethen. She made it very clear that she considered him the most interesting man she had ever met. She sat so close to Jethen Sherai wondered if she would end up in his lap before the evening was over.

As for Jethen, he relaxed as the evening wore on, and seemed to enjoy Hodesh's flattery, and open flirtation. Sherai heard him laugh as he used to laugh with her. Sherai saw a side of Jethen she had never before seen, the gracious host. Jethen saw to it that both Opar and Bethba felt comfortable, and welcome in his home. He even made some effort to get to know Maachi, and Heber.

Heber, on the other hand, devoted himself to Sherai. He told about his wife, whom he must have greatly loved. He talked of his devotion to his family, and his vast interests in religion, music, and people. In fact, he was everything that she could have wanted in a companion for herself. At least he fit every criterion she had made in Jerusalem. He even admired Jesus. There was only one problem with him, at last she admitted it to herself–when Jethen laughed again at some remark Hodesh made and she found herself grinding her teeth–he just wasn't Jethen.

Heber was a good man, and an attentive dinner partner. He made certain that every delicacy was available for her approval. She watched as he also devoted himself to Omini and Opar long enough to elicit an invitation to visit their home later that week. He let it be known that he was not averse to seeing Sherai again so soon.

Miriam sat on her cushions simply beaming. Every time she caught Sherai's eye, she winked. Sherai could have kicked her, but that wouldn't have been loving her as she loved herself. Miriam went out of her way to extend every courtesy to Hodesh, but the young woman mostly ignored the older woman. She would have liked to kick Hodesh, too, or perhaps scratch her eyes. Bethba was an absolute angel in comparison.

The evening eventually wound to an end. Once again Miriam and Jethen stood at their gate to bid their guests God Speed. Miriam pulled Sherai aside long enough to whisper, "How do you like Heber? I believe he is taken with you."

"He certainly is a good and kindly man," Sherai admitted.

"And a widower," put in Miriam.

Jethen, who stood beside her heard their remarks. He was stunned. So, his mother wasn't merely matchmaking for him. She had a husband picked for Sherai!

THE FRUIT OF THE VINE

'I am the true vine and my Father is the husbandman. I am the vine, you are the branches. If you abide in me, and I in you, you will bring forth much fruit, but without me, you can do nothing. If you abide in me and my words abide in you, you can ask what you will, and it shall be done. My Father is glorified if you bear much fruit.'

"How do you know if you are bearing this fruit he speaks about?" Jethen asked Sherai.

"Jethen, you of all his disciples show evidence of bearing fruit. Look what you have done. There is a synagogue where there was none. All the poor and needy have food and clothing. You spend hours pouring over the scriptures, studying, and memorizing. How can you ask a thing like that?"

"I suppose that I feel there is so much more to do."

Miriam spoke up from her usual corner, "When are you going to find the time to do more, my son?" In the months she strived, she was no nearer seeing her son married. Heber had been most attentive. Since he learned that Sherai spent nearly every afternoon except the Sabbath here, he had been a frequent visitor, and Hodesh often accompanied him.

"I see what you mean," Jethen laughed. "I'd better get on with my studies, then. Did he say more about this vine and branches?"

"No, then he began talking about love. *'As the Father loved me, so I love you, continue in my love. If you love me, keep my commandments. If you keep my commandments you abide in my love. I keep the Father's commandments, and I abide in his love.*

'These things I have told you that my joy might remain inside you and that your joy might be full. This is my commandment that you love one another as I have loved you. Greater love has no man than this, than that a man lay down his life for his friends. You are my frien . . .'

"What? What did you just read? A man lay down his life for his friends? Did Jesus say that?" Jethen had a memory of Jesus' eyes as he stood across the court watching the sacrifice. He felt as though a giant hand was squeezing his heart.

"He said, 'Greater love has no man than this, that a man lay down his life for his friends,' yes."

"Jesus doesn't ask much, does he? That sounds like he wants you to die for your friends." Miriam listened avidly to every word they studied.

"I don't think he means it literally, I think he means we should be willing to do it, and that we should love our friends like that," Sherai defended.

Jethen wondered. The words 'willing to lay down his life,' kept playing over and over in his mind. "I don't think I can absorb more today. Since it isn't raining for once, let's take a walk in the vineyard. I'll feel closer to his words looking at the vines and branches. Coming mother?"

"You two go ahead. I'm expecting Heber this afternoon. I'll tell him you are out."

"Heber is coming again?" Jethen felt the familiar stirring of jealousy.

"I rather imagine that he is bringing Hodesh again," Sherai replied tartly. "Why don't you ask for the girl and cease these endless visits?"

"If I were to ask for her, I suspect that the visits might increase. I don't think she would be adverse to a few scripture studies with us. What do you think mother?" Jethen teased.

The dismay that covered Sherai's face made Miriam chuckle. "I think that young lady could use some study, but I doubt that much studying would get done in her presence. Does this mean you are considering her, Jethen?"

He heard Sherai draw in a breath and hold it as she waited for his reply. "I'm going for a walk," he changed the subject. "I think I'll take the clippers, I might see a barren branch. Are you coming, Sherai, or do you want to stay with Mother to entertain Heber?"

"I'm coming," she managed to choke out.

Despite the fact that the weather was settling into the winter month of Kislev, there were still a few of the deep purple grapes on the vine. These were past due to be picked, but they had been left on the vine to become overripe, and would make the sweetest wine, and dried fruit. Sherai plucked a bunch of them from the vine, and they were so ripe many fell from the stem into her hand. "These grapes are more than ready for the press," she commented. They had mostly walked in silence, and she felt she must say something to break it.

Jethen had stopped along the rows to snip here and there, even though it wasn't time to trim the vines yet. He mostly snipped off branches that had been missed from the year before. "I think Heber is going to ask for you, Sherai," Jethen said what was uppermost in his mind.

"I think he wants *you* to ask for his daughter," she replied.

Jethen was exasperated, "I can't believe you and mother want me to ask for that preposterous . . . that child."

All at once Sherai's heart felt lighter. "She isn't a child, Jethen, but at times she does seem very young. I think your mother is more in favor of the match than I."

"Does that mean you aren't scheming for me to marry her?" Jethen stopped walking, forcing Sherai to stop. They were between rows of grapes, trimmed low for easy gathering. The leaves were beginning to turn, and they were covered with wet drops.

"Oh, I'm getting wet, Jethen. Have a care where you step." When she met his eyes she saw that there would be no putting him off, he was determined to have it out with her. "I have no wish for you to marry Hodesh," she admitted.

"Then are you encouraging Heber so that he will ask for you?"

"Jethen," Sherai answered him honestly, "I have no desire for Heber to ask for me. He is a good man, but . . ."

Jethen gripped her arms tightly, and gave her a slight shake. "Isn't he everything you told me you wanted that day on the hill? There's no question that he can provide for you, that he is a worthy Jew."

"Are you trying to marry me off, Jethen?" Sherai whispered.

"Trying to . . ." he sputtered, then, as if he could bear it no longer, he pulled her into his arms. "There is a time to embrace, Sherai, remember those beautiful words? A time to love and you said that now was my time. You are mine. God has given you to me. If we are to ask and it is to be given us, you are already mine. *'Love one another,'* he said." He was so intent on persuading her, he didn't notice that her arms were holding him as tightly as he held her.

"You have asked God for me? Oh, Jethen," she breathed, "you still want me? After all I've said?"

Sherai's eyes were wet with tears.

"There is no word large or grand enough in any language to describe the immensity of my love for you. Will you accept me Sherai, so that together we can spread the word of God? Together we can continue to do good, and study the Torah, and the prophets? Why are you crying? Are you still going to tell me no, Sherai?" He went to push her away from him, but realized that she was holding him.

"Why would I say no, when God has given you to me?" she laughed through her tears. "Jethen, I have come to realize that I do care for you. I suspected when it broke my heart to say no to you that day on the hill. At that time I was certain that you should marry another. I even wanted to help you find someone. Since then I have missed you, and longed for you. I told your mother I would help her persuade you to marry another, but I can't bear it if you do." She clutched him even tighter, and this time he was fully aware of it.

"If I had known, I would have set outside your door howling until you said yes."

She laughed a sound of pure joy. "Perhaps it's just as well you didn't know. I'm so happy, my heart's desire."

Jethen's voice was choked with emotion, "I will go today to speak with Omini about the kiddushin. Do you suppose we might forgo the usual twelve months and be married at once?"

"Twelve months does seem long to wait. Perhaps we can be granted a special dispensation by a rabbi considering our circumstances. You must find one and ask him."

"I have already met with the rabbi here in Sychar. I wanted him to take advantage of our synagogue, and come teach us. He seemed pleased that I would seek him out. He told me he heard Jesus speak when he was here, and that he healed his daughter. I'll go see him today."

"You are going to have a very busy remainder of the day, first Omini, then the rabbi," Sherai teased. "I should go home at once."

Jethen's arms tightened to keep her with him when she made a play to go. "I never want you to be further from me than the reach of my arms," he declared unsteadily.

Sherai laughed again, another laugh of pure joy. "Then neither of us will ever get anything done. I somehow don't think that is part of Jesus' plan for us. Do you think he will be pleased we are to marry?"

"I think," Jethen considered, "he might have had that in mind when he sent us here together to Sychar and told us to study. His commandment is to love one another after all."

"That part will be easy," Sherai admitted. "Do you think Heber has come and gone? I'd like to return to your mother, and tell her."

"There will be no need for words, she will know by my face."

"I hope she won't mind that I'm not Hodesh. She was rather set on that young woman. Jethen, what if I can give you no children?" Sherai clutched his robe. "I have been barren since Talitha."

"It will be as God wills, but we are to ask, remember? I think when we ask God for children, he will grant them to us."

"You have great faith, Jethen. It's one reason I love you."

"You love me, Sherai?"

"Why did you think I called you my heart's desire?"

Jethen sighed, and released her from his arms. "I have waited so long for you, Sherai. I often wondered why my father didn't ask for you when we were children."

"You moved to Jericho. Perhaps he expected you to come for me like our father Jacob went to Laban."

"I don't know, he never said. When I did come for you, on my own, you were already Reuel's."

"Did you come for me Jethen?"

A look of pain accompanied his quietly voiced, "I did."

"I am sorry, I didn't know. I just thought you had come as my childhood friend. It wouldn't have changed anything, I was already promised to Reuel. My father wouldn't have gone back on his word."

"No, he wouldn't."

"Oh, Jethen, you asked him?"

"I did. I had even brought my bride price," Jethen reddened. "I ended up selling it to Omini. I think he ended up giving a portion of it to you and Reuel."

"I never knew." Sherai thought of all the time wasted, then remembered Tobiah and Talitha. They weren't a waste. They were a part of her, as was the gentle Nathan. Tears came to her eyes. "I'm sorry I can't come to you as a young bride. There is so much between that young girl and me."

"We aren't that old, Sherai." Jethen seemed to understand her heart as his next words proved, "I wish Talitha had lived. I could show you that I love every part of you, even her. When I first saw her, I saw you as a child again, and I wished she were mine."

Sherai's heart was too full to speak. She hugged him to her in a wordless embrace.

There was so much to talk over and say that it was much later when they finally made their way back to the house. "Mother," called Jethen in time honored tradition.

Miriam called to them from her usual corner, "You certainly took your time. Heber, Hodesh, and Aichri have come and gone long since. When they entered the room she exclaimed, "It has happened at last, praise be to God! Sherai, I love you as a daughter, but I began to think you would never come to your senses."

Sherai left Jethen's side and ran to fall at the old woman's knees. "You mean you are *happy* that Jethen has chosen me?"

"Happy? I have schemed for it this year and more. I can hardly wait to tell Hodesh," her voice dripped satisfaction. Jethen laughed and came and stood behind Sherai, bending over to plant a kiss on his mother's cheek. Miriam reached out and unclasped the veil from Sherai's face.

Her hand cupped the younger woman's cheek. "You are happy also, my daughter. My happiness is full to overflowing." She fastened her veil again before adding, "You must be brought to Jericho to marry at Jethen's father's house. It is tradition. We will feast and rejoice for seven days. Jethen, you must arrange the kiddushin at once. I'll walk with you to Omini's. There is a pattern I want to discuss with Opar, and some sweets I promised her girls."

30

KIDDUSHIN

Opar was bustling about seeing that everything was ready. "This is my first big event since marrying Omini. I want everything to be perfect," she told Sherai. "I wish I were surer of how many people to expect."

Sherai shook her head as she inspected each item for the fifth time. "Everything is better than perfect, Opar. I knew many of our invited guests would send regrets. Since Omini was baptized by Jesus' disciples, many of his former friends, at least the more devout Samaritans, have avoided him."

"Then I guess it's fortunate that other of our friends aren't so devout," giggled Opar. "They are avid to come."

"Yes," Sherai agreed, "partly to eat this generous and lavish array of food, and partly to see the scandal of the city–Sherai and Jethen." Opar had told her that many had voiced the opinion to her that it was time they were making official what had been going on between them for years. Opar said she explained that nothing had been going on, but no matter what she said, they didn't believe it.

"At least your closest friends and relatives accepted with alacrity. They're probably as curious as the others, but at least they know most of the story already. I can hear them saying it, 'Imagine converting to Judaism!'"

Opar agreed, "The kiddushin is as close as they will get to the wedding since you will wed in Jericho."

"I hope that at least you and Omini will come to Jericho for the wedding," Sherai said. "You are all the family I have left." She had been pleased since Opar's conversion to count the young woman as her friend. They discovered they had a great deal in common. They both loved needlework, children, and their family.

Opar blushed with pleasure at the compliment. "I'm sure Omini would be pleased to come."

Sherai looked over the table, and reset a candle into its stick. Goat's cheese rolled in various herbs, by Opar's own hands were flanked by toasted flat breads sliced thin. Poached quail's eggs crowned rounds of sliced brown bread peppered with rye. Smoked fish lay on long platters surrounded by grape leaves. Dates, figs and honeyed and nutted pastries filled smaller dishes. Several bowls of olives, some stuffed, and others not, dotted the table. Small cakes slathered with honey were piled high. Linen napkins were placed beside pronged silver forks to spear delicacies.

These offerings were placed on a long table interspersed with candles, late blooming flowers from the garden, and fronds of ripe wheat.

Decanters of wine and brass goblets adorned another table along with unshelled nuts on a layer of small palm fronds.

It was time for the guests to arrive. The rabbi came first. Rabbi Zichri was an elderly man who had spent his life among the Samaritans, Greeks, and Romans of Sychar. There were very few Jews in his congregation. His face was kindly, his stomach was slightly bowled, and his eyes were keen. When Jesus had come to Sychar, he had been among the first to accept his teachings. His own sermons were filled with Jesus words. Omini pulled him into his private room for a quiet talk before all the guests arrived.

"So, Rabbi Zichri, you now have a synagogue at long last in which to gather," Omini said as he ushered him into his room.

"Almost," he responded. "It has a roof, and walls, but no door, windows, or floor. I suppose I am impatient, but Jethen is building it as fast as the materials come. Will you be attending the synagogue when it is finished, Omini?" The rabbi knew that Omini had embraced the Jewish faith along with his baptism by Jesus' disciples, but had yet to convert.

"I will come, Rabbi. I plan to go to Jerusalem during the Passover, and make my first sacrifice. You will come with me as my guest, with your family, if you like. You shall be a witness of my baptism for the priest."

"It would be my honor," the Rabbi answered with a bow. "My wife will accompany me, I'm sure, but my children are all grown with families of their own."

"Splendid, I will write at once and secure rooms. I know you plan to go to Jericho to perform the wedding ceremony for Jethen."

"Yes, Miriam has most generously invited me to her home."

The noise of other guests arriving drew the men from the room into the largest room where the guests were now waiting. Jethen paced the floor in front of the hall that led to Omini's room, but when he saw his host, he laughed. "I should have known the rabbi would be with you. Have you already begun celebrating, Omini?"

"I began celebrating when you came to ask for Sherai, and waived a dowry, Jethen," Omini answered in kind. To the rabbi he said, "Let us hurry and begin the ceremony before he changes his mind and demands what Sherai is truly worth."

"You don't have that much money or property, Omini," Jethen responded, "that is why I asked for none. Instead, I am offering a bride price, as you will learn when the ketubba is read."

Jethen stood before the rabbi dressed in his best new robes. His hair was neatly washed and combed, and wonder of wonders, he was sporting the efforts of a trim new moustache and beard. He had chosen to merely outline his jaw, lips and chin. It was a good choice, and showed the firm lines of his face and his grey eyes to advantage.

Omini turned him around, and observed his finery from every angle. "You look like a worthy betrothed, Jethen. The facial hair does him credit, doesn't it Rabbi Zichri?"

"Well, it isn't as luxurious as ours, brother Omini, but it is good for a start," chuckled the rabbi stroking his own luxuriant beard.

"Please," pleaded Jethen, "I am having a difficult enough time getting used to it as it is. Why did no one tell me how it itches?"

"That will only last for a short while. You will soon get used to it, and ignore it as does everyone else."

Sherai studied Jethen across the room. It had been several days since she saw him, for the Sabbath intervened since they declared their troth. Afterward, she had been too busy getting out invitations, and preparing for the festivity to attend their usual study time. He looked very handsome in his beard, she decided.

Miriam had come over to help with the baking, and had told Sherai he was growing one. Since then she had been anxious lest the Jethen she had come to love disappeared under it. She was glad to see that he was simply Jethen, and her heart beat faster just seeing him, beard or none.

Her robe was given her by Omini upon learning she was to be wed. It was of the finest linen, and dyed a soft yellow to compliment her eyes. Her himation was a deeper yellow. Her veil, a gossamer blue, matched the sash that cinched her waist. Tonight she fastened the veil with a jewel, one given her by Tobiah. She felt she wanted to share this night with him. In her heart she felt that he would understand her love for Jethen, and approve. When she presented herself to Omini and Opar for a final inspection, Omini recognized the jewel and his eyes had filled with tears. "You honor my son on this night, my daughter?"

"I will always honor your *sons*, Omini," she had replied.

Right now, she felt the night belonged to Jethen, that she belonged to Jethen. This ceremony would only put God's seal on what she already felt in her heart. The rabbi requested that they wait until after the Passover to perform the actual wedding, and it seemed like it would take forever for the three months to pass. She and Miriam would return to Jericho soon after the ceremony tonight. She and Jethen would be parted. The rabbi told her that she needed to feel like the waiting bride. Many brides did not see their husbands from the time of the betrothal until the marriage, and this separation would be good for them both. It was a time to reflect, study, dream, and prepare for their married life together.

Sherai bowed to his wisdom, and knew it to be in her best interest. Yesterday she visited all her old haunts. The homes of her former husbands, and the places they had gone together. Particularly she mourned Tobiah, and Nathan. They had been so good for her. She did need the time to separate her old life from what was to be. It was important to think only of Jethen after tonight.

Jethen had resisted the idea at first, but came to see the wisdom of it. A short wait, then she would be his–all he had ever dreamed.

The guests talked and laughed, and ate. They drank the wine, and watched the dancers and other entertainments, but eventually the time came for the important part of the evening. The rabbi walked to the corner of the room where a long white cloth had been draped. A small table covered in white held only a shining brass pitcher, and a menorah. He called, "Jethen, son of Amos, come forth to read your ketubba. Sherai, daughter of Ashah, come forth to hear and read your ketubba."

A hush fell over the room, and silently the guests gathered around leaving a path for Jethen and Sherai to walk to the rabbi. Hand in hand they walked toward him. Joy radiated from them both.

"My children, this covenant which you are about to enter is one most sacred to God. You take upon yourselves vows of obedience and commitment that extend beyond earthly power to seal. Your vows are to God himself." He looked to Opar who stood beside Omini with a tray on which a goblet and two thin scrolls resided. She stepped forward and presented the tray to Jethen.

Jethen reached for the scroll on the right. It was an expensive roll of parchment thinly outlined in gold, and decorated with sheaves of wheat, pomegranates, and grape twigs and leaves. It was a beautiful and artistic piece. To the surprise of the guests, he began reading slowly in Aramic, "I, Jethen, do offer to Sherai all my self and my worldly goods, save the house in Jericho, and the vineyard which I own jointly with my mother and sister." The audience who understood Aramaic gasped. This was unheard of in a marriage ketubba. Sherai, who had been steadily looking upon Jethen as he read, felt tears slide from her eyes and wet her veil. "Also in this regard, I waive the right to a dowry from Sherai. Any properties coming to our marriage from Sherai will be given in trust to our children.

"I promise to love, honor and cherish her all the days of her life. For her welfare, and that of our family, I will work, and provide for their welfare as long as I am able.

"I promise to obey the law of God, and live righteously. Our children will have cause to honor and emulate our commitment to one another. During her lifetime, I will seek no other wife," again the audience tittered.

Jethen ignored the interruption and said tenderly, "She is a good and righteous woman, and her price is above rubies. I only regret that I have no wealth sufficient to pay her bride price. Nevertheless, Sherai and I offer Omini, three camels, twenty sheep, six donkeys, and ten talents. My heart and hand are hers."

Jethen then handed the scroll to Sherai. She continued reading, "I, Sherai, give the property in Capernaum to Jethen in behalf of any future children we may have together. Also the property bequeathed me from Tobiah will be set aside for those same children in his name. All other bequests, will be returned to those generous donors, and all titles and property likewise bestowed." Sherai took the other scroll from the tray, and handed it to Omini. She leaned forward and whispered, "Thank you, father of my husbands, but I won't need this any longer." Thus Sherai gave back the overly generous stipend from both Omini in behalf of Reuel and Maachi, keeping only the one from Tobiah.

She continued reading with great emotion, "I promise, Jethen to honor and obey you as you obey our God. Your kindness and generosity of spirit will be an inspiration to me and to our children. Before God, I vow to raise our children in righteousness, and according to the laws of God. I will love and cherish you all the days of your life.

"Our life together Jethen and I dedicate to the service of God. Amen."

Opar wiped her eyes with a large kerchief she pulled from her sleeve. There were a few other sniffs in the house. Jethen appeared unashamed of his own moist eyes.

From the tray in Opar's hands, the rabbi took a quill, and dipped it in ink. "Jethen, you will be the first to sign the ketubba. Then you will give the stick, dipped once again to Sherai."

Jethen walked to the table and signed the paper carefully. He then walked back to Opar, dipped the quill, carefully wiped it, and carried it to Sherai who repeated his procedure except when she had signed, she left the quill on the tray, and carried the ketubba to the rabbi.

"Will the witnesses come forth and sign," he said. Omini and Miriam came forward and signed the ketubba, each dipping the quill and wiping it.

Taking the scroll and sprinkling it with sand to dry it, he then rolled it and gave it into Miriam's keeping, "You, Miriam, as mother of the groom, will keep this scroll sacred until the time of the nisuin." Miriam stepped forward and accepted the scroll.

"In as much as you have so vowed and declared yourselves betrothed before this assembly, you will now seal your promise." Taking the goblet from Opar's tray, he filled it with the pitcher from the table.

He took the goblet in his two hands, and bowed his head offering this blessing, "Blessed are You, O Lord our God, King of the Universe, Who creates the fruit of the vine. Amen."

Everyone said, "Amen."

Rabbi Zichri then before handing the goblet to Jethen, admonished him, "This wine you drink together this day is by a foreshadowing of your marriage vows. You will not drink of the fruit of the vine again together until your marriage." Jethen took the goblet in both his hands, sipped from the cup, then handed it back to the rabbi.

The rabbi then handed the goblet to Sherai which she accepted with both hands, and sipped before handing it back.

The rabbi then blessed, "Blessed art thou, O Lord our God, King of the Universe,
Who has created everything for His glory.

Blessed art thou, O Lord our God, King of the Universe,
Who has created mankind.

Blessed art thou, O Lord our God, King of the Universe,
Who has made mankind in thy image, in the image of thy likeness and prepared for him - from himself - a building for eternity.

Blessed are You, O Lord, who fashioned the mankind. Amen"

Everyone said, "Amen."

"I believe you wish to seal this betrothal with a ring. Jethen you will take the ring from the first finger of your left hand and place it on the first finger of Sherai's left hand."

Jethen took the ring, a plain ring of thick gold, from his finger. It only fit as far as his first knuckle. He took the ring and kissed it before slipping it over Sherai's finger. It was a perfect fit. Sherai also kissed the ring. He said to her, "Behold, you are consecrated to me with this ring according to the law of Moses and Israel."

"The conditions are met," shouted the rabbi, "let the rejoicing continue unabated." Rabbi Zichri escorted the couple to the dining table, and sat between them on the long pillowed bench reserved for them. The long wait until their marriage or nisuin began.

31

PROPHECY

There was nothing else to do. Winter had come at last, and the driving rains discouraged and even prevented working outside except to attend to the animals. The small synagogue was finished just in time to protect it from the weather. He smiled to find himself standing at the window gazing down the road on which Sherai left Sychar three days ago.

His smile faded when he realized that Sherai was really gone. He hoped they arrived in Jericho before this heavy rain. His mother was too old for a soaking. As they departed, they looked like a small caravan, but he was glad he sent Levi with his Mother, Sherai, and their maids. Three other servants also accompanied them for safety's sake.

He doubted that even robbers would want to be out in this weather, but remembering Matthias, he wanted to take no chances. Still, he suspected that Matthias' own servants robbed him since no sign of them had since appeared. What Matthias thought of the matter, he kept to himself. Whatever happened on the Jericho road, that godly man bore malice toward none.

Jethen ruminated over the surprise given him by Mazar who elected to remain in Sychar. One of her younger sisters, Naomi, had offered to go with Sherai to Jericho to await her wedding day. That thought led naturally to think of their wedding. In three months he would go to Jericho and fetch his bride home.

Meanwhile, he sighed, he had work to do. He was grateful to Sherai. Besides the notes she had written of Jesus' teachings on her own, she had served as a scribe much of the time John and Jude visited him in Jericho. From him she had gotten an account of the baptism of Jesus by John the Baptist. It contained that phrase that had so haunted him since that day in the temple.

Searching among the scrolls, he found the one he wanted. He made room on his table, and spread it out. Sherai made a good scribe. Her words were clear and legible. He began to read.

Andrew was a disciple of John the Baptist until Jesus came to John to be baptized by him. On that day John taught the people that he was preparing the way for another who would come after him. When Jesus came later John said, "Behold the Lamb of God who will take away the sins of the world. This is he of whom I spoke. He is coming after me, but he is preferred before me, for he has the fullness, and grace for grace; for Moses gave the law, but grace and truth come by Jesus. And I saw and bore record that this is the Son of God." *Andrew heard him say that, and afterward followed only Jesus.*

Jethen looked up. "That is the phrase John said that day on our way to Jericho. It unsettles my heart. *The Lamb of God will take away the sins of the world.* Lamb of God. Is there some other prophecy that talks of the Messiah being a sacrifice for his people? I must remember to ask the rabbi."

Jethen returned to the scroll and read on. John told it like a story, but Sherai had written it in her own words. *Shortly thereafter was the Passover, and Jesus went to Jerusalem with his* disciples. *He went into the temple, and seeing the moneychangers there, and the sellers of doves for sacrifice, he made a scourge and tipped over the tables, scattered the money, drove animals and the moneychangers out. Jesus said that they were making his Father's house a house of merchandise, and not of worship. When the Jews asked him,* "What sign are you showing us by doing this thing?"

Jesus said, "Destroy this temple, and in three days, I will raise it up."

His tormentors said, "This temple was built in forty-six years, and you will build it up in three days?"

Jethen remembered that conversation the day John said those words. At that time the only thing on his mind was Jesus divinity. Instead of asking what Jesus meant by the three days he recalled saying to John, "I am more interested in John the Baptist calling him the Son of God. Tell me, did your prophets prophesy of this?"

Now he wondered what Jesus did mean by saying such a thing. Jethen knew that he could perform mighty miracles, even so his mind couldn't comprehend building such a structure as the temple in three days. It had taken him considerably longer just to construct the small synagogue.

He wished Sherai would have included his question, it would make the subjects not seem to jump about so. At least she always left a small space before beginning another topic. At the start of this passage Sherai noted that John quoted Isaiah. He said. *"The Lord, himself, shall give you a sign; a virgin shall conceive, and bear a son, and shall call his name Immanuel."*

John also said, again quoting Isaiah, *"For unto us a son is born, unto us a child is given, and the government shall be upon his shoulders and his name shall be, Wonderful, Counselor, the mighty God, the Everlasting Father, the Prince of Peace.*

Of the increase of his government and his peace there shall be no end."

'Isaiah, that is the prophet I should read,' Jethen thought. He laid down Sherai's scroll, and walked over to the long rack he built to accommodate his many scrolls. He sought out the scroll of Isaiah. Isaiah was one of the more popular of the Jewish prophets. There had been more scrolls available from his writings than any other. Even John recommended that prophet when they had gone to the stalls to buy scrolls.

Patiently he sorted through the rack, and found the one labeled prophecies of Isaiah. It was one of the larger scrolls, and great care had been given to the copying of it. It was on a more durable medium than mere parchment, and the ink used was a deeper and more expensive blend of dye.

The scroll looked bigger even than he remembered. He sighed, and wished again for Rabbi Zichri. He would know where to find what he was looking for within the large volume. It was not going to be, however. That worthy man had taken his wife south to her mother's family for the rainy season as she suffered so from pain in her joints during the winter months. He promised to return in good time for the wedding journey, but until then, Jethen was on his own.

He took the great scroll and carried it to the table. Pushing aside the other works, he opened it and smoothed it over a large space. This was going to take some time. Impatient that want of food or drink would interfere with his study, he called in Rebbah. "I am going to be reading and studying all day," he told her. "I want neither food nor drink to interrupt my fast. Let none disturb me unless on a matter of extreme necessity." She dipped a bow in his direction to signify that she understood, and Jethen pressed on with his reading.

The first thing mentioned was the reign of four different kings of Judah. Jethen sighed. History was not one of his favorite subjects. He rose again and went to retrieve a scroll dealing with the lines of kings. The Samaritans knew of the kings of both the north and south kingdoms because it was also a part of their heritage. According to his lines, this prophecy was first received over seven hundred years before the present. Not so long ago as Moses, of course, but still quite some time past.

It was around this time that the northern kingdom was defeated by the Assyrians, and taken into captivity, never to be heard of again. Only Samaria and Judah escaped that route. Now having established the when of Isaiah, he was ready to study.

He found the spot that John had first quoted. There had been many places where he had stopped reading and wrote a bit in the special scroll he and Sherai had begun in the study of prophecies about the Messiah. It took him the better part of the day to get that far. He felt almost an urgency to read Isaiah's words. Life intruded and kept him from his study.

First the east pasture where the sheep were feeding flooded, and the flock had to be moved to higher ground. That took a week. Then the wolves broke into the pens, and they had to build a shelter in the midst of the rain. He hired several shepherds from the city to protect the sheep until it was finished. Next, a neighbor's barn fell in from the heavy rains, and Jethen helped repair it.

It seemed there was a conspiracy on the part of the weather to keep him from his studies. Neighbor after neighbor, mostly the poor who were his especial care, due to the heavy rains, had leaking in their homes, and the roofs needed to be shored up. All the men once again turned out to fix the problem, but nearly a month passed before Jethen could return to Isaiah.

The second month was nearly at an end before he at last came to the passage he had been dreading to find.

For he shall grow up before him as a tender plant, and as a root out of a dry ground: he has no form nor comeliness; and when we shall see him, there is no beauty that we should desire him.

He is despised and rejected of men; a man of sorrows, and acquainted with grief: and we hid as it were our faces from him; he was despised, and we esteemed him not.
  Surely he has borne our griefs, and carried our sorrows: yet we did esteem him stricken, smitten of God, and afflicted.

This hasn't happened yet, thought Jethen. He isn't despised, except by the priests, and the Sadducees, and maybe a few rich Jews. Then he recalled his own early feelings toward Jesus. The lawyers, scribes, and Pharisees who follow him only heckle. He took the scroll on which he listed the prophecies and began writing before he bowed his head to read on:

But he was wounded for our transgressions; he was bruised for our iniquities: the chastisement of our peace was upon him; and with his stripes we are healed.
  All we like sheep have gone astray; we have turned every one to his own way; and the Lord hath laid on him the iniquity of us all. He was oppressed, and he was afflicted, yet he opened not his mouth: he is brought as a lamb to the slaughter,

There it is. His heart felt like a stone in his chest. Jesus was to be the lamb. What else would happen? He read further,

  and as a sheep before her shearers is dumb, so he opens not his mouth. He was taken from prison and from judgment: and who shall declare his generation? for he was cut off out of the land of the living:

This says he will be killed. This entire passage should be included in our scroll, but I think I will first read to the end.

for the transgression of my people was he stricken. And he made his grave with the wicked, and with the rich in his death; because he had done no violence, neither was any deceit in his mouth.

"That is the God's truth."

Yet it pleased the Lord to bruise him; he hath put him to grief: when thou shalt make his soul an offering for sin,

Jesus is to be our ultimate sin offering. I can't bear it. He is going to die for me, and not just me, but all of us. One thing about Isaiah appeared clear to Jethen. Isaiah believed that God was God for all the nations, not just the Jews. That meant that any act of the Messiah was also for all nations.

he shall see his seed, he shall prolong his days, and the pleasure of the Lord shall prosper in his hand.
He shall see of the travail of his soul, and shall be satisfied: by his knowledge shall my righteous servant justify many; for he shall bear their iniquities.

Isaiah says it, right there. How can he do this?

Therefore will I divide him a portion with the great, and he shall divide the spoil with the strong; because he hath poured out his soul unto death: and he was numbered with the transgressors; and he bare the sin of many, and made intercession for the transgressors.

A transgressor, he was numbered with the transgressors, what does that mean? There is no more holy and righteous man on this earth than Jesus. In spite of bearing our sins he will intercede for us? The truth he had glimpsed that day in Jerusalem finally rose to overwhelm him. Jethen buried his head in his arms right on the scroll, and wept. He kept saying over and over in his mind, "Why? Why? He is so good, and he does only good, how can they despise him enough to kill him?"

Jethen didn't know how long he wept when he became aware that a gentle peace had stolen over his soul. A soft voice seemed to be whispering in his mind, "Destroy this temple and in three days I will raise it up."

Jethen raised his head and listened. "Read Sherai's scroll."

He looked down. There was still a portion of Isaiah he had not yet read. He was torn with wanting to finish it, but he set it aside and once again picked up Sherai's scroll. Immediately his eyes fell on the words, *"Don't let your heart be troubled. In my Father's house are many mansions. I go to prepare a place for you. And if I go and prepare a place for you, I will come again and receive you unto myself so that where I am, you may come."*

The voice in his head whispered, *'I do this for you, for all men. It is the will of the Father.'* The testimony burned brightly, searing Jethen's very soul. Jesus was the Lamb of God. Jesus was the Son of God.

There was one other thing of which Jethen was fairly certain. His hand shook and he laid down Sherai's scroll. His whole being seemed afire. Neither John nor Jude said anything to him of Jesus being the ultimate sacrifice for the world. While Sherai had inadvertently mentioned some straws that seemed to point in that direction from the things Jesus had said, she had never discussed it with him, and he knew that she would have. That raised more questions in his mind. Why hadn't they said? Did they realize it? Did Jesus want him to bring it up since He was the one who started him on this path to learning of it? Tears filled his eyes again at the biggest question of his heart–When? He slipped to his knees beside the chair, and began to pray.

In the weeks that followed Jethen read many more prophecies about the Messiah. Even Isaiah had more to say, but none touched him as that passage had. Jethen read, studied and prayed every day except the Sabbath. On that day he prayed and studied the Law of Moses. There were so many observances he had forgotten.

Rebbah came and brought him food, or drink, but often it sat forgotten as he poured over the scriptures, and the prophets. Many of their words he memorized. He read and reread the words of Jesus that Sherai had so painstakingly written. In the light of his new knowledge Jethen noticed many segments where Jesus seemed to be preparing his disciples for his death.

As he read, studied and prayed it became clear to him that Jesus wasn't going to be the kind of Messiah that the Jews, and even his own people had been expecting. He wasn't going to shake his rod and destroy the Romans, or any other conquering race. He wasn't going to establish himself as King of Palestine, at least, not at this time.

It seemed to him that the prophets spoke of another time when he would come, it would require much more study. He promised himself that he and Sherai would set aside some time each day to study this.

Sherai! In just three more days he was going to leave. He would get the Rabbi, and they would journey on to Jericho. Omini and Opar were also going to Jericho with them, then back to Jerusalem for the Passover. He and his new wife would also do this, and the Rabbi and his wife. It would be a glorious wedding celebration. If he knew his mother, and he did, it would be a wedding to remember.

TEACHING IN THE TEMPLE

The twisted Shofar made from the horn of a Great Kudu sounded its bass note at intervals along the mile-long, winding path that led from Jethen's father's house to the house built on their property for his sister and her husband. According to tradition Jethen sent criers sounding the Shofar ahead of him and had the man call, "Behold, the bridegroom comes," on his midnight journey to his sister Miriam's house. This practice allowed the guests assembled there, waiting with Sherai for the summons, to know that he was coming to claim his bride. As the horn came increasingly closer to the house the guests lit their small oil lamps, and awaited his coming with almost as much anticipation as Sherai.

With a shout, Jethen arrived at his sister's door, and entering, sought for his bride in every room. "Where is my bride?" he shouted. With much laughter, and dodging about, Sherai was kept from him as they moved her from group to group. At last finding her hidden among the guests, with a whoop he scooped her into his arms and made for the door. Hastily the other members of the wedding party grabbed their lamps and the procession to Jethen's father's house began.

"Please, Jethen let me walk."Sherai begged to be put down as the procession wound its way to the estate.

"What? And take the chance you might elude me again?"

Sherai laughed and submitted to the delicious feeling of being kidnapped by her own husband to be. Once inside the gates, Jethen did set Sherai on her feet, and the two proceeded together to the sala where a white linen open tent like structure had been stretched over poles. Rabbi Zichri waited for them beneath it.

From there the wedding continued along lines much the same as other Jewish marriages of their time. Jethen stood arrayed in his white robe before the rabbi. Sherai had chosen to wear a soft yellow nearly the color of rich cream. The rabbi chanted his seven blessings, as Jethen wrapped a corner of his prayer shawl around Sherai so that it covered them both. They shared a sip of wine from the sacred goblet, and at the culmination of the ceremony, the rabbi, along with the other guests escorted the bride and groom to their nuptial chambers. Jethen and Sherai entered as man and wife, and the door was shut, symbolic of shutting out the world from their world of two.

Rabbi Zirchi left the door and went to find his wife, Judith. Those two stood in a corner, conversing with guests. The rabbi held a goblet of wine, and as each guest came up to speak with him, he smiled and bowed, endangering the contents of his goblet more with each dip. He was to be congratulated, however, for the seven blessings he chanted during the ceremony had rolled off his tongue with more heartfelt sincerity and spirituality than many of the guests ever heard. His words to the bride and groom elevated the oft repeated words to new heights of joy and future felicity.

Omini and Opar beamed as though they were the actual parents of the bride. Opar looked particularly lovely in her lavender robes and veil. Many of Miriam's family in Jericho came to meet them. Miriam was a happy vision in blue. Now that her fondest wish had come true, happiness shone from her eyes. That evening she chose to wear every jewel her husband had presented her with during their married life. Her arms were covered with bracelets nearly to her elbows. Large tear drop lapis lazuli hung from the lobes of her ears, and draped about her throat. Clips of ruby decorated her sash. Yellow diamonds set in intricate filigree decorated her veil. Jethen's sister, Miriam, wearing blue robes also, wore only a few gold bracelets, and modest earrings made from rubies. It was her duty to make certain that the servants were providing drink for their guests as they waited for the bride and groom. Her robes were a replica of her mother's.

The guests made their way back to the main rooms where tables groaned with food. They waited for Jethen and Sherai to reappear before the feasting would begin. This was the first night of the seven promised nights of rejoicing, and no one planned to miss one morsel of it. Miriam was well known for her lavish banquets. Jethen and Sherai's married life began.

The camel ride to Jerusalem was filled with joy for Sherai as she openly stared at her new husband. She had not known the world could be filled with such happiness. Who could have known that when she left Sychar nearly four years ago that such bliss awaited her?

Jethen was everything her heart could desire in a husband. He was a friend, provider, and profound love of her life. She hoped that she gave him as much happiness as he gave her.

Feeling her gaze, he looked over at her and smiled his special smile. It shook her heart. She felt as though she were a young maid again, blushing in the presence of her groom.

To calm her beating heart, and to appear casual before the rabbi and his wife who accompanied them, as well as Opar and Omini, she asked, "Jerusalem will be very crowded during Passover, won't it?"

"Yes, and perhaps more so with Jesus being there. I'm glad Omini suggested that I procure rooms early. As it is, most likely Omini, the Rabbi, and I will share one room while you women share another."

"Truly?" Opar seemed a bit uncomfortable with the arrangement.

"Fear not," Judith, the Rabbi's wife comforted her. "We will all be too tired at the end of each day to worry about where we place our heads."

"It is simply too crowded to expect rooms for two, Opar," Omini explained. "I did try to secure rooms, but was told that everyone doubles up during Passover."

"Where will we eat the Passover?" she wondered. Sherai had wondered that as well. It was Jethen's first Passover as a Jew, though the Samaritans strictly observed it.

"I have arranged for our wedding party to partake of the Passover with the innkeepers."

"It will be my first Passover without our children," mentioned Judith. Her voice quavered only a little.

"At least we will still be together, my dear wife," the Rabbi patted her hand. "Think of those widows, and widowers without children. With whom do they celebrate the Passover?"

"You are right Zichri, I will cease to murmur."

The city was fairly seething with the excitement. Roman soldiers were everywhere making certain that there were no riots or uprisings. They made an imposing array standing as they did along either side of the gates, and atop the walls.

Jethen's group entered the Sheep Gate and made their way to their lodgings on foot.

Omini had taken it upon himself to find them all lovely rooms in the upper city. Their rooms overlooked the road that led to the Dead Sea. From the rooftop they could see the watchtower on Zion's Gate, also manned by soldiers, and the long aqueduct from the Serpent Pool.

After placing their goods in the rooms, they set out through the lower city for the Beautiful Gate. They had decided since John told Jethen they would enter the city from that direction, they planned to walk toward the Mount of Olives to watch for Jesus' coming. It was a pleasant walk on a spring morning.

It was a relief for Sherai to stretch her legs after sitting astride a camel for two days. They had walked less than a mile when she heard a loud commotion on the road ahead of them. People, a large crowd of people, were shouting and waving large palm fronds in the air.

"Let's wait and let them come to us," Sherai said to Jethen. He nodded and raised his arm to stop their group. As they stopped and waited for the crowd to come up to them, she heard, "Hosanna, to the son of David, Blessed is he that comes in the name of the Lord, Hosanna in the highest."

Then she saw Jesus. He was astride a donkey piled with cloaks. On the road before him people were strewing their cloaks or himations for him to trod upon. The white colt stepped on the proffered garments as though they were his due, as he was carrying a king.

One of the Pharisees among his disciples said, "Master, rebuke your disciples."

"If I forbade them to speak, and they held their peace, the stones would cry out unto me."

Jethen said for her ear alone, "He is fulfilling prophecy coming into Jerusalem on a white colt. The prophet said, 'Behold your king coming to you on an ass with a white colt of an ass.'"

"You mean we are seeing prophecy fulfilled before our very eyes?" She was awed and wished she had a palm of her own to wave.

Instead she waved her arms and sang with the rest of the crowd which soon swept past them, and they joined the throng who continued singing and praising God. As they reached the last knoll before entering the city, Jesus stopped, and looked out over Jerusalem.

Sherai could see tears falling from his eyes. As if the emotion was too much to contain, Jesus lamented, "Oh, Jerusalem, Jerusalem. I would gather you as a hen gathers her chicks, but you do not know me. If you only knew even on this day the things which belong to your peace, but they are hid from your eyes. Your enemies will build a trench and encompass you round about to keep you in on all sides. They shall lay your walls even with the ground, and your children within you. They will not leave one stone upon another because you did not know the time of your visitation." Jesus openly wept over Jerusalem, and none who stood with him could comprehend his sorrow.

Lazarus walked up to Jesus, and said gently, "Master."

Jesus looked on Lazarus and smiled through his tears. He soon clucked to the donkey, and they continued on their way to the temple.

Sherai wondered at his weeping, and whether he intended to declare war on the Romans, or level the city with his power.

Jesus alighted from the colt and entered the temple where he immediately began once again to chastize the money changers. He tipped over their tables, and cast them out. No one dared lay a hand against him. The crowd with him prevented anyone from molesting him. The blind and lame made their way to Jesus, and he healed them all. It was glorious. Their King was among them.

Little children danced about Jesus and sang "Hosanna to the son of David." The chief priests and scribes were sorely irritated by this and came and remonstrated with Jesus. "Do you not hear what these children are saying?" they asked.

"Have you never read, 'Out of the mouths of babes and sucklings, you have perfected praise?'" Jesus answered them.

Sherai looked at Jethen. He had a worried look and the lines above his forehead were creased. "What is it, Jethen? Why do you look so?"

"I fear he is goading the priests. It is his hour of triumph, but look at their faces. They wear their envy and malice plainly for all to see. I fear for him. I see absolute hatred in their eyes."

"Jesus has power beyond their vain imaginings," Sherai comforted him.

"I know that he does, but will he summon it against them?"

The next morning, Jethen hurried them all to the temple. There was no need to hasten them, for they were as excited to hear Jesus' words as Jethen. The courts of the temple were full to overflowing. People stood about talking and rejoicing that the Messiah had finally come. Weaving through the crowds were the scribes and priests, occasionally they would stop, and listen to the words being said. If anything, their scowls grew more fierce as they listened.

They stopped by Sherai and Jethen while John was telling them about Jesus raising Lazarus from the dead. "He was in the tomb four days," John was saying. "Jesus bade some men roll the stone from the door, but many of the people protested saying that he would surely stink after four days. Jesus just ignored them and waited for the stone to be moved. When it was, he stood at the doorway and called, 'Lazarus, come forth.' We all heard a shuffling noise, and Lazarus shuffled out of the doorway still wrapped in his burial rags and ointments. Jesus told Mary to take them off him, and loose him."

Sherai's eyes were like stars, "He had been dead for four days, and still he called him back? How did Lazarus look?"

"He looked well. Completely whole. You saw him today. How did he look to you?"

"I don't know him," replied Sherai.

"Nor I," Jethen told him.

"It was the man who came to Jesus as he wept over Jerusalem."

Just then their attention was diverted to movement in the crowds. Sherai knew it was because Jesus had entered the courtyard. She, Jethen and John made their way to Jesus. He smiled at them, as he smiled on others, and steadily made his way more toward the center so that he could be heard by all. Immediately, the chief priest who had been listening to John came with them to where Jesus stood. It was then Sherai noticed that many of the scribes and priests of the temple stood around Jesus.

The one who stood near them asked, "Where is it you get your authority to do the things you do?"

"If you will first answer a question of mine, I will readily answer your question."

"Well, what is your question?"

"Where did John's authority come to baptize? Was it of God, or of Man?"

Sherai looked at Jethen and her eyes smiled. Jesus had confounded the priest. He did not dare to say that John's authority came from God, for then Jesus would have asked him why he was not baptized by John. If he said John was of the devil, the crowd would mob him and perhaps stone him for many of them believed on John.

"I cannot tell you where John got his authority," the priest answered.

"Then I cannot tell you where the authority comes from to do the things I do." Jesus told him.

Jesus began teaching the people. "A certain man bought a vineyard and hired husbandmen to care for it. He then took a journey to a far country for a long time. When the season came to harvest the vineyard he sent a servant to the husbandmen to be given the fruit of the vineyard. The husbandmen beat the servant and sent him away. The lord of the vineyard sent another servant, and he was beaten and treated shamefully and cast out, the third servant the man sent was likewise wounded and cast out.

When the last servant returned the Lord said, "What shall I do? I know, I will send my beloved son. It may be that they will reverence him when they see him. When the husbandmen saw the son they said among themselves, "This is the heir, come let us kill him and the inheritance will be ours." So they cast him out of the vineyard, and killed him. What will the lord of the vineyard do to the husbandmen? He shall come and destroy the husbandmen and give the vineyard to others."

Sherai heard the priest say, "God forbid." Then she knew that Jesus was speaking of them, of the leaders of the temple. Jesus was the son he was speaking about.

She looked at Jethen and saw that his eyes were teary. She reached out a hand to him, and he clutched it until her knuckles shone white.

The priests left along with their scribes, and Jesus continued preaching to the people in the courtyard. Sherai knew that the priests sent spies to listen to Jesus, she had seen such men before who came in all piety to listen, but spoke out only to ridicule or scorn.

One such man asked Jesus, "Is it lawful to give tribute to Caesar, or not."

Jesus perceived their craftiness and answered, "Why tempt me? Show me a penny. Whose portrait and inscription does it display?"

The man answered him, "Caesar's."

"Then render unto Caesar that which is Caesar's and unto God that which is God's."

Jesus continued teaching, and by and by moved into the Court of the Women. There he saw a rich man cast money into the offering. As he watched many others came and slipped offerings into the treasury. Shortly thereafter a widow came in and thrust in a mite.

Jesus observed this and said, "I tell you truly that this widow has given more than them all. For they gave of their abundance, but she has thrown in all she had." Some of the disciples standing around him were looking upon the stones and artistry of the temple. They commented on how beautiful it was, and how fitting for a place of worship. Jesus looked around at the beautiful court and said, "As for the beauties that you behold, the time is coming when one stone that rests upon another will not be thrown down."

"When will this be. Give us a sign."

Jesus gathered his special disciples about him, and Jethen and Sherai crowded with them, as did several others.

A voice spoke at Jethen's elbow. "Well met, Jethen." Jethen turned as did Sherai, and before them stood Matthias. He was completely well, and with him stood Lydia. Matthias put forth his hand and shook hands with Jethen. "Thank you my friend for your succor." Then Matthias took in Jethen's robe, and prayer shawl. His eyes widened.

"I see that you have embraced our Lord," he rejoiced. "Praise be to God."

"Praise be to God," Jethen echoed. "Matthias, I would like you to meet my wife, Sherai."

"I have seen her following the Master, but I did not know she was your wife."

"We were only recently wed," Sherai admitted.

"Then I congratulate you both. May God's blessings shine on your union."

"I am certain they will with that sanction," Sherai told him as she smiled.

Jesus voice rose a bit, and they heard him say, "they shall lay their hands on you and persecute you, delivering you up to synagogues, and into prisons, being brought before kings and rulers for my name's sake, and it shall turn to you for a testimony.

"Settle it in your hearts not to meditate before what to answer, for I will give you a mouth and wisdom which all your adversaries will not be able to gainsay or resist.

"You shall be betrayed by parents, brothers, and kinfolk and some of you will be put to death. You shall be hated of all men for my name's sake, but let patience possess your souls. When you see Jerusalem encompassed about with armies, know that the desolation is nigh. Then let all Judea flee to the mountains."

"It's the sign given for the destruction of Jerusalem," Matthias said quietly.

"There are worse things ahead," Jethen added.

"What do you mean?" Sherai asked.

"Not here, my heart. I must listen to Jesus while I may. Later we will talk, I promise you."

All that day Jesus taught in the temple. Those about him never tired, or seemed weary. It was as though he was cramming into a few days a lifetime of teaching. When the day was finished, he told those nearest him that he would retire to the Mount of Olives until the next day when he would resume teaching at the temple. Many visitors to Jerusalem during the Passover camped there.

When Jesus withdrew, Sherai realized how tired she really was. While she was with Jesus, she was buoyed up by his words, and his spirit of goodness. When he left, it was as thought the very light had gone from the sky, and her limbs were too weak to hold her up. When she sagged a bit, Jethen caught her arm. "Here, my girl, you need some food. Let's go down to the stalls and find something. I'm famished myself. I think we stood there all day without a thought for food."

"That's the way it is with the Master. When he speaks, his words are the bread of life to our ears."

"The mouth needs a little encouragement to live, also," said Jethen practically. "Let's go find a tidbit for it." The crowd, along with Jesus and his disciples had already dispersed as if they too remembered food and drink.

"Jethen, what worse thing is to come?" Sherai asked as soon as they got to the temple steps.

"Let us eat first, and refresh ourselves. Later we will take a walk in the garden. There is a beautiful garden called Gethsemane, it will give us time to be alone together before we go to our separate rooms. I'll tell you then."

"Where is the nearest food?"

Jethen lifted his head and sniffed, "That way," he pointed north.

SPITEFUL MEN

"I tell you he openly declares himself to be the son of God, and we do nothing," Caiaphas ranted. "He raised that man from the dead, and he walks about telling everyone about it." He walked about his father-in-law's palatial grounds like a tiger in captivity.

"If he raised him at all," Annas sniffed. He was seated on one of his plush lounges that reclined. His feet hung over the end as he stretched out. A servant stood above him with a large fan protecting his face from the sun. Annas waved the servant away. He didn't want talk of their meeting being gossiped about all over the city.

Caiaphas restrained himself until the servant was indoors then he growled through gritted teeth, "Oh, he came out of a grave alright. Some of my people were there in disguise and saw it. Two of them now follow him. My priests tell me that they are calling him King, and raining praises on the son of David. I tell you he is dangerous. If he raises up, with the thousands following him, he just might throw down the Roman soldiers, and just where would that leave us?"

"Yes, yes, you've told me before. Well, do something about it."

"He deserves to be stoned to death for his heresy. You know as well as I that I can't take the necessary steps for that with the Passover almost upon us, and the Romans breathing down my neck. Pilate would have a fit."

Annas looked up at his son-in-law. The man was exuding jealousy from every pore. He hated Jesus because he had thousands of followers, and Caiaphas had to pay everyone to be loyal to him. Perhaps it had been a mistake to make his son-in-law High Priest. His ambition and greed for power, instead of sharpening his senses, made him grasping and treacherous.

"If he rises against Rome, he will soon be put down. They won't hold with some upstart calling himself a king, Caiaphas."

"And if he doesn't rise against Rome, what then? The discontent and voice of the people will demand he take my place. I tell you, I see it in their faces."

"If he doesn't rise up against the Romans soon, his popularity will die out, as it has with all the others before him. The people will lose interest in him. When they see he won't feed and clothe them for free, they will abandon him." Annas rose from his seat, and said, "Walk with me into my garden. I don't want a chance ear to hear this." They descended some steps and walked about the cultured walkways filled with flowers and fountains.

"Today one of his followers came to me and asked me what it would be worth to me to know where Jesus of Nazareth might be taken," Annas confided.

Caiaphas whirled to face Annas. He grabbed his arm and pulled him to a stop. "What did you say to him? Who was it?"

"I told him," he said simply, "that I had no personal interest in the matter, but that if he would return tonight I would take him to one who might be willing to pay him for the knowledge. His name is Judas Iscariot. He is the one who carries the purse for the disciples of this Jesus."

"I can't see him," Caiaphas said eagerly. "He would know who I am. I would rather some of my lesser priests would confer with him. They could offer him the traditional pay for information. I could hide myself and listen."

"Thirty pieces of silver for a king that would be about right. Yes, hiding would be best," Annas said blandly. What had he ever seen in this man for his dearest daughter? "When you find him, plunge a knife in his heart and have it done. The others will run off readily enough when their leader is dead. Then bury him stealthily. The matter will be over tonight."

"No, he must be brought to face his accusers. It must be a public repudiation. We must make of him a spectacle. Expose him for the fraud he is." Caiaphas couldn't decide who or what he hated more, Jesus of Nazareth, Rome collectively, or Pontius Pilate, personally. "I'd appeal to the Tetrarch, but Herod Antipas is merely a weak fool compared to his great father. That weakling wouldn't dare kill a rodent in his own palace without permission from Rome. We'll get the Romans to kill him for us. That's much the best way."

"How will you manage that?" Annas asked.

"Oh, leave it to me. I've thought about what I'd like to do to this false prophet for a long time, I'll wait until just after the Passover when everyone is sated, and sleeping. There will be just enough time to get it all done before the Sabbath. First, he will face me with his lies. I will sentence him to death." Caiaphas preened himself, and strode along the pathways like a conquering hero.

Annas sighed. "You'd better bring him to me first. I still think a quick, quiet death would be best."

Caiaphas acted as though he didn't hear him. "Yes, tonight we will meet with this Judas Iscariot, and in two days, Jesus of

Nazareth will be ours." He clenched his fists as though Jesus' neck might already be between his hands, then he rubbed his hands in anticipation.

Annas turned his face away to hide his contempt.

"I see," said Annas slowly, "then your hands are to be clean of his blood. It's just as well."

GETHSEMANE

At the foot of the Mount of Olives in the Kidron Valley a short walk from the city of Jerusalem was Gethsemane. It was an old olive orchard, but it had been enhanced with walkways worn by the feet of those who walked there. Random wild flowers like the anemone, or as Jesus called them, the lilies of the field, and the chamomile grew here and there in the grass. The Kidron brook wound through the trees giving life to their roots. After the winter rains, the old orchard was awash with flowers in the tall grass.

It was wild, primitive, and peaceful. Perhaps once an old oil press had been built there, but if so, the building had long fallen into ruin. Now large stones, scattered through the trees were the only reminder of it. The trees themselves were old and gnarled from years of growth. Some had a profusion of branches, and served for a shelter at night. Others had long since given up their lower branches and leaves sprouted from the higher top branches like hair springing from the top of the head.

Other growth was more shrub, or hedge-like, and housed small animals. This more dense vegetation formed walls of privacy and divided the garden into smaller nooks where people could walk and talk without others intruding. Now, during Passover, even though people used the area to camp at night, there were still nooks where people could gather, or walk in comparative peace.

It was here that Jethen led Sherai for a private walk. They had little privacy in their accommodations, and being newly married, they naturally gravitated toward places where they could be comparatively alone. This evening, however, Jethen had important news to impart to his wife, and he felt that this old orchard garden was the perfect spot.

"With the excitement of our wedding, and the subsequent journey to Jerusalem, and our lack of time alone together, there is much for us to talk about," he opened the subject.

"What is it that I need to know?"

"After you left Sychar, I continued to study. A phrase that John mentioned in Jericho kept echoing in my mind, and I wanted to discover what it might mean."

"Which phrase is that? He taught us so many while he was in Jericho."

"The one that kept nagging at my mind was "Behold the Lamb of God, referring to Jesus."

"Yes, I remember that John the Baptist called Jesus that. I believe he was referring to him being born of God."

"There was more to that phrase. You copied it down on one of your scrolls. Have you forgotten it?"

"I'm afraid I have. Lately I have been greatly distracted by a new husband," she teased, and dared to hug the arm entwined in hers.

Jethen refused to be diverted from his concern. There was so little time for them to be alone, and he wanted to tell her what he knew before . . . "Sherai, the complete phrase was, Behold the Lamb of God who takes away the sins of the world."

"I remember. I thought at the time that it was a peculiar phrase even for so unusual a man as John the Baptist to use. I assumed it meant that Jesus' teaching would change the world. Isn't that what you mean?"

"I know I told you and Mother of my conversion that day in the temple. What I didn't tell you was that during the Sacrifice, I saw Jesus across from the Priest's court, and that phrase came into my mind again. 'Lamb of God.' I suppose it was looking at the Lamb being sacrificed that made me think of him being the Lamb of God in a new way. I know that my heart gave a lurch, and it was like being stabbed. Jesus looked at me just then, and it was as though he . . ."

"Why did you never say?"

"I needed to find out for myself if it was true first."

"I know you met him later that morning at the inn, why didn't you ask him?"

"I couldn't. John and Jude were there, and it didn't seem like a good subject to bring up before them. He told me to search for references to him in the Torah, and the prophets. I felt like he was telling me to discover what I needed to know in prophecy."

"You could ask him now, while he is here in Jerusalem."

"I don't need to ask him, Sherai. I know what it means. That's what I brought you here to tell you."

Jethen stopped and looked at his wife. Her dark brown eyes were filled with dread. She knew that he was going to tell her what he had discovered, and that it was going to be hard to accept. "I'm listening," she whispered.

"Let me recite to you what I found. In fact, I found several references, but the one that pointed out to me the meaning of the phrase was contained in Isaiah. Do you remember when Jesus said, "Destroy this temple, and in three days, I will raise it up?""

"I do. I thought that it was a strange thing to say. I know, because of the tour, that it took over forty years to build."

"I don't think he was speaking of the temple, I think he was speaking of his body as the temple of the Lord."

"His body? You mean you think he was telling them that if they destroyed his body he could raise it up in three days?"

"That is what I think. Before you say anything else, let me tell you the rest." He began to recite, with heart-felt clarity, the poetic and terrible words, *'For he shall grow up before him as a tender plant, and as a root out of a dry ground: he has no form nor comeliness; and when we shall see him, there is no beauty that we should desire him.*

'He is despised and rejected of men; a man of sorrows, and acquainted with grief: and we hid as it were our faces from him; he was despised, and we esteemed him not.

'Surely he has borne our griefs, and carried our sorrows: yet we did esteem him stricken, smitten of God, and afflicted.

'But he was wounded for our transgressions, he was bruised for our iniquities: the chastisement of our peace was upon him; and with his stripes we are healed.

"All we like sheep have gone astray; we have turned every one to his own way; and the Lord has laid on him the iniquity of us all.

'He was oppressed, and he was afflicted, yet he opened not his mouth: he is brought as a lamb to the slaughter, and as a sheep before her shearers is dumb, so he opens not his mouth. He was taken from prison and from judgment: and who shall declare his generation? for he was cut off out of the land of the living: for the transgression of my people was he stricken. And he made his grave with the wicked, and with the rich in his death; because he had done no violence, neither was any deceit in his mouth.

'Yet it pleased the Lord to bruise him; he has put him to grief: when you shall make his soul an offering for sin . . ."

Sherai began to tremble. Her body folded over in pain as she clutched her stomach in grief. Tears ran down and soaked her veil. She turned and buried her face in Jethen's shoulder.

Jethen held her as she wept. How could he have expected anything less? He had wept when he had discovered these words and they had stricken his own heart. His own eyes were moist as he again felt the impact of the words he'd said, and his heart contracted at Sherai's grief. Since they had become one it seemed that every emotion she experienced, he felt within himself. She had pricked her finger on her needle, and his finger had throbbed in response. She had laughed with joy as she received a smile from Miriam's baby, and he had laughed. Now he shared her grief as she shared his. Would it always be this way between them he wondered?

At last she withdrew from him, and fumbled in her himation for a kerchief. Finding it she blew her nose, and wiped her eyes. "You are right, I knew as you said it that the passage refers to Jesus. It sounds like his Father is putting him through this, but that the deed will be done by people. Didn't you say, *'when you shall make his soul an offering for sin . . .'*? He's doing it for everyone, Jethen, but how? The Sadducees, Scribes, Priests, and a few wicked Pharisees may hate him, but surely they won't lay him on an altar and kill him."

"I don't know how it will happen. I only know that it will. There is a little more."

"Tell me."

"*because he has poured out his soul unto death: and he was numbered with the transgressors; and he bore the sin of many, and made intercession for the transgressors.*"

"What does that mean?"

"I think it means that he will be killed with other criminals, but his death, unlike their's, will be a sacrifice."

"Jethen," she clutched his robe, "We must tell him. Let's go find him."

"I think he already knows. I saw it in his eyes that day in the temple." A new wave of grief engulfed Jethen as he admitted to Sherai what he had long suspected.

Her voice was urgent as she pleaded, "Then we must tell the others, and protect him. It isn't safe for him here in Jerusalem."

"He knew that when he came here, my love. We can only pray for him. Listen to what he says in the temple tomorrow. It is what he came into this world to do. You wrote it yourself in one of your scrolls. *'I came forth from the Father, and am come into the world: again, I leave the world, and go unto the Father.'*"

"When, when will this happen?"

"That I do not know, but my heart tells me it will be soon. There is one hope."

"What is that hope?"

"He said he would rise up after three days."

"Can a man raise *himself* from the dead?" she asked, and softly began crying again.

"No, but a God can."

PREPARATION

Sherai's heart was heavy that morning when she woke. Since Jethen shared the results of his study with her the evening before, she couldn't shake off the inner wail of impending doom in spite of his hope. She knew that Jethen was worried for all his talk of hope. It was as though they alone, of all the people in the world, knew the bitter truth.

Tomorrow the first day of unleavened bread would begin. That meant that today and most of tomorrow Jesus would be teaching. He and his chosen disciples would be celebrating the Feast of the Passover together, but that didn't begin until sunset tomorrow. Jesus would take advantage of the crowds gathered for Passover to teach his Father's message.

The innkeeper's wife was busy that morning cleaning her inn. The rattle of crockery and the slapping of wet rags invaded ever corner, even the hallway off the room where her guests slept. Evidently the innkeeper's wife felt that one day for cleaning was insufficient.

The day of Passover, one's home was to be thoroughly cleaned and swept so that no particle of leaven might remain.

To the devout innkeeper's wife, it must have taken on the order of a challenge to leave no speck of dust anywhere. Surfaces were being cleaned that had lain in winter's coat of dust from floor to ceiling. Rugs were taken to the roof, and beaten. The inn was such a hive of industry that Sherai felt indolent by comparison.

She greeted her husband with a brief embrace in the common room where a cold buffet had been laid out for the guests. Cold mutton was not to Sherai's taste, but she did nibble on some figs, and took a bit of bread the cook had sliced to tempt the patrons to rid her of its leaven before it would have to be thrown out.

Omini suggested going to hear Jesus speak, but Opar protested, "I have seen nothing of Jerusalem. This is my first visit, and I have only been to the temple amidst large crowds, and had no tour. I dearly wish to visit the market. And I hope to visit the temple grounds so that I might see it in all its splendor. Since the crowds of people are going up on the Mount of Olives to hear Jesus of Nazareth, the city won't be as crowded as yesterday. You'll come with me won't you, Sherai?"

Sherai really wanted to be alone to pray so that peace might settle her heart, but it was not to be. She would just have to find some way to find the peace she sought while at the temple. "You won't be able to see much more of the temple than you saw yesterday, Opar, but they do conduct tours. I think you would find the Bethesda Pools beautiful. If my husband will excuse me for the day, I will go with you. Judith, can we persuade you to come with us?"

"I'll never pass up a chance to go to the market. I'd like to see the city, too. I haven't been to Jerusalem since I was a girl. I think the housekeeper will be glad to see the back of us so that she can get on with her cleaning in peace."

"I think you're right," chuckled Sherai. "They were banging pots outside the doors this morning to wake everyone early. I don't think her cockerels had crowed yet."

"Was that what it was?" Jethen jested. "I thought it was a thunderstorm. I will go with you to the Mount, Omini. What about you, Rabbi Zichri?"

"As tempted as I am to go to the markets, I will simply give you my purse, my dear wife, and go up the Mount with Omini and Jethen," he teased his wife.

Sherai filled her waterskin in the kitchen and carried it back to the room she shared with the other women. It was a large room, and very likely was given to whole families for a common room when Jerusalem was less crowded. Her own cot was behind a screen in the far corner. A large wash basin stood on a narrow table beside the cot. Judith's occupied another corner, and Opar's still another. There was room enough remaining in the center for a low table and several cushions. She took a thin strip of leather and strung it through the slits in a small bag. Into the bag she emptied the coins she had brought into the city. The rest of her goods remained at the caravansary tied up on the camels under the watchful eyes of Jethen's trusted servants,. This bag she tied around her neck, slipping it under her robe. The strap for the waterskin she drew over her shoulder.

"I'm ready," she announced. When she saw Opar's purse tied about her waist, she indicated her own, and Opar quickly hid it in her robes. Judith had already done so. There was no sense in tempting thieves. The three women and their servants made their way to the upper market near Herod's palace.

Sherai was anxious to see Jethen and hear what Jesus had said. The other women retired early, but she was languishing in some cushions waiting to hear the men at the door. At last a key rattled in the lock, and she heard their voices in the hall. "Jethen," she called softly, and he came to her side. "I have waited to hear what the Master taught this day."

Let us go into the common room, it will be empty." Jethen kept his voice low.

Sherai matched him in tone as she asked, "What was your overall perception of Jesus' teaching?"

"My first and lasting impression was that he was following up on his chasing the money lenders out of the temple by rebuking the scribes and Pharisees."

"What? He openly flouted them?"

"He spoke to them specifically. Let me give you an example, 'Woe be unto you scribes, Pharisees, Hypocrites!'"

"He said that?"

"Not once, but several times. Not only did he call them hypocrites, but also blind guides, cups clean on the outside but full of extortion and excess within, and white sepulchers–beautiful to look at, but full of dead men's bones."

"Mercy, did anyone challenge him? That would almost amount to heresy to most of them. Were there many temple priests and scribes there?"

"Yes, I'd say that all those not serving at the temple that day were there. I felt as though the Master was defying them to disagree with him."

"Did anyone challenge him?"

"No one challenged him, but he made some enemies, if the looks on any of the men's faces was enough to go by. He certainly angered them with his words. He criticized some of the lesser laws, accusing them of straining at gnats and swallowing camels."

"What sort of lesser laws?" Sherai wondered.

"Oh, like the laws governing swearing by the gift on the altar of the temple, or swearing by the gold of the temple. He told them that swearing on the temple itself was worse because God dwelled there."

"That makes sense."

"I know it does. After he picked apart their petty laws about how many steps to take and so forth, he concluded his rebuke by telling them that they were the sons of those who had stoned the prophets, and killed those who came in the name of the Lord. Jesus also told them of the destruction of the temple and the desolation of Jerusalem. Many of the scribes and Pharisees left him then, white-lipped and angry."

"What did the Master do?"

"He continued teaching those who remained. He told again some of the parables you wrote down that he taught in Galilee. The day was mostly taken up by men questioning the meaning of some of his parables."

"Did he explain them?"

Jethen chuckled, "Mostly he countered with another parable."

"That's what he did in Galilee. Simon Peter told me he did that so as not to cast his pearls before swine. He would often explain his meaning more clearly to his chosen ones later, in private. I was glad for the explanation on some of them myself."

"I wasn't aware that you were one of the chosen ones, Sherai," Jethen teased her.

"I wasn't," she smiled in the candle's light, "but I wheedled the explanations from James, or John so I could write them."

"I recall reading the one you wrote on the sower and the seeds. I appreciated knowing what that meant."

"That's the one I was thinking of also." Sherai laughed. It was good to have as her husband one who shared her thoughts.

They talked for a while of what Sherai had done that day, then Sherai asked, "Was there anything else I should know that happened with you today?"

"Only that Jesus mentioned he was going to Bethany to Simon the Leper's house to dine, but that he would return to the temple tomorrow. Rise early and we will go together."

"I will," Sherai promised. "God be with you through the night, my husband."

"And with you."

36

SHEEP AND GOATS

Sherai woke the next morning to the same commotion that wakened her the previous morning. Though she had waited up for Jethen last night, she was awake at once. She hurriedly washed and made her way to breakfast.

On this morning the common room was empty. She'd hurried too much. She noted that today there was no loaf of bread on the counter. The remains of yesterday's loaf was hanging over a lamp, tied in a bundle with a cleaning brush and scoop, to signify that the house had been cleaned of leaven. Later that morning it would be burned in the fireplace. In the place of honor was a plate of unleavened bread.

Sherai knew that Jethen would not be eating because as the eldest born son of his family, he was fasting. Perhaps that was why the room was empty, they might all be first sons. Fasting was in memory of the first-born being spared by the death angel when God sent the seventh plague to Egypt.

Tonight all the men, even the innkeeper, would attend a meeting at the synagogue, then return to a lighted house, with the Seder or Paschal Table prepared.

During the day, however, the guests would leave the innkeeper and his wife to prepare the Passover Feast for that night. They all planned to go and hear Jesus speak at the Temple. The day was promising to be clear and warm, so Sherai did not wear her cloak.

She knew at once when Jethen peeped into the common room looking for her. He gave a low snap of his fingers to catch her attention. She walked swiftly to his side.

"Let's go before we are stopped," he tugged her hand.

Feeling only slightly guilty for leaving without their friends, they both hurried out the door with as much quietness as they were capable. In the hallway just inside the outer door Jethen caught her to him and gave her a lingering kiss. His kiss said that he had missed her, and she tried to convey the same. "Good morning, wife."

"Good morning, my husband," she returned. Without another word they slipped out the door into the already busy street. "I wonder what the Master will teach today?"

As they neared the temple grounds they ceased speaking and instead absorbed the sights, sounds, and smell of the city. The smell of smoke and burnt offerings filled the air. The steps and surrounds of the temple were as crowded as the inner courts. Many of the people offering sacrifices were crowded either in the Court of the Women, or the corridor leading to the priest's court. This left the Court of the Gentiles open to those crowding around Jesus. He was talking quietly to his disciples.

When the disciples moved back from Jesus so that he faced the crowd, whatever murmuring or angry words might have prevailed, the courtyard around him became silent.

He began on his favorite theme of the kingdom of God, "The kingdom of heaven shall be likened unto ten virgins, which took their lamps, and went forth to meet the bridegroom. Five of them were wise, and five were foolish. They that were foolish took their lamps, and took no oil with them: But the wise took oil in their vessels with their lamps.

"While the bridegroom tarried, they all slumbered and slept. And at midnight there was a cry made, 'Behold, the bridegroom cometh; go ye out to meet him.'" Sherai squeezed Jethen's hand to remind him of their own wedding procession. They exchanged a smile while Jesus continued, "Then all those virgins arose and trimmed their lamps, but the foolish virgin's lamps had gone out.

"And while they went to buy oil, the bridegroom came; and they that were ready went in with him to the marriage: and the door was shut. Afterward came also the other virgins, saying, 'Lord, Lord, open to us.'

"But he answered and said, 'I know you not.' Watch therefore, for you know neither the day nor the hour wherein the Son of man cometh."

"That seems a harsh judgement," commented one man. The crowd murmured agreement. "They did come to the marriage, even if they were late. How is it they were denied? Tell us another example so that we may compare one to another."

Obligingly, Jesus began another parable, "The kingdom of heaven is like a man traveling to a far country, who called for his servants to impart his goods to them. He gave to every man according to his ability. One he gave five talents, to another two, and to another one; and left on his journey.

"The servant who received five talents went and traded with them, and increased the five talents to ten. Likewise, he that received two also gained another two. But he that received one went and dug a hole, and hid his lord's money in the ground.

"After a long time the lord of those servants returned, and called them to a reckoning. He that received five talents said, *'Lord, you gave me five talents: behold, I have gained five talents more.'*

"He also that received two talents said, *'Lord, you gave me two talents. Behold, I have gained two more talents beside them.'*

"Last, he which received one talent came and said, *'Lord, I know you are a hard man, reaping where you haven't sown, and gathering where you have not strawed. I was afraid, and went and hid your talent in the earth: Here is your talent.'*

"Their lord said to the first two, *'Well done, good and faithful servants; You've been faithful over a few things, I will make you ruler over many things. Enter into the joy of your lord.'* To the other servant he said, *'You wicked and slothful servant, you should have put my money to the exchange, and then at my coming I should have received it back with usury.'*

"Then said their lord, *'Take the talent from him, and give it to the servant who has ten talents. Cast the unprofitable servant into outer darkness where there shall be weeping and gnashing of teeth.'"*

Many of the crowd listening to the parables shook their heads and walked away.

"It seems that they want to hear not of shut doors and taking away, but of giving only," Jethen commented to Sherai.

"Yes, when the kingdom requires something it isn't so desirable to them as when it gives," Sherai answered.

"Hush," someone behind them said, "He's telling another."

It was true, Jesus continued his subject with, "When the Son of man shall come in his glory, and all the holy angels with him, he shall sit upon the throne of his glory. Before him all nations shall be gathered, and he shall separate them one from another, as a shepherd divides his sheep from the goats. He shall set the sheep on his right hand, but the goats on the left."

"And which nation shall be the goats?" called one man in a heckling tone.

"Surely you will be a goat, Asa," his friend replied.

There was some laughter, but Jesus ignored him and continued, "The King will say unto them on his right hand, *'Come, blessed of my Father, inherit the kingdom prepared for you from the foundation of the world: For I was hungry, and you gave me meat: I was thirsty, and you gave me drink: I was a stranger, and you took me in: Naked, and you clothed me: I was sick, and you visited me: I was in prison, and you came to me.'*

"Then he'll say to them on the left hand, *'Depart from me, you cursed, into everlasting fire, prepared for the devil and his angels: For I was hungry, and you gave me no meat: I was thirsty, and you gave me no drink: I was a stranger, and you took me not in: Naked, and you clothed me not: I was sick, and you visited me not: I was in prison, and you did not come to me.'*

"Then shall the people say, *'Lord, when did we see you hungry, to feed you? or thirsty, so that we might give you drink? When did we see you as a stranger, to take you in? or naked, and clothe you? Or when did we see you sick, or in prison, that we might come to you?'*

"Then shall the King answer them, saying, *'Verily I say to you, Inasmuch as you do such to one of the least of these, my brethren, you do it unto me; and when you do not, you do so unto me.'*

"These on my left go to everlasting punishment, but the righteous on my right hand go to life eternal."

After saying this he lifted his hand to signal that he was done with his teaching that day. Jethen took Sherai's arm to lead her away, but she pressed closer to Jesus and heard him say as he turned to his disciples. "You know that the time has almost come for the Son of man to be lifted up. Go and prepare the Passover that we may eat together."

Then and only then did she allow herself to be led away. "Jethen, I heard him tell the disciples . . ."

"Yes, I heard also. Lifted up," he mused and then his face whitened, "Sherai, I think he means crucified! Crucifixion is the death of a transgressor. It is performed by the Romans on their prisoners."

"Is that where they hang them on cross boards and . . . What should we do?" Sherai felt none of the peace she managed to find at the temple.

"We should go and prepare for the Passover as Jesus is doing," he answered her last question, and ignored the first. "We will seek him out afterward and see what he wishes us to do with our knowledge."

PASSOVER

Sherai let the peace of worship settle over her as she, Opar, and Judith helped the innkeeper's wife prepare for the feast that night. The men had gone to their meeting at the synagogue. First the women prepared the table. Since all the guests at the inn that night would be eating the Passover, all the tables were pushed together into one long continuous table. The head of the table was given a special chair on which cushions and pillows had been set to make it comfortable.

Then it was time to prepare the dishes. One large flat dish was set before the chair. On that dish was placed, one at a time, three large unleavened breads or matzoth wrapped in individual napkins stacked one atop the other. Then another plate was set upon the bread. It wasn't as large as the first plate, but it was large enough to hold a shank bone of lamb with some meat still attached. It had been roasted over coals. Also on that same plate they placed an egg that had been roasted in the ashes.

The roasted shank represented the Paschal lamb, and the egg represented free offerings made daily in the temple.

Next the women set the individual prepared bowls of bitter herbs, charoseth (mashed fruit mixed with vinegar), and salt water around the bread on the lower plate. Also all up and down the table cups were set at each place, and an individual wash bow filled with water, flanked by a snowy clean napkin. Decanters of wine were set at intervals along the table. At the opposite end of the table from the plate was an empty place set and reserved for Elias who was expected to come as a forerunner to the Messiah.

The ceremonial portion of the Passover was now ready. The women bustled off to the kitchen to put the last finishing touches on the food served during the feast.

The men soon returned to the inn, and took their seats around the long table, as did the women. Even the servants of the house had a place at the table. Wine was poured into each cup. The headman of the house then rose and thanked God for the fruit of the vine. After offering that prayer he sat and reclining back on his left arm drank the cup. Everyone at the table also drank.

After drinking the first cup, Thomas, for that was his name, rose and washed his hands. After seating himself again he took a small portion of the bitter herbs and dipped it in salt. Reclining back on his left elbow, as a free man and not a slave, he ate it. After Thomas ate his portion, he passed out portions to each of his family and guests, and they ate.

After this was done he removed the top plate and set it aside. He then took the middle unleavened loaf and broke it in two hiding half of it under a cushion to be eaten later. Then he returned the other half to the plate. The people immediately around him, members of his own family stood with him and helped him lift the plate, and everyone stood at the table recited, "This is the bread of affliction that our fathers ate in Egypt. This year here, next year in Jerusalem. This year slaves, next year free."

The plate was then set back on the table, and the plate above it was returned to its place, and everyone sat down.

The youngest son of the innkeeper then turned to Jethen and asked, "Why is it that on this night, of all nights, we eat bitter herbs and unleavened bread? And why is it we recline as we eat?"

Sherai felt so honored to see Jethen singled out to tell the story of the deliverance. She watched as he took the wine and filled the second cup, and began the story of father Abraham, and the children of Israel in Egypt. He told of the boy baby, Moses, who was saved from the water, and how God through Moses led the children of Israel out of slavery in Egypt to be free men. He concluded, "Free men may recline and take their leisure as they eat."

Jethen then praised God for his mercy to his children, and led the others at the table in the Hallel, (or the recitation of Psalms 112 and 114).

After the recitation was over, all drank the second cup.

All washed their hands, and the host took the bread, blessed it, and dipped a portion of it in salt water, and reclining again on his left elbow, ate it. He then prepared portions for each one at the table. Thomas also took bitter herbs and dipped them in the mashed fruit and vinegar and passed them around to be eaten. He then sandwiched bitter herbs in bread, and passed them around in memory of the Temple.

After this, the meal was served. Everyone left the table to bring in soup, fish, meats, and other dishes of great flavor. When everyone had eaten their fill, Thomas stood again, filled his cup for the third time, and blessed the meal. Everyone then drank the third cup. The children ran to their father's chair and searched for the bread he hid. When they found it, he tore pieces of it and gave it to them. This was then divided and shared out among all the guests.

Thomas stood once again, and filled the cup of Elias. This was a solemn moment, and everyone at the table was silent for some time.

Last of all, the fourth cup was filled, and everyone recited the great Hallel (consisting of Psalms 115 through 118), and the prayer of praise, then the last cup was drunk. Afterward Thomas said a prayer asking the Lord to accept what they had done, and the Passover was complete.

BITTER CUP

John was watching his Master. Of late Jesus seemed preoccupied, and given to more introspection than usual. They had been invited to Simon's house, near Jerusalem, for a feast. Right now the Master was studying his disciples. He'd kept his eyes on Judas the longest. John saw the man look up and catch Jesus' gaze, then flush and look down.

Jesus must have felt him watching, for he looked at John then, and smiled, "Simon is blessed to have such an able cook, and the means to provide such a feast. The meal was good."

"You haven't eaten that much of it," John replied. He wanted to ask what was troubling his Master, but they were interrupted by Mary. She entered the room carrying an alabaster box decorated with gold leaf. It was very ornate. She came up to Jesus and broke the seal, opening it.

Instantly a delicious small stole through the room. It was an expensive spikenard. It was earthy, carrying the scent of trees, fallen leaves, soil, flowers, and balm.

It reminded him of Gethsemane. To John's surprise, she poured it on Jesus' head. It ran down his hair, and dripped onto his robe. He breathed deeply of the fragrance, and smiled at her.

A few of the disciples grumbled at this excess. They didn't seem to be pleased with her action.

"Why was this waste of the ointment made?" Peter asked her.

"That box of ointment could have been sold for three hundred pence or more," Nathaniel chastised.

"The money could have been better used to distribute among the poor," Judas protested loudly, and several others murmured too low to hear.

Mary was beginning to feel distress. She knelt at Jesus side, and faced her accusers with tears in her eyes.

"Leave her alone," Jesus said in a mild reproof. "The poor you will always have with you, and you can help them as you will. I will not always be with you. She has done what she could, and she has anointed my head, before time, for my burial. In the future when the gospel is spread over the world, this act will be told, and it will stand as a memorial for her."

Mary looked up at him with gratitude. She rose to her feet, and left the room. She gave of her best to show her love for her master, and the gift had been accepted.

"It's getting late," John leaned over to say to Jesus with a yawn.

"Yes, and early in the morning I must be at the temple to teach one last time. I will soon take my rest."

Jesus raised his hand to signal to his disciples that he had concluded his speaking for that day. They gathered around him protectively. He turned away from the multitude and said, "You know that the son of man is to be betrayed and crucified. Let us take the lamb." They took the lamb they had purchased, and offered it in the priest's court. It was now ready to prepare for the Passover.

"Where shall we go to prepare for the Passover, Master?" Peter asked.

"You and John go into the city. You will meet a man carrying a pitcher of water. Follow him, and when you get there say to the goodman of the house, "The Master says, 'My time has come. Where is the guest chamber that I may eat the Passover with my disciples?'" He will show you an upper room. There you may prepare for our coming in the evening." Peter and John took the lamb and left the temple.

Jesus walked about the temple grounds with Jude and the other disciples. He was stopped by a few people, and he listened to them, but he rarely spoke. It was more often one of his disciples who answered them.

Once Jesus said to Jude, "You are ready, as ready as you can be until the Comforter comes to you."

"Ready for what, Master?" Jude was used to his brother's enigmatic statements, and barely listened to the reply.

"Ready to teach the word," he replied. "How beautiful the temple is." Then he shuddered.

This Jude wasn't accustomed to seeing. "What is it?" he asked. "What's wrong?"

"I saw the temple's beauty for only that first instant. In the next moment I saw its destruction, when one stone would not be left upon another. I saw the holy of holies desecrated, and the priests driven from their place."

Jude digested that vision for a moment before saying, "You see the destruction of the temple in vision?" He couldn't contemplate such an event, and sought to change the subject, and shake Jesus from his mood. "I see that Judas is back. He left for a while this morning."

"Yes, he is back," Jesus said, but he didn't look at Judas. "I will be with you a little while, then I will go away, but I will return and be with you for a while longer."

Jude looked confused, and saw that his friends looked the same. Jesus had said this before, but they no more understood his meaning now than they had then.

"This evening, after the Passover, we will go to Gethsemane," Jesus told them and Judas.

The sun was sinking in the sky as Jesus and his disciples, led by Peter, entered the upper room where the feast had been prepared. All was in readiness, the loaves of unleavened bread, the bitter herbs, the salt water, the lamb. All were there. Jesus took his place at the head of the table.

Jesus began the ceremony of the Passover by filling his goblet with wine. "I very much desire to eat the Passover with you this night, before I suffer," he told them. He blessed it and thanked God for the fruit of the vine and said, "Take this and divide it among you, for I will not drink of the fruit of the vine until the kingdom of God comes.

"When the time comes," he added, "you will all be scattered and fearful. When I am gone, I will send a comforter to you who will explain all things."

"I don't understand," John told him.

"I know, but you will remember my words later."

When all was accomplished, the meat and specially prepared foods were brought in to them. As they ate Jesus said, "One of you sitting at meat with me will betray me. It was better for that man that he never had been born."

John looked about him at the disciples. They all appeared troubled by what Jesus said.

John, who sat nearest him leaned over and said quietly, "Who is it who will betray you? Is it I?"

Jesus answered him as softly, "The one who puts his hand to the sop with me." In the next instant, Judas placed his hand with bread in the sop as Jesus did.

The other disciples began asking, "Lord, is it I?"

"Is it I who will betray you?"

At last Judas, who was the only one who had not inquired said, "Lord, is it I?"

Jesus looked at him and replied, "You have said it."

Then, as though they hadn't understood his words, his disciples began to contend one with another who would be greatest in his kingdom. He had spoken to them on this subject only yesterday. "He who is the greatest is the servant of all," he told them again, patiently. He rose from the table and tying a towel about his waist proceeded to take a basin of water, and kneel down at John's feet. He began to wash his feet.

In turn he went to each disciple and performed this service, but when he came to Simon Peter, he protested against his Lord serving him. "Lord do you intend to wash my feet?"

"What I do you don't understand now, but you will later."

"I will not have you wash my feet."

"If I do not wash your feet you will have no part with me."

"Then wash my feet, my hands and my head," said Peter.

"There is no need to wash but your feet. You are wholly clean. All save one."

Jesus looked up at Judas and saw that Satan had entered into him, "Go and do what you intend quickly," he said to him. Judas got up and left.

John watched him go thinking that Jesus had sent him to perhaps pay for their feast. Then he thought no more of it for Jesus went back to his seat, took off the towel and asked them all, "Do you see what I have done? The master is no greater than the servant. If I have washed your feet, you ought to wash one another's feet. No one is greater in the eyes of God."

He looked at Simon Peter, "Simon, Simon, Satan would have you and sift you as wheat. But I have prayed for you that your faith won't fail, and when you are converted, strengthen your brethren."

Peter protested, "Lord, I am ready to go with you both to prison and to death."

"Peter, the rooster will not crow twice before you have denied me three times."

He washed his hands and took up the bread and broke it, and passed it out to his disciples, "Take it and eat, for this is my body which is given for you. Do this in remembrance of me."

He then took the cup, and filled it. "This cup is the new testament in my blood, which is shed for many."

They all partook of the bread and wine, then Jesus began a hymn of praise to God. They all sang, and then departed for the Mount of Olives.

As they neared the mount, John realized that Jesus walked slower and slower. "What is it, Master? What is troubling you so? Is it the priests at the temple today? Jude told me of your vision of the temple, is it that?"

"I am so bowed down with grief, I can barely move, John. Peter, why do you wear a sword?"

"I wear a sword to defend you, Master."

"There is no need for swords." Jesus and his disciple's feet turned naturally toward Gethsemane. "I do feel the need to pray, to gain strength from the Father. Sit here; watch with me, pray that you are not tempted." John could see that they were sleepy from the meal, and from the wine they had consumed. He doubted they would do much but sleep.

"Peter, James, John," Jesus interrupted his thoughts, "come with me a little way. My soul is very heavy unto death. Pray with me." Peter, James and John settled a bit apart from the other disciples. John vowed in his heart not to forsake his Master.

He watched as Jesus walked about a stone's throw away from them, and threw himself down. "Father, if it is possible, may this hour pass from me? Abba, I know that all things are possible. Is it possible that this cup might pass from me? Nevertheless, heed not my will, but your will be done."

John heard his plea, and watched as an angel came down from his Father to strengthen him. He looked up and saw him come. Then he felt a deep sleep overcome him.

Jethen raced through the city. He couldn't understand his feeling of urgency, he only knew he must go at once to the Mount of Olives and find the disciples. He didn't even know how he knew they were there.

All through their Passover dinner the feeling had grown that he must tell Jesus of the prophecies he uncovered. He feared that Jesus' words the day before had sealed his fate with the leaders of the temple. Sherai, after their dinner, had left earlier than usual to her room for the night. Jethen was too nervous to retire, and he didn't want conversation. He muttered some excuse to Omini, leaving the common area where the men sat and talked.

He let himself out the door, taking his cloak, for the night seemed chill. He carried a small clay lamp with him to help him keep to the path, but in the darkness he still stumbled over rocks. Once he fell spilling some of the precious oil. It ignited a few dry weeds, but he quickly stamped it out and went on up the mount. Each moment was precious. He must find Jesus.

With unerring accuracy Jethen made his way to the exact spot where the disciples slept. Where was Jesus? He carefully stepped past them, and not far beyond he found Peter, James and John also sleeping. There ahead of him was the Master.

He seemed to be weeping, or in torment of some kind. He was alone, with his face to the ground. It was apparent that he was suffering. That much was evident from the lamp's meager light. Jethen made a move to go to him when he was stopped by his spiritual eyes being opened to the sight of an angel bending over him giving him comfort.

With the angel's ministrations, Jesus had risen to his knees, but with his departure the agony seemed to return. Jethen heard him pray more earnestly. Still, he couldn't move from his spot as he witnessed Jesus' untold pain and suffering. He saw sweat as great drops of blood dripped from him, falling to the ground.

All at once Jesus rose from his knees, and went over to Peter, James and John. He didn't seem to see Jethen standing in the shadow of a tree. Jethen heard him say, "Can you not watch with me one hour?" He roused them with his words, "Why do you sleep? Rise and pray lest you enter into temptation."

John shook himself and knelt, but the other disciples slept through his words. Soon John, too, fell over once again in sleep.

As for Jesus, he went back and knelt again. Jethen listened as he prayed "Father, if it is possible, may this hour pass from me? Abba, I know that all things are possible. Is it possible that this cup might pass from me? Nevertheless, heed not my will, but your will be done."

It seemed to Jethen that he wrestled with the heaviness on his spirit again for quite some time. Jethen was unable to move from his spot to go pray with him, so he prayed where he was. "Father, can't you hear him?"

Jethen wasn't sure how long he stood there, or how long Jesus wrestled with whatever burden he carried. He only knew that watching the struggle was terrible. He wanted to go to him, or call out some comfort, but his ability to do so was frozen as were his legs.

At last Jesus rose to his feet again. Heavily he walked to his disciples. They were still sleeping! "You are sleeping? Rise and pray with me." This time not even John roused.

Jethen could feel the sorrow in his voice. He knew he forgave them as he said, "The spirit is willing, but the flesh is weak."

This time Jesus seemed to have no ability to kneel. He fell to his knees. Whatever Jesus was suffering, he was alone. Jethen began to feel that some evil spirit had rooted him to the ground. He tried once again to go to Jesus, but was still unable to move. He could only stand and watch as the waves of agony and pain washed over him. The fragment of scripture came to him, "suffer for the sins of all people."

"Father, if it is possible, let this cup pass from me. If it is not possible, your will be done." Jesus prayed the same words again! Jethen's chest filled with the pain of repressed tears. There was no need, nothing for him to tell, Jesus knew the prophecies better than Jethen. He knew the cup from which he must drink. Jethen felt the tears burn his throat, and sting his eyes. Rooted as he was to the spot, he prayed silently and watched.

Jethen wondered if the same thing that had kept him standing under the tree had overtaken the disciples–keeping them from their vigil. He stiffened when he heard a noise and commotion in the garden. He looked over and saw lights winding up the hill. People who had been sleeping were awakened by the passing of a large multitude from the chief priests, scribes and elders. Some were brandishing swords, and some staves. They were led by Judas Iscariot.

Jesus bent and shook his disciples awake. "Rise up, let us go. He who betrays me is at hand." While he was speaking and walking toward his other disciples, who had already been wakened by the noise, the multitude reached him.

Judas came straight to Jesus and kissed him saying, "Master, Master." The priests, at this signal from Judas, came to lay hands on him and take him.

"Whom do you seek?" Jesus asked them.

"Jesus of Nazareth," spoke the chief captain.

"I am he." The guards stepped back, and some fell to the ground.

Again Jesus asked, "Whom do you seek?"

"Jesus of Nazareth."

"I have told you that I am he. If you have come to take me, let these others go." He indicated his disciples.

The soldiers of the temple came up and tied his hands, and took hold of him.

Jethen stepped forward. The terrible weight holding him to the ground seemed broken. He noticed that his lamp had gone out. He stopped when Peter rose up, taking his sword from its scabbard, took off the ear of one of the guards holding him. Jesus reached up and healed his ear.

"Do you think I could not call upon the Lord," he asked Peter, "And he would give me more than twelve legions of his angels to assist me? Put up your sword in his place. How then shall the scriptures be fulfilled if not this way?" Jethen knew exactly what Jesus meant. He was to go like a lamb.

Jesus then looked out over the multitudes and said, "How is it that you come with swords and staves to take me like a thief? Have I not daily taught in the temple? You stretched out no hand against me then."

"We are taking you now," snarled one of them.

"You'll answer for your devil words," said another.

Muttering and breathing threats, they took him and began to lead him down the hill toward Jerusalem. Jethen stumbled along behind as he watched his disciples flee. Then he noticed that though John and Peter fled at first, they doubled back and followed them afar off. He slipped off to the side and let them pass him. Stark fear, anger and bewilderment suffused their faces. They didn't even notice him standing there.

Jethen followed behind them. He was too heart sore and weary to speak to anyone. Jethen's breathing was rough and ragged. They took Jesus to a palatial house far from the temple in the upper city. What was going on? The guards chased everyone away, but Jethen saw that John somehow managed to be allowed inside before he, too, was turned away.

Running with all his might, he made for the inn. Jesus didn't need him, nor want his help. Staggering into the inn, he made his way to his room. The other two men were sleeping soundly. They didn't hear his ragged breathing, or his sobs.

Falling into his bed, he succumbed to exhausted slumber. His last thought was that tomorrow he would have to tell Sherai all that had happened. What would she think of him for deserting Jesus?

CROWN OF THORNS

As they led Jesus through the streets, John knew that being taken and bound was only the smallest indignity he was to suffer. They were passing the gate that led to the temple, and going south. It appeared they were going to the upper city, not the court of the High Priests at the temple. 'No,' a voice whispered in his mind, 'Annas, first.'

John looked around, to see who spoke, but realized he was too far from Peter to have heard him speak. At least he was no longer mind numbingly sleepy. The terrible deep exhaustion of the garden was gone. New determination filled John's mind. He knew a few people in this city, Annas was one of them. Straightening his back, he followed where the crowd led him.

He knew they had arrived when they came to the door of the gate. There were guards on the gate who only allowed a few through the door. John nodded to one of the guards, and was allowed inside. He grabbed Peter's arm, and followed the group past the courtyard.

Through the house they went until they came to a large room well lit by lamp and candle. Jesus was brought to a large throne-like seat where a large man sat alone waiting. It was Annas. He was past his middle years, but he had lived long and sumptuously as his girth attested. John drew nearer to Jesus.

"Tell me of your disciples and your doctrine," said Annas. He shifted in his seat, and adjusted a cushion behind his back. A servant rushed over to assist him, but he waved him away. His eyes stared intently into those of Jesus.

"I spoke openly to the world. I taught in the synagogue, and in the temple where the Jews gather, and in secret I have said nothing. Why ask me? Ask those who heard me. They can tell you what I said."

A guard stepped forward and slapped Jesus. "Why do you answer the High Priest so?"

John looked in surprise at the guard. Jesus had not spoken servilely, it was true, but he had not been insolent. He saw that the guard sincerely perceived some insult to the High Priest, and because of that, unto God. The guard undoubtably believed he was doing the will of God.

Jesus evidently decided the same, for he told him, "If I have spoken evil, bear witness of the evil. If I have spoken well, why do you smite me?"

Annas sat quietly and studied the man before him. Jesus neither spoke, nor asked any questions. John realized Annas was trying to force Jesus to speak and betray himself. This was all wrong. Annas had no real power in this matter; Caiaphas was the one who should be questioning him. Jesus being brought before Annas was merely a delaying tactic. He was a dangerous man for all that.

After about a half hour of scrutiny, Jesus stood silent before him, and at ease. He was unafraid. It gave John courage, and his fear diminished. At last Annas withdrew his gaze and said to the guard who smote him, "Take him to the High Priest." John knew then that for whatever reason Annas detained them, it had been fulfilled.

They marched Jesus out of the house and down the streets to the High Priest's palace. It was ornate and showy, as all the palaces were, but it was not so grand as Herod's Palace. The wall around it was higher by half again than a man's head. The postern was high and ornate. As they led him through the courtyard, and beyond to the inner rooms, John noticed that Jesus looked back and saw him following behind. Jesus knew that John was acquainted with the High Priest, and seemed unsurprised to find him there, but he looked with a question in his eyes.

John nodded his head as though Jesus had spoken. Jesus had realized Peter didn't know anyone here, and had been left outside the wall. John turned back to the door, and spoke to the servant who stood guard there. "I know that man, Justus, he is with me," said John, pointing out Peter. The servant opened the bars and allowed Peter to slip inside.

"I'm leaving you in the courtyard, Peter. I am known to the servants in the house, but you aren't. Here come over to the fire, and wait for me."

Peter nodded, but said nothing. His eyes kept darting about in fear and mistrust. John left him and followed Jesus inside.

It seemed that the multitude that captured Jesus in the Garden had disappeared. Jesus was surrounded only by the temple guards. He was taken into what was obviously their guard room in the palace. A company of about ten stood about him, and mocked him. They struck him, spit upon him, and reviled him. John stood outside the guardroom door listening, but not daring to enter. When Jesus made no response to their taunting, John dared to walk past the door and look inside. He saw Jesus standing there making no sound.

The guards tired of their reviling, and tried a new tactic. None of them noticed John standing at the door. He watched as they blindfolded him, and then struck him sending him off balance. They taunted him saying, "Prophesy and tell us who struck you."

"Call the Father to come and save you," one derided.

"Nay, let his disciples cut off our ears," another sneered, and tugged Jesus' ear.

"Call down your legions of angels," blasphemed another as he spit in his face.

A soldier brushed past John and entered the room. He came with the order, "Unfold his eyes and take him to the solar."

John stepped back behind a large palm near the door. When they led Jesus out of the room, he was still bound, but the blindfold was off his eyes. The guards took Jesus once again past the courtyard where John had left Peter.

He heard Peter before he saw him. He was swearing and saying, "I tell you I never knew the man." Just then, a rooster ruffled up his feathers, and crowed. Peter looked wildly about, then buried his face in his hands, and wept. Before John turned into another portion of the house and lost him to sight, he saw Peter out of the courtyard. The cock crowed once again.

Jesus was ushered into a large room. They were waiting for him. It was an impromptu court. That was why they had gone to Annas, to give Caiaphas time to call a synod. The high priests, many of them, circled about a large room. Accusers, men he had seen in the temple, and on the Mount the day before stood in a group near a large throne-like chair at the far end of the room. The guards led Jesus to the man seated in the chair of authority, Caiaphas, and left him standing alone.

One by one his accusers stepped forward and bore false witness against Jesus. They should have found better liars, John thought, for no two of them could even agree. They accused him of casting out devils by the power of the devil. They accused him of fraud in his healing. They accused him of saying that he would destroy the temple built by hand, and build it up again in three days without hands. It was obvious that all they had done was listen to his sermons so they could distort his words, or find something with which they could condemn him.

At the last, tiring of the poor witnesses the High Priest stood to his feet and addressed Jesus directly. "Are you going to say nothing? What is it they witness against you?"

Jesus said nothing.

There was only one way they could condemn him to death. Caiaphas puffed himself up and asked, "Are you the Christ, the Son of the Blessed?"

Jesus said, "I am, and you shall see the Son of man sitting on the right hand of power, and coming in the clouds of heaven." John gasped. They wouldn't understand that Jesus spoke the truth to them. They were blind to truth.

The thought was barely in John's mind when Caiaphas tore his robe and screamed, "Blasphemy, he speaks blasphemy. What need have we of any further witnesses? Many of the priests in the circle stood and yelled, "Blasphemy." There were a few who abstained. John ran to old Nicodemus, and looked to Joseph of Arimathaea, and a few others. He knew they believed Jesus, but they did not dare to say it.

Caiaphas was spurring on those he had already stirred to frenzy. He yelled, "You have heard his blasphemy. What is your judgement against this man?"

Many yelled out, "Death,"

"He deserves death."

"Death to the blasphemer."

Many of them came up and slapped him. One covered his face as though he could not bear to look upon him. Some spit on him and slapped him.

"He must suffer death under Jewish law."

"Then we must have a consensus. How do you say, aye or nay," Caiaphas wanted to carry his point without further delay, there was much more to do.

The priests took their seats, and each one cast their vote. Two abstained, and three said nay, but the majority carried the vote.

"There is a consensus," Caiaphas glared at those who disagreed. He might have known that Nicodemus would nay say him. That was why he had started the count on the other side of the room from him.

"We have no power to carry out a death sentence," Nicodemus pointed out.

"He's right," said another one of those who had abstained from condemning Jesus.

"True," acceded Caiaphas, he had prepared too long to be put off by pious old Nicodemus, "but one who does sits in yonder palace." He waved toward the Antonia.

"We will take him to Pilate and demand he be put to death."

"We'll take him before Pilate," others took up the cry as if on cue. John hadn't known despair until that moment. Pilate didn't know Jesus.

Again they marched through the town. This time they went through the temple courtyards. John had no eyes for the proud columns standing in graceful rows, nor for the inner wall that enclosed the temple itself. Jesus had said that the temple would fall. John shuddered in the morning chill.

The sun was indeed rising when they stood in the outer court of the Antonia. The sun shone upon its smooth walls and darkened the interior from their eyes. They stood without and called, for they could not enter this place of Gentiles without becoming defiled. If they became defiled, they could not partake of the Passover that day. Therefore, they stood without and yelled for Pilate.

Eventually Pilate came in answer to their summons. He was irritated because it was early morning, and he was tired of the squabbles the high priests cooked up trying to usurp his power.

Pilate asked Jesus, "Are you the King of the Jews?"

"You say it."

This riled Caiaphas again, and he yelled. "He is no more a King than I am."

"He calls himself the Son of God," yelled another.

"In our religion this blasphemy is punishable by death."

John looked at Pilate who was listening with his head down. Pontius Pilate was a man of intelligence. He could see that the man saw through the priests' charges to the envy within them. Pilate raised his eyes and looked at Jesus.

Still holding Jesus' gaze he told them, "I see no fault in this man."

This riled Caiaphas to a new frenzy. "This man has stirred up Jewry against the Romans. He has said it is unlawful to pay tribute to Caesar. He has stirred up the people starting in Galilee and spreading to this place."

"This man is from Galilee?" Pilate asked. "Then he is under Herod's jurisdiction. Herod is in Jerusalem, I will send him to Herod." He called for some of his soldiers. They took Jesus into their custody and marched him to Herod's palace.

John had slept some the night before, but as far as he knew, Jesus had not slept. Yet he stood silent and regal before Herod. Here was the man whose father had forced his family to flee to Egypt when he was but a babe. Here was the reprobate who had beheaded John. He looked old, disappointed, and dissipated. He also looked excited to see Jesus, curious perhaps. No doubt Herod had heard much of him, and hoped to see him do some miraculous thing in his presence.

Jesus stood silent before the tetrarch while the chief priests accused him again of things he hadn't done because they refused to believe the one thing that was truth.

Herod listened to all their accusations, and questioned Jesus at length. John felt that Herod would have liked to hear Jesus speak, and his questions were varied and eager. Jesus apparently had nothing to say in Herod's presence. He was completely silent.

John actually approved of Jesus' silence in this instance. He might have wished that he would defend himself before the Sanhedrin, but the son of God need not explain himself to a man who had no majesty, and no power except that granted him by Rome.

Herod at last became incensed, and bored by the clamoring of the chief priests. He turned Jesus over to his own soldiers. There he was mocked, and reviled, and Herod called for them to place a sumptuous purple robe on him. Thus robed, Herod caused Jesus to be paraded around his court, allowing others to abuse him as they would. Receiving no satisfaction from Jesus' reaction, Herod tired of the game and ordered him returned to Pilate.

Pilate heard from his servant that Jesus had been returned to him, and came out to face him once more. "Are you the King of the Jews?"

Jesus looked him in the eyes and said calmly, "Do you say this thing of yourself, or did others say it to you?"

"I am no Jew," Pilate exploded. "Your own nation and chief priests have delivered you to me. What have you done?"

John held his breath, would Jesus at last defend himself? Jesus opened his mouth and said, "My kingdom is not of this world. If my kingdom were of this world, then my servants would fight so that I would not be delivered to the Jews, but my kingdom is not here."

Pilate asked him, "Are you a king then?"

Jesus answered him kindly. "You say I am. For this reason was I born, and for this cause was I brought into the world, to bear witness to the truth. Everyone who is true understands me."

"What is truth?" Pilate shook his head and walked away seeking out the priests. "Call your people together," he told them. "I will address them."

Pilate left Jesus waiting inside the Antonia while the priests gathered all the people they could find to fill the courtyard outside the fortress. John, did not speak to Jesus, but waited there inside the great hall of the gentiles to be near him. They hadn't waited long when a contingent of soldiers came and bore Jesus away to a smaller court outside the fortress. There they stripped him of the purple and his own homespun robe. Chaining him to a post, they took turns striking his back with a barbed whip.

With each slap of the whip, John winced as though he suffered the lash. Thirty-nine times they flayed him. Still, he did not speak, nor cry out. John was weeping before they were done. The beating was over, and still Pilate had not called for Jesus, so the soldiers amused themselves by plaiting a circle of thorns for his head.

A bush grew in the outer court, and they pulled long stems from it. There was much cursing and jeering as the thorns pierced their own fingers. When it was finished, they jammed it on Jesus' hair. The blood from the thorns mingled with the last of the spikenard Mary had spilled over his head. They hung the purple robe over his bleeding back and declared him king, mocking him.

It was getting on to noon, and the High Priest wanted Jesus condemned to death. His priests worked feverishly to find people who would be swayed by their words against Jesus. Many strangers from foreign lands were brought to the yard, and many whose jobs were in jeopardy from the courts, or those who owed favors to the temple. When the courtyard was filled, the priests again called out for Pilate.

He came at last leading Jesus out before the people in his purple robe with the crown of thorns on his head. Blood was trickling down his face from the thorns.

John followed Jesus out, and slipped into the crowd. He went over to stand beside Nicodemus. The old man looked ready to faint from fear and grief. John supported him.

"What now?" he whispered.

Nicodemus said sadly, "The time is at hand. The final betrayal of our Lord by his own people is about to be accomplished. There is nothing I can do but go stand beside him, and I have not the courage."

Pilate issued an order, and a large hairy man with the eyes of a zealot was brought out to stand beside Jesus. He was struggling and fighting against the soldiers so hard they had chained him, and bolted iron to his feet.

Pilate stood between them at the top of the steps. "Here you see before you two men. Both of them are Jews. This man," he indicated the hairy man, "Barabbas is accused of robbery, sedition, and murder. This man," he indicated Jesus, "in him I find no fault at all. Herod found no fault in him. Twice you have brought him before me, and still I find no fault in him. During Passover it is our custom to release one prisoner to you. Who would you have me release, this Barabbas, a known murderer, or Jesus of Nazareth?"

Caiaphas screamed as a cue for his people, "Release Barabbas, kill Jesus."

The people took up the cry, "Release Barabbas, crucify Jesus."

John's cry for Jesus seemed feeble. He heard his own voice in his ears trying to yell above the roar of the crowd. Nicodemus tugged at his arm, "Do you want a knife in your back?" he warned.

Pilate called the people to silence by raising his arm. Once again he tried to reason with the people, offering them Barabbas.

"I find no fault in him," Pilate told them, but the crowd, led by the chief priests cried, "Crucify him, crucify him."

Pilate ordered Barabbas freed. The man leaped into the crowd and was gone. Pilate ordered that a bowl of water be brought to him. When it was brought he washed his hands before the people. "This man's blood is off my hands. I order his death by your will, his blood will be upon you."

"Let his blood be upon us, and our children," screamed Caiaphas.

"So be it," said Pilate, and ordered the crucifixion.

"No!" cried John as Jesus was led away from the screaming mob. Urgently he grabbed Nicodemus when the man would have left the courtyard. "Send messengers," he pleaded, "tell the brethren what is taking place."

"Where will I find them?" asked Nicodemus, bewildered. "They have hidden themselves."

"They will be at Joseph's inn in the city. You know where that is. If they aren't there, he will know where they are. They won't leave Jerusalem. Tell his mother," John managed to get out before he ran off after the soldiers, and Jesus.

KINGDOM OF SORROW

Sherai tapped her foot lightly on the bare floor while she waited for Jethen to stop pushing the food about on his plate, and tell her why he had slept so late she had sent a servant in to waken him. He had come to the common room looking as though he had slept in his clothes, and his eyes were trimmed in red. Dark circles like bruises rimmed the red.

She was about to ask him what was troubling him when Jude entered the room. Jethen stood to his feet when he saw Jude, because the normally calm and composed man was distraught. He knew very well why his friend was so upset. What he hadn't expected was his wild appearance. Jude's hair lay about his face in dank, dark straggles. His robe was also damp, and he wore no cloak. His feet were soiled with the dust of the streets mixed with water.

When he saw Jethen he swayed and would have fallen had Jethen not rushed to hold him up. "Sherai, fetch him some wine," he cried. She rose at once to do his bidding.

"The chief priests of the temple have Jesus," Jude blurted. "They took him before the Chief Priests. They accuse him of blasphemy!"

Sherai brought him a goblet of wine, and he drank it down in gulps, then coughed because it was stronger than he was used to drinking. Jude had been shaking when he came in, but the wine seemed to calm him somewhat.

"What do you mean?" Sherai cried.

"They arrested Jesus last night, Sherai," Jethen told her.

Sherai didn't even have time to wonder how Jethen knew, before Jude continued as though neither of them had said a word. "Then they took him to Herod. Herod wouldn't do anything, so they took him to Pilate. They said that he was an enemy of Rome."

"How do you know this, Jude? When was he taken?" Sherai wanted an answer.

"He was taken late last night in the Garden. He was praying when they came like thieves in the night to arrest him."

"How did they find him?" Jethen asked for Sherai's benefit, though he knew full well.

"It was Judas, Judas betrayed him. He told us at the supper that one of us would betray him, and then Judas left. The rest of us stayed with Jesus. Judas came with the temple guards, and he kissed him."

Sherai sounded horrified, "Judas betrayed Jesus with a kiss?"

"Where is John? Where are the others?" Jethen wondered how Jude had found out all this when he had run away with the other disciples at Jesus' command.

Jude drew a deep ragged breath, and then said in a tone too terrible to belong to such a good man, "John is with Jesus. Our mother, and some of the women are with him, but the men, the other disciples have fled in fear. I was told he was carrying his cross to Golgotha. He is to be crucified. I know what happened because John sent a servant to seek us out. He found some of us at the temple looking for Jesus. I sent the servant to our mother, and she and the other women went to the Antonia where they held him. They were barely in time to follow him to Golgotha." The chill of his voice as he said the word warned them of its danger.

Jude's voice was filled with sorrow, "He told us to flee. He knew . . . he knew he would be crucified. He warned us . . ." Jude sank onto a chair. "I think John is the only one who believed him." Tears coursed down the man's face. "The rest of us are just afraid."

"It seems to have happened very quickly." Jethen looked helplessly at Sherai. His foreknowledge was making him feel slightly ill.

"They've been plotting against him since before he raised Lazarus from the dead," Jude reminded him. "We tried to persuade him to stay out of Jerusalem, but our pleas were in vain. They accused him of blasphemy because he said he was the Son of God. Blasphemy is punishable by death. Why didn't he stay in Galilee?"

"But he *is* the son of God," protested Sherai. "It isn't blasphemy if it's the truth."

Jethen caught his breath on a sob. Bless Sherai for her simple sublime faith. It was too bad there was nothing they could do. The knowledge Jesus had commanded them to discover helped no one.

Evidently Sherai thought differently, "Jude, listen to me," she urged, "John wasn't the only one who believed him. We believed him, too, Jude, Jethen and I. Remember he told us to go home and study the prophets? It was prophesied long ago. The prophets told of his birth, and that he would be born of David, but they also foretold of his death at the hands of his friends. It was one of the minor prophets, Zephania. '*One said to him, what are these wounds in your hands?*'" she quoted, "'*Those with which I was wounded in the house of my friends.*'"

Jude looked up at Sherai with hope, "Did these prophets say he would rise again?"

"The prophets said that he would come with power and great glory; that his kingdom would never end. What do you think? Has he come with power and great glory to this world yet?"

"What about his entry into Jerusalem?"

"Jerusalem isn't the entire world, Jude." She waited for him to grasp what she said.

Jude answered her hesitantly, "He did say he would leave for a while, then come back for a short time. I must go and tell the others." Jude spoke with more calmness, and his voice carried a little hope. He added, "It is completely dark outside. Did you know? The heavens have shut their face against this atrocity. I must go and tell others," He got up to go to the door, but turned back. "You are of us," he told Jethen and Sherai. "Would you remain in Jerusalem?"

"We will." Jethen promised.

"Would you care to come with me now?" The man tentatively offered.

"We can't come with you just yet. Where are you staying?"

Jude told him the location of the upper room where they had last supped with so much joy.

"We'll know where to find you. Will you keep the Sabbath there?"

Jude nodded, "It should be safe there for a while. The owner is a follower of Jesus."

"Then I think we will go to Golgotha, Jude. Our friend may have need of us."

"We must stand as his witnesses," Sherai added, as though it was the most natural thing in the world.

"Tell John you saw me, and Peter, if you see him." Jude raised his hand in farewell, and left as abruptly as he came.

"I don't think you should come with me, Sherai. It won't be . . ."

"We are one, Jethen. You did say, 'we,' remember?"

"It is nearly the Sabbath. We will have to return here before sunset."

"They may need help with Jesus." Sherai grabbed her cloak from a rack near the door. As they stepped outside she understood what Jude meant by dark. "I'd best go in and fetch a lamp," she told Jethen.

"Stay, I'll fetch one for each of us, although I doubt its light will penetrate much of this darkness." Jethen went back indoors, and took his own cloak from the peg. He was so upset he wasn't in the least cold, but Sherai might have need of it later.

They made their way through the dark streets. It seemed that everyone was indoors now probably to escape the darkness, or to prepare for the Sabbath, and it was also the second day of the Passover. They couldn't see lights from the windows until they were almost up even with them. The darkness was like a thick mist. For all they knew the sun might have left the sky.

Jethen took a deep breath and told Sherai all. She was totally silent for a few minutes then she said, "I'm sure you did all you could." She hugged him to her for an instant of comfort. Then releasing him she said, "Why is it dark? There is no rain, only this thick mist," Sherai shuddered and drew her cloak close around her. "I've never seen anything like it."

"You've never seen a God being killed," Jethen reminded her. "Sherai, what about my deserting Jesus?"

"Jethen, I am upset that you didn't tell me. If you had come and told me of your concern, I would have gone with you. That is my only complaint. I would have done exactly as you did in the circumstances. If the guards sent you away, they would have sent me away as well," She said as if that settled it, and maybe it did. Jethen drew the first deep breath in relief. Then she said,

"You are right, Jesus is a God, I know it. You know it, too. How will they be able to kill him? Aren't Gods immortal?"

"I don't know, I haven't much experience in this, myself," he shook his head, but doubted Sherai could see it. "I don't mean to make light of your questions, Sherai, but I don't know the answers. Didn't Jesus say that no man had greater love than one who would lay down his life for his friends? What if he was speaking of himself? I think he was. There must be some way he can lay down his life and die. He will then take it up again. What did he say at the temple that day, that in three days he would raise it up?"

"He did say that. I should have reminded Jude of it," she berated herself.

"I doubt if Jude would have accepted it. He was more ready to listen to the prophets than to his own brother, remember?"

"I imagine it would be difficult to think of your brother as the son of God." Sherai admitted.

Privately, Jethen agreed. They traveled on for several more minutes. "I never thought to ask where Golgotha is," Jethen commented. "How is it that you know where to go?"

"I was following you."

"We really are the blind leading the blind. Let's stop and think a minute." Jethen drew Sherai under an awning which dripped moisture from the mist along the edges. "It makes sense that they would execute prisoners outside the city, and outside their fortress. I suppose I've heard mention of the place, before today."

"Tombs are always located outside the city walls, my guess would be northward of the Antonia." Sherai volunteered.

"Yes, let's make our way to the temple. At the least there should be someone about there who can tell us where to go." They stepped out into the street, and kept going until they reached one of the gates.

"Here we are at the temple. How still it seems. It's so quiet its almost like a large tomb. I don't think there is anyone about to ask."

Sherai shivered, more from reaction than to chill. "Where do we go from here?"

"Let's cut through the courtyards. It will take some time off our journey and I feel a need for haste. We'll stop at the Antonia." Jethen told her.

Their instincts were correct. A detail was just leaving for Golgotha as they arrived at the Antonia Fortress. They simply followed them out of the city, and met with others on the road intending to observe the spectacle.

They knew when they had nearly arrived, for lightning began plying the skies. Though Jethen knew what to expect, the sight of the three occupied crosses tore at his heart. His breathing hastened like the night before, as though he ran. From afar off it looked wrenching, up close would be worse. Wanting to protect her from the sight he urged, "Sherai, I have seen enough to witness it. Let's go back and wait with the others."

"You wish to leave John to face this alone?" Sherai said the one thing to stop selfish flight. Jethen clenched his jaw, and trudged forward. If she could bear it for John's sake, he could.

The detail left the road, and moved up the incline behind the crosses. The trusses that supported the cross were built of beams. They looked like whole trees stripped of their bark and branch. Soldiers were loitering beneath their skeletal remains. A few soldiers knelt down casting lots.

"Look," Jethen pointed them out. "They are casting lots over his raiment, just as one of the prophets said."

Sherai didn't say anything. She was steadily looking up at the man she had followed from the well in Sychar. The man, who had given her living water, so that she might never thirst again, was hanging suspended from a cross with *nails* driven through his hands and his feet. That gentle loving man who had healed the sick, and raised the dead wore a crown of thorns jammed on his head. His head, there was something above his head, a sign of some sort. She moved closer, and waited for a streak of lightning to read by.

"This is Jesus the King of the Jews." She caught back a sob. The Romans were killing more than a king.

Jethen heard her sob, and drew her close to him as much for his comfort as hers. He looked up at Jesus, and noted that he said nothing. His blood slowly and steadily dripped to the ground.

His outstretched arms must have ached trying to hold up the weight away from the nails ripping at the flesh in his hands. His feet were nailed to a small platform affixed to the cross, and that bore his weight, for as long as he still had the strength to push against it.

Into the silence of grief one of the thieves hanging beside Jesus derided him, "If you are Christ, save yourself and us."

The thief on the other side rebuked him, "Don't you fear God? You are suffering the same condemnation as he. We are justly punished for our deeds, but this man has done nothing amiss."

Then that same thief looked to Jesus and said to him, "Lord, remember me when you come into your kingdom."

Jesus turned his head toward the second thief and said, "This day you will be with me in paradise."

At last Jethen noticed John. "John," he called to him with a depth of sadness in his voice Sherai had never before heard.

"Jethen, Sherai, you shouldn't be here." John said something low to the woman beside him, and came over to them.

"Neither, my friend, should you, nor should he," Jethen jerked his head toward Jesus.

"I couldn't leave him to go through this alone," John told him. "When he told me what would be, I determined then that I would follow him come what may. They didn't want me, only him."

He nodded toward the priests and scribes from the temple. "They've been here the entire time. You should hear what is coming from their lying, hypocritical mouths."

Sherai said, "It will only be for a little while, then he will come again. Remember what he said at the temple? In three days he said he will build the temple back up."

Just as she said it one of the priest's nearer Jesus called out in impudence, "He said he would destroy the temple and build it up in three days, why can't he save himself."

"Do you believe that, Sherai?" John asked her.

"Yes," she said, "I do."

"Earlier," John choked, "he asked the Father to forgive them. He gave me the care of his mother. Still he thinks of others before himself."

As the words fell from his lips, the man on the cross opened his eyes. He looked down upon his friends, and though it was obvious he was in agony, he seemed to study them.

When the chief priests who were standing near by noticed his eyes opened, one mocked him, "If he is King of Israel, let him now come down from the cross, and we will believe him."

Another mocked, "He saved others; himself he cannot save."

The soldiers also came up offering him vinegar and saying, "If you are king of the jews, save yourself."

Jesus ignored them, and spoke not a word. Instead, he concentrated his effort in a look of compassion upon them.

As the time wore on, and more people passed by they heaped scorn upon him. Another time one of the priests called out to the people standing about, "If you be the Son of God, come down from the cross." It was nearing the ninth hour, and still they called out to add as much as possible to his suffering.

Jethen clinched his fists, he wanted to go over and punch the priests' words down their throats. While it may have relieved his feelings, it would not have helped his Master. Instead, when he calmed himself, he looked up at Jesus. The man hung there in obvious agony, yet he neither whimpered, nor spoke. All at once Jethen found he wanted at that hour to be as much like his Master as he could.

Rather than hate those men, he remembered what Sherai had written that Jesus said in one of his sermons, *'Blessed are you when men shall revile you and persecute you and say all manner of evil against you falsely for my sake.'* He had also admonished his disciples to love their enemies and do good to those who despitefully used them. Taking a deep breath he said, "I can do that."

"What did you say, my husband?" asked Sherai.

Tears flooded her eyes as he answered her, "I can love my enemies if he can." Jethen stood a little taller, and looked up at Jesus as if he could commune all his love and admiration for him without words.

How long they stood there Jethen never knew. It was the worst lightning storm he could ever remember in his entire life. It played over the hills, striking the ground. The lightning repeatedly struck Jerusalem.

There was no rain, just darkness, the lightning, and that terrible thick mist. Near the end they saw Jesus lift his head to the heavens and call, "Father, Father, why have you forsaken me?" Jesus head sank once again on his chest when no answer from the heavens seemed forthcoming.

It tore Sherai's heart, she sobbed, seeking comfort in Jethen's arms. "This awful darkness," she wept, "It *is* as though God turns his face from this wickedness."

"Perhaps he has. The heavens certainly seem to reflect his displeasure. I've never seen such darkness as this."

They stood together watching, bearing witness to the tragedy. They were determined to remain until the end. Both of them prayed quietly.

It wasn't long afterward when Jesus lifted his head one last time and in a clear voice said, "It is finished. Father, into your hands I commend my spirit." He then closed his eyes, and sagged on the cross.

A centurion stood nearby, and heard Jesus say it. He then muttered, "Glory be to God, certainly this was a righteous man."

Sherai wept softly, as did Jethen. He knew it must be drawing on toward the Sabbath, because the soldiers at the far cross, to hasten the death of the malefactor, broke the thief's legs. They then marched to the other thief and broke his. When they came to Jesus the centurion said, "This man is already dead."

A soldier remarked, "He cannot be dead so soon." He took his spear and thrust it into his side. Blood and water gushed out, but Jesus was dead.

"Is he dead?" One of the temple priests came up to the centurion and asked.

"He is dead," the centurion answered. "You can go and tell Caiaphas that the deed is done. The King of the Jews is dead."

"He's not our king," hissed the priest in anger. He called to his fellow priests, and they drew their robes about them and left Golgotha.

People standing about smote their breasts, and then departed. Jethen went to John who was comforting Jesus' mother. Sherai wept with the other women who stood there mourning Jesus. The lightning stopped as suddenly as it came, the mist began to dry, and the clouds rolled away.

JOY IN THE MORNING

Since the Sabbath had come so quickly after Jesus' death, they barely had enough time to take his body and wrap it in linen. Joseph of Arimathaea, a priest of the Sanhedrin who had not supported Jesus' arrest, begged Pilate for his body. Permission was granted, and he helped them carry the body of Jesus to his burial in Joseph's own tomb.

The hardest thing Jethen had ever done in his life was help the men roll a stone over the door of that tomb, and leave Jesus. Even leaving Sherai on the mount that day in Capernaum hadn't been as difficult. The priests from the temple posted a guard to make sure that none of his followers would have the opportunity to move the body during the Sabbath, and claim he had risen from the dead.

Jethen and Sherai kept the Sabbath with the other disciples in the upper room. That night they gathered one by one as if drawn to the room where last they talked with their Master. Peter was the last to arrive. He came to the door, noted who was there, then walked to a far corner in the shadows. He didn't move from his spot.

They discussed every word John told them of the arrest, trials, and crucifixion. When John was finished with his story, Peter confessed that he also had followed Jesus, and how he had denied him. Again he wept, but his countenance was not as bleak. The disciples came to him in a great outpouring of love, and told him of their own fears.

John clasped Peter to him, and said, "Don't grieve over your mistake Peter, Jesus would not want you to let it ruin your life. He understood your fear."

"I thought I was so strong," Peter sobbed. "I was the first to betray him."

"No," Thomas growled, "Judas was the first."

"You are our leader, Simon Peter, now that the Master is gone. He was the one who gave you the name Peter, and you are to be our guide."

"You have chosen a poor guide," he murmured.

"Not so," James told him. "You will be the stronger for your repentance. You have taught us all the way."

One by one they confessed their own fears of that night. They each forgave each other their weaknesses, and resolved to follow Jesus' commandments from henceforth. There was healing in the room. The chosen twelve, only eleven now, drew closer to one another. The others in the room rejoiced to see their merging strength in the face of the severest trial of their lives.

The next day they prayed, sang hymns, talked of Jesus, and wept. Each person in the room, even the children, repeated those sayings of his which were their most favorite, and his parables. They discussed what they felt the meaning of each was, and how they could live to obey. They talked of his miracles, his faith, kindness, and all they knew of his life.

No one had felt much like eating all that day. Those in the room with children saw that they were fed, but even the children seemed hungrier to talk about Jesus than eat. During that evening they had a light supper offered them by the man who lent them the room. Peter stepped forward then and blessed the wine, blessed and broke the flat bread, and passed it among those present. It was the third day of the Passover. Rather than recite together, Peter repeated what the Lord had said during their last supper together.

After the last hymn was sung, most of the people took to the walls, and laid out cloaks. Those with children put them to bed. Most of the women soon retired, whether or not they slept was another matter. Most likely they listened to the men as they sat talking quietly in the center of the room.

The next morning, Sherai was still sleeping on her cloak when Jethen awoke at the sound of the women gathering linens, spices, and herbs to attend Jesus' body. There had been time for nothing else the evening before the Sabbath, that was why the women left as early as sunrise this first day of the week to attend to his body. This was their first opportunity to tend to his burial.

Jethen arose and saw Matthias was already awake, and sitting at the table in the center of the room.

"You are awake early, my friend."

"I couldn't sleep, Jethen. My old bones don't care much for the floor," Matthias said.

"I still prefer the floor to the ground with sticks and rocks to poke holes in me," Jethen told him. "The women are off early to the tomb. Who went?"

"Mary Magdalene, Mary the mother of James, Salome, Joanna, and a few others. Nicodemus gave them a hundred weight of herbs and spices for the burial. Do you know Nicodemus?"

"No, I never met him. Is he here?"

"No, he is one of the high priests of the Sanhedrin. He has followed Jesus teachings from afar. He is one of his most ardent believers. He and Joseph of Arimathaea are at least two of the priests we spoke of yesterday who did not condemn Jesus as a blasphemer."

"That must have made them quite unpopular in the court."

"Unpopular with Caiaphas at any rate." Matthias sighed, "I haven't felt this old since the morning I woke up from the beating you saved me from."

"Let us speak no more of that, my friend. Jesus healed you, didn't he?"

"Yes, I felt the renewed vigor of a much younger man. How could Jesus' goodness be interpreted as anything other than what it was?" Matthias buried his face in his hands, and slow tears leaked through his fingers.

Jethen moved to put his arm about the shoulders of the older man. "Envy and a lust for power can deny any good thing. Take heart, Matthias, all is not lost."

"I fear all my dreams are lost with the death of that great man," he said through his tears.

"Do you forget so soon what John said? Jesus gave up his life, they did not take it from him. I believe there is hope."

By this time others in the room had begun to stir. Sherai sat up in her spot and began combing her hair with her fingers beneath her veil. The children were clamoring to be fed, and the servants of the house chose that moment to enter with bowls of steaming grains, and pots of honeycomb.

The breakfast was cleared away, and many were making ready to return to their own lodging with the agreement to meet again that night when a stir from below stairs captured their attention. Someone was running up the stairs.

Mary Magdalene ran into the room, and collapsed on a chair completely out of breath. She clutched her side and drew deep breaths. Her breathing was ragged, tears coursed down her face. Everyone gathered round her to hear the news.

When she had recovered herself enough she told them, "The tomb is open! What should we do? Jesus' body is gone."

"What? Where are the guards?"

"They lay on the ground like dead men," she told them.

"Who could have taken him?"

"When?" Everyone awake was questioning Mary's report. She ignored them to listen to Peter.

Peter said, "John and I will go and see. James, you remain here with Mary and the others."

"No, I am going back with you. The other women went to inquire where they had laid him, but I came to tell you. I'll go back with you." Mary was adamant.

"I'll remain here in case the other women return and bring word," James told Peter. "You two go."

John took off at a run, and Peter was not far behind him. Mary ran out after them.

Sherai came to Jethen. "What is it Jethen? The tomb is empty? What is happening? Is it as we thought?"

"I believe so, wife," Jethen almost shouted in his joy. "Let's go to the tomb and see for ourselves."

THE EMPTY TOMB

John was the first one to reach the tomb. It was as Mary had said. The stone was rolled from the door. There were no guards lying as dead men, evidently they recovered, and were gone. He went to the sepulcher and did not enter it. Stooping down, he looked in and saw the linen clothes lying there folded on the slab.

Peter caught up with him at last. He could hear him coming from a way off because his breathing was ragged, and labored. He ran past John, and ducking his head went right into the tomb. He looked about him wildly, and saw what John had seen from the door, that the tomb was indeed empty. The napkin that had lain over Jesus' face was neatly folded and lay in a place by itself at one end of the slab, while the linens were at the foot.

"It is true," he whispered, but the acoustics of the tomb sent his whisper out to John.

John entered into the tomb then, and looked at the linen lying neatly folded. "It is true," echoed John quietly. "He has risen. He is the Christ, the Son of God, just as he said."

Peter rubbed his eyes, they were smarting with tears. They had ignored Mary who still stood outside the tomb weeping. Peter and

John told her that the tomb was empty, and that Jesus had risen. "We are going back to tell the other disciples," Peter told her.

They left the tomb, and began walking back to the city. They encountered Jethen and Sherai as they approached the tomb.

"It is empty, isn't it?" Sherai rejoiced.

"It is," Peter laughed.

"Praise be to God," shouted Jethen. Jethen and Sherai, passing Mary, went to the tomb and looked in, but they didn't enter. They tried to comfort Mary but she remained behind, weeping.

When everyone had gone, Mary bent and looked into the tomb for herself. It was no longer empty! Two angels sat inside on the slab, one at the head, and one at the foot where Jesus had lain.

One of the angels said to her, "Woman, why do you weep?"

Crying she said, "Because they have taken away my Lord, and I don't know where they have laid him." She loved him so, he had changed her life.

The woman was so distraught with grief she didn't acknowledge the presence of angels. She withdrew her head and turned to start back to the upper room when she saw a man had been standing there behind her. She supposed he was the gardener. He was standing in the sun, and her eyes were filled with tears. Her heart was desolate. The man who saved her soul from endless torment, and filled her life with purpose and meaning had been senselessly murdered. She felt like her own life was over.

He said to her, "Woman, why do you weep? Who do you seek?"

She said to him, "Sir, if you have taken him away, will you tell me where you have laid him so that I may go and recover his body?"

Then the man said, "Mary!"

Mary ceased her weeping. It couldn't be true. She wondered if grief was destroying her mind. That voice! No one said her name quite like that . . . He said her name, she realized–it was *Jesus*. Mary's eyes were opened, and she saw the man clearly. It *was* her beloved Master. Eagerly she reached out her arms to him, "Rabboni!"

Jesus, ever compassionate could not bear her grief. He stepped back from her and said, "Do not touch me. I've not yet ascended to the Father. Go to the brethren for me and tell them that I ascend to my Father and their Father, to my God and their God." Then he vanished from her sight.

"But there's so much more I want to know," she found herself wondering whether she said it aloud, or cried it in her heart. How long she stood there staring at the spot, she didn't know. What she did know was that her heart rejoiced while her mind reeled at the unexpectedness of his appearance to her.

Then it came to her that those beings she had seen in the tomb had most certainly been angels. She ran back to the tomb, but it was dark and only the linens remained. "Thank you, Father God," she said. She must return to Jerusalem and tell everyone that she had seen Jesus alive and well.

The other women who had gone to inquire after Jesus, Mary, Salome and Joanna, having no success in finding anyone to tell them anything, returned to the empty tomb. They encountered something they didn't expect.

They discovered a being in shining white sitting on the stone outside the sepulcher! They trembled in fear to see the man as bright as the lightning that had split the earth three days before. His raiment was as white as the sun shining on newly fallen snow.

The angel said to them, "Don't be afraid. I know you seek Jesus who was crucified. Why seek the living among the dead? He is not here. He is risen as he said he would. Remember when he said to you in Galilee, 'The Son of Man must be delivered into the hands of sinful men, and be crucified, and on the third day rise again?'"

"I remember," said Mary the mother of James.

"Yes, I remember, also," said Salome.

"And also I," Joanna agreed.

"Come and see the place where the Lord lay," said the angel.

The women timidly entered and found the tomb empty. When they came back out the angel still sat upon the stone.

"Go now," said the angel. "Tell the disciples that Jesus goes to Galilee, and he will see them there."

The women left the tomb. "I never thought to see an angel until I died," said Salome.

"I still can't believe an angel told me that Jesus is alive!" exclaimed Joanna.

"It's time we're getting back to tell his disciples what we've seen and heard," urged Mary. "Rejoice, our Lord has triumphed over death!"

"Praise be to God," they were saying among other rejoicing. They were hurrying to Jerusalem when they met Jesus.

He greeted them, "All hail!"

The trembling women came up to him and fell at his feet. They touched those feet[1], and worshiped him. "Fear not," he told them gently, "go and tell my disciples I will see them in Galilee," and then he left them.

"We saw him, we touched him," they rejoiced to one another. Filled with joy and happiness, the women made their way back to Jerusalem to tell the glad tidings to the disciples.

---

[1] Although Biblical text does not mention why these women could touch him and Mary Magdalene could not, perhaps by this time he had returned to his Father and could accept their touch.

43

BELIEVE

It was drawing nigh to dusk. It was the fourth day of the Passover, and many had returned to their homes. Cleophus, his wife Mary, and their friends left for Emmaus. Other of the followers of Jesus also returned to their homes leaving the eleven after hearing tidings from Mary Magdalene and the others. It was as if they hadn't believed what the women told them.

Matthias and Lydia remained, as did some of the others. Most of them didn't believe the women, but that didn't stop them from questioning them over and over. At least they were willing to hear further. Jethen told John that he wanted to hear from them before they left for Galilee. He and Sherai were planning to go with them and see to their house in Capernaum. Besides, if Jesus said he was going to see them in Galilee that is where they wanted to be.

"What is Simon Peter going to do?" asked Sherai.

"He asks us that we all call him Peter, for that is the name Jesus gave him, and he will not suffer to be called by any other, now." John told them.

"Where is Peter?"

"He has gone to talk with the man who allowed us to use this room. Since most of them are leaving this morning, he wanted to secure the room for a couple more days. He doesn't think it is wise to be about in Jerusalem just now. The priests are on the lookout for us, or so Nicodemus told John." Jude added.

John came up to them to take leave of them. "Peter, James, Andrew, and I are going to Bethsaida where we live. A few of the disciples will most likely come with us. You are welcome to come join us there after you have seen to your house."

"Thank you, John. I believe we will come to you. We want to be a part of whatever you decide to do."

"That you will," John shook his hand warmly.

Jude also bid them farewell. "God be with you until we meet next," he said.

Jethen and Sherai returned to their inn. Omini, Opar, Judith and Zichri met them at the door. Since rooms were freed by people leaving the inn, they each now had rooms of their own, and Opar led them to the one given them. The large room where the women slept had now become their common room where they could meet, she told them.

"Omini has been worried for you, especially after we heard about Jesus. Your little maid, Abagail, has wandered about like a little ghost."

"Oh," Sherai was stricken, "I should have told her something."

"She's well, I took care of her. She has been sleeping with Eliza in a little room off the kitchen. Come over to the common room as soon as you can, and tell us what happened."

"We'll be down as soon as we've refreshed ourselves. Have Abagail send hot water. A change of clothing is greatly needed." Jethen told Opar.

Sherai hugged Opar. "Thank you for caring for Abagail. I'm so sorry we worried you. Thank you for getting us this nice room."

"Yes," Jethen added, "Tell Omini we'll settle up accounts later." Opar nodded, and left them.

They entered their room and shut the door. They were alone together for the first time in over a week. Their move toward each other for comfort was as natural as the sun rising. "So much has happened," Sherai said through tears.

"You are exhausted, my dear wife," said Jethen, and took her in his arms. "Shall I go down and appease our friends while you rest?"

"No, I want to be with you," Sherai pulled herself out of his arms after several kisses. "I can't let you face the wrath of Omini alone," she laughed.

Pleased to hear her laughter after so much sadness Jethen said, "You really do believe he rose from the dead, don't you Sherai?"

After so much weeping at his cruel death Sherai was pleased to answer, "Yes, don't you?"

"I couldn't mistake the joy on Mary Magdalene's face or the joy of the others as they spoke of the angels. Yes, I do believe, but will the others? Some of the disciples didn't believe, you know."

"I don't know if our friends will believe, but the sooner we get down there to tell them, the sooner we will find out."

Omini scolded, "You left the inn without a word to any of us. The next thing we know it is being noised at the temple that Jesus of Nazareth has been crucified. We returned to the inn to find you gone. We have worried about you, for all we knew you had also been arrested."

"You should have left us word, children," said the Rabbi.

"I am sorry to cause you so much worry," said Jethen. "Sherai and I felt that John had need of us after we learned that Jesus was arrested. Let us tell you all. You will be content."

"Come and sit here by the fire, and I'll go out to the kitchen for some food. You both look half starved," Judith told them.

Jethen and Sherai obediently sat, and related all that had taken place since they left the inn on Friday afternoon. They also told them what Jude had said to them to make them leave in the first place.

Food came, and they all ate while they talked.

"The tomb was empty?" the Rabbi asked in shock.

"Yes, I tell you Jesus has risen from the dead."

"That's not what we heard," denied Omini. "The guards are noising it about at the temple that his disciples came in the night and stole his body to make it appear that he had risen."

"You may be sure that did not happen. Sherai and I were with them all night, and no one left. It was the Sabbath, after all."

"That's why when you returned you didn't look as sad and grieved as we expected you to look," mused Rabbi Zichri.

"We were saddened by his cruel death, Rabbi, but we were too exulted about his glorious return to grieve long."

"Let Jethen tell you what the women said who went to the tomb to tend to the body this morning," Sherai urged them.

Jethen told them every word that the women had related to them about the visit of angels, and seeing Jesus in the flesh standing before them.

"The women saw angels? I've always wanted to see one." Opar breathed in rapture.

"You surprise me, my dear," said her husband. "I see one every day." He took her hand and kissed it. Opar blushed a thousand shades of red.

Judith didn't say anything. She just looked stunned, and thoughtful. Eliza and Abagail, who were also there for the telling, looked shocked as well.

"It seems odd that he didn't appear to the men who followed him so ardently," commented Rabbi, Zichri. "I think I will believe your story when *they* have seen him."

Omini nodded his head in agreement. Surprisingly, Judith disagreed with them. "There is no reason not to believe the account of the women. Knowing the kind of man Jesus is, he would not want the tender-hearted women to suffer his death a moment longer than they had to. Think what a comfort his resurrection is to his mother," she added.

"That is what I think, too," Sherai supported her.

Their discussions were interrupted by Omini and Judith's servant coming to announce dinner in the common room of the inn. They all went down to dinner, but they didn't stop talking about the events of the past three days.

It almost seemed natural when the meal concluded and they still sat at the table talking, that John should enter the room. His face glowed, and his eyes sparkled with happiness. "I have seen him," he announced. "I wanted you to be the first to know. Jethen, you and Sherai believed before anyone, and I wanted you to know that I've seen him."

"Praise be to God," shouted Jethen.

"Do you mean to say that Jesus, himself, appeared to his disciples after his death?" questioned Rabbi Zichri. "Was he a spirit?"

"No, Rabbi," John answered him, "he appeared in the flesh. His body was a solid as yours and mine. It happened this way. Cleopas and Simon left for Emmaus this morning after the women came and told us about the empty tomb. They were on the way when they were met by a stranger who joined them and asked them what they were talking about.

"They told him they were speaking of Jesus who they had believed would be the one to ransom Israel, and they told him how he had suffered and died on a cross. They told him what the women had said that morning, and how surprised they were.

"The stranger then began speaking to them of what the prophets had said concerning the Christ, and expounded scriptures to them. When they reached Cleopas' house the stranger made as if to continue on his way, but Cleopas invited him in to sup with them.

"While they were at the table, the man took the bread, broke it and blessed it, then they knew him. It was Jesus himself who had walked with them. He then vanished from their sight just like he had done with the women."

"Just a minute," interrupted Omini, "young man, you told us you had seen him."

"I haven't had a chance to get to that part yet," said John. "If I may continue?"

"Please continue," begged Jethen. His heart was becoming lighter with every word John uttered.

"They talked among themselves that they should have recognized Jesus because every word he said burned in their hearts just as it did when he taught us here or in Galilee."

"I know that feeling," commented Sherai.

"Yes," replied John, "we all do. They decided to return to Jerusalem at once and tell us what had happened to them. Thus it was that we were all sitting together in the upper room talking about his appearing. The doors were locked, for we were afraid of the priests from the temple looking for us. Suddenly Jesus was there in our midst, through the locked door!"

"And you say he was not a spirit?"

"No, he was not a spirit. The first words he spoke were, *'Peace be to you.'* Several of the women screamed, and the men muttered and looked afraid. Then he said, *'Why are your hearts troubled? And why do doubts arise in your hearts? Look at my hands and my feet. A spirit doesn't have bones and flesh as you see I have. Handle me and see.'* It was then he showed us his hands, and his side.

"When everyone had touched him, and wondered at his presence he said, *'Have you any meat?'*

They brought him a bit of fish, and a honeycomb, and he ate it!"

"He ate food," marveled Rabbi Zichri. His face took on the glow of wonder and astonishment. "A spirit would not ask for food, nor eat."

"Did anything else happen?" prodded Jethen.

Omini had listened in skeptical silence. He was not yet persuaded. "And you touched the prints in his hands? How was this?"

"His wounds were beginning to heal. They had covered over and come together. The scab that formed on them had fallen off and the flesh beneath was new, and tender. They were still there, and visible, but they were healing.

"He told us more. He recalled to our minds words that he told us while he was with us about how all things must be fulfilled that were written in the law of Moses, by the prophets, and in the psalms about him.

"Somehow he opened our understanding that we could now understand his words, and then he explained that the scriptures said that the Christ must suffer, and rise from the tomb on the third day. He continued talking to us of our preaching and spreading the word, and he proposed to walk to Bethany. When we were almost to Bethany, he was carried up into the sky, so we returned to Jerusalem. I stopped here to tell you, but the others went on to our rooms."

"I believe every word of it," said Jethen.

"That is why Jesus told us to study the prophets, he knew that we would understand, and believe," Sherai told him, and hugged him.

"I believe, as well," admitted Rabbi Zichri. "I wasn't baptized when he came to Sychar, but I want to be baptized now."

"So do I," agreed Judith.

"Well I was baptized, but I just can't believe it." Omini sounded as though he wished he believed it.

"You aren't the only one," John assured him. "Thomas wasn't there tonight. He is one of the twelve, eleven, I mean. He won't believe it either. I bear you my witness that everything I have told you is the truth."

"I didn't say that I didn't believe you believe it. I think you do. I just can't believe that Jesus is the Christ who was promised to us. Now Sherai, I know that you and Jethen believe it, but reading has not led me to believe that Jesus was meant to die for our sins. I'll have to study what you have found before I make a decision of that sort." Omini doubted.

"Jethen, we decided to return to Galilee the fourth day of the week, so we won't be on the road during the Sabbath. Can you be ready to go with us by then?"

Jethen looked at Sherai who nodded her head. "Yes, we can be ready."

"Meet with us at the room early in the morning. We'll take advantage of the coolness of the day to begin our journey."

"We'll be there," Jethen assured him.

GALILEE

Jethen, Sherai, and their servants celebrated the Passover for the last time on the road with the disciples. They were interested to discover that the eleven kept the ceremony as Jesus taught them, and not as the Jews did. In fact, Jethen mentioned to Sherai that the disciples seemed to withdraw themselves from the Jews since the crucifixion.

When he asked John why this might be, John told him what the Savior, as they lately referred to Jesus out of respect to honor his name, said concerning his fulfilling the law of Moses. He said, "The other disciples and I feel that we now have a higher law to obey. This will not take away from those commandments that God gave Moses, but they will supercede them. He told us more about how we should establish his church when he is gone from us. It is different from the way the Jews worship. I can't explain it more than that."

"Then all Jesus, the Savior's, disciples should follow this," suggested Jethen, meaning himself.

"It may come to that," admitted Peter who overheard them. "You will learn of our ways as you associate with us. That is as it should be."

More men than John had first indicated elected to accompany them. It seemed that they were reluctant to part company now that they saw Jesus again after his crucifixion. Just like Jethen and Sherai, they felt a strong connection with each other, and would not be parted. They didn't know themselves whether it was because Jesus had admonished them to love one another, or because his loss was so new to them, and they were used to being together.

Peter, with his natural abilities as a leader, often talked with them of the scriptures cited by the Savior concerning his foretelling by the prophets of old. His teaching had taken on new authority as if he had gained strength from Jesus appearance. He commented, "I think we should commit those passages to memory so that we may refer to them." He didn't say when they would need to refer to them, and Thomas was the only one who grumbled and asked why.

Thomas reminded Sherai and Jethen of Omini, for he had declared many times that he didn't believe they saw Jesus. The theory he espoused was that in their grief they imagined his presence, and talked of him so much that he became real to them. Thomas remarked more than once that he wouldn't believe until he saw and touched the nail prints in his hands and feet, and thrust his hand to his side, then he would believe.

On one such recital John looked over at Jethen and winked. Then he said to Thomas, "It may be that you will soon have that opportunity, Thomas. Jesus said for us to go to Galilee and he would meet us there. You can tell him then that you think he is a product of your imagination."

It seemed that none of the disciples loved Thomas the less for his doubts. They seemed to understand that he would need to see their Lord just as they had.

They parted company on the day before the Sabbath. The rest of the disciples planned to press on to Bethsaida, and invited Jethen and Sherai to meet them there on the first day of the week. Peter warmly invited them to his home. "It's a large house, and only my wife's mother and I are left to rattle about in it. You are most welcome."

"You are welcome in my home, also," invited Andrew.

"You both will have a place in my home," echoed John. "It is really my father's home as I have not yet married," he blushed, "but you will be welcome."

"I thank God daily for you all," Jethen said. "My heart is warmed by your kindness. By that same token you are welcome to come to our home in Capernaum and keep the Sabbath with us."

"No, we want to push on now that we are so near," Peter told them. "The women are anxious to see their homes now that we are so near, and John wants to settle Mary in his home and make her welcome there."

Since John had not said so, Sherai wondered how Peter knew this with such certainty. Some of Jesus' followers had already left them along the road as they journeyed through their villages.

As they reached the bend that led to Capernaum, they bid one another farewell. Peter lifted his large hand and said, "God be with you, May he bless your going and your coming." He then turned and left Jethen and Sherai to make their way to their home. The other disciples all followed his lead.

Jethen was glad now that Sherai had purchased such a large house in Capernaum. It didn't seem as large with the servants all settled there with them. His animals had to be quartered elsewhere. However, it was a good house, and the first home they had been alone together in since their wedding. They didn't take much time for living in it, even so. Since they would soon be joining the disciples in Bethsaida, they laid up provisions for the servants they would be leaving behind. Rather than take camels and servants with them, they determined to leave the servants in Capernaum. Instead, Jethen spent some time refitting a mule named Sly with their travel tent, and some provisions.

Not knowing how long they would be gone, they each took several changes of clothing. Sherai left Abigail to clean and dust, and prepare dinner, the men she sent to purchase food and provisions, and leaving Jethen to his packing, she went off to see Mary. There was much to tell Jacob's sister about her journey, and her new husband. Jacob, who had gone on to Bethsaida, left word for his wife with Sherai. He wanted her to know he would return to Capernaum after he received instruction from the Savior.

That was how certain most of the disciples were that they would see Jesus again. They refused to make any new plans until they had received further instructions from him. They regarded themselves as very much still his followers. Jethen also seemed to join them in this idea. He had spent his time as Jesus instructed him, and now he was ready to devote the remainder of his life to doing whatever it was Jesus wanted him to do.

Sherai didn't know whether to be amused, resigned, or jealous over Jethen's devotion to Jesus. When they first spoke of it in Jerusalem, after their wedding, she had realized that his commitment to the Master was as deep as her own. She found an echo of her own dedication to his words in Jethen. It was only then she understood how jealous Jethen had been of her devotion to Jesus and her new religion before his conversion.

A part of her wanted Jethen all to herself. She wanted to explore their new relationship, and to devote herself entirely to him.

On the other side of that desire of wishing to be the most important person in his world, was the desire to continue to follow Jesus as Jethen did. Not until he clarified his feelings for her on their first night in their home in Capernaum did she fully understand her own emotions on the matter.

That night they began their Sabbath worship, and partook their first meal together in their own home. They gathered all their servants about them, and held prayer together. Their servants seemed settled in their home, and content to remain behind to care for the house. Sherai intended to take Abigail with her to Bethsaida. She was too young to leave alone.

At last Sherai and Jethen were alone in their room with the curtain drawn. Jethen, who had doors on all his rooms in Sychar said, "The first thing I will do upon our return from Bethsaida is see a carpenter about making a door for this room."

"A door won't be necessary unless we remain here in Capernaum," Sherai, ever practical, responded.

"My wife," he said with all the tender love and wonder of which he was capable. She thrilled to hear those words on his lips. They had never sounded so lovely from any other. Not even Tobias called her "wife" with such love, longing, and reverence.

"My husband," she responded to his embrace.

"You are right to doubt our remaining, or even soon returning to this house or any other. I wish that we might forever remain as we are now," he punctuated that thought with a kiss, "but I know in my heart that we cannot. Our love and devotion is partially founded on our love for the Messiah. It was because of him that we are now one. We owe him everything for our new happiness. Our lives are his, and not our own to spend. Do you feel this?"

Sherai hugged him to her possessively for a moment before she answered, "Yes, I know what you are saying. I thought about this earlier today. Our lives belong to him, and not to ourselves. I felt more that way myself before your love filled my life to overflowing."

That statement called for several more kisses, but soon Jethen broached the subject again. "I don't know what the future holds, but I have the deepest feeling that we will live unsettled lives, seeing our home rarely, and traveling a great deal. Our children will be nomads along with us, for I have no intention of being separated from you ever again," he admitted. "I don't know what John and Peter mean about building a church, but I must be a part of it."

"I also must be a part of it as being so readily a part of you." She didn't voice her concern over them ever having children, or the need to journey with them. Somehow she allowed his simple faith to bolster hers.

"Then we are agreed, my wife. Our lives together for the Messiah. It may come to mean that we don't live as lavishly as we do now. We may sell all as Matthias and Lydia did if Jesus asks us."

"Then we will still have everything in each other," she responded. They sealed their devotion with another kiss, and shut themselves into their world of two for that night.

The day after the Sabbath they walked to Bethsaida. It was a beautiful spot on the north shore of the lake. Peter's house, when they found it, was large. It covered a bluff overlooking the lake, and was situated to take in the sun from every direction.

Peter welcomed them to his home, and took pride in showing them over the whole of it. He took them up on the roof for the spectacular view of the lake and showed them the exact spot where his neighbors let down a man through the roof to Jesus for healing because his house was too crowded for them to come in through the door.

He even showed them his cellars where salted fish and grains were stored for his household. It was a lovely house, and Jethen could understand his pride and simple joy in it. Peter then took them down to the shore where his boats were docked. There was one small boat, and two larger ones. "I ran the boats with Zebedee and his sons," he told them. "They look neglected now. I imagine old Zebedee takes out the small one from time to time, but with both his sons following Jesus with me, he hasn't much use for the larger boats. I doubt I will ever really be a fisherman again. I should sell them."

"I was wondering much the same about my own business," Jethen confided. "I have several camels, and mules to carry goods from place to place for trading, but I . . ."

Peter put his hand on Jethen's shoulder in sympathy. "We all feel the same," he said simply. "We are waiting for instruction. I know we are to build a church, but I don't know where, or how. I feel most inadequate to the task. Why don't we just wait on the Lord before making any decisions?

"I feel it will not be long," he added. "That is why I wanted you all to come to Galilee with the eleven. I was disappointed when some went to their homes as though it was all over. I know that it isn't."

"We appreciate you opening your lovely home to us, Peter."

"You are most welcome, Sherai. Come, I will show you where you may sleep."

Jethen took a deep breath of the air from the lake, and told his host, "I would be as content to sleep here with the sound of the water lapping the shore, and beneath the stars."

"You may, Jethen," laughed Sherai, "but I am looking forward to the comfort of a real bed after weeks on the floor. Two nights in a bed have spoiled me."

"I will give you a room with a balcony that overlooks the lake," Peter promised. "Then you will both be content."

The next day proved to be a full and happy one. They were introduced to Peter's mother-in-law, and found her to be a charming, gracious lady full of wisdom and simple goodness. She told them that she had suffered greatly with pain in her joints until Jesus healed her. Bedda, for that was her name, talked a little of her daughter, and lamented that she and Peter had no children to enliven her old age.

The next day Peter walked them all over Bethsaida, and surrounding villages, gathering up the eleven who had dispersed themselves to various households. He wanted to have a meeting that night at his house. It seemed that he was impatient to begin whatever it was he was to do, and his restlessness communicated itself to the other disciples.

They found Matthias and Lydia at Andrew's house, and they renewed acquaintance and spent some time there learning from the older couple more of Jesus words and teachings. Even Sherai learned new things, for there had been many times when she was unable to accompany Jesus as he traveled.

She came to love and appreciate Matthias as much as Jethen did. He was such a wise and gentle old man. His face radiated love. He was the most like Jesus of all the disciples. At least Sherai felt it to be so. His wife Lydia she also came to love and they spent much time together as couples.

Jethen and Sherai spent the afternoon with them, talking and learning, then walked with them back to Peter's house on the bluff. There they had a lovely dinner cooked to perfection by Bedda. They were all sitting together talking among themselves when they all sensed the presence of another. They looked up from their talking to see Jesus standing in the midst of them.

Sherai gasped aloud, and clutched Jethen's arms. He turned to look at what the others were staring at so steadfastly, and fell to his knees in worship. Sherai also bowed with him.

"Peace be unto you," Jesus said.

"God's peace be with you," some answered automatically. But Jesus was intent on one of their number who had not been with them before. He walked over to Thomas who was staring at him as one stricken. "Take your finger Thomas, and trace the scar on my hand. Take your hand and thrust it into my side, and be no longer faithless, but believing."

Thomas's face crumpled and he fell to his knees, "My Lord and my God," he voice broke as he murmured. All the disciples and those in the room then fell to their knees, praising and thanking God for the Messiah.

"You are blessed, Thomas," said Jesus, "to *see* and believe, but blessed also are those who have not seen," he smiled at Jethen and Sherai, "and yet have believed. There will be many you will tell of me, and they will not see me, yet they will believe. They must come to the knowledge that I am the way, the truth and the life, and that no man may come to the Father but through me.

"I believe there have been questions among you as to what you should do now that I am no longer always with you. It is the will of the Father that you spread the good news abroad. Thomas, you doubted, but doubt no more.

"A sign will be given you what you should do. Watch, wait and pray for that sign. I will come to you again, and I will have further instructions," he promised them. Then once again he vanished from their sight.

Several more restless days followed, and the disciples began once again to murmur, and wonder in their hearts what they should do. Some had families, and others had brought their family with them, as had Matthias and Jethen. All wondered what sign they should look for, and when it would be given.

No one was very surprised when Peter was the first to break under the pressure of waiting. "I am going fishing," he announced.

James, John, and several of the other disciples including Thomas decided to go with him. They all seemed as tired of waiting as Peter. They got some nets, and gear, and took off for the shore. Jethen and Sherai, along with several others decided to remain behind. When the disciples returned they wished they had also gone, for Jesus appeared to them again.

John told them the story as they all walked toward Jerusalem, for Jesus had told them that he would visit them again there, on the Mount of Olives, and teach them all that they should do.

"We were fishing all night," he recounted. "We hadn't caught anything. I think we all knew that we should be waiting as Jesus told us to do, but it was good to be out on the water, and in good fellowship. We were in the small boat, so it wasn't very roomy, as you can imagine."

Jethen acknowledged that he could imagine it, he had seen the boat. Sherai was content just to listen.

"We decided to row to shore, and see if we could catch anything with our nets. Well, it was getting on toward light and we noticed a man on the shore. He had lit a fire, and as we neared he called out to us, *'Children, do you have any meat?'* We called back that we had caught nothing.

"*'Cast your nets to the right,'* he called out to us. By then I knew who it was, and I told Peter, "That is Jesus there waiting for us." You know Peter, he pulled on his fisher's coat, and jumped into the water making for shore.

"The rest of us cast the net, and we were hard put to pull all the fish into the boat. We counted when we reached the shore and there were one hundred fifty-three fish. We pulled the boat to shore, and pulled out the nets and began counting the fish. Peter and Jesus were talking, and cooking some fish.

"Jesus had some fish cooked, and some bread, but no one dared ask him where he got them.

"He blessed the food, and broke off some bread and offered it to each of us. We were ravenous after the long night of hauling wet nets, and we gladly ate. It was good to be in Jesus' company again, just as we used to be, and we were content. All the questions we asked ourselves when he was not with us seemed to disappear in his presence.

"Presently Jesus asked Peter, *'Peter, Simon, son of Jonas, do you love me more than these?'* He swept his arm over the heaps of fish drying on the shore. We could all sense that this was the most important question Peter would ever be asked.

"Peter said, "Lord you know that I love you."

"Then Jesus said, *'Feed my lambs.'*

"We all looked at each other. What was Jesus telling Peter to do? Jesus had no lambs that we knew of, and Peter looked like he wanted to weep.

"We finished eating, and cleaned up. We took care of the fish. And sat around the fire waiting, I suppose, for Jesus to teach us as he used to do.

"That was when Jesus said to Peter a second time, *'Simon, son of Jonas, do you love me?'*

"This time Peter's voice broke as he said, "Lord, you know that I love you." I think Peter thought that the Lord was questioning his love because he denied him that night at court."

"Do you think that's what it was?" Sherai interrupted.

John replied, "I don't think that was it, because this time he said, *'Feed my sheep.'* I began to get a glimmer of what the Master was really telling Peter.

"Then Jesus said to him, *'Come, Peter, let us walk together.'* They got up from the fire and walked away. I followed them, and I heard Jesus say to Peter a third time, *'Simon, son of Jonas, do you love me?'*

"This time there were tears in Peter's voice as he answered Jesus, "Lord, you know that I love you."

"Jesus said, *'Feed my sheep. When you were young you girded yourself and walked wherever you would, but when you are old, they will lead you by the hand wither you would not go.'* He was telling Peter that this love of him would lead to his own doom.

"Peter knew I was following them, and he thumbed back at me and said, "What about him. What will he do?

"Jesus said, *'What is it to you if I allow him to tarry until I come again? You follow me.'*

"Peter said, "I will follow you. Where is it we are to go?"

"*'I want you to go to Jerusalem. We will meet often before I leave you. Go to the Mount of Olives and wait there. I will instruct you there how to build my church, and what to do. I want you to no longer call yourselves disciples, but apostles. You should be twelve. Choose another from among you to take Judas' place. You twelve will lead my people, and build my church.'"* John finished his narrative with those words.

Jethen felt brave enough to ask, "Who will you choose, John?"

"We won't know until we are all together in Jerusalem. We will gather all the eleven together, and we will decide. I imagine there will be much prayer and fasting. Jesus refused to name the one, we are to decide ourselves. He is preparing us for when he will no longer be with us."

"What did Jesus mean that *you* will tarry until he comes?" asked Sherai.

"I think he means that I will be allowed to remain on this earth to await his second coming in great glory," replied John.

"That is a great gift," Sherai commented.

"Yes, sister of the kingdom, it is. I cannot comprehend it."

45

WAIT ON THE LORD

The sky was a clear blue that morning, and the spring sun was warm on their faces. Very soon Sherai removed her cloak, rolled it up and placed it among Sly's bundles. Jethen wore his cloak slung back at the shoulders like a cape, and ignored it. Sherai was free to notice the new lambs frolicking in the hills as they made their way to Jerusalem. Shepards dotted the hills along with their flocks.

Bedda had offered to keep young Abigail with her for the summer until Jethen and Sherai had resolved what they were likely to do. Sherai was grateful to the woman. With their lives so unsettled, and camping along the road most of the time, it was difficult to have a young girl along. Abigail seemed content to remain and work in the beautiful house on the shore for her keep.

Jethen pondered John's words all the way to Jerusalem. He was unaware that he was inattentive to his new bride. He was trying to puzzle out what it was that the Lord wanted of him. Sherai heard him pray often to ask the Father what he would have them do. Since his prayers always included her, she was content. Her own prayers were often for him.

In her innermost heart, it seemed dangerous to travel back to Jerusalem so soon after the crucifixion. The High Priests would not yet have forgiven Jesus for taking their congregation. It was unlikely they would welcome his followers still clinging to his teachings. Sherai, for one, had been relieved to have them all leave the area. As it was, the Mount of Olives was less than half a mile from Jerusalem. Ten times that distance would have better pleased Sherai.

As before, along the way they collected all the disciples of Jesus who had left them. Some chose to remain in their homes rather than journey into danger. Some of the men left their families and journeyed alone.

Peter selected some of their number to be messengers to those who lived in Emmaus and Bethany, and any other nearby city around Jerusalem. "Go to these cities and give the Master's call." To his fellow apostles he said, "Those who answer that call will be the future leaders of the church. Those of you who are with us today will be central to its establishment in Jerusalem."

"What more can you tell us of this?" asked Justus. He was a righteous man who had traveled with Jesus from the beginning of his ministry and still continued on with the apostles.

"My friend, I know no more to tell you," Peter answered honestly. "I beseech my Father in Heaven for insight just as you do."

When they reached the Mount of Olives, they set up a camp. Jethen knew Sherai didn't like camping on the ground, so he carefully groomed their spot free of rock and branch, and erected a small tent for her, and placed a comfortable bed with a narrow tick of cloth he'd packed on Sly. He also set up a bowl and pitcher for her to bathe.

The apostles took a site apart from the others. They felt the need to separate themselves as Jesus had often done. Sherai knew they did this to pray together as a group, and that they often fasted. It was also that they needed time together to discuss what they needed to do. When she shared her thoughts about it with Jethen he remarked, "This seems only right to me. It is upon those eleven that so much responsibility descended with Jesus' death." When they had all set up camp at the Mount, a thick mist came down suddenly on the ground near the apostle's camp, and Jesus walked out of it. He communed that day mostly with the eleven, and left in the same manner he came.

Jethen still wasn't talking much, the day after Jesus returned to them, and Sherai was worried. "My husband," she called him from his thoughts, "what is it that troubles you so?"

Jethen looked relieved to talk about it, "Lately I have been thinking that I should send word to Omini, and to Rabbi Zichri to come here. They are disciples of the Christ. They should be here to see him, and take instruction from him."

"Are you thinking of going to Sychar to get them?" she asked.

"If there were only someone I could send," he mourned. "I dislike leaving here when there is so much to be learned. I strongly feel that Jesus' sojourn with us won't be for long."

"I could go," Sherai offered.

"Bless you, no, my wife. I couldn't part with you, and I would never send you alone," he took her hand and brought it to his heart.

"Why don't you ask John or Peter what you should do? We have only been here two days, yet more people have been arriving. Perhaps there is one among them you might send," she suggested.

"I have thought we might go to Jerusalem and hire a messenger. My mind is in turmoil because I feel this so strongly."

"Perhaps this is a matter that we must pray about and trust in the Lord, Jethen."

John came to them often with bits of news from here and there. After Jesus left them the next day he came and told them, "We heard news from those who lived in Jerusalem concerning Judas. He repented of his actions and went back to the priests. He wanted to give the money back that he received for betraying Jesus. Nicodemus said the priests refused it, and they heard that he used the money to buy a field. Later they discovered that Judas hung himself in that very field."

"That is terrible news, but it seems just that he would punish himself for his wrongful deed." Jethen commented. "John, while I have you here, I want to tell you my thoughts." He told him of his impression that his friends should be here.

"If you have been impressed to do this, send for them. Others have been telling the Apostles the same sort of impressions. I think these people are meant to come. They are being called, in a way. Send for them, by all means."

"I have no servant to send, is there any other way?"

"Look," John pointed to some men trudging up the hill with a laden mule. "People are coming in daily by twos and threes. We didn't send out messenger to all of them. Yonder come some now."

The men came in sight, and Jethen sprang to his feet with a glad cry. "Rabbi Zichri, Omini! Did the Lord call you here? My heart has longed to send for you these many days."

Omini came huffing and puffing to their camp. "I had a dream," he told Jethen, "in which the Lord told me that you wanted me here. The next day Rabbi Zichri came to me and told me he, well, let him tell you. I am winded."

Rabbi Zichri took up his part, "I had a dream in which Omini and I were to make a journey. I was to go to him and convince him to travel with me to Jerusalem and go up the Mount of Olives. The dream was so urgent it woke me in the middle of the night.

"The next morning I went to him and told him my dream, and he told me his. We decided to travel here at once. So you see us."

"He left out the part where he cajoled me, persuaded me, and nearly threatened me with my soul's salvation if I didn't come," added Omini. Jethen laughed for joy, and hugged each of them in turn.

John smiled and said, "As I said, people are being called. Welcome, my brothers in the Lord. Set up your camp, tomorrow the Savior is speaking to us all."

Omini asked Jethen, "The Savior? Does he mean . . .?"

"Yes, my friend, he means that Jesus the Christ is coming to teach us. I have seen him, he lives!"

Omini looked to Sherai as if to ask her if Jethen was fine in his head. She nodded, "I have seen him too, my father. He lives."

"Hallelujah, Praise be to the most High God!" exclaimed Rabbi Zichri. He did a small dance and spooked the mule.

Omini calmed the mule and said, "I'm afraid I will have to see him for myself."

"Come with me," said John. "There is someone I'd like you to meet. I think you and he will become fast friends." John led Omini straight to Thomas who at that moment was coming toward them.

Jesus came to them in his usual manner, through the mist. He found all his disciples who had come at his command seated down the hill waiting for him to teach them. Jethen could tell that his heart was touched when they knelt before him, and bowed their heads to the ground in worship. He sensed his eyes upon him as if searching his heart and mind.

Before Jesus spoke to them he offered a prayer. "My Father, I thank you for these people you have given me. I pray that you will send the Comforter to them, and strengthen them. There is a work for each of them to do, and I pray they will come to know it. Keep them safe from harm until their work is finished."

When his prayer was done, he looked upon them again and said, "As you have seen me do, do likewise. I was sent into this world to bear witness of the Father, and to suffer for the sins of the world. This I have done. My work is finished, but your work is about to begin.

"There need be no more blood sacrifice. I have paid the price for all. You will stand as a witness to me and the Father in all places. Repentance for the remission of sins much be preached in my name, among all nations, beginning in Jerusalem. You are the witnesses of these things.

"Behold, I will send the promise of the Father to you, but you must tarry in Jerusalem until you are endued with power from on high. Then will you preach and teach in my name. He that believes and is baptized shall be saved; he that does not shall be damned.

"These signs will follow those who believe in me: in my name they shall cast out devils, they shall speak with new tongues; they shall take up serpents; if they drink any deadly thing it shall not hurt them; they shall lay hands on the sick, and the sick shall recover.

"Now I will speak with you concerning the kingdom of God. The kingdom is now in your hands. I have appointed my apostles to build my church. You are the workers, as are they. I cannot always tarry with you. They will lead you and guide you when I have departed."

Jesus talked on to his disciples all that day instructing them, and teaching them of his kingdom, and themselves as a part of it. So absorbed were they in his words, they took no thought of food or drink, only of him. His words were the bread and water of life.

There was such harmony and love among there number that all felt as one.

That night Jethen and Sherai suddenly remembered they were hungry. In their tent they feasted on bread and cheese. They talked over what Jesus said about them knowing what it was they should do for the kingdom. "I am beginning to think that I know," Jethen told her.

Sherai held her peace. She also thought she knew what their calling would be, but she wanted to hear Jethen tell it. Together they prayed, and sought the will of the Father.

Daily thereafter Jesus came and taught them, or the apostles. For thirty days after they arrived on the mount, he came and dwelt among them, often returning to his father in the mist. When with them, he prayed with them, taught them, exhorted them, but when he was away, he was always in their thoughts and in their hearts. It was a glorious time. Christ had triumphed over death, and by so doing had given them the hope of doing the same. He said, "I am the way, the truth, and the life."

Jethen seemed to grow in stature as he listened to his Lord day after day. Sherai saw him grow from a babe in Christ to a mature man. No longer did she feel that her years of experience and sorrow outweighed his maturity, or spiritual insights. She watched and supported him as he humbly took his rightful position of the head of their house. She rejoiced to see his growth, and his new found wisdom. Here was a man she could honor, next to her Savior only, as a man of God.

One evening, about thirty days after they had reached the mount, Jesus was again teaching the group.

He was preparing to leave them for the day and he said, "Go now to your meals, and tend to your families. I must go. Tomorrow I will take leave of you, but not before I give you my last message. Prepare this night for your journey to Jerusalem where you will wait. Peter will lead you in my place, I have charged him with this duty."

The people all cried out in distress and dismay. They had become used to their Lord among them again.

Sherai cried along with many others, "Don't leave us, My Lord God," and shed tears. Jethen comforted her, but there were tears in his own eyes.

Many openly wept at his announcement. Jesus was moved by their distress, and said, "I will not go and leave you comfortless. Pray that the Comforter, even the Holy Ghost, will soon come." So saying he took his apostles back to their secluded place, and left them.

The next morning the sun rose, and was shining as though their Lord God was not leaving them alone in this world. Peter came and roused them all. "It is time to awake," he called. "I will lead you up the mountain as our Master commanded me."

When all of them had assembled, there were about one hundred twenty souls. Peter, James and John led them up to the top of the mount. There they met Jesus. He was dressed in spotless white. His face shone more than the light of the sun that fell upon him. When they had all gathered around him, he raised his arms high, and blessed them. His love for them was obvious in his face.

Then in a clear voice, he charged them, "Go into all the world and preach the gospel to every creature. Baptize them in the name of the Father, the Son and the Holy Ghost. Teach them to observe whatsoever things I have commanded you. And Lo, I am with you always, even to the end of the world.

"Do not depart from Jerusalem, but wait there for the promise of the Father which you have heard from me. John indeed baptized with water, but you shall be baptized with the Holy Ghost and with fire. You shall receive power after the Holy Ghost is come upon you, and you shall be witnesses of me both in Jerusalem, and in all Judea, and in Samaria, and to the uttermost part of the earth."

Jethen looked up at his Savior God, and knew in that instant that his own thoughts were precisely what his calling was to be. He was to teach in Samaria. Jesus had told him that on the day he had first spoken to him. He wondered if others were receiving their calling on that day. They were first to teach in Jerusalem. This would be a test of their faith, for most feared the Sanhedrin.

While Jethen looked steadfastly at the Christ, he saw him rise in the air above him. He continued to ascend until he was covered by a cloud. When he could see him no more, he reached out for Sherai and drew her to him, but he continued to look upward. In his heart he knew he was bidding him farewell. He would see Jesus walk no more on this earth.

Everyone on the mountain that day seemed transfixed on the sky. Two men stood among them dressed in white, and called for their attention. They said, "Why do you men continue to gaze upward? This same Jesus that you saw depart will come again in like manner as you have seen him go to heaven."

Jethen turned Sherai, "Yes, we have his promise that he will come again. There is much to be done before that great day."

"Yes, my husband, there is much to be done."

"Then we'd best go about obeying his first command to us," he told her. Taking her arm to guide her over the rough terrain, together they made their way down the hill to their mule packed and ready for the journey into Jerusalem. Omini and the Rabbi stood nearby packed and waiting for them.

Jethen, Omini, and Zichri all shared a moment together. They took comfort in their friendship. Zichri offered a prayer for their journey, and asked the Father to give them patience to wait. Sherai stood and watched them. What excellent men they were. You might have thought Omini had another son.

Peter, James, and John came down the mount along with the man who owned the upper room where they had kept the vigil after Christ's crucifixion.

"Our brother Joseph is the owner of the house where our Lord administered the Passover to us," Peter introduced the man. "He has graciously invited us to wait with him once again. We will go first and prepare the way. Those of you who don't know where Joseph lives, follow us," he announced. "The rest of you will come by two's and three's. We don't want to alert anyone to our presence. Bring food. Buy extra if you have the means. We must prepare for a prolonged stay, and not be a burden to our host." With those words the men turned and made their way down the mount. A few, unfamiliar with the location of Joseph's house, followed them.

Jethen told Sherai and his friends, "There's no need to follow them, I know the way. Let's go into the market. We also need to stable our mules. I know just the place. Then we'll purchase some food, as we were asked."

"I wonder what power from on high we shall be endued with." Zichri wondered aloud.

Omini, the doubter no longer, said, "Why the power to spread the good news, without fear, that Jesus lives."

TONGUES OF FIRE

They were all together in the upper room. All one hundred and twenty people filled it to overflowing. Their voices were raised in prayer continually. They were of one mind, and one accord. All of them were waiting. Not one of them actually knew what they were waiting for, they only knew that Jesus told them to wait and pray, and they were obeying.

They all looked to Peter for leadership. Even the apostles deferred to him. He was their spokesman. On one of those days of waiting Peter stood up and called for attention. He said to them, "Men and brethren, the scripture must be fulfilled. The Holy Ghost filled the mouth of David and he spoke concerning Judas who was a guide for the priest who arrested Jesus.

"Judas was numbered with us, and he obtained part of this ministry. He took the money and bought a field, but his blood was spilled on that field, and hereafter it will be called the field of blood.

"Psalms says, *'Let this habitation be desolate, and let no man dwell there, and his bishopric let another take.'* Therefore, someone among us, who was with us from the baptism of Jesus by John until the resurrection, must be chosen to take his place. Who will you name?"

Several called out various names. Peter was happy to hear that these choices had also been voiced by the apostles. "The apostles should choose from among those names," he declared. After conferring with his brethren he announced, "The two names we have settled on are Joseph called Barsabas, and Matthias."

"Matthias," whispered Sherai to Jethen, "I just knew it."

"It will be Matthias," he whispered back to her, squeezing her hand.

The eleven apostles knelt before them, and prayed among themselves calling on the Lord, "You, Lord, know the hearts of these two men. Which of these good men have you chosen that he may take part of this ministry and apostleship which Judas has transgressed, that he might take his place?" After the prayer, the apostles cast their lots, and Peter rose to tell the results. "The lot falls to our brother, Matthias. Matthias come forward and be received by us in fellowship."

Just as Jethen and Sherai predicted, so it was. Lydia was beaming through her tears, and as she sat by Sherai, Sherai was able to give her a quick hug. Matthias rose and took his place at the front with the other apostles. Tears were falling down that dear man's cheeks as he took his place. His hands were shaking as he was grasped by each hand in welcome.

That evening Jethen and Sherai rejoiced as Matthias took his place, and presided over the blessing of the bread and wine. No bread or wine ever tasted sweeter to their lips.

During those days of waiting, Peter, conferring with his other apostles, set down certain guidelines taught to them by Jesus for the establishment of his church. Those among the one hundred and twenty were appointed to the seventies.

Jethen was appointed as an evangelist to Samaria. He would accompany John and Jude through Judea, and Samaria teaching the gospel. Jude would continue on to Idumea, and Syria, but John would remain in Samaria teaching. They would return and report to James the Lesser who was appointed bishop of Jerusalem for two years.

Jethen beamed with happiness, and offered his home in Sychar as a base. Rabbi Zichri was appointed as a seventy, and he was also sent to Samaria. Omini was called as a teacher in the synagogue in Sychar to take Rabbi Zichri's place. Omini began tutelage at once under Zichri.

All the men were appointed to various duties under the guidance of the apostle who was assigned to their area. All was done without haste and in order after much prayer. The work took considerable time, and all was written down, and each person was set apart by the apostles as Jesus had taught them to do.

They proceeded on with each calling, and the women were also given responsibility to care for the church, and see to the poor and needy among them. All this organization took time, and when the group were not worshiping or praying, they were working to build up the kingdom of God–and they were waiting.

The day of Pentecost had fully come. It was the fiftieth day after the first day of Passover. The congregation in the small upper room was again praying.

Jethen was kneeling beside Sherai in a small group with those who were going with John and Jude to Samaria. They were praying for the people of Samaria when Jethen felt his hair begin to blow about his face. In his ears sounded a rush of wind so strong that he reached out to grip Sherai lest she be blown about by it. The wind rushed to each member in the congregation, and it filled the room where they were. In the wind were small cloven tongues of fire, and they whirled about the room and settled on each person in it.

As the tongue of fire settled on Jethen's head, he felt his body begin to shake. It started at the top of his head, and flowed down to his feet. It was a mingling of the power and glory of God. It filled every particle of his being. He felt as though he was on fire. His heart was nigh to bursting with joy. He was immediately filled with the Holy Ghost, and he began praising God in a pure stream of words. Everyone in the room was doing the same. They were all shouting and praising God. Soon they were on their feet, pushed upward by the joy and exuberance the power had given them.

In every heart was confirmed the sweet knowledge that Jesus was the Christ, the Son of God. Their hearts were overflowing with love, gratitude, and confidence in the gospel of Jesus Christ. The spirit within witnessed to them that they must fulfill the last commandment of Jesus.

Almost as one every person in that room made their way out the door, down the stairs, and out into the streets. Singing and rejoicing, singly or in pairs they walked to the large courts below the stairs leading up to the temple. It wasn't until they reached this court that they heard the people around them exclaiming and following them to listen.

One fellow called out, "Behold, they are drunk."

Others took up his cry and laughed and pointed as the disciples continued to shout and praise God. Peter, stepped forward out of the group with great majesty and authority, and said for them all, "Men of Judea, and all who dwell in Jerusalem, let this be known to you, and harken to my words. These people are not drunk as you suppose being that it is only the third hour of the day. But this is what was prophesied by Joel 'In the last days I will pour out my spirit on all flesh and your sons and daughters shall prophesy, your young men shall see visions, and your old men shall dream dreams. And on my servants and my handmaidens in those days I will pour out my spirit and they shall prophesy.'"

The crowds gathered around, and began to listen to Peter as he continued preaching. It was just then that Jethen realized Peter was speaking in fluent Greek. Peter, the man who had never spoken anything but the roughest Aramaic was speaking perfect Greek.

A man standing near Jethen and Sherai said, "Aren't these men from Galilee? How is it they are speaking my tongue like a native?"

Jethen answered him and said, "He is filled with the spirit of the Holy Ghost."

They listened to Peter as he recounted the words of the prophets, and the promises for the Messiah, and they heard him say, "Therefore let all the house of Israel know that this same Jesus that you have crucified God has made the Lord and Christ. Repent and be baptized every one of you in the name of Jesus Christ for the remission of sins and you shall receive the Holy Ghost."

Then the apostles and disciples dispersed, and began talking with the crowd.

Two men near Jethen grabbed his arm and said, "How can we receive this Holy Ghost?"

Sherai, who had never spoken a word of Arabic, turned to the man and said in that language, "First you must believe on the Lord Jesus Christ."

"Then," said Jethen, "you must repent of all your sins before God, and you must promise to keep the commandments of Jesus Christ." Sherai understood his words, though he was speaking Ethiopian, and translated for the man in Arabic.

Another man standing nearby asked, "How is it that you know the tongue of Ethiopia, young man? Have you resided there since your youth?"

Jethen replied, "I speak only as the spirit directs me. Jesus Christ is the Son of God, and it is through his suffering and dying, and his resurrection, and by the power of the Holy Ghost that you understand me in your own tongue."

"What are these commandments?" asked a woman nearby asked eagerly in the language of India.

Jethen answered her in her own language, "To love the Lord thy God with all thy heart, mind and strength, and to love your neighbor as yourself."

"You testify that Jesus lives. But he was crucified." She protested.

"That same Jesus who was crucified lives again. I saw him, and I bear witness that he lives."

"I believe," said the man from Ethiopia.

"I believe," the Arab told Sherai, who had continued to say Jethen's words to him in Arabic.

"I believe," the woman from India agreed. "What must I do?"

"What must we do?" They all cried.

"You must repent of your sins, and be baptized in the name of Jesus Christ," Jethen answered them.

All over the square people were asking the same questions, and receiving the same answers in their own native languages. Ethiopians, Asians, Greeks, Armenians, Romans, and Arabs, all heard the gospel for the first time in their own tongue.

"Where must we go to be baptized?" they asked.

Jethen and Sherai shared a smile with each other. This was what they had waited for in Jerusalem. No more hunger or thirst for righteousness would exist, ever again, for anyone on earth who would accept Jesus Christ. They would be filled with the Holy Ghost.

Thought to thought their hearts spoke to each other in endless harmony. The unspeakable joy they felt radiated on their faces, and sent hope to those looking upon them.

"Permit me," a voice interrupted them. It was a man from Asia. "What must I do to be saved in the life to come?" Jethen began to tell him.

The Arab told Sherai, "I must go fetch my brother. He will want to hear these words."

All that day Jethen and Sherai taught the word of God. Together they added many converts to the fold.

That evening the apostles called the people to the Jordan to be baptized. It was a glorious sight to see, thousands came forward to be baptized into the church of Jesus Christ.

Jethen and Sherai sat on a rock near the water's edge rejoicing as each new convert was baptized. When they came out of the water, each one was given the gift of the Holy Ghost by one of the apostles laying hands on their head.

"Here is a part of the kingdom of God," marveled Sherai. "It is truly sublime."

"When he comes again," Jethen added, "his gospel will cover the earth. We will be a part of that, my wife."

"Our family will be a part of it, my husband." Sherai put her hand to her stomach in protective love. "God has answered our prayers."

Jethen was stunned. "Sherai, are you with child? How long have you known?"

"Not long," she assured him. "My time came and went about two weeks past. I've waited to tell you until I was sure."

"I've been so preoccupied with other matters, I never noticed," Jethen mourned. "I wanted to be the first to know."

"You are the first I've told, dear husband. A woman always knows first, that is God's gift to us."

"There can be no greater happiness than this," Jethen avowed. "I never dreamed anything could make me happier today than all these baptisms. I hope we have a little girl like Talitha."

"I hope we have a son who can carry on his father's work," she contradicted him in happy argument.

"Then I hope we have both," tears came to his eyes, and Jethen put his head down on Sherai's shoulder, weeping with pure joy.

Sherai held him to her. Her cup was full and running over, just as Jesus had promised. She was so profoundly moved she could not speak.

With his head still buried in Sherai's shoulder, Jethen recollected that his dreams and hopes had more depth and meaning than he ever imagined.

'How good God is to those who love him,' he thought. 'How can I ever repay such blessings?' He prayed silently. 'Thank you, Father God. I give my life to you. And it may be in small measure, compared to your goodness, but I will find a way to repay you,' he promised as he prayed in his heart.

The End

GLOSSARY

Abigail - sister to Mazar, maid to Sherai
Abinah - a seller of scrolls in Jerusalem
Ahi - husband to Sachi, servants to Jethen
Aichri - son of Heber ben Gera
Amos - father to Jethen, deceased
Amos - son of Mishob
*Andrew - a follower of Jesus
Anna - woman with the issue of blood
*Annas - high priest in Jerusalem
Ashaah - father to Sherai, distant relative of Amos, and partner in business
*Bartholomew/Nathaniel - follower of Jesus
Bedda - name of Peter's mother-in-law
Bethba - first wife to Maachi
*Caiaphas - The High Priest of Jerusalem
Caprias - a cloth merchant in Hippos
Deborah - shopper in Jericho
Eliphaz - second son of Omini and husband to Sherai
Eliza - Opar's maid
Frisk - a lamb Jethen loved as a boy
Halakah - Jewish law
Heber ben Gera - suitor of Sherai
*Herod - son of Herod the Great, tetarch of Galilee
*Herodias - first wife to Philip, then to Herod
Hodesh - daughter of Heber ben Gera
Isaac - lawyer in Jericho
Jacob - brother to Mary, who sold her house to Sherai in Capernaum
*Jacob - prophet whose name was changed to Israel
*Jairus - ruler of synagogue, daughter raised from dead
Jakim - merchant in Jericho

*James - son of Zebedee, follower of Jesus
*James - Jesus' brother
*Jesus of Nazareth - rabbi, teacher, son of God
Jethen - son to Amos, distant relative of Sherai and Ashaah
*Joanna - woman who went to the tomb
*John the Baptizer - baptized Jesus
*John - son of Zebedee, follower of Jesus
Judas - man in shop
*Judas - follower of Jesus
*Jude - brother to Jesus
Judith - wife of the rabbi Zichri
*Laban - father-in-law to Jacob
*Lazarus - man Jesus raised from the dead
Levi - servant of Jethen
*Levi/Matthew - tax collector, follower of Jesus
Lucius - owner of a caravansary outside Jericho
Lydia - wife of Matthias, follower of Jesus
Maachi - fifth husband of Sherai
Mary - sister to Jacob, sold her house to Sherai in Capernaum
Mary - wife of Mattheu the innkeeper
*Mary Magdalene - woman at tomb
*Mary - wife of Cleophus a follower of Jesus
Mattheu - owner of an inn in Magadan
Matthias - husband to Lydia, jewish merchant who intends to sell all he has and follow Jesus
Mazar - young maid of Sherai's, sister to Abagail
Mikveh - baptismal font
Miriam - mother to Jethen, wife to Ashaah
Miriam - sister to Jethen named after mother
Miriam - daughter of Miriam, named for grandmother and mother
Mishob - Jethen's father's cousin, and chief overseer
*Moses - prophet of Israel
Nam - mule belonging to Jethen

Nathan - fourth son of Omini, husband to Sherai
Nibble - mule belonging to Jethen
Omini - father to Reuel, Eliphaz, Nathan, Tobias, Maachi, husband to Paaba, and Opar
Opar - second wife of Omini, mother of two daughters
Paaba - first wife of Omini and mother of his sons, deceased
*Philip - an older man who followed Jesus
Rebbah - servant of Jethen's in Sychar
Reuel - oldest son of Omini, husband of Sherai
Rama - servant to Jethen
Rima - friend to Sherai
Rulla - Rima's daughter
Sachi - one of Jethen's servants
*Salome - woman who went to the tomb
Sheba - Jethen's camel
Sarah - maid to Miriam
Sherai - daughter to Ashaah, wife to Reuel, Nathan, Tobias, Maachi, daughter-in-law to Omini and Paaba, distant relative of Jethen
Shy Bit - mule given to Lydia by Jethen
*Simeon - follower of Jesus
*Simon - follower of Jesus (known as Zealot)
*Simon/Peter bar Jonah - follower of Jesus, son of Jonah, own of boat, partner in fishing with Zebedee
Tah - servant of Jethen
Tahan - husband to Miriam daughter of Miriam
Talitha - only child of Sherai and Tobias, died when about two years old
*Thomas - follower of Jesus
Thomas - innkeeper where Jethen, Omini, and Rabbi Zichri stayed during the Passover
Tobiah - third son of Omini, husband to Sherai, deceased
Trinius - a merchant who bought all Jethen's cloth from Lydda

*Zebedee - name of father of James and John, owner of a boat, partner with bar Jonah
Zichri - rabbi of Sychar
Ziriz - Second overseer under Mishob

* Actual persons living before or at the time of Christ